Loki

S.J.A. Turney is an author of Roman and medieval historical
fiction, gritty historical fantasy and rollicking Roman children's
books. He lives with his family and extended menagerie of pets
in rural North Yorkshire.

Also by S.J.A. Turney

Tales of the Empire

Interregnum
Ironroot
Dark Empress
Insurgency
Invasion
Jade Empire
Emperor's Bane

The Ottoman Cycle

The Thief's Tale
The Priest's Tale
The Assassin's Tale
The Pasha's Tale

The Knights Templar

Daughter of War
The Last Emir
City of God
The Winter Knight
The Crescent and the Cross
The Last Crusade

Wolves of Odin

Blood Feud
The Bear of Byzantium
Iron and Gold
Wolves around the Throne
Loki Unbound

LOKI
UNBOUND
S.J.A. TURNEY

CANELO

First published in the United Kingdom in 2024 by

Canelo
Unit 9, 5th Floor
Cargo Works, 1-2 Hatfields
London SE1 9PG
United Kingdom

A CIP catalogue record for this book is available from the British Library.

Print ISBN 978 1 80436 779 7
Ebook ISBN 978 1 80436 780 3

Cover design by Tom Sanderson

Cover images © ArcAngel, Shutterstock

Look for more great books at www.canelo.co

Printed and bound in Great Britain by Clays Ltd, Elcograf S.p.A.

1

MIX
Paper | Supporting
responsible forestry
FSC
www.fsc.org
FSC® C018072

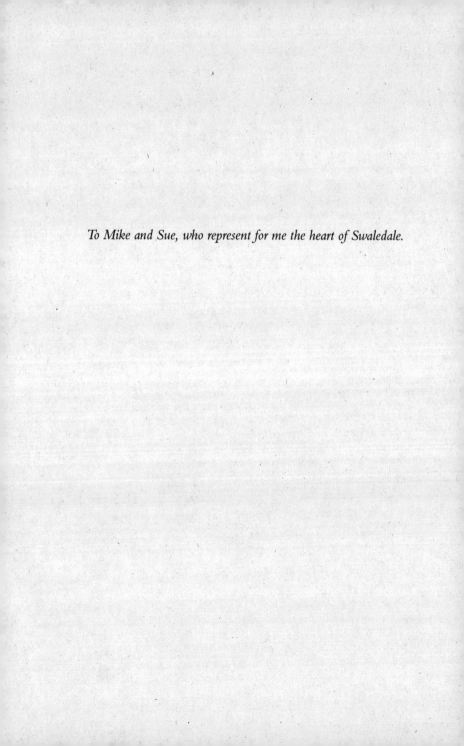

To Mike and Sue, who represent for me the heart of Swaledale.

A note on pronunciation

Wherever possible within this tale, I have adhered to the Old Norse spellings and pronunciations of Viking names, concepts and words. There is a certain closeness to be gained from speaking these names as they would have been spoken a thousand years ago. For example, I have used Valhöll rather than Valhalla, which is more ubiquitous now, but they refer to the same thing. There is a glossary of Norse terms at the back of the book.

Two letters in particular may be unfamiliar to readers. The letter ð (eth) is pronounced in Old Norse as 'th', as you would pronounce it in 'the' or 'then', but in many cases over the centuries has been anglicised as a 'd'. So, for example, you will find Harald Hardrada's name written in the text as Harðráði (pronounced Har-th-rar-thi) but it can be read as Hardradi for ease. Similarly, Seiðr can be read as seithr or seidr. The letter æ (ash) is pronounced 'a' as in cat, or bat.

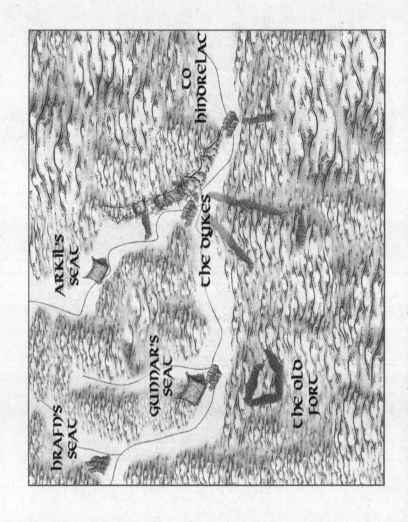

Three years ago

Gunnar looked left and right. It was difficult to make out much detail, what with the black smoke boiling up out of both stone and timber buildings, curling like the grasping hands of gods into the evening sky. It was almost over. Every figure he could see now was one of his *hirð*, their victims almost all gone. Two warriors charged from the tithe barn, whooping as a great gout of golden flame burst forth behind them and the roof exploded with a crash like that of Thor's own hammer. Two more were carrying a great, heavy timber cross, fitted with gold ornamentation, while a third followed on behind, trying to stuff a brass plate into a sack already full of loot.

This, Gunnar mused, must have been what it was like in the days of his ancestors, when they loomed out of the mist on the great, grey whale road, setting eyes on this island for the first time, and aiming for a monastery on an isolated spit of land. This must be what the heroes of old felt, the coursing of Odin's might through their blood, the power of the Northman in a world unprepared for their strength of arm and of will. He smiled, grimly.

'Gunnar,' someone yelled. Sounded like a warning. The tall, grey haired, yet impressive jarl of Swaledale turned to see one of his men pointing and followed the man's gesture. Arkil Bear-shoulders, a mountain of a man by anyone's standards, had just emerged from the church doorway, carrying half a priest as though it were some sort of puppet in a child's entertainment performance, using his free hand to manipulate the arms and mouth as though the dead dismembered man was still moving and speaking. It was not a pretty sight, even to a man as inured to war as Gunnar Thorkilson. Others yelled warnings, pointing at Arkil as they gave him a wide berth. The jarl rolled his eyes. What did they expect *him* to do about it? When Arkil Bear-shoulders went the way of the *berserkr*, only an idiot got in his path.

A noise drew his attention and he turned again.

Another priest had been brought out, this one intact, whimpering, held by the shoulders. For a moment, Gunnar considered intervening. Personally, he could not fathom how anyone could bend knee or neck to the White Christ, but he had striven to bring some sort of uneasy peace between the men of the old ways and the children of the nailed god, who seemed to probe ever deeper into the wild places. As such, he wasn't sure he entirely approved of what was about to happen. Still, that was why they were here, burning monasteries as though it was three centuries ago and they were fresh off the dragon boat from Nordland: to send a message.

A very clear message: Swaledale is ours, protected by the Allfather, by Thor and by Loki. The endless advances into the great valley by the evangelising priests of Jorvik would no longer be tolerated. The time had come for the stand to be made.

He hardened his heart as he focused on the scene before him and straightened, refusing to even blink. The priest clearly knew his time was up and that his end would be a grisly one, and Gunnar had to acknowledge the man's bravery, for he had stopped whimpering, and not moved to a womanly shriek like most of his kin. Instead, he had fallen silent, pale as ash, muttering his mantra to his nailed god under his breath over and over as he was pushed to his knees before the most impressive of all the hirð.

Hrafn stood still, her staff in hand, the bird's skull atop it bleached white, empty eye sockets locked on the figure being forced to the ground. Black feathers whipped and swirled around the staff, driven by flurries of wind and ash, as the woman who held it lifted her face to the sky and thrust out her free arm, the grey and black sleeve of finely embroidered linen disguising the ash flakes settling upon it. He shivered as Hrafn's man handed her the weapon, an unusual form, a single hand axe with a haft only as long as her forearm, and a bearded blade almost half as long. She hefted it a little, changed her grip as the men before her, men who were nominally Gunnar's but who, he knew, held a more specific loyalty to the *völva*, pushed the priest face down into the mud. He was still chanting quietly, saying his prayers to a god who, if he did exist, didn't seem to be paying much attention.

Hrafn examined the blade, looked up once more, and croaked her offering to the gods as she stooped and brought the axe down with all her might. The priest's mantra now gave way to a scream as his ribs exploded into shards, the edge cutting deep into the flesh of his back. But even had he the strength to tear himself free of the grips that held him down, now the smashed bones would prevent it, and he could do little more than shriek his desperate plea to his unseeing god as she brought the gleaming red blade back up, then struck again. Again. Again. Each time with precision.

The man's back was little more than a smashed field of blood, gore, innards and shards of white bone by the time his howling stopped and she passed the gore-rimed weapon back to her man. She reached down to the quivering mass of flesh and then rose, holding the dismembered heart.

'Hear me, Grey Wanderer,' she cried. 'Hear me, Queen of Fólkvangr. I give you the body and spirit of the priest of this place, but not the heart, for the heart is *mine*.'

And with that she bit into the glistening organ, tearing piece after piece from it until there was nothing left but the blood coating her hands and running from her chin. Her eyes glittered as she turned to Gunnar.

'It is done, Jarl of Swaledale.'

Gunnar nodded. The message had been sent.

Part One

ᚹᛟᛚᚠᛖᛋ ᛟᚠ ᛟᛞᛁᚾ

Jorvik

I preached the precious faith,
no man paid heed to me;
we got scorn from the sprinkler
– priest's son – of blood-dipped branch.

And without any sense,
old troll-wife against poet
– may God crush the priestess –
shrilled at the heathen altar.

Þhorvaldr's Verse from the *Kristni saga*,
trans. Siân Grønlie

Chapter 1

A lifetime ago. Unnamed village,
half a day's ride west of Skara, Geatland.

'Off with you, Bjorn Bjornsson. Out from under my skirts.'

Bjorn stumbled away as his mother's hand swatted at him, missing by just a breath. He almost stepped into the way of his father, an immense figure in furs and a chain byrnie, as the man strode across the house with axe in hand, examining the braiding of his beard in the blade. He ducked under the big warrior's arm and dodged to the lopsided table, where his older sister sat with bread and soup watching events.

'Sit down and shut up, Blaand,' she sneered, a common insult of hers comparing the ubiquitous fermented milk drink to her albino brother's complexion. Ingiríðr was never particularly nice to him.

Bjorn pushed himself into his seat and reached for the wooden platter of bread, which Ingiríðr predictably slid out of his reach. He sighed, not even bothering to reach for the soup bowl, given the wicked mischievous look in her eye.

'Why must he go?' he asked.

No one answered. His question had been nominally directed at his mother, though she was busy making the last moment arrangements for his father, who was still stomping around testing weapons and shrugging his chain shirt into a more comfortable position before belting it around the middle.

'Why must he go?' he begged again, eyeing his father. This time he did get one answer, though all it did was irritate him.

7

'Grown-ups have to do things,' Ingiríðr replied airily, as though she were already as old as their parents. In truth, she was just three years older than Bjorn, though since she had already been promised to Ari, the son of the blacksmith, she lorded it over Bjorn as though she were a married woman. Some days he wished their younger brother Baldr had survived his sixth year, so that someone else could take some of the verbal assault Bjorn suffered daily.

'Da? Why have you got to go?'

His father, stuffing a blanket into a hiking pack as he lumbered past, paused as he finally noticed his son calling to him. 'What?'

'Why are you going?'

'A man must heed his jarl's call,' was all the man said, before stomping off.

'Ma? Ma? Maaaa!'

'What?' his mother snapped, turning back to him again.

'Where is he going?'

His mother waved the question away as though unimportant, and Bjorn sighed again, reached for the bread, only to see it move out of his reach once more. As he sat, dejected, looking down into the scratched surface of the table, a new voice cut in.

'He must go, because the cross-kissers in Magnus's valley have sworn to remove the Odin stone.'

Bjorn looked across at the source of the scratchy, parchment-thin voice. His grandfather sat with both hands on the top of his stick, white eyes with no sight but the sad internal view of his own past settled on Bjorn unnervingly, as though he knew what he was looking at even through lost pupils.

'Grand-da?'

'The men of this village go to war with Magnus's people to defend the old gods against the serpent of the White Christ, Bjorn, my boy. Had I eyes, I would be with them. Had you balls that had dropped, so would you.'

To some extent, the old man's words warmed Bjorn. His grandfather was the only one that ever seemed to treat him well, but then the old man could not see the pale milky skin and pink eyes of his malformed scion, and consequently perhaps, did not realise quite how hideous Bjorn was, or so his sister said, anyway.

'Will he come back?'

'Of course he'll come back,' snapped Ingiríðr irritably. 'He is one of the jarl's best, a champion in his own right. He is Thor's chosen.'

'He's also a fool,' their mother grumbled, then smacked their father on the shoulder with her spoon. 'Don't make a liar out of your daughter. You make sure you come home.'

Their father muttered something affirmative and then hurried out to retrieve his shield from the shed. 'What happens if he doesn't?' Bjorn whispered.

'Pray to every god you know that he does,' Ingiríðr said in a low whisper. 'If they lose this fight, then Magnus and his men will come for their prize.'

Bjorn shivered.

'Please, Odin...' he began.

Late February 1044. Yore River, Angle land.

'Ah, Jorvik, at last,' the white-clad figure announced from the ship's prow, clinging to the carved dragon head.

Bjorn grunted. It seemed to him that they had been rowing forever. It didn't particularly bother him, though. He was built like a ship himself, after all, a great oak and pine construction of a man, solid and impressive, the muscles in his arms shifting visibly beneath the skin as he worked. And it wasn't boring either, as Lief sometimes complained. There was something simple and soothing about the rhythm: dip, pull, raise, swing, dip, pull, raise, swing...

He was getting quite good at estimating distances these days. It must have been eighty miles or more since they pulled their way into the river between the reaching arms of the feature-less flat land, the first half of that up a tidal channel heading more or less west inland, the second half becoming a winding, narrower river, though still of good size and flow for shipping, that meandered its way slowly north.

His gaze, full of suspicion, wandered from their guest to their surroundings and back repeatedly as he dipped, pulled, raised, and swung. Trust was a sparse, and precious, commodity in this world, and Bjorn had long known of himself that he had at best a limited supply. He'd extended it over these past few years, as one of the Wolves, to include men who had come to them from various disparate sources to take the place of the crew they had lost in Georgia. It had been easy to trust those men who had come with them on the *Sea Wolf* all the way from Sigtun, who gripped their Thor amulets and prayed to the Allfather as they portaged their ship like raiders of old. He'd had a little more trouble extending his trust to cover the Varangians they'd picked up, Rus warriors who prayed to the nailed god in their eastern manner. They were good men, and while they stuck to that ridiculous *draugr* god of theirs, at least they respected that the heart of the Wolves still lay in Odin's grasp. Then they had picked up those Normans who served William Iron-arm in Apulia. He'd had even more trouble extending his trust to embrace *them*, for they were not only Christians, but proper foreigners, whose ties to the North were old enough that even their grandfathers had forgotten what it was to be Norse. Yet, again, they had embraced the Wolves and become part of the crew. Now, in truth, there were far more children of the nailed god in the ship than there were sons of Odin.

But despite the multicultural nature of the crew, still their guest stood out as something different, and it was Ælfric Puttock, Archbishop of York, who they had saved from a siege at William the Bastard's Norman castle, who Bjorn found he simply did not have enough trust to cover.

The bishop was like a beacon of the nailed god. Wherever he went, men turned and bowed their heads to him. Bjorn didn't like that. Wolves of Odin should not be bowing their head to some priest, no matter how important he was. The man was, by his very presence, undermining the solidarity of the crew.

And Bjorn did not like the nailed god. Did not like his churches, or his priests, or his hypocrisy, telling his people not to kill, then sending them out with a sword to enforce that law – to the death if necessary. No, he did not like the nailed god.

His da, leaving the house, heading to war against the Christians of Magnus the Good...

His twitching gaze slid from the archbishop to the terrain behind him. This land seemed to be largely flat and featureless, but the city of Jorvik rose from it like a great grey fortress. On the east bank, a huge city, houses of timber and of stone clustered tightly together, surrounded by heavy walls, with the tower of a large church rising above them all, smaller versions dotted about. On the west bank, another town apparently, with its own wall, rising up a gentle slope from the water's edge to the embracing ramparts, more, smaller church towers visible there. It was, Bjorn admitted, the largest city he'd seen since at least Taranto, if not Miklagarðr. But it was also the most visibly Christian, which made him twitch.

His gaze slid back to the archbishop.

They were going to work for him.

Bjorn was not keen on the idea.

Somehow it was different to the other jobs they'd done so far.

Serving alongside the vile Jarl Yngvar had been part of a grander purpose of seeking revenge, and that was fine. Revenge was a good thing. Though if it had been Bjorn's father the man had killed, Bjorn would simply have torn his head off and been done with it. Still, it had been an adventure. Even fighting the war for King Bagrat on behalf of the maniac Yngvar had been fine by Bjorn. He liked a good fight, and when the enemy were also Christians, that was perfectly acceptable.

And serving in the Imperial Guard, the Varangians, in the great Byzantine city had been all right. The emperor may have been a bag of shit, and his empress far too wrapped up in the nailed god, but the guard was full of men of the old world deep in their hearts, and it was only a job. They had been, to Bjorn's mind, mercenaries. They'd been dragged into too much politics for Bjorn's real liking, but there had been bloodshed and gold, and though they'd fled, they'd fled rich.

And then working alongside the Norman lord Fulk in Apulia had been fine too, despite their being ever further from the Allfather's grasp, for that was simply a matter of hunting treasure. Though those Normans had once been good Northmen, these days they all seemed to be treacherous children of the nailed god, so killing them had been no great struggle, and the gold with which they'd escaped was the stuff of legend.

He'd been less impressed with their time in Nordmandi, with the warring Norman lords and the politics and that young Duke William and his plans, but again it had been a means to an end, making it back to the North. And it had given Ulfr the chance to make their new ship.

But now, here, he was more than a little uncertain about what they were doing, and the fact that it seemed they would be doing it for one of the nailed god's high priests.

He watched the archbishop suspiciously as they slid between the two urban sprawls and to a wooden jetty on the right. Halfdan and Ulfr gave out calls and orders, and the rowers let up as they drifted in close to the timbers, raising and then shipping the oars.

'What's eating you?' Lief asked from the bench beside him.

Bjorn pulled a face. 'Not a rosy-cheeked little woman, I can tell you that,' he replied in a leery tone, causing the small Rus to roll his eyes and look away, though his glance fell briefly on Anna, and he flushed.

He had long since learned to use ribald humour as both weapon and shield. He went through the automatic motions as the ship bumped into place against the jetty and ropes were slung out and tied, watching the archbishop and his jarl together.

That also worried him. The Wolves were the closest thing Bjorn had had to a family since he'd come of age, and Halfdan was more than his jarl. Halfdan was his friend. His *brother*. A man Bjorn would throw himself into the mouth of Fafnir to protect. To see him so at ease with a hated priest of the nailed god was troubling. Constant exposure to these people seemed to lead to conversion, as though their worship was a disease that could be contracted with too much proximity.

Men were busy discussing the city of Jorvik around him, pointing to buildings ancient and modern, but Bjorn remained quiet. It was the best way. With the exception of humour and insults, which he could sling out with ease, he had always found that important conversation was something that needed to be considered before release.

Men were waiting on the riverbank for them. Some sort of signal must have gone up as soon as the *Sea Dragon* had been spotted coming upriver. Three men in the robes of the nailed god's priests awaited, along with a score of men in chain shirts with spears and large, round shields, bearing quarters of red and white just like the tunics beneath the chain. An army. Only the nailed god would need his own army.

'My lord archbishop,' one of the soldiers greeted the new arrival, head bowed, while the priests fawned over their master.

'Edgar, well met. Please, though, these good men who have escorted me back to this fair city must be as famished as I, more even, since they also rowed, while I stood at leisure like a guest. Have word sent up to the episcopal palace ahead of us. Have the hall made ready for a feast.' The archbishop looked up into the greyness above. 'I suspect the time for evening meal is almost upon us anyway. Are the kitchens at work?'

The man called Edgar nodded. 'The hogs have been roasting for hours, my lord archbishop. All can be made ready swiftly.'

'Then see to it, my good man.'

That, at least, eased Bjorn a little. He was definitely hungry. He wondered what they drank in Angle land. Did they have beer like the Danes, or wine like the southerners? But they were back in the North. Maybe they had blaand.

The word made him twitch as always, and he refocused on what was happening.

'Farlof,' Halfdan called, waving to the man, who gestured back.

'My jarl?'

'It's not that I do not trust our host,' Halfdan announced, eyeing the archbishop, 'but that I know how troublesome cities can be. I have no intention of leaving the ship unprotected. Pick six men and keep them here to guard the *Sea Dragon*.'

Farlof bowed his head.

'I'll stay too,' Ulfr said, and Halfdan nodded. 'I'll make sure a meal is sent down, and we'll arrange a change of watch before bed.'

The archbishop turned from where he'd been in quiet conversation with one of his priests on the jetty. 'Everyone else, you must join us for sustenance in the palace.'

There were general murmurs of affirmative across the ship. Bjorn joined in.

'I could eat a whole hog,' Lief announced, rising from his bench and stretching.

'Did I ever tell you about the time I did just that?' Bjorn muttered conversationally, though his gaze was not on the small Rus, but on the priests still.

'Let me guess,' Lief replied with weary disbelief, 'it was whole and still moving.'

'No,' Bjorn countered, 'but *I* was in the raw, and the hog's owner wasn't pleased when he came back from polishing his crown and found his dinner gone and his wife naked and shagged out on the rug.'

'You do talk shit sometimes, Bjorn.'

'And sometimes I tell the truth.'

14

'If you say so.'

With a grin, Lief leapt ashore and followed the others. Bjorn did the same, falling in with the core of the Wolves as they stepped onto dry land and tried to adjust their stance to the lack of a rolling deck for the first time in many days. He stayed quiet once more as they moved onto a street of the city, with the red and white guards leading the way, the more important priest and most senior guard sharing tidings with the archbishop at the head.

'Things have only become worse since you left,' the priest was saying.

At least their language was easy. After so many years of listening to Byzantines, Italians and Normans, with their Grikkjar and bastardised northern tongues, it was refreshing to hear something so familiar and old. Their tongue was not *quite* that of the true Northman, but where it differed, that was because of a scattering of German in there, and there was plenty of such in the ports of southern Geatland, so this was nothing new to Bjorn. He found that he understood almost every word with the ease of a native, which was good.

'Worse?' the archbishop asked his man. 'Worse how?'

'Godwin's new castle has not put the fear into them that we had hoped. Indeed, it seems to have made them fortify their own positions further up the dale. Reports have them manning ancient pagan ramparts and forts long since abandoned.'

'They can be winkled out. That is why I brought our new allies, my friend.'

Bjorn's lip wrinkled. He didn't much like the sound of that.

He half listened to updates that meant nothing to him as they walked toward a large stone church that stood at a meeting of several streets. The ruins of some ancient complex, a massive stone building, surrounded them, columns rising like bony fingers into the grey evening sky. The church had been built within the ruins of some earlier place, and apparently built out of those ruins, too, by the look of it. Still, it was not to the church they were being led, but to one of a number of timber cruck buildings clustered nearby, a hall of some size, tall and long and impressive. A jarl's mead hall of some sort, Bjorn decided. Perhaps these nailed god high priests lived like jarls. They had their own army, after all.

The hall's interior was just as impressive, great timber beams hanging with red and white banners, a cross the size of two men at the eastern end. Even as they made their way inside with their host and his escort, servants or thralls of some sort, were hurrying this way and that, settling huge trestle tables into position in a great 'U' shape, carrying long benches and placing wooden bowls and mugs around the set-up. They were doing an extremely efficient job, and by the time Bjorn reached the seat apparently appointed to him, between Ketil and Lief, he had everything he needed for an evening of food and drink, barring the actual food and drink itself.

He stood behind the bench for a moment, and in the busyness of the hall, Halfdan finally broke off his almost constant conversation with the archbishop and looked around himself, seemingly checking on everyone else. Bjorn threw a hand out in his direction and crossed close enough to murmur in his jarl's ear.

'I don't like this. Why are we working for the nailed god?'

Halfdan shot him a look loaded with warning, made a motion with his hand that indicated this was not the time or place for such a conversation, and then shuffled off back toward their host.

Bjorn bit down on his irritation. Few things annoyed him more than the nailed god, but one of them was being left out of things. He turned to Gunnhild, who was moving further away from the priests.

'I want to know—' he began, but she waved the question aside and carried her place setting three spaces down, turfing Thurstan from his seat in an exchange.

Bjorn found that he was growling gently under his breath.

'I imagine this will be a good spread,' Lief announced, straightening the spoon and knife beside his bowl in anticipation of the main event.

'That reminds me of a joke about a Danish whore,' Bjorn said, formulating the old story in his head so that the punchline came out right, but Lief shook his head.

'Look around you, you big oaf. This is not the place for such a joke.'

Bjorn felt the tension snap inside him. This was becoming too much.

'Bollocks,' he said, loud enough that the nearest four seats to either side turned to look at him in surprise. Lief frowned.

'Bjorn...'

'No. I'll not sit and be a good quiet boy because we're in a nailed god hall, eating nailed god food with nailed god priests. Fuck, Lief, but you know they call bread and wine the flesh and blood of their god. I'm no cannibal.'

Now a large number of people were glaring at him. He caught the gaze of Halfdan and held it, defiant. After a moment, the jarl nodded once, very lightly, and Bjorn understood. Halfdan knew. Halfdan felt the same. But Halfdan was also better at hiding his displeasure. Bjorn had never learned the art of subterfuge. His was a straightforward life, and that was how he liked it. Three spaces along, Ketil was giving him a look loaded with agreement and sympathy.

After a long moment, the tension faded and the others went back to their conversation. Bjorn sat, irritated, and it took time for him to realise that Lief, next to him, was giving him a very odd look.

'What?'

'You've got to be more careful, my big friend. We don't want to insult the archbishop.'

'Why?' demanded Bjorn. '*I* might want to.'

'For now, we need him. We need the deal Halfdan struck.'

'Why?' Bjorn demanded again. 'What is so important that this priest can offer us that makes it worth fighting for the nailed god. And if I understand it properly, we're to fight a good son of the Allfather. I'd rather eat my own cock than fight Odin's people for the Christ.'

Lief acquired that long-suffering look Bjorn knew well, and nodded. Lief was, of course, a Christian himself, and Bjorn often forgot that, so solid was the man. He was about to apologise, a rare thing, when the little Rus turned to face him directly, knife in hand, tapping it with his finger.

'It's not about whether the man we hunt is one of your old pagans, Bjorn, or whether he's a blessed son of the Theotokos. And it's not about fighting for Christ, either, or for Odin. This is about an exchange. We are doing a favour for a man, in return for his help. We're going to kill a warrior in return for a prize we'll get nowhere else. *That's* why Halfdan has agreed.'

'I still don't understand,' Bjorn huffed, though he often found it hard to argue with the clever little bastard.

'Excommunication. Only someone as powerful in the Church as the archbishop has the power for such a thing at such a level. Halfdan is unlikely ever to find another man as important as the archbishop, and such an offer will never come again.'

'So the Church says it doesn't want Hjalmvigi any more. What difference does that make?' Bjorn grunted.

'*Every* difference,' Lief replied. 'Hjalmvigi is the personal priest of the King of Sweden now. He has more power than any priest in the North, and his power derives from his position. His position affords him a fortress of his own, a bodyguard, a place in the court. He is practically untouchable now. Halfdan will never get within a thousand paces of the man armed. Even you, my big friend, could not just walk into the court, find him, and tear his head off.'

'I'm willing to bet I could.'

'No, you couldn't. Halfdan knows all this. But when official confirmation reaches Uppsala, the zealot Hjalmvigi will be stripped of all his authority, and even the pope in Rome will turn his back on him. And if a man is cast from God's flock, then no true Christian will lend him aid. He will lose the king's trust and support. He will lose his church, his palace, his fortress, his men, all his power. He will be nobody. Not even a priest any more. *That* is why we do what the archbishop asks. That is why we will find this troublemaker and we will kill him. That is why we would do it whether he was pagan or Christian. For Halfdan. To get to Hjalmvigi. Do you follow me?'

Bjorn nodded sullenly. He understood what Lief was saying, though he was still unsure why this was the case. How could one priest stop another priest being a priest? Especially just by writing a few copies of a note and sending it to his friend? It all sounded a bit far-fetched to him. He spent the next few moments trying to word this in his head, and finally unleashed his thought to Lief.

'Still sounds like bollocks to me.'

Lief chuckled. 'You, my friend, are a man of simple vision.'

Bjorn mused on the value of the written word for a time as the hall settled and food was brought. Despite his misgivings that this might be some official nailed god meal of wine and bread, it turned out to involve three whole roasted hogs, enough vegetables for a man to hide behind, and, yes, bread, but no matter how much he sniffed or poked at it, it appeared to be just ordinary bread, and, when he finally decided to taste it, it tasted just like bread, too.

Best still, rather than wine, what they brought in was small barrels of beer and of mead, and Bjorn, not wanting to miss out, stole three extra cups while their owners weren't looking and fetched himself two cups of each. They were not at all bad, and though he occasionally paused to look suspiciously at the cups and the bread and wonder if a man could be poisoned into believing in the White Christ, he found he was hungry and thirsty enough to take the chance.

'Tell us what you know,' Halfdan said in a lull in the murmur of conversation, and the hall fell silent. The archbishop put down his knife and finished chewing, then leaned forward, steepling his fingers.

'We hear a lot of rumour. What is fact is less certain. The leader's name appears to be Gunnar. He is Norse by blood, I think. His people have lived in the upper reaches of the Swaledale for generations. My predecessors came to a sort of understanding with his forebears that they could stay untouched where they were, as long as they did not come down the valley and cause trouble. I had intended to hold to much the same agreement, but it appears that this Gunnar is of a different mind, and much, I think, is the fault of the lead.'

'The lead?'

The archbishop nodded. 'Swaledale is one of the land's most abundant sources of lead, from the mouth of the dale right up into Gunnar's lands. We need the lead, and we have been very careful not to push mining operations up to Gunnar's border, but we have come close to them. And to support the industry, of course, we need people. A monastery at Ghellinges that had been abandoned for generations has been reoccupied, the village of Hindrelac on its hill, the first settlement up the dale has been extended and settled from Jorvik and surroundings. But it seems Gunnar is not happy for us to even extend into the end of the dale, as though the whole region belongs to him.'

'So this is a border dispute,' Halfdan surmised, leaning back.

'It was. A few years ago we were still willing to talk and negotiate with Gunnar and his people. Then they took things a step too far. They raided Hindrelac and took the newly appointed parish priest prisoner, killing several locals, and then, in a moment that broke any hope of negotiation, they sacked and burned the Ghellinges monastery, killing every soul within, some in the most gruesome of manners. Since then, they have retreated up the dale, but now any time we try to reoccupy the lead mines in Swaledale, they are attacked. Gunnar has made himself my enemy now, and this can only end one way.'

Halfdan nodded. 'So Gunnar and his people have to be removed.'

'Yes. Simply, that. Though I have a small force of armed men, it is just that: small. I do not have the men to lead a campaign into the dale and dislodge Gunnar from his seat. In other times, I might have been able to call upon the king's men, or upon the local reeve, but I am not the most popular of men in my position at the moment, and I doubt I could raise sufficient support. So, you see, I can only rely upon the aid of mercenaries. You know what I offer in return for your aid, but I shall make the deal ever more palatable. Your ship will have to stay here – the river is not navigable beyond Ripun, I'm afraid – but in your absence I shall have it loaded with supplies for your ongoing voyage.'

'So that you can be rid of us as fast as possible once the job is done,' Ketil put in, shrewdly.

'I would not have put it so callously,' the archbishop smiled, glancing across at the Icelander. 'In fact, if you are back any sooner than June, I will do all I can to keep you in Jorvik until the summer, for the sea between here and Norway is brutal and treacherous in the spring.'

'We will need to leave men with the ship, you understand? I lost one ship to a thief in the great city of Miklagarðr. I will not risk losing another in Jorvik.'

The archbishop nodded. 'Of course. I am a man of my word, and I give that word freely in the sight of God. I shall uphold my end of our bargain. You return to Jorvik with proof of Gunnar's fall, and I will see your wicked priest removed from the Church, your ship safe and loaded, and grant you leave to stay in the palace until the seas are safe.'

Halfdan turned and glanced past Bjorn, to Ulfr, who nodded. 'He's right, Halfdan. The open sea between here and home will be rough as a new-sawn timber until summer. Better to stay here. Besides, I still have a few finishing touches to put to the *Sea Dragon*.'

Nodding, Halfdan turned to Lief, seeking confirmation that the archbishop's word would be good. The little Rus nodded his agreement, so Halfdan seemed content. 'Alright. How do we go about this?'

'I will have horses made ready for however many men you take, and documentation that will see you safe in my lands. The journey is simple. The old Roman road from Jorvik connects with Deira Street, the great way that runs from south to north through the land. Follow that road north to the village of Catraeth, and there you will find my liege man, Godwin. He will give you any more local and up-to-date information on the situation in Swaledale, and will be able to give you further directions.'

Bjorn leaned back.

It sounded simple enough.

He still didn't like it.

Chapter 2

Halfdan gripped his sword and glanced up again.

The skies, red as blood, shook and boomed, as though being torn apart. A black crack loomed above him as he stood, sword in hand, watching his enemy emerge from the doorway of the stone hall. On a bleak hillside, a world of men watched as Heimdallr and Loki met.

The guardian of Bifrost was tall, in a glittering shirt of silver. His eyes shone almost gold in the reflected light of the dreadful sky; in his right hand he held a sword that was the death of men, and in his left was a beautiful and terrible horn. It was that which transfixed Halfdan, even deep in the dream, for the very sight of the horn made the Loki serpents on his arm burn, as though he were aflame with the war-fire of the Greeks.

He stepped forward, and so did Heimdallr, and their swords met with a ring that cut through the earth, awaking giants, sending a call to the halls of the slain that the time was nigh.

Loki unbound...

—

Halfdan awoke, shaking and sweating. As usual, he knew it was a dream, yet he also knew it was *more* than a dream, for it was far from the first time he'd faced his doom on that hillside dreamscape. Four times now, always the same dream, always the same figure, yet he was still to see the end, which might, of course, be a blessing.

No, he realised, it wasn't *exactly* the same every time. One thing was different, so vague that one could almost miss it. It

23

was the *feeling* of the dream. The first time he'd had it, back in Nordmandi, the dream had been a looming, portentous thing, vague and warning. The other times it had felt similar, if perhaps a little more detailed, a little more real. This time, though, it had felt truly immediate, direct. As though it was actually happening, right now, here, to him.

That made him shiver.

Any hope of further sleep had been torn from him and he rose, pushing back the blankets, and found his belt, and his boots and cloak. Even here in the guest hall, with the embers of the night's fire glowing deep orange in the grate, the cold of February gripped Jorvik. In some ways, it felt almost like home here in Angle land, insofar as he'd ever really known a home. The weather was not dissimilar to the land of his youth, and the terrain was familiar. Blink and he could be in Gotland, watching his father die and their village stone being torn down.

Stepping between the beds of snoring and farting men, he approached the door and slowly, trying not to wake anyone, turned the key. The door opened with the gentlest of creaks, out into a corridor. Three rooms filled this place, each opening off that timber corridor in a line, each a bunk room for guests. It seemed that part of the nailed god's monastery was always given over to guests, and the Wolves were split between the three rooms, two filled with burly warriors, the third given over to the three women.

That had been interesting. The archbishop seemed to have come to terms with the trio during their time in Falaise, and then on board the *Sea Dragon*. Two of the women followed the nailed god, but in some slightly different way – for the Byzantines did everything a little differently – and one he considered a witch, and yet somehow accepted on tentative terms. The archbishop was, however, alone in that. Since their arrival in Jorvik, every other pair of eyes, from the lowliest thrall in the street, to the most richly draped priest, watched her with a barely concealed mix of revulsion and fear. Only her position among the crew and the strange off-hand respect that Ælfric Puttock accorded her prevented any trouble.

Halfdan passed the second room of men, the sounds of night-time issuing forth, and reached the third. He paused. He didn't want to knock, in case he woke all the three women, when it was only Gunnhild he wanted to speak with. But the door would likely be locked, and it was hardly fitting to just walk in.

Unable to decide, he reached out and grasped the handle, gently testing the door. To his surprise, it opened smoothly and quietly, and he immediately felt a wash of guilt at sneaking so into the world of the women. He paused, door open, and looked into the darkness. He could make out the beds, only two of them occupied, and then noted with a start the figure of Gunnhild. She was not abed and asleep, but standing at the room's window, looking out into the darkness, fully dressed, her back to him.

She must have heard him enter, and so he said nothing, trying not to disturb the figures of Anna and Cassandra in their beds. He slowly, quietly, clicked the door shut once more and padded across the room, coming to a halt at the window beside Gunnhild. She made no move to acknowledge his presence, and he leaned on the windowsill beside her, resting his arms next to the runes she had carved into the sill to prevent unwanted figures using the window for entry. Rarely had she not considered such things.

'I am troubled,' he whispered.

She said nothing, gave a single nod.

'I had the Heimdallr dream again.'

This time she turned to him. 'You do not need to whisper,' she said in low tones. 'Cassandra trained herself to sleep on board ship, surrounded by loud warriors, and when Anna is not talking, which is rare, she is oblivious. That girl could sleep through *Ragnarok*.'

Ragnarok. That did not help.

'I had the dream again,' he repeated. 'Only this time, it felt nearer. Almost now. If it *is* prophecy, a work of *Seiðr*, I think we're approaching the time and place. Gunnhild, I'm worried.'

She turned to him then, and he realised that whatever his concerns right now, they were far from alone. 'I have spoken to Lief about this matter,' she said. 'He has this thing he calls a metaphor. He does not believe that it is *actual* Ragnarok for which we are heading, but that your dream is giving you some sort of *personal* Ragnarok, an end of *your* world, an unmaking, and the birth of a new.' She straightened. 'Of course, Lief is a dreamer and an idiot, born of the White Christ.'

Her eyes took on their more usual twinkle, and that brought some relief to Halfdan.

'It might help, perhaps,' she added, folding her arms, 'to think of your life in a series of cycles, each like the world serpent, bound around your life, consuming itself. You have already faced a series of powerful men, and each has brought about its own ending, its own change to your life.'

'What do you mean?'

'Yngvar the Far-travelled. He killed your father and tore down the Odin stone in your village. You trekked across the world, built a crew, bought a ship, and faced dragons and giants and *draugar* to bring him down, even following him in his crazed quest in order to do so. And in facing and defeating Yngvar you changed your whole life, from seeking revenge to seeking greatness, something that has cemented your hold on the Wolves.'

He shrugged. 'I did what needed doing, but still Hjalmvigi escaped, and if anything, he should have been even more my enemy, for he was the one who drove Yngvar to his crimes.'

'Hjalmvigi awaits you at the *end* of your journey, I believe. After all, for what are we doing all of this if not to see his fate fall upon him?'

Halfdan could only nod at that. Somehow things always made a little more sense when Gunnhild said them.

'You faced the anger of *Norns* and Gods in the imperial city by refusing what I advised, and forcing me to defy the Norns myself. You lost so much in Miklagarðr, but what you gained, you probably did not even notice. The man who led us to Miklagarðr was a young warrior with a hirð behind him. The man who *left* Miklagarðr was a jarl, who others flocked to.'

'That was more or less necessity.'

'The same is true of the Norman lords. Each of your quests to overcome a powerful enemy has changed not only you, but the world around you. Each has been a Ragnarok of sorts. Now this encounter with Heimdallr you fear is coming, what is different? All I wonder is what new Halfdan Loki-born will walk away from this?'

Halfdan gave a sigh of surrender. 'Perhaps you're right. Will you walk with the goddess for me?'

Gunnhild turned, then. 'It is not a good time or place, Jarl Halfdan.'

'Oh?'

She pointed into the dark window, and Halfdan glanced out. The view here was of the magnificent stone church, across a wide courtyard. He almost jumped as his gaze fell upon the watcher. One man in the robes of a priest, standing bathed in weak winter moonlight, a gentle drizzle soaking him as he stood, eyes locked on their window, eerie, unmoving.

'How long has he been there?'

'All night. This whole city is smothered beneath a blanket of the nailed god. Freyja is not welcome here. She may not hear me.'

Halfdan chewed his lip. He had to know whether he was dreaming some sort of whatever-it-was Lief had talked about, and that it was his own mind warning him that things were going to change, or whether very literally they were soon to meet the guardian of Bifrost, so that Ragnarok could begin.

She glanced sidelong at him. 'I will tell you this *without* the aid of the goddess. Yes, you are Loki. You always have been, for the marks on your arm branded you as the trickster from birth. And since the day we travelled with Yngvar the Far-travelled, Loki has been bound. First to the King of Georgia and to his oath of vengeance, then to the Varangoi and his oath to an empress, then to his men and to Fulk the Norman, and even to William the Bastard so recently. And you are *still* bound, Halfdan, just now to the archbishop of Jorvik. Loki remains bound. But some day soon your bonds will fall away, perhaps when you kill Gunnar for the archbishop, for then you will owe nothing, be beholden to no one. Then, Loki will be free.'

He did not find that at all comforting. 'Gunnhild, please.'

She looked around at him, that appraising gaze of hers, and folded her arms. 'All right, but not here. Somewhere where the nailed god holds less sway. Somewhere the song will not wake the others.'

Halfdan nodded and noted with interest as she stepped away from the windowsill that she already wore her shoes, and her cloak was draped at the end of her bed ready. She had expected to be up and about.

'Tonight is not a night for sleep, I think,' he mused as he looked out once more at that wet priest standing in the moonlight, watching their window. He turned and followed her from the room. She did not bother locking the door. He smiled. One of life's constants was Gunnhild's self-confidence.

She opened the outer door, leading away from the guest house, and the cold hit them with a vengeance, swirling eddies of drizzle blowing into the corridor on the icy blast. 'This way,' Gunnhild said, pointing toward the end of the church. Halfdan frowned, but followed. The various halls and ancillary buildings that seemed to serve the great church of Jorvik were kept separate from the main streets of the city by a wall of their own. It was a smaller, less military looking affair, yet still it kept the world of the nailed god apart from the world of the mundane, and it was with some trepidation that he followed her toward the small gate that led to the city beyond.

A soldier of the archbishop in red and white livery stood guard there, even at this time of night, and he looked confused as they approached. The man presumably had standing orders to prevent the entry of unknown or unwanted folk, but perhaps had never been told what to do about people unexpectedly *leaving*. He faltered, but Gunnhild simply swept past him. 'We will return shortly,' she told him, leaving him floundering, unable to do much but nod his understanding.

She led Halfdan with purpose, then, and he followed, fascinated, through the saturating drizzle and a darkness illuminated only partially by poor, wet moonlight. Around the church they went and into the ruins of that building they had seen when they arrived, some great ancient structure with the stumps of columns, timber and stone houses built into the shattered remains, making use of the age-old strong walls. One place amid the buildings stood silent and untouched, close to the church that was built over part of the structure, an ancient room in the complex apparently shunned by those who followed, and it came as little surprise when Gunnhild made for that chamber.

Half the roof had survived intact, and so the rear half of the stone chamber was cold and dark, but at least dry. A set of steps led down into the darkness below, but someone had covered the steps with an iron grate with its own lock, so whatever was down there was of little concern.

'What is this place?'

'I know not, Halfdan, but it remains in the shadow of old gods, and the crawling fingers of the White Christ have yet to touch it.'

He marvelled. There were faint hints of a painted wall in the rear, though it was too dark to make out any detail. He stepped back a little, to where he was just under the shelter, but could see out into the open square outside, among the houses. Smoke belched up from a few of the roofs into the wet, dark sky, but it was late enough into the night that the majority of Jorvik's population would be fast asleep.

Her song began, then, and he divided his time between keeping watch outside and observing the timeless ritual of the völva calling upon her goddess. Her song was muted, and he wondered how much of that was out of respect for the sleeping folk around her, and how much was an attempt not to raise the ire of the nailed god whose stronghold this city was.

As her song wound and wove, rising like the sun on a winter morn, Halfdan found himself, as always, entranced. That was why, when he turned back to the door, he almost jumped to see the figure. A priest, surely the same one who had watched their window, stood in the street. He felt a moment of irritation. Was this the hospitality of the archbishop, to be watched like some untrustworthy stranger?

With a last glance at Gunnhild, to be sure she was safe, he marched out into the rain, straight across to the robed figure, who looked up at him on his approach, but made no attempt to move away.

'Leave,' he snapped.

'Witchcraft will not be permitted in this city of God,' the man said, officious and spiteful.

'Unless you want to meet your White Christ in person, fuck off.'

The man's eyes narrowed. He turned, looking back toward the gate that marked the boundary of the nailed god's complex, then to Gunnhild in the room, then back to Halfdan. 'Your horses will be ready in the morning. Be gone at first light. Even the archbishop cannot protect heathens for long.'

With that, the priest turned and walked away. Halfdan watched him go for a long moment, and was about to turn back to Gunnhild when he heard a cry and his heart lurched. He spun, focusing on the room, and saw her fall. In a heartbeat, he was running, splashing across the puddled flags and in through that door. Gunnhild lay in a heap on the dusty ground at the rear of the room, shaking wildly. Panic gripped him, and he ran over, dropping to the stone flags beside her. His hands reached out, but he paused, uncertain. Could he do more harm than good if he interfered? Her eyes were closed again now, or perhaps were *still* closed. Her shaking gradually subsided into trembling, and he bit down on his nerves, reaching out and grasped her, gently manoeuvring her to the room's shadowy back wall and sitting her up against it. He lifted stray locks of her ash-blonde hair from her eyes and tucked them with the braids behind her ears.

Her eyes opened then, perfect emerald green, but looking *through* him, looking through the whole world and into something else, as she shivered a few times more and slowly became still.

'What happened?'

She shook her head, her mouth moving slightly, not enough to form words.

'Is it this place? The nailed god and his priests? They are everywhere in Jorvik.'

Her head shook again. Still, she was silent, and his worry came afresh. What could do such a thing to Gunnhild? Even Bjorn, a powerful mountain of a man with Thor in his heart, was but a scrawny child beside the power of the völva.

'I cannot see,' she managed eventually, and her voice was shaky, which worried him further.

'It is this place. We can try again when we leave Jorvik.'

'It is nothing to do with the nailed god and his weak children,' she said, then. 'Our threads form the weaving of the Norns from this place, but I cannot see where they lead. The future is a shadow, and no more. I can see *nothing*. Worse: I am being *allowed* to see nothing.'

'That happened before, with Yngvar. It will clear in time.'

She shook her head. 'This is not uncertainty, as with Yngvar. There is something, *someone*, out there, who deliberately stops me, who cuts my bond with the goddess.' She turned and focused on him, and he was shocked to see what appeared to be fear in her eyes. 'Halfdan, something out there is more powerful than me, and it waits for us.'

31

He shivered, but forced down the fear. A jarl had a duty to his people, and part of that was to be their courage when their own failed. He grasped her by the arms and lifted, pulling her to her feet against the wall. He fixed her with what he hoped was a look filled with strength and confidence, a look that was entirely façade.

'There is always someone stronger out there,' he said, calmly. 'There are jarls in the world with more power than I. There are warriors with more strength than Bjorn. There are faster runners than Ketil, there are better engineers than Ulfr, and there are wilier thinkers than Lief. Of *course* there will be more powerful völva than you, Gunnhild.' He'd never believed that, of course, and desperately hoped that it wasn't true, but it sounded good.

'That is not much of a comfort, Halfdan.'

'But it *should* be. Because no matter that there will always be someone better, what there is not is any hirð out there who can beat us when we are together. A wolf alone can be cornered and killed. A bear can beat it. A man can beat it. But show me a *pack* of wolves, and I'll show you something that no one, nothing, can corner and kill.'

He held her gaze, and finally she nodded acceptance of his words, straightening. 'We should get back,' she said quietly. 'Sleep might be difficult, but we should try. We have a long ride ahead of us.'

He took a deep breath and followed her once more as she stepped out of cover and into the rain. Amid the ruins of a forgotten world, he dogged her heels back toward that gate. The guard did nothing to stop their return, simply stepping aside and bowing his head. Halfdan looked ahead and spotted for a moment that priestly figure, across the square. The man watched them for a heartbeat, no more, and then disappeared into a building. Returning to their own guest quarters, Halfdan opened the door for Gunnhild, who entered without a word, bidding him good night with a nod as he closed it behind her.

The past hour had not gone well, he mused as he turned and walked back toward the far door, his own room. He had woken from a very troubling dream, filled with worry and uncertainty, and had gone to the one person in this whole world he felt would always have the answers, would always be a pillar of strength amid any uncertainty. Unfortunately, in seeking strength and confidence in her, he had instead seemingly brought her into his own world of fear and confusion.

He almost jumped from his skin for the third time that night when the middle room door opened at the very moment he passed it. He even yelped in a tiny breathless voice, so taut and nervous was he. He breathed out heavily and leaned against the wall, filled with relief at the great comforting shape of his big albino friend in the doorway.

'Bjorn Bear-torn, are you trying to stop my heart? What are you doing awake?'

Something about Bjorn's expression did little to improve his mood. The man looked just as unsettled as Halfdan felt. 'I saw you and Gunnhild coming back across the yard,' Bjorn said quietly.

'But why are you awake?'

'I am troubled, Halfdan.'

Bjorn? What in Odin's name could be troubling the giant? 'Tell me.'

'What makes a *thrall*?'

Halfdan frowned. What sort of question was that? 'I don't follow you, Bjorn. Thralls are born into slavery, or captured in war, or sold to it, or suchlike. You know all this.'

'I've been watching these nailed god men.'

'So have I.'

'I think they are thralls, Halfdan. Slaves to their cross. I think they are thralls, but so meek that they don't even know they are thralls. They are so deeply enslaved that they think their slavery is freedom.'

Halfdan blinked. Philosophy? From Bjorn? What kind of weird night was this turning out to be?

'You might be right,' he admitted. 'But I fail to see—'

'Halfdan, if we hunt our own at the command of the nailed god, that makes us what they are. That makes us thralls to the White Christ. I will *never* be a thrall, Halfdan.'

The jarl's brow furrowed further. He tried a reassuring smile. 'Go to sleep, Bjorn. We have a long ride, tomorrow.'

'*Never*, Halfdan,' Bjorn repeated. The jarl gave him one last encouraging smile and walked on down the corridor to his own room. There, Halfdan opened the door once more, entered and locked it. On a whim, he crossed to the window, running his fingers across the protective runes carved there, and looked out into the night, where the light drizzle was rapidly turning into a deluge. At least the priest had stopped watching them and the square was empty. His gaze drifted across to the church, windows lit and warm even at this time of night. This place was as much the heart of the nailed god's world as that great temple in Miklagarðr where the emperors were crowned.

One by one, the Wolves were being plagued with doubt and fear. Halfdan and his dream of the final war; Gunnhild, her sight blocked by something she believed more powerful than herself; and even ever light-hearted Bjorn worried about their path and was dark of thought. Thank the gods for solid Ulfr, crazed Ketil and clever Lief. In the morning, he would have to speak to them all, seek their help in building strength and confidence in the pack once more.

His gaze danced along that great church.

Perhaps they *were* thralls now to the nailed god. Maybe Bjorn was right. But then so was Gunnhild. He – Loki – was bound, as he had been ever since the Wolves first sailed, but those days of bonds were coming to an end. And when they did, when their thraldom ended and they broke free of the nailed god, he promised himself here and now that he, and anyone who came with him, would never live in the debt of any man again. They would kill this Gunnar and earn the archbishop's help, then they would sail the whale road once more as free men of the North.

They would find Harðráði and take the *Sea Wolf* back from him, they would hunt down Hjalmvigi and bring to a close four years of vengeance and blood oaths. And then he would take them somewhere the nailed god could not touch them.

Somewhere they could live free.

It was a single thread to hold on to in this difficult time, and he gripped it like a drowning man clings to a branch as he returned to his blankets and eventually fell into a still, untroubled sleep.

Chapter 3

Bjorn stumbled, fell, was dragged for a time, painfully in the dust and grit, and finally managed by some miracle to pull himself back up to his feet as the ropes that bound his wrists, and also bound him to the children both before and behind, tugged and jerked. His wrists were red raw, bleeding, his feet sore, his legs beyond aches.

He looked at his fellow prisoners. Bjarni, Akil's son, in front of him, tall and willowy, and Erne the butcher's son behind, bulky and ruddy-faced. Both looked as hopeless as he. And that was as it should be, for hope had been torn from the world when a wounded warrior had staggered and lurched back into the village, his gut coils sliding free of a great slit in his belly.

'Lost. All lost,' were his last three words before he fell face first into the dirt by the Odin stone, desperately gripping his sword so that the Allfather's maidens would know he was worthy when they came for the fallen.

The village had exploded into panic. Many had run. Others, led by some of the older men, pulled old, nicked and rusty swords from lofts, or pitchforks from hay stores, and gathered in the square to await the inevitable arrival of Magnus and his victorious butchers.

Bjorn had not known what to do. First, he ran to the house, only to find it empty. The neighbour, busy packing all she owned into a bag in a desperate rush, told him that his mother had swept up Ingiríðr and fled, knowing what

36

victorious warriors would do to the women when they found them. Bjorn had panicked, then. His father had clearly fallen in the fight, and his mother and sister had gone.

Then he found his grand-da. The old man, though blind as a bat, gripped his spear and joined the feeble defence in the village square. What else could Bjorn do? He found the wood axe from their garden and stood by his grand-da, a shield wall of the too-old and the too-young. The enemy came soon, and there were so many. They ran into the square and began butchering the old and young alike, crying their nailed god slogans as they killed. Bjorn watched his last surviving relative fall, those sightless eyes never to close again.

Bjorn did fight. He was only a boy of nine years, and untrained in war, but he was quite big, even at that tender age, and a wood axe combined with impressive body size made a formidable foe for anyone. He thought he had killed one man, and maybe ruined the leg of another, before something smashed into the back of his head and he fell to the dirt, everything going black.

The next thing he'd known, seven boys seemed to be all that remained of the village, roped together as he groggily returned to the waking world, in time to be dragged back to the valley of Magnus the Good.

The village was, in truth, not much different from his own, other than the lack of old carved stones, which had been replaced with a great wooden cross at the centre of the village. As Bjorn was dragged with the others into the village square, the folk of Magnus's village emerged to watch with interest. The half-dozen warriors accompanying the captives hauled them to a halt at the centre, close to the cross, and an old greybeard with a scar that ran across both cheeks below his eyes and left a furrow across his nose, stepped toward them, both fists balled, resting on his hips.

'You are nothing,' he said. 'You are *less* than nothing.'

As if to illustrate his words, he took a single step, his boot sinking into a pile of fresh-ish horse manure. He then took four more steps and wiped it on the leg of one of the boys.

'Shit has more value than you. Shit is more useful. There are seven of you. By year's end, at least half of you will have died. Those that survive might finally be more valuable than shit, but not by much. Obey. Work hard. Survive.'

Then the bidding began. 'Nine silver coins for the church fund if I get the big redhead,' announced one warrior.

'Six for the bandy-legged blond.'

'I'll give seven for bandy-legs.'

And so it went, each of the victorious warriors offering to give funds for the construction of their new village church in order to take one of the thralls home. Of course, the money they were donating had all been stolen from Bjorn's village anyway, so no one really lost out.

It came as no great surprise that no one seemed interested in bidding on Bjorn. He'd always been something of an outcast, even among the boys in his own village. A man with no colour was marked for something, and not everyone was interested in finding out what.

'I'll take the ice giant for three,' someone finally said.

Bjorn looked up, and his stomach flipped. The speaker was the greybeard with the shit-covered shoe. It was highly unlikely that anything good would come of this.

Three lads suddenly scurried forward from the surrounding crowd, clawing at the old man.

'No, Da, not him.'

'How can you?'

'He's cursed. Look at him.'

The family resemblance was clear. The three boys, each at least three years older than Bjorn, were either the man's sons, grandsons or nephews.

'It matters not,' the man told his boys. 'If you buy a cow, you don't worry how God feels about it. All this is is a cow on two legs, who can chop wood too.'

No one was about to argue. No one else wanted Bjorn. He looked across at his new masters. The greybeard he knew he could deal with. The man would be cruel, but Bjorn was an investment of a sort, and as long as he behaved himself, he would survive. The three boys were a different matter. One look at their eyes, and Bjorn could see years of torment lying ahead.

'Take him.'

Late February 1044. Burgh town, Angle land.

'This land reminds me of my home, when I was a child,' Bjorn mused, looking about himself at the low, rolling slopes, covered with farm fields, woodlands dotted here and there, a river winding along off to their right.

'Isn't that nice,' Cassandra said with a warm smile.

'No,' Bjorn replied flatly. 'It isn't.'

'You've never spoken of your home, Bjorn,' Ulfr noted conversationally.

'No.'

'And now is not going to be the time?'

'No. Childhood is shit. The only good thing about it is being able to grow out of it.'

Ulfr shrugged. 'Some men never truly grow out of it.'

Bjorn narrowed his eyes at the shipwright for a moment, unsure of whether that was a dig or a general comment. In the end, he just grunted and turned his attention to the road once more.

By Halfdan's estimate they had travelled some fifteen miles from Jorvik that grey, cold morning, everyone keen to leave the city and get on the road where dangers were obvious and visible at a distance. The road had been good, and more or less straight, running through a couple of roadside hamlets of no real note, but they were approaching their first direction change. The rain was holding off for now, but skies the colour of lead and speeding clouds suggested it was only a temporary reprieve. Lief leaned closer as they rode. 'I know you don't like working for the archbishop, but just think of it as a job. It's just like working for Yngvar, or the empress, or Maniakes, or Iron Arm. And the archbishop took the oath on the holy book. He's a man of his word. He will give Halfdan exactly what he needs. This is a deal, not slavery.'

'I still don't like it,' Bjorn grunted, surprised that the little Rus understood as much as he did.

The more he thought on the matter, the more it was bothering him, and Bjorn would be the first to admit that he had only a limited scope of thoughts to work with. Their current predicament was occupying much of his mind.

'Did I ever tell you about the day I tore the arm off a troll?' he asked.

Lief sighed, catching sight of his Anna rolling her eyes. He shook his head. 'Your tales are getting taller even than Ketil.'

The Icelander threw them a glance that warned them to leave him out of their comparison, which only made Lief smile.

'It's true,' grumbled Bjorn. 'He was a good two feet taller than me, and broader at the chest. So hairy, I thought he might be half dog, and there were runes of power burned into his flesh, like brands. He'd been terrorising the area. Now, I was doing some fair terrorising myself, and I have nothing against such a thing – everyone needs a hobby – but this troll was treading on my territory. I met him in a fighting pit. He was eating the remains of someone's foot, and the first thing he did was to throw the foot at me. First time I was ever kicked by someone with no body. Not the last, but that's another story. Anyway, he came at me, speaking his troll tongue, growling and swiping his claws back and forth. Big claws, they were, too. Maybe half the length of a sax blade, on hands like shovels.'

Beside him, despite his scepticism, Lief was entranced.

'Go on.'

'There was a door into the pit. Didn't fit very well, and they'd left it open when we went in. The thing came after me, and I know I'm not the sharpest sax on the shelf, but I had a moment of Loki cunning. I was still young, you see, not the big-cocked scourge of warriors and whores I am now, and I knew I couldn't win. I ducked under the thing's first swing and got behind it. I ran through the door and half closed it. The troll couldn't quite get to me, and it kept shoving its arm through whatever gap it could. It got its arm between the door and the frame, and I slammed the door as hard as I could. Broke its arm. And while I held the door shut with one hand, I yanked its arm this way and that with the other, till it tore free.'

Lief was looking at him with an odd expression, the one he reserved for trying to determine whether there was any truth to Bjorn's stories. 'Then?'

'Then I opened the door again. I beat the thing to death with its own arm and in the end, I stuffed it up the troll's arse so that only the fingers were showing.'

'You almost had me sold on that one until the end.'

As Lief went back to contemplating his world, Bjorn fell silent again and looked this way and that. They were approaching a town of sorts. It had probably been a thriving place long ago, but now it was a village of timber houses, built within the ruins of an ancient, much grander town. It was a village pretending to be something more. Much like Bjorn's tales. His friends would marvel to know that every one of his stories *always* had a core of truth. He just liked to embellish them. When a man had been through what Bjorn had been through in his life, a little fantasy was important from time to time, to take the weight of destiny off.

His bad mood started to return as they drifted into the settlement. Halfdan made some enquiries and they were directed to another road that was, apparently, the great Deira Street that led north. Bjorn's already irritable mood continued to slump as he watched the locals glaring at them with barely disguised dislike.

They were approaching the ruinous town walls and the way north when the column stopped at a call from Halfdan. Bjorn, who was three horses back from the jarl, looked up, frowning. A number of armed men in chain shirts had stepped out into the road, led by a man in a fine, high quality cloak.

'Yes?' Halfdan said, curtly.

'I am Cyneric, a representative of the Reeve of Ripun.'

This was delivered with such a flourish that clearly Cyneric expected them to know who he was, or to be impressed in some way. Halfdan did not look impressed. Bjorn very much wasn't. In fact, with his mood the way it now was, wallowing somewhere in a black pit, he was more inclined to tear a man's head off than bow to him.

'So?'

Cyneric frowned. 'You are foreigners, I see. It is the responsibility of the reeve to keep the great roads of this land safe for travellers, to apprehend criminals and to dispense justice where required. You are not locals, yet you ride with weapons bared as if to war. Such a sight might easily draw the attention of the authorities.'

Halfdan nodded. 'We are here on official business.'

As the conversation progressed, Bjorn felt a tickling sensation on the back of his neck, and, turning, found one of Cyneric's men staring at him, goggle-eyed.

'I take it you have some form of identification?' the official asked Halfdan.

'I have.'

'And?'

Bjorn was only half listening. The armoured man by the roadside was still watching him, though what had been a fascinated stare was now sliding toward an unpleasant glare. Bjorn decided that all the man needed to do was say the wrong thing, and he might just give him a second arsehole.

Ahead, Halfdan produced the document they had been given by Archbishop Ælfric and held it out. 'This should tell you everything you need to know.'

Bjorn narrowed his eyes dangerously at the man watching him. That soldier's lip had curled up into a sneer that Bjorn decided would look just fine smeared across a rock.

'Halfdan?' he murmured, blood starting to boil.

The jarl waved his comment down without even turning, his own attention on the man with the document.

'This has the look of a forgery to me,' Cyneric announced, waving the document.

'It is genuine, and you know it,' growled the jarl.

'Halfdan?' Bjorn tried again. His blood was starting to fizz and thunder in his veins the way it did when he was *really* ready for a fight. He was known for the times he had truly surrendered to the berserkr and fought like a madman, like a bear or a troll. But the simple fact was that just being Bjorn was more or less halfway to berserkr anyway. It did not take much to set him off, and though he had of necessity learned a little better control over recent years with the calming influences of Halfdan and Gunnhild, even he knew that he was only ever one insult away from punching a man's face through the back of his head.

'Not now, Bjorn,' Halfdan snapped as he turned back to Cyneric. 'That seal came straight from Jorvik. We are tasked with finding the lord Godwin of Catraeth and helping him remove troublemakers from the valley beyond.'

This seemed to change things. Cyneric frowned, tucked the document away in its case, and held it back out for Halfdan. 'There are less than thirty of you.'

'Yes.'

'And you're going after Gunnar of Swaledale?'

'Yes.'

'Then you're either brave beyond measure or mad as a frog.'

'Halfdan?' Bjorn tried again. The soldier was giving him a look now that suggested Bjorn reminded him of something that fell out of a cow's arse.

'Not *now*, Bjorn.'

'Yes,' the soldier sneered quietly, 'sit quiet. There's a good freak.'

Bjorn couldn't help himself. In his defence, he'd tried to ask Halfdan to do something three times now, and been ignored each time. There wouldn't be a fourth.

For a big man, Bjorn was fast enough that it often surprised people. That, of course, was a symptom of his awful childhood, when being fast was a large part of staying alive.

His axe was tucked in the back of his belt, quite loosely and lightly, for otherwise it caused trouble when riding. As such, it came free with a simple whisper as Bjorn's fingers closed on it and brought it out and round and then over, all in one fluid, graceful move. It hit the sneering man on the top of the head, butt-end first, blade reversed. The sheer power of the blow and the weight of the weapon damn near killed the man in an instant as his conical helmet crumpled and slammed down into flesh and bone, carving a line around the man's skull with its edge, the nose piece bending and cutting his chin. The man's neck had vanished, his head squashed down into his shoulders under the immense thump.

Bjorn lifted his axe and frowned at it as though it were not working properly while his victim, far beyond hope of a sneer now, staggered this way and that, his helmet jammed onto his head so tight it was touching bone, blood sheeting down his head in every direction as he bumbled, making 'urk' noises.

Bjorn looked at the man.

'Shut up,' he said, and swung again. The man turned at the last minute, blinded by iron and blood, and so the butt of Bjorn's axe now caught him on the back of the head, sending him sprawling into the road.

Bjorn looked up.

Everyone was staring at him, all the Wolves, and all the Reeve of Ripun's men. There was silence.

'Well,' Bjorn said, 'he was being a prick.'

'We're supposed to be on these people's *side*,' Halfdan hissed.

'I'll be on *his* side,' Bjorn said, pointing at the official in his cloak. 'Unless *he* starts being a prick too.'

Halfdan was glaring at him, giving him meaningful looks. Everyone else registered somewhere on a scale between shocked and horrified. Everyone except Ketil. The Icelander was trying to hold in explosive laughter as the badly injured soldier managed to get to his feet, but walked straight into a wall, still blind, unable to prise his helmet off his head.

'At least he used the *back* of his axe,' Lief noted. 'Could have been worse.'

Bjorn nodded. Could have been worse. Should have been, really. He'd drawn his axe and struck too quick. He'd intended it to be blade first. The butt end was an accident.

'Your man will owe *weregild*,' Cyneric announced. 'Normally I would have him taken to a cell and let the reeve pass judgement. It might well be death,' he added, 'but in the circumstances, I fear you'll need your killer ape when you meet Gunnar of Swaledale.'

'What's weregild?' Lief put in, leaning forward.

'A payment of compensation for injury inflicted. Ideally, I would like a doctor to look at him, but there is not time. I set the weregild at a sum of fifty silver pennies, payable immediately.'

Bjorn frowned, looked down at the injured man. 'How do you know he *has* fifty pennies?'

Halfdan turned in his saddle. 'He means *you*, Bjorn Beartorn. He wants *you* to pay the man, to apologise for braining him.'

'Then he can fuck off,' Bjorn said airily. He could feel his mood lifting every moment now. He was starting to enjoy this.

'Bjorn...' Halfdan said, his tone a warning.

'No. Not a penny. In fact, if I have to pay any money, I'm going to make it worthwhile and pull his tongue out through his arsehole first.'

Halfdan winced as other soldiers put hands on sword hilts now, and Cyneric's expression became dark. Ketil looked to Bjorn and then Halfdan.

'Choose your battles, my jarl. This one—'

45

'Pay the man,' Halfdan insisted, eyes still locked on the albino.

'No. *He* should be paying *me* this weird-gild. I only hit him. *He* looked at me funny.'

Lief gave a light chuckle. 'That alone might be considered just cause for our big friend.'

Halfdan's eyes narrowed. 'Pay the man, Bjorn. You have the silver.'

But Bjorn had no intention of doing anything of the sort. Not because of the money. He didn't really care about the fifty pennies. But a fight was a fight. He'd enjoyed it so far, and the way the tension was rising, if there was any luck, they'd all be involved in a massive ruck with the soldiers any time now. He grinned and looked at the man next to 'helmet head'.

'You. Are *you* looking at me funny now?'

To the man's credit, he moved like lightning, stepping back and disappearing behind his friends, out of sight. Bjorn felt slightly cheated.

It was Lief who brought the whole episode to an end. 'Halfdan, you're a jarl in your own right. You have the authority to dispense justice when it involves your hirð.'

Halfdan nodded, grinned as he caught on, and turned back to Cyneric.

'You have levelled a weregild sum of fifty pennies for the injury Bjorn did to your man. But among my people, an insult can be worse than any injury, and your wounded man brought this on by insulting Bjorn. As such, I hereby demand a weregild sum of fifty silver pennies from your injured man for his insulting behaviour toward Bjorn. So, if we were to consider both sums as paid and cancelling one another out, then there is no injury outstanding, nothing owed, and we can get on with our journey.'

The official frowned at what he clearly considered a dubious bit of legal logic, but after a look along the line and a little consideration, he clearly reached the conclusion that this was as good as things were likely to get unless he was willing to risk a proper fight.

'Very well. We shall draw the matter to a close.' He gestured to the man who still could not see past his blood-stained helmet. 'Osgar, take him inside and get that thing off him.'

As the injured man was helped through a door into an adjacent building by two men who kept looking back at Bjorn nervously, Halfdan and Lief engaged in a quiet, urgent conversation with the nobleman. Bjorn sat back in the saddle. It had been a fun little diversion, but the others had put paid to it going any further. Bjorn liked a good fight, and he'd been missing one ever since Nordmandi. He sat there, feeling the elation gradually subsiding, and the gloom of his earlier musings rising once more to take its place. Cassandra tried to say something to help, but her chirpy little comments were just irritating.

In the end, by the time they rode off again, Bjorn was more or less back to his glum state.

They rode out from Brough on to the great north road, crossing a sizeable river on a timber bridge of some antiquity, and heading north. They could see now that they were in some immense valley, for distant lines of hills kept pace with them, blue-grey, to either side. Bjorn wondered idly whether they might get jumped by bandits, but decided with a sigh that men like the Reeve of Ripun and his soldiers probably kept the roads clear of such opportunities.

'You look miserable.'

He turned to see Lief riding beside him.

'And you look like a man. Appearances can be deceiving.'

The diminutive Rus ignored the deliberate jibe. 'There will be plenty of fights. Plenty of men in the coming days that you can break the skulls of.'

'*Good* men,' Bjorn countered. 'Men destined for Odin's hall. Men I would proudly stand by in battle. I want to fight these snivelling little *Christian* soldiers.'

'Careful,' warned Lief. 'My tolerance goes only so far. You know that Anna and I are both children of Holy Mother Church.'

'Yes, but with you I always think it's some kind of mistake. Like you got dropped on your head and your brain stopped working for a while. One day you'll come to your senses.'

Lief snorted. 'In the perfect world, what would be the perfect fight, Bjorn?'

He turned to the Rus. There was something in the man's expression. He knew something Bjorn didn't. He was not far from grinning.

'What?'

'A fight makes you feel good, but what fight would make you feel better than any other?'

Suspicion weighed deeply on Bjorn now. He ruminated on the question. 'Fighting my way into a whorehouse through a door made of beef, over a moat of ale.'

Lief rolled his eyes. 'I mean in the *real* world.'

Bjorn thought some more. 'A challenge. Something that tests me.'

'And what could test you most of all?'

More thought. Finally, Bjorn shrugged. 'There's only one man I could fight and not be sure I'd win.'

'And that is?'

'Me,' said Bjorn. 'Of course.'

Lief chuckled. 'Then maybe you have something to look forward to after all.'

'What?'

'Cyneric told Halfdan and me that Gunnar is lord of Swaledale, but that it is his champion, his right-hand man that the region quakes in terror of. It is this man that wins Gunnar's fights for him. And you know what they call him?'

'Bjorn?' Bjorn hazarded, not entirely sure where this was going.

'No, you fool. I don't know his *name*. Only what they *call* him. They say he wears the bear shirt.'

'A *berserkr*?' Bjorn's eyes all but lit up. Only once, ever, had he fought a true berserkr. It would be the closest thing in the world to fighting himself.

Lief did not reply, but his knowing smile said it all as they rode on north, along a road as ancient as the hills that lay to either side. According to the archbishop, their first stop, at a place called Catraeth, should be another twenty or so miles, just nicely granting them a place to stay as the sun set on their first day of travel. After that, the distances would shrink, but the difficulty of the terrain and the danger awaiting them would grow by the mile.

Bjorn spent the day in a sort of limbo, periodically dragged down into irritation at their thrall-like service to a Christian priest, and then occasionally lifted by the thought that somewhere, in this Swaledale ahead of them, lay a fight with the makings of legend, a tale to be told by heroes in mead halls from now until Ragnarok.

Some time in the mid-afternoon, as a very fine drizzle began, the road descended a gentle slope, granting an excellent view north along the wide vale, then crossed a bridge over the narrow flow. The long-flattened ramparts of some fortress lay to either side of the metalled way, and a single timber house sat on the far side of the bridge, smoke curling up from a fire within.

After a brief discussion at the head of the group, Halfdan dismounted and approached the door. As he neared it, it opened, and an old man, with a long beard countering the complete lack of hair atop his skull, lurched into the open, leaning on a stick. He wore ragged clothing and a threadbare cloak, yet a decorative gold torc around his neck told a different story. Bjorn grinned to see Ketil eyeing the prize speculatively.

'We seek Catraeth and the lord Godwin,' Halfdan said to the local. 'Are we on the correct road, old man?'

The fellow nodded. 'I don't know this Godwin of yours, but Catraeth lies an hour or more that way,' he said, pointing on north. He looked along the line of warriors. 'You go to war?'

Bjorn, sitting back, already bored by the conversation, scratched his buttock idly. Ketil was drumming his fingers on his axe haft.

'We do,' Halfdan said. 'Against the Northmen of Swaledale, for the archbishop of York.'

'Find more men,' the old fellow advised, and then slipped back inside and closed his door.

Halfdan walked back to his horse and mounted once more as Lief straightened in his saddle. 'He's the second person today to make more or less that suggestion,' the Rus noted. 'I'm starting to think we may have bitten off more than we can chew.'

Bjorn snorted. 'A *thousand* men cannot stand against the Wolves of Odin.'

'A theory I'd rather not test,' added Lief.

'It is not about numbers,' Halfdan told them both. 'The dangerous part of a snake is the head. Crush the head and you needn't worry about the rest. Our remit is to kill Gunnar, remember, not to depopulate the whole of Swaledale. We will fight as we must, but I will do what I can to minimise the risk to our people. Focus on their leader, and we can win this fight.'

But Bjorn had other ideas. He didn't really care whether this Gunnar lived or died. Cyneric had said that the one to truly watch for was Gunnar's champion. Bjorn had his own path to take now.

Once more, his spirits began to lift at the thought.

Sure enough, as the sun began its descent, they closed on their destination. Catraeth, like Brough earlier, was another of those places of great antiquity that had fallen into disuse but had risen again as a lesser, timber village, this time outside the ruins, but close by. A church, built of old, re-used stones, sat on a rise above the cluster of wooden houses, and across from it, on a second slope, stood a palisaded enclosure with a sizeable cruck hall at the centre and a number of smaller buildings around it. Bjorn simply plodded along as Halfdan led the way to the fortress that had to be their destination.

A glance to the west revealed that those hills which had been marching along on the horizon had gradually come closer, and now there was a distinct gap in them, signalling the entrance of a wide valley.

Swaledale, home of the renegade Gunnar...

...and his berserkr.

Chapter 4

Halfdan approached with care. They were greeted at the fortress gate by a warrior wearing the same red and white as the
archbishop's guards, a man terse and not initially welcoming,
though a swift perusal of the document they carried granted
them access.

'As the archbishop's men,' the soldier told them, 'you may
keep your weapons on your persons, but be advised against
drawing them in my lord's presence, lest the garrison take
against you. Osmær will take your horses and stable them.'

Halfdan nodded his understanding, and looked about those
in his hirð to make sure the instruction had sunk in all round.
Everyone seemed content with this, though Bjorn still looked
unsettled, tense. Halfdan knew the big man was uncomfortable, and he'd have to keep an eye on that. When Bjorn was
uncomfortable, people tended to die, horribly.

As one of the younger warriors approached the horses,
Halfdan looked to Ulfr. 'I trust you, old man. Make sure the
horses are safe. Without them, we walk.'

Ulfr nodded with a smile. Halfdan tried not to echo the
smile. Ships, wagons and horses, when it came to moving the
Wolves from one place to another, it was always to Ulfr they
turned.

Ulfr helped the young warrior, and their horses were led
to a stable, while the party themselves were escorted to the
great hall. As they were ushered through the door into the
great building, Halfdan reflected upon the excellent timing they
seemed to be maintaining. They were arriving at the homes of

lords in this land just as feasts were being set out. Either the gods were truly favouring them, or these lords of Angle land lived fat and well and feasted like this daily. If the latter were the case, then no wonder the Norse had spent so many centuries crossing the treacherous sea to raid and settle here.

The hall was on two floors, though the upper was a mezzanine, reached by a timber staircase guarded by another red and white soldier. The ground floor was one enormous room, laid out with tables around a central fire pit. Hounds lay in the straw on the flagged floor, and servants hurried this way and that, bringing out the settings for the meal, coming in through another small door from some ancillary building.

The master of the hall sat, as expected, in a slightly larger and more ornate chair than any other in the place, at the centre of the head table. He was a tall man with pale features and a flat nose, clean shaven and with neatly clipped, short hair, in a tunic of rich green, draped with jewelled belts and chains of gold. He clutched a wine cup as though to steady himself, and the eyes that played across the new arrivals were wary, suspicious. His gaze slid to the soldier escorting them, who came to a halt before him, bowing, and offered the archbishop's document.

'My lord, guests from Jorvik.'

'Jorvik?' the man mused, taking the document and opening it, looking down the contents. If Halfdan was any judge, the lord didn't like what he found, any more than he did a bunch of armed pagans walking into his hall, but it seemed that the archbishop's name was still sufficient to buy them at least grudging goodwill. Finally, he handed the letter back. The soldier passed it on to Halfdan and, at a nod from his master, bowed once more and retreated from the scene.

'I am asked,' Godwin announced, 'to offer you all hospitality, and any useful information or supplies for your mission.' He frowned. 'It does not, however, explicitly state what that mission *is*. I would like to know more before I comply.'

One of the more senior servants appeared with a silent question for the master, looking back and forth between him and

Halfdan. Lord Godwin nodded, and extra places were swiftly laid for the Wolves. Halfdan took a couple of steps forward to where the soldier had stood to face Godwin.

'We are to remove the threat of Gunnar of Swaledale.'

It seemed the lord almost laughed as the entire room fell silent and motionless, the only disturbance a surprised thrall dropping a small stack of wooden plates, and hurriedly stooping to scoop them up. Godwin looked from head to head among the Wolves.

'I count twenty-seven of you. There are no more outside?'

Halfdan shook his head.

'Then I fear,' the lord said, 'that the most likely accommodation we can grant you is a decent burial, if any parts of you come back.'

Halfdan managed not to snort derisively. The same could not be said for some of his men, and he heard a murmured string of invective from Bjorn. 'We've faced kings, emperors and dukes,' Ketil called across, 'and beaten them all. Jarls should be no different.'

'You have no idea,' their host said darkly.

'I would caution you not to underestimate us,' he warned Godwin.

'And I would caution *you* not to underestimate *Gunnar*.' Godwin took a swig of his wine and replaced the cup, folding his arms. 'I have near thirty men myself, and they are just about sufficient to prevent the heathen bastard from raiding this far east. And my men are a trained and disciplined force, too.'

Halfdan didn't have to give a command, and he winced as the throwing axe whirled through the air and slammed into the wooden seat a finger-width from Godwin's ear. The lord's eyes bulged.

'I have *never*—' he began.

'My men take insults to their skills and strength rather personally,' Halfdan said, cutting him off. 'Let us get to business. You do not want us here. You see us as little better than those we hunt. You do not believe we can win. That is your concern. We do not want your men, and we do not need your friendship or respect. All we need is whatever information you can give us that will allow any advantage, and perhaps two- or three-days' dry rations for the road. Then, when the sun rises, we will be out of your hair. If we fail, you need not worry about us, and if we succeed you need worry about neither us nor Gunnar. I do not see a downside for you. Am I correct?'

Godwin's eyes narrowed as he reached up and with some difficulty plucked the embedded axe from the chair beside his head. When it came free, he looked at it for a time, then held it out. Ketil stepped past Halfdan and retrieved it, and the lord of the Catraeth rubbed his hands together as though to remove something unpleasant from them.

'Sit. You and your people.'

They did so, Halfdan taking the nearest place to Godwin. As they settled in, a small, rotund priest entered the building, went pale at the sight of the guests, crossed himself three times, and then hurried to a seat carefully selected to be close to Godwin and his guards, and as far as possible from the armed and scarred men openly bearing the symbols of old gods. Halfdan had to at least acknowledge the likelihood that any time these people usually saw such things they would be on the raiding men of Gunnar.

'Tell me about the raids,' he said.

Godwin nodded slowly, took another sip, and then straightened. 'They have been increasing of late. The heathen and his people have been at the upper end of the dale for several generations. There had always been something of an uneasy peace between them and the locals, who were, of course, good God-fearing people. They even traded. The Norse raised their animals up there, and even brought out lead from the old adits for tools and weapons, but they stayed in the upper end of the dale. The problem is that these lands belong to *us*, not Gunnar, who is an invader, and those sources of lead are much needed.

When we opened our own mines further up the dale, they began to raid us.'

'They broke the peace?'

Godwin had the grace to look abashed. 'It may have been my predecessor who started this, in truth. He was adamant that, these being our lands, we had prior rights over any invading pagan. Still, since my own arrival, I have attempted to make temporary peace with Gunnar, through messages with his people. He is unwilling to listen. He considers our people settling the dale to be a Christ-driven occupation of his lands and a threat to his people. We re-established an old colony at Hindrelac five miles up the dale, and the settlers had been there less than a month before the first raid took every man of fighting age from the village. I assigned a small garrison of five men there, presuming that the simple presence of soldiers would deter them. I was wrong. My men were butchered and left in— in such a state that it defies description.'

Halfdan nodded. He was not entirely sure he disagreed with this Gunnar yet. Generations settled implied at least a claim to land ownership. If Halfdan had been jarl of Swaledale and the archbishop's people began to settle the area, he might well have taken the same steps. Still, he held his tongue. Now was neither the time, nor the place.

'The old abandoned monastery at Ghellinges was reoccupied by monks from the abbey of Dunholme, as part of our attempt to bring a little more civilisation to the wilder parts of the region. Ghellinges is not even within Swaledale, and lies some distance from Gunnar's lands, to the north of Hindrelac, yet the heathens butchered the monks and raided the place. I fear that was the moment that any possibility of coexistence with Gunnar's people ended. The archbishop will not countenance such actions, and I support him in this.'

'And so you sit at the end of the dale and hope he stays far away and stops raiding?' Ketil interrupted from a little further down.

Godwin gave the Icelander a cold look. 'I have but a small garrison. My remit is to protect the settling of the flat arable lands in the lower dale and to reopen lead mines as I can.'

'And in this it appears that you are failing,' Ketil sneered, earning a sharp look from Halfdan.

A flash of anger greeted this. 'I do not have sufficient manpower to take the fight to the heretic. I do what I can, while preserving my men as far as possible. This, I presume, is why the good archbishop has given the task to pagan outsiders. You are, I think, dispensable. Perhaps when you and Gunnar have thinned one another's ranks sufficiently, the bishop will grant me extra men and I can finish the job.'

Halfdan brushed this aside with a wave of his hand. 'So you keep settling and pushing up the dale to take the lead, and Gunnar's men raid and kill to keep you away. Yet the way you speak, you have apparently never met this jarl of Swaledale face to face? What can you tell us of his people, his strength, his positions?'

Godwin glared at him silently for some time, and then took a deep breath and another swig of wine. He looked to the man at his side, another figure in a rich tunic, though this one of red. Another noble, perhaps, or a trusted man. 'Cuthbert, do the honours with a map.'

The other man nodded, rose and grabbed a long stick from near the wall. He then came round to the grime and dust of the floor in front of the tables, close to the fire pit. Herding lazy dogs from the area, he had two thralls clear away the straw and add three shovels of ash from the edge of the fire there, smoothing it out into a surface. Cuthbert then began to draw a map with a stick.

'This is us, at Catraeth,' he noted, creating a mark. He then drew a wide shape leading up from it, with a branch off to the right some way up. 'This is Swaledale. Gunnar is based here,' he added, dropping a second point some two thirds of the way up the valley. 'The side vale is controlled by his monster.'

Here, Godwin took over once more. 'The lead mines become more common and more profitable the closer we come to Gunnar's seat. Therein lies part of our problem. Gunnar has a small settlement on the hillside, overlooking the valley. None of my men have seen it directly, of course. This comes through intermediaries from the dale itself. Gunnar has perhaps two to three hundred warriors at his command, if estimates are to be believed. Since our disputes began afresh, he has started to fortify the dale. Just where the side valley branches off are a whole system of dykes, of ancient ramparts and ditches from some long-gone pagan people, as well as several fortified positions. These have been heightened and manned now against any incursion. They effectively sealed off the upper end of the dale.'

He leaned back. 'Gunnar has absolute power over his people and they will fight to the death for him, that much we know well. Beyond this, though, he also has companions. A witness from the massacre at the monastery brought us a clear description not only of Gunnar and his warriors, but also his associates. One, a monster of a man, goes by the name of Arkil Bear-shoulders.'

Halfdan instinctively glanced round at Bjorn to find his big friend suddenly alert, listening intently.

'Tell us.'

'They say he is a berserkr like the Norse of old. If the tales are true, then this Arkil is so dangerous and unpredictable that even Gunnar will not have the man at his settlement. Arkil lives in this side valley,' he said, pointing to the branch that led off right from the dale. 'There he commands alone, though these days, that is also behind the defended dyke systems.'

'A jarl, a berserkr and two hundred men or more,' Halfdan mused.

'And a witch.'

Again, Halfdan's head snapped round. This time, his gaze fell upon Gunnhild, who was intent on the speaker, leaning forward, tense.

'A witch?'

'They call her the raven. *Hrafn*, I think, in your tongue. They say she has the power of the Devil himself at her command. More so than Gunnar's warriors, or Arkil's rage, the people of the dale and beyond live in fear of the foul magics of Hrafn. I cannot tell you of her home or what she is, for the only surviving direct witness, the monk they let live at Ghellinges, was hopelessly mad by the time we found him, and much of his raving may have been plucked from his own mind. However, there are many tales from the dale of her evil and her power.'

Halfdan nodded. 'Anything else you can tell us of value?'

'Only that Gunnar has begun to place watch posts further down the dale in the past few months. I doubt you will get far beyond Hindrelac before you encounter the first watchmen for Gunnar. Simply, you will be walking up Swaledale into the waiting arms of a small army behind impressive defences, who will be well aware of you long before you are of them, and who sport a crazed killer and a witch among their number.'

'What of other approaches? If these dykes seal off the dale, what of ways over the hills from other valleys?'

Godwin shook his head. 'There are ancient ways over the moors, but even in the most peaceful of days they can be treacherous at this time of year. With rain, fog, gales and even snow, getting caught up on the heights could end your mission far more certainly than any sword. Moreover, it is said that Gunnar and his witch keep the highways sealed against us, and given what we have heard of her, I would suspect that only a fool would attempt such a thing. The only ready access to the dale from outside is from the north, but that is a considerable distance around, and would bring you straight to Arkil's house close to the dykes. You would gain little for your efforts.'

'So you are suggesting that the only realistic approach is a direct assault up the dale.'

'No,' Godwin replied, 'I am not suggesting it. I am *telling* you this as a *fact*. Only a suicidal madman would attempt another approach.'

'Is this witness, this mad priest, in your fortress? Can we speak to him?'

A shake of the head. 'The man was raving. He was taken to the motherhouse of his order at Witeby for convalescence. The most local accounts you will receive will be from the people of Hindrelac as you move into the dale.'

Halfdan nodded.

'I have no love for heathens,' Godwin said, suddenly. 'In truth I care little whether you live or die, and if the latter, then there will be no salvation in the kingdom of heaven for you, and your bodies will moulder on the hills of Gunnar's lands. But as a Christian, I like to think myself a good man. I will give you one piece of advice. Whatever deal you have made with his grace the archbishop, I urge you, for your own sake, to return to Jorvik and renounce the deal. Go your own way, for in Swaledale you will find death, and, perhaps at the hands of Bear-shoulders or the witch, even worse.'

Halfdan shrugged. 'I mean no offence to you or yours, Lord of Catraeth, but these men are the Wolves of Odin, and just *one* of them I would comfortably pit against your whole garrison.'

'You go too far,' Cuthbert replied. Having returned to his seat after his cartography, he now rose from it once more, angrily. Godwin did nothing to stop him.

'You doubt me?'

'*I* do,' barked a man in the red and white of a soldier, stepping in from the shadows behind the noblemen. He was a big specimen, well-armoured and mean-looking, with a scar across his forehead as though someone had tried to lift the top of his head off.

Lord Godwin waved the man back. 'If these heathens intend to march into the dale, they will need every man, Heard. Step down.'

Halfdan, knowing what was coming next, turned to see Bjorn already half-risen from his own seat, ready to take on a challenge. He threw the big man a look. Bjorn was twitchy at the moment, ready to pull the arms off someone for just looking at him wrong, as that little incident with Cyneric had proved. The last thing he needed right now was Bjorn blood-eagling the lord's best man. That would hardly improve relations. He gave the great albino a small shake of the head. Bjorn looked extremely irritated, eyes narrowing dangerously as he sank back to his seat.

'If your man seeks humiliation,' Halfdan told their host, 'then let him come. I will meet him.'

Godwin frowned for a moment, then shrugged and gestured to the large warrior, who made his way forward, between the tables. Halfdan looked at the man. He really was big, and dressed in a chain shirt that came down to just above the elbows, up to the collarbones, and down to mid-thigh. He had his hand on a belted sword, his head bare, protected only by thick blond braids. His boots were of soft leather. Halfdan glanced for a moment at his own waist, where his sword and sax were sheathed. If a lesson were to be administered here, he had to do it at the lowest cost to his host. He looked around as the big man approached, and found a large bowl on the table, awaiting contents, a long metal ladle lying beside it. He picked the ladle up and gave it an experimental swish through the air, then turned back to his approaching opponent.

The man was strong, heavy, big and well armoured. Such a man was likely also slow and lumbering. That was not a given, so Halfdan would have to be careful, but if he was right, then he had the advantages of speed and agility. He stood still, watching the man. The soldier favoured his left leg, but his sword was worn for the right hand. His eyes were on Halfdan, but on his face, not his movements. He expected the jarl's eyes to betray his plans. He did have the grace to look a little confused when Halfdan picked up the ladle.

The big man drummed his fingers on his sword hilt, but then drew a knife, a sax of sorts, from the other side of his belt. Gripping it tight, he came to a halt facing the jarl.

'You do not have to do this,' Halfdan advised, calmly. Though his eyes were on the man's face, he was paying attention to his peripheral vision, and watched the man's left foot shuffle very slightly, into a position to brace himself.

'Heathen,' the man snapped, and made his move.

Halfdan was prepared, had seen the attack in the planning. He pivoted as the man lunged, letting the big warrior lurch past. As he came round, he lashed out, catching the man a solid blow on the back of the head with his ladle, a clonk ringing out around the room, raising a few laughs from the Wolves.

The soldier was incensed. That made Halfdan smile. A man losing his control was even easier to outwit. The big warrior staggered to a halt and turned, knife raised. He snarled something incomprehensible and lunged once more. This time, he was anticipating a dodge, and so did not allow his momentum to carry him past, but Halfdan was not where the man expected. He had dropped into a roll even as the man leapt forward. As he tumbled past his opponent through he scattered ashy remnants of the map, he delivered his second ladle blow, this time to the man's kneecap. The big warrior howled for a moment, lurching and staggering as he came to a halt and turned once more.

Halfdan looked down at his left hand that had collected a thick coating of ash in the manoeuvre. With a smile, he reached up and drew Odin's *valknut* upon his forehead in black, adding a line across each cheek in deference to the Allfather's ravens. Then he gripped his ladle tight, swishing it a couple of times, and grinned at the soldier.

'Heard, back off,' the lord of Catraeth told his man.

'My lord?' the big warrior frowned as he limped back to face Halfdan, knuckles around the knife white and tight.

'You are embarrassing yourself.'

Halfdan smiled. The man was not ready to quit yet. One more should do it, though. A good blow could end it. He saw the warrior tense, saw him sizing Halfdan up. He would be prepared for anything now. Indeed, the man came slowly this time, eyes darting. Halfdan let him come. The man was wary. That could be an advantage in itself. Heard came within knife reach and tensed. He was plotting a blow that Halfdan could neither duck nor sidestep. The jarl smiled. Back, down and to the side being out, there was only one way to go. He drew his big, heavy spoon back.

The soldier lunged. Halfdan was ready, while the man's eyes had been on his own, trying to anticipate a move, Halfdan had subtly changed his footing. As the knife came forth, Halfdan stepped a pace forward, inside the blow, his left arm sweeping up, knocking the man's arm aside, safely out of the way. Even as the knife was shoved aside, the ladle came out and smacked the man straight in the face, between the eyes.

Halfdan danced three steps back, smiling benignly. The big soldier looked confused. He took a step, and his legs seemed to fail him. His eyes had turned in as though trying to look at the site of the blow that had ended the fight. He dropped to his knees, the knife falling from his fingers, reaching up and touching the space between his eyes. At even the lightest touch, he whimpered.

Halfdan left the man there, confused and bruised, and returned to his seat.

'Your point is made,' Godwin of Catraeth said, quietly. 'While I maintain that this task of yours is the utmost idiocy, I will acknowledge that you are perhaps more than you appear. I will wish you good fortune on your mission for, as you say, your success is mine, too.'

Halfdan bowed his head as two other soldiers helped the confused Heard to his feet, gathering up his knife, and escorting him from the room.

The conversation resumed, and now extended to include other figures in the room, both locals and visitors. Halfdan continually probed for further information throughout the talk, and even through the meal that followed, though he learned little more of any use than that which they had already been told. He was careful throughout the evening not to provoke Godwin, for the man was not only their host that night, and the source of supplies for their journey, but also, when this was over, it would be to Catraeth that they would come once more on their return.

He spent much of the evening, too, paying attention to his own hirð. Bjorn's eyes were almost dancing with every new thing he learned of Gunnar's berserkr, and the man had a growing hunger about him that made him look more like himself all the time. That was good, on one level, but also brought to the fore the violent unpredictability that was Bjorn Bear-torn. His attention was also on Gunnhild, who had sat straight and attentive at news of this 'witch' of Gunnar's, and who had been silent and inattentive ever since, her concentration seemingly upon her own inner monologue. Ketil, he noticed, was sitting beside Bjorn, nodding along to the albino's excitable predictions about what he was going to do to Arkil. Ulfr, sitting across from them, was watching them both carefully, with a slightly worried expression. Lief and Anna sat huddled together a small island of normalcy in the assembly.

When the meal was over, they were shown to a large bunk-house in the fortress grounds, and there left to their own devices, though Halfdan was willing to wager that at least three soldiers would have their eyes upon the building throughout the night. In circumstances such as these, trust went only so far.

'What do you think?' he said, finally, when they were alone.

'This Arkil Bear-shoulders is mine,' Bjorn said instantly. 'I don't care whether I have to go the long way round and find him from the north, or climb over the bodies of Gunnar's hirð to get to him. If anyone here dares lay a finger on him before I get to him, I'll tear them in two.'

Halfdan nodded. 'I doubt anyone had any intention of getting in your way, old friend.' He glanced at Gunnhild, who looked up and nodded, turning to the big albino.

'I will give you what you need, Bjorn, to meet the man on level ground.' Her fingers brushed across the pouch at her belt that contained the strange compound that allowed both her to commune with her goddess, and any other warrior to reach that state beyond violence and fear men knew as berserkr.

'Dear God,' Lief breathed, 'but don't let me get caught up in *that* fight.'

'I won't,' Anna answered, squeezing his arm.

'That won't *be* a fight, that will be a *slaughterhouse*,' Ulfr noted.

Murmurs of agreement met this. Should two *berserkir* meet, the only thing to do would be to stay safely far away from them. Even the demise of one would not end the peril. The other would have to fight himself into a stupor to stop.

'And you,' Halfdan said to Gunnhild. 'Is it this Hrafn that is causing your difficulties?'

'It could be,' she admitted. 'Something here is more powerful than me. I am, after all, somewhat new to the calling, while Gunnar's völva sounds like someone from the ancient tales. I am unsure yet as to what she is. If these tales are to be believed, then she is a dangerous one, given to using the Seiðr only for power and harm. Of course,' she added rather dismissively, 'these are Christians, and their idea of such power is always that it is used for harm. They are but children at times, and see only monsters where the daughters of Freyja walk. She could be no more vile than I. Then again...'

They all nodded at that. Even the Christians among the Wolves knew how völvas were perceived by the Church and its children.

'Whatever she's like,' Ketil grumbled, 'she's the enemy for now.'

There were nods at this.

'Still,' Halfdan said in a matter-of-fact tone, 'no matter how powerful she is, she is clearly at the side of Gunnar just as much as this Arkil the berserkr. And, simply, there is none among us who can hope to face her better than you, Gunnhild.'

He was a little worried about the uncertainty that flashed across her eyes before she nodded, but before he could dwell on that, Anna was there. 'Gunnhild is not alone. This Hrafn monster may be stronger than one woman, but we are three. With Cassandra and I, no witch can stand against Gunnhild of Hedeby.'

'There are more than three of you,' Ulfr put in. 'We are the Wolves of Odin. Anyone tangles with *one* of us, they have to tangle with *all* of us.'

Ketil snorted. 'I will personally put an arrow through the woman if she tries anything.'

'Since you lost your eye,' Bjorn said in a bored tone, 'you couldn't put an arrow through a barn door.'

'I'll put a fucking arrow through *you*, Bear-torn,' the Icelander snorted.

'My point was,' Ulfr sighed, 'that we are strong together.'

Anna shook her head. 'Not when we meet the witch. That is not a fight for men. But Gunnhild walks with God's grace. We shall not lose.'

Ulfr nodded. 'I only hope we can claim half as much confidence in Bjorn's victory.'

'Fuck off,' Bjorn replied succinctly.

'I mean no insult, my friend,' the shipwright said. 'I know you for a great warrior. But over-confidence is dangerous, and this Arkil sounds like a monster.'

'Fuck off with bells on,' Bjorn said airily.

It almost made Halfdan smile. Gunnhild rolled her eyes at the exchange, but when they settled once more, there was an odd comfort in them. He had to believe that Bjorn could not lose, and with her sisters, Gunnhild *had* to be stronger than Hrafn. In their years together now, Anna and Gunnhild had struck up a sisterhood that seemed able to overcome their differences, and in more recent months, Cassandra had done the same. It was true that anyone who now stood against Gunnhild would find herself facing three strong women, not one, and though they may not have the power of Seiðr, Halfdan had seen Anna with a knife. She was not one to be dismissed lightly. Cassandra either.

'Alright. I think it is safe to say that in order to stop Gunnar, and to remove his power from the dale, we will have to also deal with those he relies on. Arkil is Bjorn's problem, and Gunnhild will have to lead our move on Hrafn whenever we find her. It is my hope that when the three leaders fall, the rest of the warriors of Swaledale can be persuaded to peace. I have no intention of fighting hundreds of warriors with our own twenty-seven.'

He leaned back. 'This, then, is the plan. We move first to Hindrelac, and there find out anything extra that we can. We move up the dale slowly and carefully. I want to find these watchers before they see us. We find their scouts and put them down. That means we can approach the upper dale unexpected. I somehow doubt, if they have fortified these ancient walls, that we can pass there unnoticed. They will be expecting an army, probably from the archbishop, or Lord Godwin. They will not be expecting us. No matter what Godwin says about the hills, the defences have to end somewhere, and at their extremes they will be weakest. That may be where we hit them. Whatever the case, we cannot plan any assault until we are close enough to see what we're up against.'

Lief nodded, producing a stick of charred wood and a piece of vellum from his pouch. 'I will try to recreate the map, and then at Hindrelac, perhaps we can fill it in a little more.'

That was it. All the planning they could do for now. In the morning, the quest could begin in earnest.

Swaledale awaited.

Chapter 5

The past. Magnus's Valley, west of Skara, Geatland.

'Step to it, Whitey. Fresh water.'

The thrown bucket bounced painfully off Bjorn's shoulder, and he glowered secretly beneath lowered brows as he stooped to pick it up. The three grandsons of Orm Barelegs were that particular brand of needlessly cruel that engenders a lifelong hate and a desire for revenge in their targets. There was more than adequate fresh water already in the trough that morning, and the only way they could fit more in was if they had been wasting it deliberately, just to give him extra work.

He settled himself in for the task, carrying the heavy wooden bucket, knowing it would be more than three times as heavy on the return journey. The trip took him through the village, across the slippery plank bridge, half a mile along the side of the steep gorge, and then across rough rock before he could reach the part of the stream that was fresh water with no one's piss or waste in it. Once, months ago, he'd cut the journey short and brought water back from below the mill, where three houses could have pissed in it, but it turned out that the boys had been watching him, and the beating he got from them and the old man had been so severe that it had been almost a month before he could walk normally once more.

Life was not about cutting corners any more than it was about enjoyment and wonder. Life was simply about surviving another day. In some ways he was doing well, really. Of the other six lads who'd been brought here as thralls after the raid, only two remained, and they had all had an easier time of it than Bjorn.

He scooped up the bucket of water with a silent prayer to Odin that the three boys might drown in it, and then worked his slow and uncomfortable way back to the village. This time, though, he was noticing things. A good hiding place bush here, a muddy deer trail there, a hunter's footprints, where the water pooled. This time, he was paying attention, because this time would be the last.

He returned to the house and tipped the water into the trough, noting the pools around it where the three boys had wasted all the clean water larking about just to give him a job.

'Hey Ghost, show us your blue dick.'

Ghost. Whitey. Snowdrift. Chalky. Names he had come to know as his own, derisive and mean. What worry, though, were mere names, when the smallest infraction had him whipped or beaten.

He stood there, dropped the bucket and then pulled down his trousers, standing half naked in the dirt behind the house as the three boys pointed and laughed. Bjorn hadn't much to compare himself with, admittedly, but was fairly sure he was quite normal down there apart from the lack of colour to his flesh. That alone made him an endless figure of fun.

Maybe the other boys who'd died had it better. They had just been worked to death, rather than being laughed at while they did it.

'Take off your tunic and stand still. One move and I'll tell Grand-da that you tried to run away.'

Without a sound, Bjorn stripped off the rest of his clothing and stood there with his trousers round his ankles, naked, as the three boys threw sticks and stones at him, hard enough to hurt and to bruise, but never quite enough to break bones. By the time they were bored, he was bleeding in half a dozen places and would grow bruises so numerous they would meet across his flesh and give him the colour that nature had denied him.

At their command, before they went off to find something else to do, he used moss to clean his wounds, then pulled on his clothes. There would be no clear evidence of their cruelty. There rarely was. Not that the old greybeard would punish them if he knew. He might give them a clip round the ear for damaging his property, but that would be the extent of their punishment.

Their last words, as they left, echoed through his head. 'Keep your arsehole tight. We might need it tonight.'

He'd not planned on running until tomorrow morning. Tomorrow, the older boy and his grandfather would be off on the hunt, and Bjorn would be under the supervision only of the younger two. He'd decided that the likelihood of them getting bored and leaving him alone long enough to get away made it the ideal time. Today, though, had broken him. That last stoning, followed by the promise of a night of sexual abuse had done for him. No more. Danger or not, the time had come.

He stood in the scrubland behind the house and peered off around the corner. He could just see the three boys, each with a three-foot stick in hand, approaching their friend's house. They were off into the woods. As long as the old man did not return for a while, this was as good a chance as he would get.

Had he kept to his plan, tonight he would have retrieved the knife and his store of dried food for the journey that he'd hidden behind a loose board. But he was going early, unexpectedly, and to delay long enough to collect what he needed risked the old man coming back, or even the boys if their friend was busy. No. No time.

Bjorn tested his muscles. He hurt. The stones had done damage. But if he'd learned one thing this past year it was that pain could be ignored, even made to serve him, to be a source of determination.

He ran.

As he left the village, the only figure he saw was the miller, and he slowed as he passed within the man's sight, looking downtrodden and miserable, as though on yet another chore for his masters. The last time he'd tried to run, he'd made the mistake of being seen doing so, and when they'd caught him, his arm had been broken in the severe beating. He considered it Loki's own luck that the arm had set right and he'd only had a niggling gentle ache this last few months. He'd learned in the two attempts he'd made early on that just running was only going to earn him pain. He needed a better plan than simple flight. And that was why he'd been preparing this for weeks.

He kept to stones and rock, to gravel or thick grass. No mud where tell-tale footprints could give him away. Across the river, he ducked into the bushes and found the first hollow. In there were fresh clothes he'd stolen from washing lines around the village, greens and browns, very miscellaneous. And best of all, a light green cloak that he'd used whatever free moments he could gather to stitch with leaves, tacked on to create the perfect camouflage. Once he'd stripped from his thrall attire, he donned these new clothes, satisfied that if he held still, only the sharpest eye could pick him out from the undergrowth. He took his other clothes with him, though, for leaving a trail of any kind would be foolish.

He ran.

He did not look back. This time, if they caught him, they would probably kill him, and he would take that over thraldom now. He was done being the slave of a cruel man and the plaything of three brash fools. He would live or die, but he would never again be a thrall.

Late February 1044. Hindrelac.

'Wait here while I make enquiries,' Halfdan called across the group, gesturing for Lief and Ulfr to join him as the others remained at the edge of the settlement, their horses snorting and stamping.

Bjorn sat in the saddle, bored. Oh, he could understand why just the three of them went, really. If the jarl wanted information, he was unlikely to get it with Gunnhild, Ketil or Bjorn at his shoulder, given that the locals lived in fear of a Norse völva and a great berserkr. But Bjorn bored easily, and riding was the easiest way to reach that state. At sea there was always action, danger, waves the size of dragon wings, sea monsters waiting to eat a man whole, fights and activity, and at the very least rowing. Riding meant sitting still for hours at a time. He'd punched Lief on the arm early on, just in the hope of starting a brawl to keep himself busy, but the Rus had just called him names and moved away.

He looked up. They'd had a brief shower of light rain as they left Catraeth just over an hour ago, crossing the ancient bridge and then following the north bank of the river up into the dale. The drizzle had stopped perhaps halfway through their journey, but the sky remained leaden grey and promised further, perhaps heavier, downpours. The cold was clearly getting to some of the men who were bred to the climate of Apulia, but was of little nuisance to true Northmen.

Along with Bjorn, the column of riders waited at the edge of the village. He looked about the place. Hindrelac was no great metropolis, smaller even than the villages where Bjorn had been born, and then reborn. A cluster of perhaps a dozen houses on a slope that granted an impressive view west up the dale, the place lacked a mead hall, or even a church, which was a surprise, given how prevalent the White Christ temples were in this part of the world. There *was* a large stone cross, carved with images of warriors and magnificent beasts, and scenes of feasts and strange gatherings of men, which probably counted as a church to the nailed god followers. That village of his youth where he'd spent the worst year of his life had been lacking a church for their strange cult, and had made do with a rough cross, too.

Bjorn had learned early to despise the nailed god's people, not because they had defeated his father's in that raid, and not even for their denial of the true gods, but because of their hypocrisy. In their trance-like rites, they seemed to do little more than vaunt the values of understanding, peace and forgiveness, yet then they would disperse and return to their houses to practise patronising brutality and casual cruelty. Not that Bjorn was against brutality and cruelty. Brutality and cruelty could be useful, and often fun, but at least *he* revelled in it and did not pretend to be some peace-loving sop. Bjorn's lip wrinkled at the stone, and he looked up again into a sky that promised a storm, silently asking Thor to lay the cross low in his fury.

Halfdan, Ulfr and Lief dismounted, walking across to an old greybeard who sat on a bench outside one house, leaning on his stick, and began to engage him in conversation. The rest of the Wolves on the periphery deliberately kept their hands far from their weapons, trying to give the impression of peaceful travellers, despite their armoured appearance.

Hindrelac was the last settlement up the dale that was under the control of Godwin of Catraeth and of the archbishop of York, and so was nominally the last friendly place they would visit. In truth it felt to Bjorn about as friendly as the other ones they'd visited, which was to say, not very. But then it didn't matter to him too much. He had no use for White Christ slave friends, and he wasn't feeling particularly friendly himself.

The people of Hindrelac scurried this way and that past them with nervous glances, despite the reassuring smile that Thurstan had affected in an attempt to make the visitors appear friendly. Bjorn did not affect a friendly smile. He knew well that his smile made him look more like a lynx about to pounce than a warm human being. Children stared until their parents dragged them from sight. A young woman watched warily as she skirted around them in a wide arc with a basket of bread. A dog wandered toward them, but even the mangy mutt stopped short of the visitors and scurried away between two houses.

Bjorn felt his lip wrinkling again.

Christians. They were all the same. All right, maybe not *all*, he conceded, noting Lief standing beside Halfdan across the square, and remembering how many of the Wolves now worshipped at the cross. But these ones in Hindrelac were just the same as the majority. The same as the Normans who had looked down on them from their figurative cross, the same as Jarl Yngvar and his pet priest, the same as Magnus and his cronies all those years ago, who had thanked the White Christ for the gift of peace and understanding even as they held Bjorn down and beat him senseless for naught but their own amusement. Bastards.

He felt his spirits dipping once more and forcibly hauled them back up, turning to Ketil with a forced grin. 'Did I ever tell you about the time I won a bet with a Finn because I managed to fit a whole pig inside another pig?'

But Ketil was going to be no distraction today. He simply rolled his eyes at Bjorn and turned away, trying to listen in on his jarl's distant conversation, uninterested at the big albino's tales.

Bored once more, and struggling to stay content, Bjorn's attention was drawn to one particular figure, or rather to a pair of them. A man with a lined, leathery face and drab tunic and trousers strode across the square from the steep, long slope that led down to the river, the same flow they had been following since Catraeth. Behind the man, a young woman was struggling with a heavy bucket of water.

In an instant, Bjorn was whisked away through many years and many lands to the village of Magnus, carrying the full bucket back to the house in time to be abused by the three grandsons of Gorm. Days of painful servitude.

His wrinkled lip was joined by a twitch in his cheek.

Of course, this *could* be different. The woman could be the man's wife, or even his daughter. Something deep within, however, told him that was not the case. He watched, tensing as if ready for action, as the two figures crossed the village square. In the background, he caught sight again of Halfdan, Ulfr and Lief in conversation with the village elder, but his attention was swiftly drawn back to those two locals at a cry of alarm. The woman had stumbled in the dirt and almost dropped the bucket of water. As Bjorn focused on the pair, the bucket swung this way and that as she desperately righted it, water slopping around. A small amount of the contents sloshed over the man's leg, spattering his calf and ankle before the woman fully regained her footing and managed to secure the bucket once again.

Bjorn was not at all surprised when the man spun, angrily. He began to rant at the woman, jabbing a finger at her. Then, when she said something in a meek tone, he took a step toward her and gave her a clout to the side of the head.

Bjorn felt his hands ball into fists around the reins of his horse as he watched.

Peace and love, eh, White Christ?

The woman cried out and stumbled at the blow, and the bucket sloshed wildly once more, a second splash soaking the man's leg. He suddenly burst forth in a stream of angry invective and began to slap the woman again, and again, and again. She hunched her back, protecting herself from the blows as she whimpered.

'What's the matter?' a voice murmured behind Bjorn. He turned to see Ketil frowning at him. He ignored the big Icelander and turned back to see the woman on her knees now, bucket spilled and rolling in the dirt as the man continued to land blows on her, calling her clumsy and a waste of good air.

Just like the grandsons of Orm Barelegs.

Bjorn only realised he had reached breaking point when he discovered he'd managed to snap the reins, the worn leather falling apart in his massive hands.

He looked about. No one was paying any attention to the display. The villagers were walking past, barely looking. Even Halfdan, Ulfr and Lief only glanced over as they discussed local matters with the elder. No one noticed or cared about the plight of a thrall.

'Bjorn…' came a warning from Ketil, but it was too late. Bjorn had slid from his saddle and was stomping across the open ground toward the pair. Even as he closed on them, the man delivered a kick that sent the woman over onto her side with a cry of pain.

The man pulled back his foot again. His second kick never connected. Instead, he gave a strangled cry as he was lifted bodily from the ground. Bjorn, easily holding the reedy man in his right hand by the nape of the neck, reached round with his left and gripped the man's bunched tunic at his throat, turning him to face his new opponent.

The man stared in shock at the huge white and pink figure that held him more than a foot above the ground, their faces on a level.

'I—' the man began. It was all he got to say.

Bjorn hit him. Hard. It was not a planned and elegant attack, not a blow struck with strategic skill in the midst of combat. Just an offhand and unexpected punch, but it carried with it decades of pent up anger, and the man's face broke in several places, bones cracking and crunching as blood and snot sprayed forth across the white-pink knuckles. In a way, the man was lucky to live through the blow which could very easily have killed him. In another way he was much less lucky, for Bjorn was not done with him yet.

'Fuck you,' Bjorn snarled as he dropped the man to the dirt, howling and clutching his ruined face. 'Fuck your wet leg,' he added, giving a kick to the damp trousers that probably broke the man's shin. Bjorn felt the rage claiming him, felt the mist descending on his reason, something that usually only happened when he partook of Gunnhild's mysterious compound. Occasionally, just occasionally, the rage was enough on its own. A berserkr was not a thing made, but a thing born.

As the man reeled, clutching his face and leg, screaming, Bjorn reached up with a great meaty hand, and then stopped in surprise as a hand gripped his wrist. He turned, the anger still coursing through him, ready to transfer the violence onto his new attacker, and realised that the figure holding his arm was Halfdan, and that the arm he restrained now held a large rock, which he'd been about to smash down on the man's head.

Halfdan's face conveyed one word.

Stop.

It never ceased to amaze Bjorn how the young jarl could cut through even a frenzy with his air of command. That, of course, was why the Wolves followed him, even men much older and with more experience of leadership.

Bjorn dropped the rock, and Halfdan let go of his wrist.

The woman on the ground was picking herself up, staring back and forth between Bjorn and the broken man with eyes filled with horror. She hurried over to the man and crouched, almost touched him, but then recoiled.

'Run, woman,' Bjorn said. 'Find somewhere new.'

The man on the ground was recovering his wits, slowly, though he was still in extraordinary pain, and had stopped shaking so wildly. Bjorn reached down to his belt and unfastened one of the three pouches he carried there. He looked inside, scooped out a small handful of Byzantine coins and threw them at the prone man, where they scattered and tinkled, bouncing from his shuddering form and rolling off into the dirt.

'For her freedom.'

He turned, and there was a question in Halfdan's eyes that he did not feel like answering right now. 'Fucking nailed god thralls,' he grunted. But then what were the Wolves right now, if not nailed god thralls?

'You are doing an excellent job of keeping our approach quiet and unnoticed, my big friend,' Halfdan said, a mild scolding writ clear in his eyes.

'If you don't want me here, I can always go back to the ship,' Bjorn grunted, and not entirely in jest.

Halfdan gave him a lopsided grin. 'As it happens, I have a better task for your particular brand of inventive violence.' Bjorn frowned, and the jarl turned and pointed at a shed beside one of the houses. 'It appears that some of Hindrelac's hunters caught one of Gunnar's scouts a few miles from the village. They have him contained, but they don't know what to do with him. If they kill him, they fear they might bring unwanted attention from the rest, but releasing him would be foolish, of course.'

'You want me to kill him?' Bjorn felt his spirits rising once more.

'I want you to make him answer a few of my questions. Then, when he's done that, we shall see.'

Things were looking good. With Halfdan leading the way, they crossed the square toward the shed, leaving Lief and Ulfr to deal with the broken man. The owner of the adjacent hovel met them at the shed door and pulled back the heavy latch. Pulling the door open, he stepped aside swiftly, away from any potential danger. Halfdan gestured to Bjorn, who stepped into the doorway.

The shed was little more than six or seven feet across, and low enough that Bjorn had to stoop to fit. Upon entry, the trapped occupant hit him at speed, in an attempt to flee in the brief opportunity afforded. A foolish attempt, of course, for Bjorn entirely filled the doorway, and no matter how strong and fast the man was, his momentum had little impact. A sheep running into a wall would have a similar effect. The man bounced off Bjorn's bulk and staggered back into the shadows. He never had a second chance, for Bjorn's hand shot out and grasped him by the neck.

'Not so tight,' Halfdan hissed, following him in. 'He has to be able to speak.'

Bjorn loosened his grip a little. 'What's your name, little man?'

The warrior grunted something.

'What?'

'Erik.'

Halfdan took over now. 'Erik, tell me where the nearest of Gunnar's watchers can be found.'

'Fuck you.'

Bjorn looked to Halfdan, who gave a small nod. Chewing his lip, trying to decide what best to do, the big man came to a decision with an unpleasant smile. Erik was clawing ineffectually at Bjorn's arm, which held him by the throat. The albino's other hand suddenly found his victim's scratching fingers, and he snapped the man's forefinger so hard it broke the bone clear through. As the man screamed, Bjorn pulled hard, tearing the flesh so that the finger came free, severed. As blood jetted and fountained across them both from the stump, Bjorn grinned again and pushed the half-finger into the man's open, screaming mouth, then slammed his hand across the jaw, holding it shut.

'Bjorn, not *quite* so inventive,' Halfdan growled. 'I need him to talk, remember?'

With a sigh, Bjorn let go of the mouth. The man spat out his own severed digit and coughed and choked, blood and spit everywhere.

'Where are Gunnar's nearest watchers?' the jarl tried again.

The man took some time to recover from the choking, but finally, still held tight by Bjorn, he coughed and shivered. 'Two...' he gasped. 'Two and a half miles. North slopes. Old mines. Four men.'

Halfdan nodded. 'And how does any warning get sent up the valley to Gunnar?'

There was a silence, and not because the man was refusing to answer, but simply because he was processing the agony in his hand and the shock it had brought. Still, Bjorn was not in a mood for messing around. He reached down and grabbed another finger.

The man's eyes bulged. 'Signal beacons on the hills,' he gabbled urgently.

Halfdan nodded. 'Tell me about the defences you've manned. The ancient dykes. Numbers, strengths, where men are to be found.'

Erik paused again. This time, Bjorn simply poked the raw, bleeding stump of the man's finger, making him howl, and then let go, allowing the man to collapse back against the wall.

'Fifty men most... of the time,' he gasped. 'Spread out, but with most of them near the centre, where the bridge and the gate are. The southern dyke has an old fort a mile behind, with another twenty men. The northern one has... Arkil.'

Bjorn grinned at that, and the man seemed to almost retreat into the wall. 'What will you do with me.'

Bjorn looked round at Halfdan, hopefully, but the jarl had that narrow-eyed look of deep thought. 'I am undecided,' he said.

'I answered all your questions.'

'This is true. Of course, you may have lied.'

'I didn't,' the man said, panic edging into his tone.

Halfdan folded his arms. 'You will stay here in the custody of the men of Hindrelac. When we return, I will know whether you were true, or misled me. Then, your fate shall be decided.'

The man began to protest desperately, but Halfdan had already stepped outside. Bjorn left the whimpering, bleeding man and followed his jarl out, the door latched behind him, containing the prisoner once more.

'I might ask,' Halfdan said quietly, 'why you felt the need to beat a man senseless for abusing his slave, while you have no problem with abusing a war captive yourself.'

Bjorn frowned. Was there a comparison there? 'The other was a woman,' he said. 'Spoils of war, probably. A victim and nothing else. This arsehole was a warrior who managed to get himself caught by feeble villagers. They are not the same. One deserves better, the other worse.'

Halfdan laughed. 'You never fail to surprise me, my friend. When I hold my first Thing, I may have to call upon your wisdom.'

Bjorn frowned again, but the subject was making his head hurt. Instead, he looked about and was surprised to see most of the village's population gathered in the square, looking at the shed with wide eyes. Clearly they had been unprepared for the blood-curdling shrieks that had rung out from it. The screams had drawn a fascinated, worried crowd.

'Why do they look unhappy?' Bjorn grunted. 'Is Erik not their enemy? I never will understand Christians.'

Halfdan chuckled. 'I think they worry that we will bring further troubles to their doorstep.' He cleared his voice, donned his most comforting smile and turned to the assembled villagers. 'We go to free you from Gunnar and his people,' Halfdan told them. 'Keep your prisoner safe until our return. Their first outpost is apparently two and a half miles away, at some old mine works. Does anyone know of this place? If so, tell me.'

One of the men of the village stepped forward. His voice quavered initially. 'The old lead mines at White Cliff. There is a small fort there. It was near there the man was caught on one of the known deer trails.'

'Can it be approached unseen? And do you know where any beacon might be held nearby?'

Bjorn drifted off as the two men discussed the watch post and its approaches. He was already bored of the details. They would find the watch post, charge its ramparts and tear the limbs off its defenders. The rest of the plan did not concern him. Besides, a name from that interrogation in the shed was echoing round his mind now, once again.

Arkil.

The berserkr.

Chapter 6

'Tell me what you see.'

Beside Halfdan, the Rus squinted into the drizzle. 'Small encampment on a terrace.'

The jarl clicked his tongue irritably. He could see that much for himself, but wanted the minutiae confirmed by someone with eyesight as good as his.

'Details, Lief.'

Lief hummed to himself quietly and leaned into the bush to get the best view possible.

'Fair enough. Cliff to the right: high, no easy access. Craggy and with some undergrowth at the base. Reasonable amount of cover for a small group, but only a small one. Signs of open mining up there. Two old forts, close together, maybe each fifty paces across. The furthest one hasn't been touched in a giant's age, just a low mound in a square. The nearest one has had the ramparts raised recently and a fence of brush and wood installed atop it. Two gates, one each side, one facing us, the other further away. Two tents. Suitable for the four people we were expecting. Nothing else on the terrace. Then a long slope down toward the river a quarter of a mile away, maybe more.' His gaze strafed the valley, then, looking further afield. 'Nothing visible then on the way up the valley bar a few small farm buildings here and there.'

'Beacon-wise?'

Lief huffed. 'The one in the fort's clear. Big enough to be seen a fair distance away. Halfway to Nordmandi at night, I reckon. Lower visibility today, though. As for any others on the hills, impossible to see at the moment.'

Halfdan nodded. 'Your opinion on the beacon in the fort?'

He had his own thoughts on that, and the danger did not worry him greatly, but Lief was Loki-clever, too, and it was always worth getting his opinion.

'It won't be easy to light. Rain's been set in here on and off for days, and it doesn't look like they've kept it covered. It'll be soaked through, but they can't be that daft, surely. They'll have a plan. I reckon somewhere under cover in that place they'll have a store of dry brush and hay, and probably a bucket of pitch or something. Then no matter how damp the wood is, there'll be a way to light it.'

Halfdan nodded. 'But it'll take time. When they're aware of danger, they'll have to retrieve the brush and pitch and add it to the beacon, then get it lit, all while dealing with that danger. Then it'll take a while for the beacon to light properly. It'll smoulder for a while.'

'That will give off a massive cloud of smoke,' Lief noted.

'Smoke will be at least partially obscured in this weather, with the cloud and drizzle. But I take your point. We need to stop them getting that far. We need to hit them fast, and that means we need to get close quietly.'

'Which means creeping along the cliff base above the fort, which means there can't be too many of us.'

Halfdan nodded. 'Thank you, my friend. And please don't take offence if I leave you to look after the others. My choice is nothing to do with your skills or bravery. Odin knows his own, and so do I.'

Lief nodded. 'Who will you take?'

'One for each of them. Me, Ketil, Ulfr, and Bjorn.'

'Bjorn?' blinked Lief. 'To sneak up on the enemy? You are aware that Bjorn's idea of sneaking is a full-pelt charge with axe in hand while he screams things about animals' private parts?'

Halfdan chuckled despite himself. 'There are times when having a man who is almost a bear with you can be advantageous. Bjorn can tear two men apart before most warriors can unsheathe their sword.'

Lief nodded dubiously. 'But he's not the subtlest of men. Sneaking is not his natural manner. Beating a man senseless with his own severed leg is his natural manner.' A worried look crossed his face. 'Also, something's bothering him at the moment. He keeps slinging his usual insults at me, and gracing us with tales that even Homer would find farfetched. But it's almost as if his heart isn't in it. Something's bothering him, and it's to do with us working for the archbishop. I know he doesn't particularly like Christians, but I've never seen him so on edge.'

Halfdan nodded. 'In fairness, after what I saw of your kind in my youth, Lief, it has taken a great deal even for me to become comfortable with most of my hirð bowing to the nailed god, and I am a lot easier going than Bjorn. But if I know the big man, the only way to cut through worries with him is to give him a target for his violence. He is, I think, only one mug of ale away from berserkr at the best of times. Still, I think I might need him when we get to the camp. His attacks are fast and brutal.'

'True,' admitted Lief. 'But get him to cover his face and hair with mud or ash. He stands out like a marble statue, even in this weather.'

Halfdan nodded, the pair returning to the hirð, and a quarter of an hour later he was back at the cover of the bushes overlooking the wide valley with his three chosen men. Ketil towered over him at his shoulder, an impressively tall figure made all the more frightening by the maimed empty eye socket that told of his time with the rebel general Maniakes. Ketil wore his monochrome black as always, though he had been persuaded to don a grey woollen cloak with a nod to blending in with the weather. Bjorn was almost as tall as Ketil, and almost as broad as he was tall. His own clothing was currently drab enough to hide him reasonably well, and a healthy layer of mud had been applied to his white face and hair to make him stand out less. The only one who'd needed no tweaking was Ulfr, who had shrugged from his chain shirt like the rest of them to allow a sneakier approach, and was otherwise already dressed for the occasion.

Attired for subtlety. Attired for the kill.

One day, Halfdan promised himself, they would all be able to wear grand and bright clothes, with no need to hide or sneak. One day they would be able to stand proud anywhere, with their valknut tattoos and their *Mjǫllnir* pendants on show, without fear of being ostracised. But until then, their time would be a white-water journey of revenge and of feats of violence sufficient to gain the fame and fortune that it was his duty as jarl to bring them. When they were draped in silver, and each had sufficient wondrous tales to fill an evening in a mead hall, they would find somewhere that could be theirs and which no one would challenge them for. A home.

He drew his attention back to the present.

'Good. You can all see the fort, yes?'

A murmur of agreement.

'And we can presume four men, as the prisoner told us. What we need to do is make sure they are all put down before they can light their beacon. If the beacon goes up, then word of our approach will race up the valley and resistance there will become far stronger. Yes?'

Nods.

'All right. We approach along the base of the cliffs, using the adits and the bushes for cover until we are close. Then we rush them in one move. Here's what I want to do: Ketil, you are faster than any man alive. When we charge them, you swing wide, at the far side, and come in through the rear gate. That way, no one can escape their fort and run for help. Put down anyone you find there, and make sure no one gets away. The rest of us will race in through the front gate.'

He looked around at the other giant with him. 'Bjorn, I want you to run to the beacon. I think someone will try to get to it straight away and light it. You need to stop them. If no one comes, try and push the beacon over, dismantle it, but stop if anyone comes and kill them. Yes?'

Bjorn gave him a fierce nod.

'Ulfr, you and I are the middle ground. We each head straight for a tent. I very much suspect the defenders will be out in the open by the time we get there, and we'll have to deal with them there, but if not, we kill them in their tents.'

He looked around at them once more. 'Remember, the priority is to stop them lighting the beacon. Kill them all as fast as possible. And one last thing: try not to scream or yell. I know it's natural in the fight, but we don't know how well sound carries in this valley, and I'd prefer us to be unnoticed as long as possible. So kill as quietly and as quickly as you can.'

More nods. The briefing done, there was no further reason for delay, and Halfdan began to make his way between the trees and undergrowth, up toward the upper slope and the cliff that rose from it. Behind him followed the other three, Ketil curtailing his natural loping stride to keep pace with them, Ulfr silent and swift, Bjorn surprisingly quiet.

The valley side rose at an increasing gradient from the river far below, past the camp and up to the cliffs, which met the slope with a border of jagged broken rocks and scree, bushes and trees growing from it, suggesting that it had been quite a while since some of the adits had been worked. The four men moved from the woodland where the Wolves waited, into the scrub among the scree, picking their way from bush to tree and from tree to bush. Halfdan traced the Loki serpents on his arm with his index finger as they walked, sending a silent plea to the Trickster that they move with his deftness and guile, while praying for the same to the Allfather through silent lips.

The going was not easy, footing being troublesome, and every step required care, watching the ground ahead and testing the rocks. Worse still, with the weather as it was, the rocks were also wet and slippery. Every now and then, one of them would put down a foot and the rock beneath would shake or move, sending a light scatter of shale away with a slight hiss. Loki was working his magic, though, for the drizzle hitting leaves and rocks filled the entire valley with a gentle hiss that perfectly masked the occasional failures in footing.

Every ten feet or so along the torturously slow way, Halfdan managed a quick glimpse of their goal. As they came gradually closer, he was able to confirm that the lookouts Gunnar had posted here were either stupid or lazy, or likely both, for there was not a single figure to be seen. The tents spoke of an ongoing presence, but it seemed the four men they were moving against were shunning their duty in favour of using those tents to shelter from the rain.

All the better for the Wolves. The Allfather was with them, clearly.

He glanced up and was not surprised to see the shape of a black bird wheeling out across the valley. A raven, presumably, one of Odin's own, watching and reporting back to its master.

Moving out from the shelter of a larch, with juniper growing beneath, Halfdan encountered their first sign of trouble. An open area of ground, where the undergrowth had been cleared and a tree felled, even the rocks moved aside, awaiting them. The rough hole in the cliff face that spoke of lead mining had been shored up recently with timbers from the felled tree, evidence of the attempts of the archbishop's men to re-open the lead workings here. Had Gunnar's men been on watch as they should be, there would be a chance of the Wolves being spotted now, but thank the gods, they remained safely in their tents, and Halfdan led the others across the clear area swiftly, visible in the open, but moving fast and quiet with no fear for their footing.

They were closing on the lookout fast now, and even Bjorn was moving with care and quiet, though radiating that ever-present need to kill something. Between further bushes and past a tree they scurried, and Halfdan found another momentary observation place. His heart pounded suddenly and he stopped dead, hidden by foliage, hand coming up to halt the others.

He'd been wrong. Not all the four men were hiding in their tents, after all. One man was outside, though far from observant. They'd not seen him before, for he crouched on his heels in the lee of the great beacon, cloak pulled up over his head to keep him relatively dry. He was in a foolish place for a lookout, since he could see almost nothing of the valley from his position, but by ill chance his decision to find somewhere out of the worst of the weather had landed him with a view of the cliffs and undergrowth above the camp. Just, by chance, where the danger was actually coming from.

Halfdan squinted. It was hard to make out too much detail through the sheet of rain and past the small hedge of brush and broken wood on the earth rampart, but he was content that the man's eyes were hidden from view below the cloak. Unless something made the man pull back the cloak and look up, he would not see them. Halfdan turned and made motions to the others, instructing them to move very carefully now. They were getting close and one bad step might make enough noise to draw the man's attention.

With great subtlety and slowness, the four men crept on until they were level with the nearest ramparts. There, Halfdan stopped them. He motioned to Ketil and pointed on, and the Icelander nodded. As the other three stepped out onto the wet grass below the scree and clear of the bushes, Ketil loped quietly along the slope past the upper edge of the camp, preparing to seal off the rear gate. Still, the man did not look up, his hood remaining in place. Halfdan glanced at the others. Had Ketil been with them, he could perhaps have put an arrow into the man and silenced him before they closed on the camp, though to do so was to risk sending up an alarm, and wet weather was no good for bowstrings anyway. Instead, Ketil was even now rounding the far side.

Judging the time to be right, Halfdan gave the signal.

The three of them broke into a run, making for the open gateway that faced the direction of their approach. They'd lost sight of Ketil now, but he would be mirroring their approach, running toward the other gate, sealing the four men into their camp. No alarm went up, for despite their sudden burst of activity, the Wolves remained silent in their work, and the hiss of the constant rain hid the soft thud of their boots on springy turf. They reached the gate with no shout of warning, and immediately split up. Bjorn ran for the beacon, his eyes alight with hunger for battle, knowing that a man awaited him there. Ulfr veered toward one of the tents, while Halfdan ran for the other.

The left of the two tents had its door open, pinned up with a stick to create a sort of porch from the rain, and as they approached, one of the camp's residents finally saw the danger, turning and looking out of the front of his tent in time to see a furious Gotlander racing toward him, sword in hand.

Halfdan fought the urge to roar with battle rage, to cry the Allfather's name, something that felt natural when charging into the fray, for now it was crucial to attract as little attention as possible. The man in the tent shouted a warning, though his cry was somewhat muted by the enclosing tent, and it was highly unlikely anyone beyond the edge of the camp could hear it, no matter how acute their hearing. Those in the camp, however, *did* hear. As the man scurried toward the tent doorway, pulling a sword from the dark recesses, the other tent's door opened and a man's head poked out, startled, looking this way and that at the warning.

The two men never stood a chance. Ulfr's sword caught the emerging face at the other tent mid-swing, the blade almost decapitating him at mouth height, wedging into the man's spine where it met skull. The barely connected head flopped and wobbled as he fell back into the tent, dead before he could even defend himself.

At the same time, Halfdan met the man who'd cried a warning at the tent entrance. The restricted environment worked in the jarl's favour, for the lookout's blade was a traditional northern sword, three feet of heavy iron, and the tip snagged on the tent wall as he tried to bring it round to face Halfdan. The Gotlander's prized Alani blade, however, was a foot shorter and wielded in the open air, and even as the tent dweller swore desperately and struggled to free his blade, Halfdan's first blow caught him in the neck, just above the collarbones, slamming deep into windpipe and throat until it touched bone.

Even as the man fell away with a wet bubbling sound in place of a cry, Halfdan peered past him, hoping to see the remaining man in the tent. The place was empty, though, and Ulfr was even now ducking into the other tent. On the assumed count of four occupants, that left the one crouched by the beacon and a last man unaccounted for. Halfdan backed out of the tent and rose, listening.

The man by the unlit beacon was done for. Despite the order for silence, he could hear Bjorn snarling imprecations as he tore the man limb from limb, somewhere out of sight, behind the carefully constructed wooden beacon. A second sound of affray came to his ears, though, signalling that a fourth man had appeared from somewhere unseen and met Ketil at the rear gate. Good. All four accounted for, and apart from two ongoing clashes and the snarled oaths of Bjorn, without too much fuss. Given the constant drizzle and the clouds and reduced visibility, it was highly unlikely that anyone who might look this way across the valley would notice anything out of the ordinary.

He stepped into the open, away from the tent, and stretched, holding the dripping sword at arm's length. A thud signalled the end of Bjorn's fight, for only silence followed. Similarly, the curses being barked by Ketil's opponent had stopped, though the sounds of blows landing suggested the Icelander was still finishing the man off, probably unnecessarily. Like Bjorn, Ketil had a tendency to overdo it.

It was over, and all had clearly gone well. He took a deep breath and turned, and their undoing caught his attention out of the corner of his eye. A fifth man had appeared as if from nowhere, and was already casting aside the bucket, having slopped pitch across the lower part of the stack of wood. Even as Halfdan registered what was happening, the man was reaching to his belt, presumably for a flint and steel. Bjorn was on the far side of the beacon, unaware, Ketil was out of sight at the other gate, and Ulfr was inside a tent. Halfdan's eyes widened as he began to run, the man at the beacon meeting his gaze, alarm rising in his eyes as he realised he'd been seen. His flint came out. His steel came out. One in each hand.

Halfdan was running.

One spark. With pitch, it would take just one spark, and even the drizzle would only dampen the fire and make more smoke.

'Fuck,' he swore as he ploughed toward the man.

The lookout struck. A spark flashed for just a moment, fizzling in the rain.

Legs pounding. Heart racing. Knuckles white on sword grip.

Strike.

Spark.

More sparks.

Fizzling, unable to survive long enough in the rain to light the beacon.

The man was brave. Many, seeing Halfdan bearing down on them while armed only with a flint and steel, would have run for their lives. Instead, the man bent low, close enough to the pitch to allow the spark to ignite despite the rain, even though there would be a damn good chance that if the beacon caught, the man would be engulfed in the flames at such a distance.

Strike.

Spark.

Halfdan hit the man with a roar. He'd meant to be quiet even now, but something primal had gripped him in that moment

91

of desperation, and he was snarling like an enraged bear as he and the man flew away from the beacon and landed in a heap on the wet ground. Halfdan wasted no time. His sword stabbed once, twice, thrice, each time rising back into the air glistening, coated with gore, and the man breathed his last, the fire-makers falling from motionless fingers into the wet grass.

Halfdan heaved cold air into burning lungs as he rose and turned.

His heart lurched. Flames were lapping the lowest timbers, and smoke was rising from them. Then, suddenly, half the beacon simply disappeared with a rumble, and in its place stood Bjorn, covered in gore atop the mud that darkened his complexion, teeth white in a mouthful of blood. Even as the fire tried to spread among the tumbled timbers, Bjorn was grabbing beams and logs and hurling them away. In a heartbeat, Halfdan had joined him, grabbing timbers and yanking them away from the conflagration, limiting what could burn. By the time he looked up again, Ketil and Ulfr had joined in.

In short order, all the untouched wood had been removed, but Halfdan was still working. He grabbed one of the burning timbers by the unlit end and pulled it away, slamming the fiery tip into the wet grass, pounding it again and again and grinding it into the turf, extinguishing it.

Bjorn and Ketil joined in, pulling apart the fire and putting out each burning timber, and moments later Ulfr appeared with a bucket and tipped water over what was left, sending a brief plume of black into the air. Halfdan was about to berate him for making the fire smoke so, but relented. Smoke had already been rising from the fire, and the small extra puff Ulfr had created hardly added much to it. Indeed, the smoke was paltry, barely visible in the grey clouds, and it would take superhuman sight to separate the two from any distance.

Halfdan stretched, content that they had done all they could do. Still, to be sure there was no sixth man lurking, he grabbed the others and the four of them moved methodically through the camp, searching it. No last man appeared, lurking in the shadows, and in moments they had cleared the place. Ketil and Bjorn set about looting, first stripping the bodies of anything of value, then moving on to the tents. Halfdan stood and looked out across the valley, silent and still, as Ulfr came over to stand beside him.

'This Gunnar is impressive. More so than any jarl I've seen, even Yngvar. More so perhaps even than Byzantine empresses and Norman dukes.'

'Oh?' Ulfr said. 'How so?'

'That last man knew he would die, and badly. He knew I was going to gut him, yet rather than run, or even draw a weapon to face me, he kept trying to light the beacon, even though he might well have burned with it. Imagine the fear or loyalty that requires. If Gunnar inspires such in his men, then he is truly a formidable enemy.'

Ulfr nodded his understanding and agreement. 'And there are perhaps two or three hundred such warriors in this valley. Do they *all* owe such loyalty and fear to the man? We are few by comparison, Halfdan. Can we beat them? I am your man, always, but I do not enjoy the idea that we might be marching to the apocalypse, to a glorious final battle, an end for us all.'

Halfdan shuddered.

The skies, red as blood, shook and boomed, as though being torn apart. A black crack loomed above him as he stood, sword in hand, watching his enemy emerge from the doorway of the stone hall. On a bleak hillside, a world of men watched as Heimdallr and Loki met.

Ragnarok.

He shook himself free of the disastrous omen that continued to plague him. So far, only Gunnhild knew about the dream, and it would be best to keep such knowledge limited to the two of them. Yet there was one small bright spot in the gloom of that vision. If he was to meet the guardian of Bifrost, who he was sure now had to be Gunnar somehow, then they had to live long enough for that to happen, which meant that crossing the defences in the dale should be possible. Of course, the Norns were tricky, almost as tricky as Loki, and a man should never count on omens, for Fate has a way of tripping the over-confident. Perhaps that was why Gunnar was so powerful? Perhaps he *was* Heimdallr, in the flesh.

Halfdan set his jaw firm, expression radiating determination as he turned to the man beside him.

'I do not believe it will end for us all here. Certainly not yet. I will face Gunnar, and I will win, for I will allow neither gods nor fate to get between me and Hjalmvigi, who will pay for his deeds.'

This seemed to be enough for Ulfr, who nodded. 'You are a great jarl, Halfdan, and you are right, I think. We *will* win.'

Halfdan stood there for a while as Ketil and Bjorn moved about the place with arms full of semi-worthwhile junk, competing with one another over their booty. He was having trouble shaking off the memory of the dream, once again. Gunnar was Heimdallr. Halfdan was Loki, marked out from birth by the serpents on his arm. If the old skalds were to be believed, even allowing for a storyteller's tendency to exaggerate, then Ragnarok would begin with the rainbow bridge being broken, and Heimdallr Goldentooth's horn blast heard around the nine worlds. Then he, the great guardian, and Loki, Thor's trickster brother, would meet in battle as around them Odin and his warriors fought the endless tide of the *Jötnar*. Loki and Heimdallr would die together, on one another's blades. Was that the fate that awaited Halfdan in this bleak valley?

An image arose in his mind of the vicious priest, Hjalmvigi, in that hall of white stone in Georgia, and the sight of the old enemy drove down the waves of uncertainty that threatened to claim him. No. He would not die with Heimdallr. He might be Loki here, in this world, but he would not fall. He would survive, and live at least long enough to see the light leave the priest's eyes. Determination flooding him, Halfdan smiled grimly.

Then movement caught his eye, and he turned to see a small group emerging from the woodland off to the east. He could see Gunnhild with her green dress and ash blonde hair leading the way, staff in hand, her two ever-present acolytes at her heels, a small group of the Wolves following on. He frowned. He'd left instructions for no one to follow them until called. Still, they'd finished here, and the next step was to move up the dale, so perhaps no harm was done. As the party approached, he spoke to Ulfr.

'I think we need to have two scout parties from now on, each of just two men, our fastest and quietest. They should each move up one side of the dale and watch for lookout posts. If I remember the map correctly, the defences across the valley cannot be more than six or seven miles from here. But the valley snakes north and south between the two, and so this cannot be the only beacon, as it could not be seen from Gunnar's hall. There must be at least one other beacon in between, if not more.'

'There are,' Ulfr said in a flat tone, hand coming up, finger pointing off to the south-west, past Halfdan. The jarl turned and looked off that way, spirits sinking. A great blazing beacon was afire perhaps two miles away, below a woodland on the opposite side of the valley.

'Shit. I could have sworn we did this well enough not to be seen.'

'Maybe they saw Gunnhild?' Ulfr suggested.

Halfdan looked back at the new arrivals and then away to the west. '*Maybe*,' he conceded, 'but I don't think so. I can't see figures moving near that fire, so I don't think they could see people moving here. Two miles is a long way. But I thought the small amount of smoke this fire caused would have disappeared in the clouds.'

They waited as Gunnhild and the others approached the gate, and moments later the new arrivals came to a halt, the völva stepping out front and walking to meet Halfdan.

'I don't understand what went wrong,' he said as she came to a halt. 'We did everything right.'

Gunnhild nodded, expression blank, though oddly dark and unsettled in some way. 'You did nothing wrong,' she said. 'This is not your doing or your fault. No one could have prevented this. Gunnar's völva, this Hrafn, knows that I am coming. It is I she has seen, even hidden as I was in the woods, and it is because of me the beacons are lit. But I do not think it will increase the peril facing us at the dykes. Far from it, in fact. It has more the feel of an invitation. I think she and her jarl are looking forward to this meeting.'

'That will change when they discover we are coming to kill them.'

Gunnhild's eyes narrowed. 'She already knows that, I think. She also knows she is more powerful than I. It is possible that Gunnar is more powerful than you, and if any man alive is more powerful than Bjorn, then it could be Arkil. I think they do not fear us, in the same way a bear does not fear a worm.'

Halfdan forced a firm, grim smile to his face, though inside he quaked at the idea that even Gunnhild thought they were all outclassed.

'Then we shall give them good reason to fear us,' he said.

Gunnhild simply looked away, toward that beacon.

'I hope so,' was all she said.

Part Two

� ᚠᚮᚱᛗᛋ ᚮᚠ ᚮᛞᛁᚾ

Berserkr

Odin could make his enemies in battle blind, or deaf, or terror-
struck, and
their weapons so blunt that they could no more cut than a willow
wand; on the other hand, his men rushed forwards without armour,
were as mad as dogs or wolves, bit their shields, and were strong
as bears or wild bulls, and killed people at a blow, but neither
fire nor iron told upon themselves. These were called Berserker.

Chapter 6: Of Odin's Accomplishments from the *Ynglinga saga,*
trans. Samuel Laing

Chapter 7

The past. Skara, Geatland.

Tonight's entertainment was to be Bjorn's death, and that was clear from the moment his opponent stepped to the edge of the round pit in the dusty open ground between the buildings. The man was perhaps ten years older than Bjorn, who had ceased to be a child at the age of nine, the day his village fell and he was taken a thrall. Moreover, the man was a veteran of raids and wars, as was clear from the network of scars across his flesh. He was muscular, broad, tall, and the most important thing of all: he had a knife.

There were few rules at Einar's pit fights. Only three were repeatedly drummed into anyone who took part: The fight was over when one man surrendered or died. The fight did not start until Einar gave the order. And the fighting had to stay in the pit, no customer was to be inconvenienced. Beyond those three rules, anything went.

The pit attracted only a certain sort: the desperate, the stupid or the mad. Bjorn was willing to accept that he may fall into all three of those categories, yet he'd been fighting here for five months now and had run up a steady string of victories. They'd started by pitting him against boys his size and age, some of them runaways, others penniless vagrants, yet more thralls bought by Einar for a song to bulk out his numbers. The crowds at the fights had been paltry in those first two months, for there was little interest in watching two boys tear each other apart. But Bjorn had discovered in the very first fight that he had an edge. The day he'd stood in the village square, he'd been panicked, hopeless, grieving, and it had been a disaster. Now, he had nothing to lose, and everything to gain. He was free again, and as that first boy had come at him, knowing only one of them could climb out of the pit, Bjorn had taken one punch, a hard one to the jaw, but it had triggered something. A hundred heartbeats later, he was holding a broken rib in his glistening hand and looking down at a ravaged corpse. Even though they were little more than boys, the crowd were howling their delight.

Others had come, then, some chosen by Einar to make good matches, others trying their luck, determined to be the one to kill the white-skinned freak that had surprised everyone that first fight. Bjorn had discovered that he had not only a natural knack for brutality, but also that it did something to him. Breaking bones, smashing heads, drawing blood, managed to instil a certain contentedness that nothing in his erstwhile life had achieved.

Killing calmed him.

He was already growing big, even at thirteen, and Einar had had little compunction about pitting him against a steadily increasing quality of opponents. The first real man he'd fought was a thief who'd been caught in Einar's longhouse, and who'd been given the choice of fighting or accepting punishment for his crimes. The man had been over-confident. He'd come at Bjorn directly, arms wide, ready to grab him and crush the air from him. Bjorn had let him come and had simply dropped and thrown one heavy punch at groin height. He knew as the blow landed that he'd ruined the man. Something had burst or unravelled in his nethers. The man screamed. Bjorn was about to deliver further blows, but the thief held up his hand for mercy, and the fight was stopped. The man was flogged for his crime in the end, and then released back into the world as a *niðing*, a creature with no place and no value, and with ruined testicles, to boot.

Three more months just saw an increase in the strength of the men, but along with it a steady increase in Bjorn's own power. He was becoming truly huge for his age, and the scars he was picking up as a result of the fights only added a fearsome appearance. Looking back, Bjorn knew when the breaking point had been. One of Einar's men decided he needed to teach Bjorn a lesson, for he was a true warrior, battle-tested, and Bjorn was becoming too powerful. As Bjorn had squeezed out the man's eyes with his thumbs, he'd looked up to see a decision in Einar as he sat in his great chair. Einar had decided Bjorn's time here was done. He was losing valuable stock.

Hence this man, clearly a mercenary type, brought in to do the job. There was no rule here against weapons, though few chose to use one. The pit was far too restrictive for swords or axes, with no room for a good swing, but a few chanced a knife. This man's blade was a foot-long sax of gleaming steel. He gripped it professionally, and came at Bjorn the moment Einar's command rang out, settling the watching crowd to a breathless, expectant silence.

Bjorn let him come, sizing him up. The man knew how to use the knife, that was clear. Bjorn was under no illusion that this was basically murder. The man had been brought in to kill him. There was no way Bjorn was going to escape this fight without a scratch. At least one knife wound loomed in his near future. So perhaps he could accept the coming blow, but use it to his advantage. He looked down for just a moment at the scar on his left arm. For fun, his master's grandsons back in that village of captivity had put a thin metal rod through his arm when he'd pissed them off. They'd driven it right through, and Bjorn had cried and howled, then wept alone, clutching his bandaged arm, but he'd also marvelled that something could go through the arm without a bone in the way.

That was why, when the man finally leapt, bringing the knife round at an angle intended to punch it into the side of Bjorn's neck, he simply raised his left arm and took the blow on that, using his body to parry. His aim was good, and the knife slammed into his forearm, driving between the two bones. He hissed and bit his lip against the pain, but he was prepared, had known it was coming, and all the agony of steel in flesh now did was galvanise him into bloodthirsty action.

The man blinked in surprise, but Bjorn was not done. Gritting his teeth so he did not bite through his tongue with the pain, Bjorn tilted his arm, feeling the knife grate on the bones. But the knife's hilt was plucked from his opponent's surprised hand with the motion.

The man's startled pause cost him his life. As he reeled, Bjorn pulled the knife from his own arm, a gout of blood bursting out into the chilly air, and struck. It was not a careful blow, just an instinctive one. He hit the man in the chest, the knife sliding between ribs. It was not a killing blow, for he'd yet to learn where the heart lay, but he knew he'd hit a lung from the sudden expulsion of air from the wound. The man staggered back, crying out, but something happened to Bjorn. All he felt was rage, all-consuming and bloody, and by the time he became aware of himself again, he was standing drenched in blood, with a thing made of broken bones and ragged skin at his feet. It was as it had been that first time. He had been claimed by Thor, given the great Thunderer's rage and power to win his fight.

The crowd were not cheering. They were staring in horror. Bjorn had not just killed the man. He had left the remains in tatters, ravaging the body, long after life had fled.

Einar rose from his chair, face bleak.

'You have had all the victories you will get in my pit, young wanderer. I'll not have a berserkr at my games.' He reached down to his belt, unfastening a pouch that gave off a metallic jingle, and cast it to Bjorn, who caught it. 'Go. Do not come back.'

Bjorn never even nodded. He climbed from the pit, slipping a little in the gore that seemed to be everywhere, and left the square, the crowd opening wide to make way for him. He returned to the small hut he had been using, little more than a shed, a lean-to of the great longhouse. There he pulled out all his winnings and his poor collection of possessions, and strode away, along the road east, out of Skara.

He had arrived in the town two years ago, lost and aimless, weak and starving, broke and broken, until he'd found the pit. He was leaving it as a warrior, with coin to spare, and utterly without fear or conscience.

He had become a killer.

And now he knew who he had to kill next.

Late February 1044. Swaledale.

'Can you make out numbers?' Halfdan asked quietly.

Bjorn glanced ahead, despite the fact that the question had been aimed not at him, but at Lief. He knew his eyesight was not as good as the little Rus's.

'Hard to determine,' Lief replied, 'but I can tell you where the strengths are.'

Bjorn looked up. The rain had slackened to a light mist, with the promise of a break in the weather. The watery, pale sun was trying with all its might to break through the grey clouds. Bjorn would be grateful for the change. It seemed to rain in this place far too much, and rain made fights unpredictable, slippery and troublesome. As the clouds shifted slightly, the sun's gleam shone through for a moment, and Bjorn reached up with his arm to shade his eyes, which then fell upon the twin scars before them, a small, circular one from the metal rod and a longer, jagged one from the pit-fighter's knife. He felt a sense of order return to his world at the sight.

Archbishops could go fuck themselves. Complicated land ownership could go hang. Destinies and weavings and grand plans could fuck off. All he needed was an enemy to fight, a beer to drink, a woman to swive, and he was happy. A man of simple pleasures. And that was why he was starting to feel a little brighter, and a little more comfortable. They were now far from the influence of those nailed god followers down in the lowlands, in a place that felt more like the true North, albeit a slightly soggy version. And the closer they came to Gunnar, the more likely Bjorn was to get a good fight.

One fight in particular.

His gaze slid off toward the right, the northern edge of the dale. There, a side valley snaked off from this one, and even with his poor grip of geography, Bjorn knew it to be the one on the map where Arkil the Berserkr was supposed to dwell.

But to get there, they needed to overcome the defences Gunnar had put in place to stop the Christians coming up the dale.

The dyke was old. Even Bjorn could see that. Centuries old, for sure. Ancient. But it was easily the height of a tall man, with a ditch of similar proportions running along in front of it, and in protecting his domain, Gunnar had had a protective palisade of timbers erected all the way along it, no mean feat considering how long the dyke was. The defence stretched from the south bank of the river, some thousand paces or so up the slope, where it met a stream gulley that was steep enough to form its own defence. The far side of the river seemed to have no dyke, but then the slope there was far steeper and began almost flush from the riverbank, and a rough fence of sharpened timbers placed there would be as hard a proposition as the dyke. One single gap had been left cut through the defences, on a level terrace, perhaps halfway up the slope, though this had been given its own gate in the recent fortifying.

'No easy proposition,' Lief pronounced. 'What did Adlard say?'

Adlard, one of the faster and more observant of the men who'd come with them from Nordmandi, was now in regular duty as a scout. Halfdan made a huffing noise. 'The upper reach of the dyke meets the stream, and above that the ground is very uneven, largely overgrown with bracken and heather, ankle-breaking dips and rocks, and blanket bog where the peat has kept the winter waters.'

Bjorn grunted, looking up the slope, then back among the trees where the others waited, their horses tethered in a clearing. The moorlands didn't sound like a place for a walk, let alone a fight. Ulfr appeared a moment later. 'The animals are settled,' he announced.

Lief apparently agreed with the scout. 'There was always going to be a reason the dyke did not go up onto the moors. So, the terrain above there is just too unforgiving. And if we *did* try to go round, since they know we're here, they could just move their forces to trap us up there. Similarly, the far bank is a narrow approach. Too easy to defend. This dyke is the only real option.'

'So let's just go hit them and climb over it,' Bjorn interrupted, getting sick of the debate. The longer they spent here, the longer it would take to get to the second group of dykes, and it was probably there where Bjorn would meet this Arkil.

Halfdan and Lief both looked round at him. 'We are few,' the jarl said. 'We need to work our tactics to best preserve our men.'

'Although,' Ketil cut in, 'Bjorn may be right. We're overthinking this. The enemy know we're here, and they're well prepared. Maybe our best chance is simply to assault the gate. It's the easiest approach.'

'And well-defended.'

'Sneaking is no use,' Bjorn pointed out. 'If they know we're here, there's no point. That means there's going to be a fight. Better to get to it quickly. The longer you debate this, the longer it gives them to organise and plan. Hit them fast. Take them by surprise.'

Lief sighed. 'Not everything is solved by being the first to throw a punch, Bjorn.'

'No,' he agreed. 'Everything is solved by being the *last* to throw a punch.'

Halfdan chuckled at that. He turned and looked back past Bjorn, musing. Bjorn turned to look too. Twenty-seven altogether, including the three women. He was still adjusting to that. In his mind he automatically discounted the women when it came to a fight, but over the past few years they were beginning to make it clear that this shouldn't be the case. Even Bjorn had been impressed from time to time by Anna and Cassandra's capabilities for extreme violence. Should anyone threaten Gunnhild, or Anna's man Lief, the women all became like polecats, hissing and violent, and even Bjorn might walk around them in a wide circle.

'All right. We're going to play this the Bjorn and Ketil way,' Halfdan said with a nod. 'There are maybe twenty of them at the gate, and twenty-seven of us. We have the edge now, but there are more further down the dyke, toward the river, and a small group higher up, too. I'm happy that we can take the gate, but we need to be secure afterwards, not swamped by more of them. We take the gate by hitting it hard and fast, but then I want Ketil and two picked men to head up the slope and discourage survivors. Bjorn? Same for you. As soon as the gate's secure, take two men and clear the rampart right down to the river. You don't have to kill everyone. Just frighten them away. They're apparently so loyal to – or frightened of – Gunnar, that they will want to hold. It's time to change that, to make them more frightened of us than they are of Gunnar. Got that?'

Bjorn nodded. Let the jarl think he was content with that. In actual fact, he had no intention whatsoever of taking two men with him. At such times, he often found that having people fighting alongside him merely meant more people to get in the way. Since the days of his first bloodshed in the pit at Skara, he liked, in the perfect world, to fight alone. More than one opponent, for preference, but no one else for him to have to work around.

He reached round and pulled the great heavy axe from the back of his belt as he smoothed down his beard with the other hand.

'How do we want to do this?' Lief asked quietly, eyeing the gate.

Bjorn rolled his eyes. Even when you'd decided on a head-on attack, the little Rus wanted to plan that in detail. He turned to Halfdan, an imploring look in his eyes. Halfdan gave a short laugh, then nodded. 'Like this,' he said, and gestured to Bjorn.

There it was. The familiar feeling of release. The moment the constraint was dropped and all there was was the fight. No more complications, no discussion, and nothing to worry about but being better at it than your opponent, which Bjorn knew he was. He gave Lief a gruesome grin, then rolled his shoulders. He took a dozen steps forward, toward the gate in the dyke, stepping out from the scrub behind which they'd been hiding. The enemy knew they were here somewhere, on the approach, but could not know numbers or precise location.

Out in the open now, Bjorn paused and looked back. The others were all following, unsheathing swords, producing axes, Ketil testing his bow. Satisfied, Bjorn walked on, heading along the open flat ground toward the gate. He stopped when he judged he was within hearing distance, for he could now see numerous figures behind the palisade and gate.

'You are good men of the North. I'm going to kill a few of you now, but who is up to you. I'm coming in, and if you want to see another dawn, be good and fuck off out of the way.'

And with that he broke into a slow jog. There was a stunned and baffled silence from the enemy gathered at the gate, but it mattered not to Bjorn what they thought. Halfdan had given him the lead, for he was the jarl's champion, and he knew it.

He studied the gate as he ran. It was formed of timbers around six feet tall. No ropes binding the logs together, so there must be braces along the back, nailed on. A solid thing. He adjusted his thinking. He'd been planning to simply barge them open, and was convinced he had the strength and bulk to do it. At most they would have a bar across, but that could only be held in place with ropes or a more flimsy wooden D shape.

The problem was that if the gates were good and solid, he might damage his arm or shoulder in the process. He would heal, but that might just put him out of the ensuing fight, and there was no way he was going to allow that. He needed some kind of buffer between the gate and his shoulder.

As he ran, he reached up and unfastened the brooch that held his cloak in place. Letting the brooch fall, for it was just a stolen thing of poor quality, he folded the cloak three times with some difficulty, axe still in hand, and then wrapped it around his upper left arm and shoulder, tucking the ends into his armpit.

He finished it just in time, turning slightly at the waist to present his left shoulder as he ran at the gate.

'Odiiiiiiiiiiin!' he bellowed.

He could hear the astonished and shocked men behind the gate, and could hear several of them moving away, sensing what was coming.

He hit the gate right at the join between the two leaves. Even with the multiple thickness of woollen cloak, sleeve of chain shirt, woollen tunic and linen undertunic, the impact was hard. Bjorn felt his entire body take the brunt of the blow, but he also felt the elation as the bar used to hold the gate, just a plank rather than a beam, splintered and gave, the twin leaves bursting and swinging inward hard. Men were knocked aside by the timbers, leaving Bjorn barrelling into an open space.

He was in the fight again in a heartbeat.

Lief had often marvelled at Bjorn's ability to take impressive punishment and yet barrel on as though he'd not even noticed. The Rus put this down to Bjorn not having any wits in the first place to be knocked out of him, though Bjorn knew damn well that the ability to completely override pain and shock, and to fight on, was a product of those months in the pit. Without that skill, he'd have died a dozen times over.

Only one figure stood before him, the rest reeling back with the exploded gates. The man was clearly the leader, for he stood with hands on hips, an axe tucked into the back of his belt in the same manner as Bjorn favoured. The man had been directing his soldiers, though now he stared, wide-eyed, at the big man who had broken his gate. The leader, recovering well, reached round for his axe.

He wasn't fast enough.

The momentum that had allowed Bjorn to break through the timbers carried him forward at breakneck pace. He hit the leader head-on before he could bring the axe round. The man was thrown backward, falling to the wet grass and rolling for some time, axe flying off into the turf nearby.

Bjorn didn't waste time. The leader was still alive, but there were others at the gate, and Bjorn might miss out if he dallied. Consequently, he allowed his momentum to carry him straight on, over the fallen man. His left boot came down heavily on the man's ankle with a loud crack, then his right slammed down onto the leader's face. Bjorn cursed for a moment as he almost lost his footing on top of the man's head, but he recovered and veered into a curve that would bring him back to the action without losing pace.

Behind him, the crippled and broken figure howled and moaned as he rolled in the grass.

The others at the gate were making a valiant effort. The rest of the Wolves had followed Bjorn into the breach, and were now spreading out, taking on the defenders with a ferocity Gunnar's men could hardly have anticipated. Most were already occupied, though two enemies were engaged with one of Halfdan's men. Bjorn angled toward them and brought his big axe back and to the side. As he reached the small scuffle, he roared and swung in passing. The axe took the arm off one of the warriors just above the elbow, an impressive feat even for an axe of such size. In its passage, it also carved a deep line into the man's side. The arm flew away into the grey afternoon, its shrieking former owner backing away from the fight, staggering off, clutching at the stump in horror.

Bjorn looked about. Everyone was occupied. Even Cassandra and Anna were busy stabbing knives into a yelling warrior over and over again, their victim a spinning tower of fountaining blood as he tried variously to get away or to at least face only one madwoman at a time.

Another scuffle came close, and Bjorn took another opportunistic swing with his axe, slamming it down into a man's shoulder. The blade bit deep into hard bone, and when he managed to pull the weapon free, pieces of his victim came with it. He looked around, hoping for a more satisfying fight, but everyone seemed busy.

A slow smile spread across his face, then. Now was his chance to get away alone without Halfdan saddling him with two helpers. He was momentarily distracted, as a figure lurched into view on his left and he turned to see that leader he'd downed hobbling toward him on a damaged ankle, his face a mess of blood and scrapes from Bjorn's boot.

The man growled, lifting the axe he'd retrieved from the grass.

Bjorn sighed, waited for the man to swing, knocked the blow aside, and then reached up with his free hand, grabbing the man's ear. He tore the ear free and then lifted it to his mouth.

'Do you lot not listen? Fuck *off*.'

The man stared, silent for just a moment, before he reached up to the bloody hole on the side of his head and began to scream. He dropped the axe once more, and Bjorn turned, leaving him to it. Nearby, he saw Lief finishing a man off. Striding past as the Rus's opponent fell, Bjorn grinned. Lief had his left hand out, rubbing a cut on one of his fingers, and Bjorn dropped the severed ear into the open palm. 'Here. Maybe he'll listen to you.'

Leaving his revolted little friend, and finally, for the first time in days, feeling truly like himself, Bjorn broke into a jog. As he raced off down the slope along the inner line of the dyke, he could just hear Halfdan back at the gate yelling to take people with him. Later, Bjorn would claim to have been too far away to hear.

He was maybe a hundred and fifty paces from the gate when he met the first resistance. Two men who'd been in the area, manning the defences, had seen him coming. One had drawn a sword and turned to face Bjorn. The other looked a little less sure and stood a dozen paces further away, weapon in hand, watching nervously.

'Come on. It's more fun with two,' Bjorn shouted at the hesitant man.

'I don't know who you think you are...' began the nearer man, haughtily.

'I am Bjornfucking Bearfuckingtorn,' Bjorn grinned. He looked up at the second man, a bit further away. 'Remember that when you're nightmaring about this, later.'

The lead warrior leapt, stabbing out with his sword. Bjorn simply turned slightly and bent at the knee, so that the blow, instead of connecting with his thigh just below the chain shirt, struck the armour directly, robbing it of its killing potential. The blow was well delivered, and Bjorn knew well that he'd ache there and have an impressive bruise later. But the man was out of luck now. The blow with which he'd hoped to open the artery in his opponent's leg had been turned aside. Bjorn's left hand shot out and grasped the man by the throat, lifting him clear from the ground. As he gagged and stared in panic, Bjorn dropped his axe, and plucked the sword from the man's hand, like a tutor removing a toy from a difficult child.

'I'd say learn to watch your tone,' he said conversationally, 'but you won't have long to learn it.' He flipped the sword in his hand and then slammed it, pommel first, into the man's face, aiming for the mouth. The warrior's teeth exploded under the iron weight, the jaw cracking.

'That was for your tone. This is for making the wrong decision this morning.'

Tossing the sword away, he reached up and put his hand in the broken mouth, a mass of blood and ruination. With a fierce grin, Bjorn gripped the man's lower jaw and pulled with all his might. The jaw came free with a click and a crunch and the grind of tearing sinews. As the man in his grip passed out from the sheer agony, Bjorn looked over the victim's shoulder at the other man. The second warrior had gone whiter than Bjorn could ever claim to be, every hint of blood drained from his face. Bjorn threw the jaw toward him.

That was all the man needed. With a cry he was off, running across the turf, back up the dale, shouting a warning to retreat. Bjorn grinned to himself. In his hand, the unconscious wounded man shuddered. With a frown, Bjorn shook the body violently until the man came round, groggily, then groaned as he realised his situation.

'Ih eee,' he said, all he could manage with only an upper jaw, tongue lolling loose.

'Happy to oblige,' Bjorn grinned, then dropped the man and reached down, sweeping up his axe. When it came back down it went two thirds of the way through the crippled man's neck, finishing him.

Bjorn rose and began to jog once more. He could see a small group of half a dozen men toward the bottom of the slope near the riverbank, clustered together and engaged in furious debate. He grinned. Six. That was more like it. He began to run faster.

His disappointment was made vocal with a great deal of swearing as the six men saw him coming and their debate ended abruptly, all six pelting away across the grass, upriver toward perceived safety. Crestfallen, he let them go. Even in the throes of battle-lust, he recognised that to follow them was foolish. He would be alone, running into the arms of whoever these men were retreating to. He watched them go until they passed through a wooded area and were lost to sight. The whole valley seemed utterly peaceful, then, the only enemies within sight now silent and still in the grass. Before he left, he crouched and put the dead man's sword back in his hand. If Odin's maidens came to this place for the slain, this man deserved his seat in the hall. Shit, but Bjorn would even be pleased to sit next to him and drink when they were on the same side.

With that, he pounded back up the slope, heaving in tired breaths. At the gate, the others had heaped the enemy bodies into a pile. Of the Wolves, three were bleeding badly, seated on a log while Gunnhild and her women treated them. Three others lay dead nearby. Not a bad toll for what they'd done.

'I told you to take men with you,' Halfdan shouted at him, pointing an accusatory finger.

'You also told us to make them more frightened of us than of Gunnar,' Bjorn countered. 'Job done.'

Halfdan held his gaze for a moment, and then broke into a weary smile. 'I can imagine.'

'No, you can't.'

The jarl laughed. 'Actually, you're probably right.' He turned and took in the scene. 'All right. That's the first line of defence crossed. The next one, I fear, will be harder.'

Bjorn nodded, but his own gaze rose to that side valley he could see in the distance.

Arkil…

Chapter 8

'This dyke is longer,' Lief noted as they peered out between the foliage.

Halfdan nodded as he too watched the defences in the distance. They had moved up the dale from the first dyke cautiously, relatively slowly, being careful not to blunder into anything unanticipated, which had largely meant keeping Bjorn under control, for the big warrior had now had a taste of blood and, as always, yearned for more. Two miles further on, they had spotted the second of the two great defensive lines that sealed off Gunnar's world from the lands of the Christians, and had found a good position hidden by foliage on a terrace of the valley side to plan.

'Not so much *longer*,' he replied. 'It's actually three dykes.'

But the result was much the same. The defensive rampart that stretched from the river all the way up to the heights on their left was more or less a repeat of what they had faced at the last obstacle, though this one was not alone. From here, they could just see a second set of defences crossing the heather moor, cutting off any hope of going around the upper flank. And on the far bank of the river another dyke arose, marching off to the hills over there, mirroring the one at hand. From their lofty position, the Wolves could see clearly across the whole valley. On this side, the dyke was controlled by maybe thirty or forty men, though positioned in three groups and concentrated most heavily at the gate, presumably based on reports of the Wolves' last encounter. There were fewer defenders on the far bank dyke, for it was shorter, but it would still be a tough proposition. A small bridge crossed the river before the dykes, connecting the two sides of the valley, and there were signs of settlement in the distance, where the side-valley branched off.

'It is my gut feeling,' Halfdan told the others, 'that our best option is to hit them somewhere along the empty line of palisade. They are clearly expecting us to come for the gate, repeating what we did earlier, but they will be prepared this time, and Bjorn's tactics will not work so well again. They have concentrated their people at the top end of the dyke system, too, so that will be a hard fight. I propose we hit them somewhere in between,' he said, pointing to a stretch of the defences where no figures could be seen.

Ulfr frowned. 'There are men close enough to respond, at the gate and the top. By the time we're through or over the works, those men can converge and meet us there. They're not daft.'

'But they *are* nervous,' Halfdan countered.

He could tell. At the previous dyke, men had been clustered at the palisade in twos and threes, even alone in places, while the gate had been defended in strength. Here, no one guarded alone or in pairs. Gunnar's warriors were gathered in larger groups, because no one was willing to stand alone and risk what might come. And given what Bjorn had done to someone just an hour ago, every one of the defenders would be shaking at the thought of facing him again, of being the next jawbone he held aloft as a trophy. These men were frightened of their jarl, and of Arkil, Gunnar's berserkr, but now they had met *Halfdan's* berserkr. Their confidence had clearly been shaken.

'That doesn't mean they won't fight,' Lief said, dubiously.

'It means that if we get in among them, there is a good chance of panic. That being the case, we need to get on their side of the defences, and fast.' He turned to Bjorn. 'Do you think you could pull apart a palisade?'

Bjorn had a strange expression, though, and appeared distracted. The big albino was quiet for a moment, then he rumbled slowly, face folding into a picture of determination. 'I'm crossing the river, Halfdan.'

'What?'

'Arkil is there. I have to kill him.' Beside him, Ketil was nodding encouragement. Bjorn and the Icelander in a planning session was always a danger.

Lief shook his head. 'Bjorn, if we're to cross these defences, we need everyone together. Without you we lack the shock we need.'

But Halfdan was already nodding slowly. Silently, inside, he'd seen this coming. Bjorn had fixated on the enemy berserkr, and it seemed to be the only thing giving him energy and will at the moment. Halfdan wasn't sure what Bjorn might do if his jarl ordered him to stay here and not pursue his opponent, though he had no intention of finding out. After all, Bjorn had followed Halfdan across the world in a blood feud against one man. He had other reasons for agreeing with Bjorn, too, though. 'He's right. If we cross these dykes and move up the dale, but we don't deal with their berserkr first, then he will be *behind* us. Think on that.'

There was a worried silence from the others. It was an old adage that a good warrior never let a healthy enemy get behind him. If the Wolves moved on against Gunnar, and Arkil came with warriors at their heel, they would be trapped. And, after all, who better to face the berserkr than Bjorn?

He fixed the big man with a look. 'Arkil is not alone over there. Take five men. And Gunnhild. You need the cunning of the goddess with you. Be safe and be careful. I have no wish to face a world without my big friend in it.'

Bjorn shrugged. 'All men die. Except Geirr the Eternal. But it's not time for his story right now, and I don't have enough turnips to tell the tale anyway.'

Halfdan laughed. 'Go with Odin's favour, and join us when Arkil is no more.'

He glanced across at Gunnhild, a single, simple look managing to convey the need for her to look after the albino and make sure he returned safe. She caught the meaning, nodded, and threw a very similar look back at him, then gestured to five of the Wolves and drew them aside. Two of them were Cassandra and Anna, of course, something Halfdan had not considered. He'd meant Bjorn to take five strong warriors. But then, Gunnhild knew what she was doing, and as Bjorn gave him a wave and wandered off to join them, Halfdan settled in to rethink his plan. Had he had Bjorn and twenty-four men, he'd thought on applying force alone to overwhelm the defences and then move against them, using the shock of speed and the charge to break their will and send them running. Now he could not rely on the brute power of Bjorn, and he was down to seventeen men, and three of those still sported wounds from the last fight. Even knowing his hirð were the better warriors, those odds were much less favourable.

He needed a new plan.

He looked up. The rain had stopped now, the sun a pale disc making its presence known between the grey clouds, but with the arrival of the sun in the drenched valley, something new was happening. Mist was beginning to rise, to coalesce. An idea began to form, and Halfdan looked across and up the valley. The same was happening everywhere. Mist was rising from the soggy ground in a low blanket. Now it was a thin wispy white vapour, but this was just the start. There was little warmth in the sun, but clearly enough to draw the moisture from the ground into the air. And the clouds were still clearing, the ground still soaked. The mist would continue to get worse until it was little more than a wall of white, if he was any judge. He'd seen as much in the fields of Gotland in his youth.

Shock and power were out. Surprise and unpredictability were still possible, though.

He smiled and turned to Ketil. The Icelander was looking bored, levering something from his teeth with a sliver of wood. He had clearly hoped to go with Bjorn and fight the berserkr and his people, and not being chosen irked him. Halfdan smiled.

A few years ago, before Apulia, Ketil would have argued with him or simply disobeyed. His time with the Byzantines had changed him, though. He was still opinionated and rash, but at least he did as he was told now. The Icelander looked up, meeting Halfdan's gaze with his one eye. 'What?'

'Ready your bow, my friend. We're going to frighten the shit out of Gunnar's men.'

He turned to the others and pointed toward one of the field walls nearby, rough farm boundaries formed of boulders tightly packed together. 'Everyone put your weapons away and grab two fist-sized stones.' The others frowned their lack of understanding, but everyone here knew their jarl, and Halfdan was now radiating confidence, so they did as he asked without question.

It was not about *killing*. It was about *fear*. Bjorn had struck a blow not so much to the military strength of Gunnar's people, but to their confidence, to their heart. And now Halfdan would continue that work, unravelling their will to resist. After all, the Wolves were in no great rush. The archbishop had not given them a time limit. Even as he found himself two good-sized rocks, just as the others were doing, he glanced back across the world. The mist was rising and thickening every heartbeat. In half an hour it would be thick. In an hour they might as well be wrapped in wool, blind.

Excellent.

While the others worked to find the best stones, he crossed to Ketil. 'Time to show us you're back to your great form with that bow, despite the eye.'

The Icelander chewed his lip. 'What have you in mind?'

'There's a big oak tree over there,' he replied, pointing off toward the dyke. 'It's about halfway, I reckon. That should be close enough for shooting?'

Ketil nodded. 'So long as I can see. The fog's getting worse.'

'That's the idea. The fog is rising from the grass. It will lie low, probably below the height of the trees. As soon as it's thick enough to cover our approach, get to that tree and climb it. From there you can see the gate. With luck you'll be able to make out the people there. At my owl hoot, start putting an arrow into anyone you can see. Make sure to leave a count of ten between every shot, and be careful not to drop them too short. We'll be in the way. Make sure every shaft goes *over* the palisade.'

Leaving the Icelander looking from the tree to the gate, now becoming wrapped in white, Halfdan gathered the others around him. 'You remember how the Byzantines use their archers?'

Some of the Wolves nodded, though others had not been with them when they had faced the Greeks in Georgia or seen them in action in the great city or Italy. 'They use something called a volley,' he explained. 'They have two or more groups of bowmen in lines, so that one group can be putting arrows into people while the other reloads. That way, the attack is constant.'

Nods.

'We're going to do the same. The fog is getting thicker. Soon, it will be hard to even see each other. If we are quiet, we should be able to move right up to the wall without them knowing.'

'And what then?'

'Then, Ketil is going to start putting arrows into the enemy from his position high in a tree. He's going to count to ten between every shot. In between, we're going to climb their palisade and pelt them with rocks. We can only do that at the gate, and that's going to limit us, so we'll make four attacks, two rocks each, eight of us at a time.'

'And get an arrow in the back of the head?' Ulfr said.

'We will have the count of ten to throw a rock and get back down. Trust me. And trust the Icelander. He knows what he's doing.'

Lief sighed. 'Let's hope he is as good as he thinks he is.'

Crouching, Halfdan found a small, sharp stone, and rose once more. Using the point, he began to scratch a Σ shape into one of the two rocks. As he finished it, put it aside, and began with the other, Lief came close. 'What is that?'

Halfdan paused, turning a furrowed brow on his friend. 'Do you not know the runes, Lief?' It seemed inconceivable, even for a follower of the nailed god, that a northerner could not know such a fundamental thing.

'I know the *runes*, Halfdan. That is Sowulo. But why scratch it into the rock?'

The jarl began to work again as he answered. 'Runes have power, Lief. *All* runes. And not just the power to tell stories or to commemorate the fallen on a rock. Have you not seen Ulfr's runes on the *Sea Dragon*?'

'Well, yes, but...'

'They give us the speed and strength we need. Gunnhild will tell you about them. All runes have power, and Sowulo has the power of sight. Of clarity. We are in a sea of fog. A little sight and clarity could make all the difference.'

Lief pursed his lips, deep in thought. As Halfdan finished and blew the dust from his rock, the Rus reached over and plucked the smaller stone from his hand, then began to carve the rune into his own rocks. 'I'm not wholly sure that God would approve,' he noted, 'but I also think he'd prefer to keep his flock alive, so I imagine he'll compromise.'

Halfdan chuckled.

'And let's hope Ketil has done the same with his arrows,' the Rus added, vehemently.

Halfdan hefted his two rocks and moved back to where he'd been observing the dyke. He could barely see it at all now in the thickening white. Indeed, the big black oak, all but bare of leaves, was fast disappearing into the fog, despite being only half as distant.

'Niflheim,' Ketil murmured, looking out into the white.

Halfdan nodded, shivering. *Niflheim*. The mist-world into which Loki had banished Hel. He could really do with not being reminded about Loki and the fate of gods and men right now, given the dream that continued to plague him nightly. But certainly, he could see how Ketil made the connection.

'Let's just hope that Hel does not await us in that white.'

'One hoot,' the Icelander said. 'Give one to start loosing arrows. Two hoots and I'll stop.'

Halfdan nodded. 'At two hoots, put your bow away and come running with your axe.' He turned to the others, who were now gathering ready, a rock in each hand, then gave a quick glance out into the mist. He could no longer see the gate, though he had its position memorised. Indeed, the black skeleton of the winter oak was fast becoming ethereal grey. 'I think it's thick enough, now. We can go.'

With a gesture, he burst free of the undergrowth. It was an odd feeling, racing out across the grass in silence. It had been weird enough attacking in silence at the lookout post when they left Hindrelac, but then they had been creeping slowly up on the place, and at least the silence made sense. It was even stranger to be *running* into battle in such quiet. Not only was each of them keeping their mouth closed, not a sound arising from the whole assault, but all had secured their weapons and chain shirts so that there was little that could clang, shush or clonk with their movement. Most of all, though, the springy wet turf deadened even the fastest of footfalls, and the enveloping white muted what sound there was. A silent, eerie, advance. In that moment, to Halfdan, the Wolves seemed to be draugar, restless spirits in the mist. The notion made him shiver.

As they moved like wraiths across the level terrace of grass that led to the gate, the billowing white all around them, Ketil gave him a wave and veered off, making for the tree. Halfdan watched the lanky fellow as he passed, those long arms and legs giving him a huge advantage as he jumped into the tree, grasping a lower branch that would be too high for most people, and pulling himself up. By the time he was some fifteen feet up, he was lost to sight, the tree little more than a grey shape now. That also meant they were close to the gate.

He cut his pace and waved the others to do the same. Their approach slowed, what was already quiet now becoming totally silent. Even as they moved at a walk, he could see the shape of the palisade before them, looming out of the white world. Following his lead, the Wolves dropped to a crouch as they approached. The palisade was perhaps six feet high, and at the moment no one was looking over it, the attackers closing entirely unnoticed.

Halfdan changed his angle of approach, spotting the gate. He'd gone very slightly off course in the fog, but not far enough to matter. Location was important. It had to be the gate. Over the length of the dyke, a ditch the height of a man sat in front of the rampart, then the palisade above that, making reaching the parapet a near impossibility. The gate, though, by necessity, had no obstacles upon approach, and the timbers sat at ground level. It was the only place they could reach.

With a quick silent call to Odin to give them victory, he crept toward the gate, the others at his heel. It took mere moments. As he fell into position, dropping one of his rocks to the turf and still crouched to remain out of sight, he tried to control his breathing and listen. It was hard not to smile. He could hear them on the far side of the gate, and from their tone as they murmured in quiet conversation, they were expecting nothing, had seen nothing, were calm and untroubled.

If only they knew.

The others arrived with him, crouching, staying low, and he motioned positions for each to fall into as they emerged from the white. The moment the last of them was in place, two groups of eight, all low, he took a deep breath and put hands around his mouth. He knew four bird calls: goose, grebe, heron and owl. They had been the things of both game and work in his youth. They had been involved in play with the other children in the village, but they had come from the hunters, who used them to great effect. As such, he was in no fear that the enemy would suspect a man's voice behind the sound. The only problem might come from the proximity. An owl in the open, in the day, near humans, was unlikely.

He gave the call and flinched automatically, ducking even further.

The arrow came less than a heartbeat later and the result could not have been engineered any better if Halfdan had included the enemy in his planning. One of the nearest of the guards behind the gate had craned to see over the timbers, trying to spot the owl so close to their defences. The arrow took him in the throat, and threw him back out of sight with a strange gurgled bark.

Halfdan began to count instantly, that standardised timing based on a rested heartbeat the Wolves had used in all their time together, even as he lifted the rock he carried and gestured for the seven with him at the front to join in. He threw his free hand up, grasping the top of the gate timbers, and hauling with all his might. He could feel the strain as he pulled himself up, but by the fourth heartbeat he was looking over the parapet. The fog might be thick, but close up it did little to hide its secrets. Dozens of men moved around in a panic behind the gate, three of them gathering around the form of their fallen companion. Halfdan chose one at random and hurled his stone. He risked disaster by staying too long to watch the result, the others throwing their rocks and then dropping back, out of potential bowshot of Ketil.

Halfdan's rock struck a man in the side of the head, and the result was both impressive and gruesome. The man's skull shattered under the blow, red, pink and white exploding out from the missile. The jarl thought he saw the eye burst, but he might have been mistaken in the spray of matter as the man fell away, his head broken.

He was barely back below the level of the gate when the second arrow came. He never saw that one land, but a squawk behind the gate suggested that Ketil's aim was as good as ever. He had delayed too long, for the others were even now swapping, the second group of eight passing the first and reaching for the timbers even as Halfdan struggled to get out of the way. A second cascade of rocks flew into the defenders, raising a chorus of panic and agony among them, and even as Halfdan began scanning the ground for his other rock, he knew damn well that no matter how good his plan had been, he had miscalculated the timing. The second wave were barely back down out of danger before the next arrow whirred across the defences.

Knowing that if this went on, someone was going to be injured, Halfdan waved to his group to wait. There was an odd silence for a time, broken only by the shouts of consternation and the whimpers and moans from behind the gate. Halfdan gestured to his men, then, and they moved up to the timbers again. Ketil's next arrow whipped overhead, and Halfdan leapt, grabbing the timbers. Pulling himself up, he spotted a standing figure and hurled his other rock, then dropped back before he saw it hit, pulling himself down out of danger.

Another arrow, and then the second group threw their last rock.

A final arrow, and Halfdan gave two loud owl hoots.

That should be it. Ketil would be dropping from the tree now, putting away his bow and running with that pace only he could manage to join them. All arrows, all rocks had been cast. Now it was down to simple killing.

He waved to Thurstan, who hurried over to join him. At a gesture, Thurstan pulled at the two leaves of the gate, and Halfdan peered through the gap. What was left of the defenders were hardly in a position to mount a counter attack, and so the jarl cupped his hands and bent, nodding to Thurstan, who planted a boot in the cradle and then launched himself up and over the gate. Halfdan followed, using both hands to grab the top and pull himself up. Without aid, he was slower than his friend, but in moments he was dropping down the inside and helping the other man pull the bar free and open the gate.

Only five of Gunnar's men seemed to have survived the assault without serious injury, and three of those were clearly panicked, dealing with their wounded comrades. Only two saw the pair of interlopers drop over the gate. They shouted, for all the good it did, and Halfdan left Thurstan to the work once the bar was mostly clear, and turned. An older man with grey hair and a face like a mashed tomato, all red and angry, was coming at him with sword held high. Just behind him and to his left, the other was drawing his own blade. Halfdan smiled. The men might look fierce, and might be trained and armed, but their approach was little more than a shuffle, neither of them keen to be the first to face this madman, both trying to let the other get ahead. Halfdan had been right: fear was now buried deep in the bones of Gunnar's defenders.

He grinned a certain grin that he knew looked more maniacal than happy, and lifted his own sword. 'I took this blade from the body of a dragon warrior of the Alani,' he said, turning the blade this way and that as he advanced. 'He died well. You won't.'

The lead man's step faltered slightly, but still he came on, the other defender at his heel. Halfdan noted a slowness to the greybeard's movements. He looked up for a moment and smiled at two faint black shapes he could see circling in the air. The world around the small group may be wrapped in white, but above, the air was clear where the two birds wheeled and watched.

'Odin sees me,' the jarl said, still wearing a madman's grin. 'I have the Allfather's favour.'

The man came close, lumbering into an attack, and swung his sword down, aiming for Halfdan's shoulder to cripple his sword arm. He was too slow, though, age putting lead into his bones, while the Gotlander was young and agile. As the swing came, Halfdan stepped left, out of the way of the swing, and as the sword passed across his vision, he stabbed out three times in quick succession, each blow hitting the man's side, below the ribs and under the sword arm. The man wore no chain byrnie, and each lunge sank into flesh, each time bringing forth a gout of blood to soak his yellow shirt.

The man gasped, staggered to the side reaching down to the wound, and Halfdan let him do so, stepping round behind him. He had a few moments before the second man could reach him, enough time to finish the first. His sword rammed into the man's back, this time higher, into the chest, and he felt it grate on ribs. With grim satisfaction and a lunatic smile, he pushed the dying man away and turned, rising, to face the other defender.

His grin slid from maniacal to genuine.

The man was gone, and so were the others, all but the dead and dying. He could just make out their retreating shapes in the swirling white. Behind him, Thurstan had the gate open now, and the others were pouring in through the defensive dyke.

'The survivors ran,' he said, pointing with a bloody sword west, into the mist, up the dale.

'What now?' Lief asked as he hurried up, Ketil going to work with his sax, walking among the wounded and finishing them off.

Halfdan mused as he peered off into the mist that had swallowed Gunnar's men. It was a difficult decision. To go on ahead and pursue the survivors risked losing touch with Bjorn and Gunnhild in this white world, yet to delay meant losing the momentum of fear they had built. If the men were running as purposefully as they seemed to be, then they were running *to* somewhere, as well as *from*. The words they had drawn from a captive came back to him, then. 'The southern dyke has an old fort a mile behind, with another twenty men.' If he allowed them the time to consolidate there with their friends, they could face a serious siege. Right now, those men carried panic with them, which could be made to work for any attack. But even Gunnhild might not be able to find them again in this. He chewed his lip, deep in thought.

Sometimes only the gods' guidance could help, and without Gunnhild's wisdom there was only one place to look. His gaze rose to the sky. The birds had ended their swirling and were making west along the dale.

126

'We follow them,' he said. 'Have Ulfr bring up the horses. We ride them down and teach them to fear the Wolves.'

'And Bjorn?'

'No fog lasts for ever, and this dale cannot be that big. Not big enough to hide Bjorn for long, anyway.'

He turned as Ulfr went to bring the horses.

They had crossed two dykes so far. It occurred to him momentarily that he'd actually never been told how many there were. People just kept referring to them as a 'system'. Ah well. They would find out soon enough. He cleaned off the blade with a rag and sheathed it, then traced the Loki serpents on his arm as Ulfr brought up his horse. Every step west now took them toward Gunnar, toward victory, and therefore toward Hjalmvigi and rightful vengeance.

Onward.

Chapter 9

The past. Magnus's Valley, west of Skara, Geatland.

Bjorn shouldered his bag. He was, he thought, on the cusp of his fourteenth year. He had been born in the summer, and spring was even now fading into the warmer days. He had grown into a big young man, and already bore scars to match any great warrior. He did not know what the Norns had woven for him in the days to come, but since he had left the fighting pit in Skara, he had known what had to be done in the meantime. He had a score to settle, but to do so, he had to unburden himself of a certain weight. He was still an escaped thrall, no matter how powerful, and that made him a niðing, a creature of no value, even as a slave.

Magnus's village looked just as it had, and despite how much Bjorn had changed since last he was here, and how far he had come, he still felt that familiar shiver of fear run through him at the sight. He stood on the game trail he had followed through the woods. The fields were lush and green, and he could see people in them, working. One thing was new, though. A small wooden church rose at the centre of the village. The sight did not please him.

He patted the axe at his side for comfort. It was not a thing of beauty or of value, no great warrior's axe or heirloom of centuries of fierce battle. It was a woodsman's tool, taken from the stump where the hapless owner had left it unguarded. But it was sharp, and it was heavy, and it was comforting.

Someone saw him coming, now, and a call went up. He'd half expected not to be recognised, for he had grown to manhood since last he had trod the earth of this place, and had acquired the face of a killer and the hide of a scarred warrior. Yet that would be too much to hope for the boy they had called Ghost, and Whitey, and Snowdrift. Even the time gone by and the changes that time had wrought could not hide who Bjorn was.

By the time he was approaching the open ground at the centre of the village, between the houses, a small group of people had begun to gather, a number of them carrying weapons. For a moment he worried that in his absence that sour old bastard, Orm Barelegs, had passed away, but the man's house remained strong and lived in, and even as he came to a halt facing the crowd, the old man himself came strolling out into the square. The gathering parted to make way for him, and the old man stopped, facing Bjorn. There was a long, uncomfortable silence, which finally the old man broke.

'You have guts, I'll grant you, boy, coming back.'

'I left here a thrall,' Bjorn said in a quiet voice. Calm. Hopefully a little menacing. 'I return a warrior.'

'You return a niðing,' Orm Barelegs sneered. 'A runaway slave is less than a thrall. You are nothing, white boy.'

'I will not spend my life with the shadow of your ownership over me,' Bjorn answered. He reached down to the pouch at his belt with his free hand, the other clutching the bag over his shoulder that held all his worldly possessions. From the pouch, he produced three coins, which he allowed all to see, and then threw into the dirt at Barelegs's feet.

'What is this?'

'That is the price you paid for me. That is the price of my freedom.'

The old man's sneer returned in force. 'If you think—'

Bjorn fished another trio of coins out and tossed them over to join the first three. 'I double your money for the inconvenience and the embarrassment I caused you when I ran. Six coins. There will be no more. I consider my debt paid and my freedom bought. No matter what you say, I am a thrall no longer. And I am not the feeble boy you wronged. I have killed more people since last I saw you than the plague. I suggest you take the coins and walk away.'

There was a strange silence, then. Not the expectant one of earlier, but a strained and nervous one. Bjorn had always known he might have to fight this out, but now he looked into Orm's eyes, he knew that would not happen. The old man looked him up and down, marking the scars, marking the axe at his side. Orm would not argue. Bjorn was a free man, no longer thrall or niðing. He was Bjorn, warrior of Skara. The old man scooped up the six coins, that sneer back on his face, though now given a strange taint by fear.

'Go, and never come back,' he said.

But Bjorn was not done. His peripheral gaze had caught sight of three new figures at the edge of the square, and the other reason for his return came to the fore. Even as Orm Barelegs stood with a nervous expression, watching him, white fingers wrapped tightly around the six coins, Bjorn turned and pointed at the three new figures. The grandsons of Orm Barelegs stopped at the sight.

'I challenge your boys to *Holmgång*.'

Barelegs's eyes widened.

'What? No.'

Another old man among the crowd cleared his throat. 'On what grounds?'

'On the grounds that they did me much harm and insult in my time here, all of which was unwarranted.'

'You were a thrall,' Barelegs snarled. 'You still are.'

'No,' the other greybeard said. 'No, he is not. You accepted his payment. The white boy is free. Whether or not he can legitimately challenge for Holmgång based on insults levelled at a thrall is a different matter. A council will be called to consider the matter.' He looked across the square at the three young men. 'Unless they wish to accept, regardless.'

There was a hint of challenge to the tone. The man was goading the three into accepting, which made Bjorn smile. The older of the three came forward, eyes slitted, considering. 'One at a time, or all three of us at once?'

'That is not the way of Holmgång,' the old man interjected, but Bjorn held up a hand to stop him.

'However you wish it,' he replied.

The older lad smiled unpleasantly. 'I and my brothers accept your challenge. It was levelled against the three of us together and so you will fight the three of us together.'

Orm Barelegs was staring in shock, but the decision did not seem to please the other old man, who was shaking his head. 'You are set upon this course of action?'

Bjorn turned to him. 'I have challenged. They have accepted. There can be no going back.'

The old man nodded slowly. 'One against three is not in the spirit of a duel. As elder of this village it is my decree that the Holmgång go ahead. However, the white boy will be given the three shields as tradition demands, while the three challenged shall take one shield each.'

Bjorn nodded his acceptance of this. He glanced across at the three lads, who wavered at the decision, but finally accepted their lot. They could not back down now, after all, once the challenge had been accepted. To do so would see them leave the day as niðings.

'The challenge shall be fought in three days,' the greybeard announced, 'on the grass before the church, in the full sight of God.'

Bjorn grinned. That suited him down to the ground. Let the nailed god watch his hypocrites die.

Late February 1044. Swaledale.

'I can't see anything,' grumbled Bjorn as they stepped from the bridge to the north bank of the river. 'Can't even make out where the dyke is.'

Gunnhild nodded. 'But it is there, and I know how far. By what I could see from across the valley before the fog came down, I would say there are a dozen men guarding this dyke. There was a small group at the upper end, where the slope becomes steep, but the majority were around the gate. Maybe nine men.'

'I can break the gate open,' Bjorn said. 'I did it before.'

And on the other side of that gate, somewhere, was Arkil, the berserkr of Swaledale. Every moment's delay now was making Bjorn twitch.

'No,' Gunnhild retorted. 'They will be expecting such a direct approach now. If these people truly do follow the old ways, we could rely upon settling this without the need for a big fight. You seek Arkil, and Arkil controls this area. Were we to know that they respected the rules of Holmgång, you could challenge the berserkr, and perhaps we could win this whole place with just one fight.' She sighed. 'However, we are still strangers in this world, no matter how much they may seem like us, and only a fool rests his neck on the chopping block of a man he does not know. Still,' she added, 'that may work for us. If neither the war-like approach of Thor, nor the wise approach of Odin will help, then perhaps it is time for the trickery of Loki.'

'I don't like trickery,' Bjorn grunted. 'It takes too long and usually involves less fun.'

Arkil was waiting.

'I do not believe they are watching the river,' Gunnhild smiled. 'Of course, they will be worried and therefore alert, so any approach will soon draw their attention. Unless they have a reason to be looking elsewhere.'

Bjorn frowned. Halfdan talked in riddles half the time, as far as Bjorn was concerned, and Lief did so *most* of the time, but neither could hold a candle to Gunnhild, whose every simple thought tended to baffle him. 'What do you want me to do?' he sighed. 'And make it quick. I want Arkil.'

'And you shall have him, Bjorn Bear-torn. But I intend to make sure there can be no other interference. I want you, Bjorn, to walk straight up to their gate and to challenge their berserkr.'

Bjorn blinked. That was more or less what he wanted to do, anyway.

'Why?' he asked suspiciously.

The völva rolled her eyes. 'Sometimes, trying to get the simplest plan into your head, Bjorn, is like trying to push a sponge into a rock. You are the distraction. You will be alone at the gate. If Arkil accepts and the gate opens, then all is well. If not, then we will make sure the gate opens for you. Either way, Arkil will await you on the other side of it.'

This, Bjorn could follow, though he still had no idea of what Gunnhild meant to do with the others, apart from it involving the river somehow. 'Where is the gate?' he asked.

Again, she rolled her eyes. 'What are you standing on, Bjorn?'

He looked down, brow creasing. 'The ground?'

'What type of ground?'

They were standing on a rough track that led down from the bridge. 'A path?' he hazarded.

'And what is the important thing about a path?'

He was getting sick of this. 'It's flat?'

'No, you big troll-turd. A path connects two places. What places must this one connect?'

Bjorn sighed. 'The bridge and... and the gate?'

'He gets it at last,' Gunnhild said with a sarcastic little clap of the hands.

Again, Bjorn sighed. If Lief had said that to him and clapped, he'd have given the Rus a dead arm to think on. If a stranger had done so, the bastard would go home in a bucket. Gunnhild was different, and he would let her get away with almost anything, but it still rankled. He nodded. 'I will follow the path and challenge to Holmgång.'

She bowed her head. 'One way or the other, we shall see you on the far side of the gate, Bjorn Bear-torn.' And with that, she gestured to the others and walked down to the riverbank. He watched for a moment, baffled, as the six of them slipped down into the water, then shrugged, turned and walked on. His job was not planning. It never was. Probably a good thing, he admitted, given the trouble he'd got into in the old days when he *did* have to plan for himself.

He walked alone into the mist. A small smile broke out on his scarred face at the realisation of what this must look like for anyone who saw him. Bjorn was unnaturally pale at the best of times, and to see such a white figure emerging from a world of white would be strange to say the least. His smile widened to a grin. He shook out his hair so that, apart from the braid, it was wild and white, and removed the colourful scarf from his neck, tucking it into his belt. What was left was a man mostly white and grey, if one counted a chain shirt as grey, anyway.

He walked on, then, with purpose. It was not long before his goal coalesced from the mist. Another dyke, for this valley seemed to be filled with them. A man-deep ditch before a man-high rampart topped with a recent palisade. And before him, at the end of the path – *damn that Gunnhild and her logic* – the gate.

For a brief moment, he considered charging it anyway. It didn't look any sturdier than the first one he'd hit, and he was quietly comfortable that he could break through it. But Gunnhild had told him not to, not knowing what to expect on the far side. Instead, as he began to approach the gate, he slowed.

He grinned even harder. Bjorn Bear-torn may not have the Freyja wisdom of Gunnhild, the Loki cunning of Halfdan or the Allfather sense of Lief, but he had his moments of brightness. Halfdan had said that half the fight in this valley would be won through fear, not iron. Let them fear Bjorn more than any other creature. He would be the thing of legend in this place, more so ever than their Arkil.

He started to sing. He knew his voice to not be the best, and 'tuneless' was about the nicest thing Gunnhild had ever said about it, so he deliberately kept his voice low and deep, allowing every crack and wheeze to infiltrate the melody, giving it an unpleasant, jarring sound. It was an old song, the *Skírnismál*, as told by the visiting skalds in his youth. A carefully chosen part, beginning on a tune of brightness...

'*I strike you, maid, with my magic staff of power, to make you obey my will.*'

The tune changed to a minor key. '*You will go where no human will ever see you again.*'

Back to a slightly happier tone, just as three faces appeared over the gate, peering into the white at this strange musical apparition emerging from the mist.

'*On the eagle's hill you will always sit...*' He allowed the tune to drop to a minor key again and acquire a hollow, dark aspect. '*And look at the gates of Hel.*' He allowed the emphasis on the last word to linger for a while, to give added eeriness to the scene. He'd been around Christians enough in his life to know that they had a Hel, too, and that they were more frightened of theirs than a good Northman was of his. Two more faces appeared at the gate as he now came close enough for them to make out every scar and scratch on his white skin. They had gone rather pale themselves.

'*Your food will become more loathsome to you,*' he finished, '*than a pale snake is to men.*'

He came to a halt.

'I am Bjorn Bear-torn, scourge of Skara, breaker of heads, child of war and wearer of the bear shirt.'

He let this sink in. He hoped it sounded as impressive to them as it did to him. It appeared so, from the draining of any remaining colour from those faces at the gate.

'I come to kill Arkil Bear-shoulders. Bring him to me so that I can face him as tradition demands, in Holmgång, one berserkr to another.'

The faces vanished as the enemy dropped back behind their gate. He could just hear the murmur of voices. There was a long pause and then, unexpectedly, to Bjorn at least, the gates swung open.

'Arkil is being summoned,' said a figure standing calmly in the open gateway, though his voice quavered, and his face was still pale.

Bjorn bowed his head and walked forward, hand away from his axe. He had issued a challenge and been welcomed in. The world remained white beyond the gate, and he could see no further than the three men around him. He frowned as his thought process slowly caught up with his senses. Three men. There had been five above the gate just now, and it was quite possible that the other two had gone to find Arkil and bring him, but Gunnhild had estimated the number of men at the gate to be nine. Four men had vanished. Of course, that was not a difficult feat in this fog, but still...

He was not entirely surprised when the fog was cut through by an unearthly shriek of pain and shock from the direction of the river. The three men with him looked that way sharply, fear painting their faces once more, then back at Bjorn, their suspicions on him, despite he not having moved.

They murmured together for a moment, and then one said to the others, 'Go and see what that is.'

'Fuck that,' was the only reply he got.

'I am your superior,' the man snapped. 'You want me to tell Arkil you're disobeying orders?'

The other two looked at one another, at Bjorn, into the mist, then back, caught in a quandary. They may well fear Arkil more than almost anything in the world, but Bjorn was comfortable that he had now edged above his opponent on that list, and what was happening in the fog that made men shriek was certainly up there too. Neither of the men were keen on disobeying orders, but that option was currently looking a lot nicer than the alternatives.

Before any further debate, though, their decision was made for them. The unearthly wailing became louder and louder until a figure began to emerge from the mist, at first just the shape of a man, then the detail became clear. Even Bjorn, who had told Lief time and again that he was afraid of nothing in the nine worlds, felt the blood drain from his face.

The man was clearly one of Gunnar's men, another of those who had guarded the dyke, and presumably one of those number missing from the gate. His howling descended into a low, hopeless moaning as he wandered roughly toward them, arms outstretched in front of him, feeling for anything, for where his eyes should be were just empty crimson sockets, twin rivers of red marring the face from the eyes down to the chin and beyond, where they had soaked the man's tunic and chain byrnie.

What had Gunnhild and the others been doing?

The two men who had been in a quandary over what to be most afraid of were no longer in any quandary. Both men turned to their superior, then turned again, and sprinted away into the fog, heading directly away from the gate, deeper into Gunnar's realm.

The remaining man at the gate was more than a little shaken. He stood watching Bjorn, eyes occasionally sliding to that grisly spectre, who had walked into the palisade and was now feeling his way along it while issuing a horrible keening sound.

Even Bjorn jumped a little when Gunnhild appeared. He never even saw her approach, gradually coalescing from the mist as one would expect. She was simply there, suddenly, right behind the remaining guard. She had her staff raised in both hands, and tapped the man lightly on the shoulder with the butt of the weapon. He turned in surprise, and then received a heavy smack in the face from the same ash pole, hard. He spun, dazed, shaking his head, trying to recover his wits. Then, suddenly, Anna and Cassandra were there too, each wielding a knife. Bjorn watched, oddly fascinated, as they both stabbed the man from different sides. As he spun, trying to get away, they simply struck him again and again, each time in a different place. By the time he dropped to the ground, dead but still shaking, pouring blood from a score of wounds, the other two Wolves with them had emerged from the mist. Both looked shocked and slightly sick. Given the state of the blind man, Bjorn found himself wondering what other horrors Gunnhild had visited upon the missing members of Gunnar's hirð.

'I wanted him alive to tell his friends how scary I was, coming out of the fog,' he complained to the völva.

'Others saw you and live.'

He nodded. Of course. The two who went to fetch Arkil. And though these nightmares had been inflicted by Gunnhild and her women, word of what was found when the fog lifted would only grow Bjorn's legend. Still, he felt faintly cheated that all he'd done was knock on a door scarily, while Gunnhild had walked through the mist, killing and maiming as she went.

Which was why, when a new figure suddenly appeared from the north, the direction of the steep bank and the dale's side, Bjorn decided that this one was his. The man had barely arrived, mouth opening wide in shock, much like his bulging eyes, when Bjorn stepped over to him. In a fluid, swift motion he'd learned many years ago in a fighting pit, his left arm came up beneath the man's upper arm, while his right dropped hard on the same limb, closer to the elbow. He was rewarded with a sharp crack, and the arm dropped as he moved his own, hanging limp from halfway up the humerus, held on only by skin and muscle. The man screamed and staggered back. His agony and shock robbed him of the sense to flee instantly, which was a mistake, for Bjorn took one more step and repeated the process on the other arm. He stepped back to admire his handiwork. The man's upper arms were jutting slightly outward, but the rest of each was hanging loose, swinging this way and that with every movement. The man was caught in endless screaming, unable to even barely take a breath.

'Go tell your friends that Bjorn Bear-torn did this,' he grinned at the man.

His victim simply stood there, horrified, in agony, panicking and staring down at his dismembered limbs. He was still screaming. Bjorn, faintly irritated now, reached up and turned the man around by the shoulders, which made the limbs flap comically, and put his boot to the man's backside, launching him into the fog the way he had come. The figure staggered off into the white, still screaming. Bjorn watched him until he was no longer visible, then turned to Gunnhild, even as the noise diminished with distance.

'See. I can be just as scary as you.'

Gunnhild rolled her eyes. 'Yes, Bjorn, you are terrifying. Not subtle, but unsubtly terrifying.'

He frowned for a moment, not quite sure whether that was a compliment or an insult. Deciding, knowing Gunnhild, that it was probably both, he shrugged.

A new noise was cutting through the mist now, and he turned to face that direction. A few moments later, shapes began to emerge. More warriors. It was possible that two of them were those who had witnessed his approach in the mist from the safety of the gate, though he could not tell. There were maybe a dozen, but it was what – or who – they were escorting that interested Bjorn.

Arkil Bear-shoulders was a giant.

Even Bjorn, a man rarely impressed, had to admit to being the tiniest bit intimidated by the new arrival. Arkil could easily be *jötunn*, one of the ice giants who would come at the end of days to bring the death of the gods. He towered above the men with him by a clear two feet, possibly more, and those men were not small themselves. From shoulder to shoulder, he was as wide as the two men in front of him together.

He wore only trousers, his chest bare, even in the chilly fog, and while his beard was long and black and braided into a tight tail, he was entirely bald. The most striking thing about him, other than his sheer remarkable size, though, became visible as he moved closer. His entire body was decorated with tattoos in an off-putting fashion. His face was inked with a black skull, mirroring what lay beneath the flesh, and the rest of his body was covered in runes, not in ordered lines, as text, but each within its own decorative pattern.

Runes of power.

No wonder Arkil Bear-shoulders was so feared by all. The man was the size of a frost giant, and his very skin was marked with power. Even Bjorn felt a single shiver ripple through him. As the group approached the gate, several of the accompanying warriors veered off and made for Gunnhild and the others. Their leader had his hand on his sword hilt as he approached, but faltered as the völva's hand came up, an accusatory digit levelled at him.

'I am Gunnhild of Hedeby, völva of Jarl Halfdan Loki-born, and daughter of Freyja, and any man who touches me will spend the rest of his days feeling his flesh slither from his bones, like a snake shedding its skin.'

Everyone approaching her stopped dead, faces blanching, as Anna and Cassandra and the two other warriors stepped to her shoulders in support.

The mountain of a man that was Arkil ignored the exchange. His gaze had fallen upon Bjorn, and he strode straight toward him.

'What is this?' the man said in a thick, heavy, deep voice, accented with some strange tone from beyond these parts. 'The Christ thralls finally send a *warrior* against me.'

Bjorn felt a little twitch tug at his cheek. He straightened in the face of the oncoming thing and held himself strong. 'My jarl has a deal with your enemy. He will see Gunnar fall. But me? I do this because I have travelled from the land of the Svears to the lands of the Grikkjar, from Apulia to the dukedom of the Normans, and I have yet to find a man worth fighting. Are you a man worth fighting, Arkil Bear-shoulders, or are you all mouth and flab?'

The huge man broke into a wide grin. 'I shall look forward to adding your skull to my collection.' He turned to the men with him. 'Mark us out a field for Holmgång.'

Bjorn studied the man. Arkil had no obvious weakness. Every inch of him was covered in runes of power, and beneath them all, enormous muscles bulged. Bjorn only became aware that Gunnhild was hissing his name when she had been doing so for some time. He tore his gaze from his opponent back to the völva.

'What?'

She reached down to her belt as she stepped toward him. When she lifted her hand once more, she held a small pouch that Bjorn recognised as one of those in which she kept the compound she used to walk with the goddess, and which, when employed by a bear-shirt, could instead be used to bring him into the deepest of battle lusts.

He looked down at the pouch, then up at Gunnhild in surprise. She guarded the stuff jealously, and rarely even let Bjorn within eyesight of it. And he had to admit that it was true that he did not generally need any such enticement. Bjorn Bear-torn lived every moment of his life halfway to berserkr anyway. And he knew what taking the compound would do. Yet she was proffering it to him.

She nodded.

He took the pouch, and was about to open it, but she shook her head. 'Not yet. Wait until your ground is ready. You will breach the rules of Holmgång if you begin the fight before everything is ready.' She locked him with her gaze. 'Do not take too much. You need a certain amount of control of yourself. If you are both berserkr, I doubt anyone will try to keep you to the traditional rules, but you need to not be the first one to break them. Are you sure about this?'

Bjorn simply nodded. This was what he had been looking forward to, *yearning* for, even. When he stood over the body of Arkil Bear-shoulders, there would be a new tale to tell in the mead halls of this island, and Bjorn's fame would grow. And no one would call him a thrall any more, of the nailed god, or of *anyone*.

He removed the axe from his back and then undid his belt, dropping it to the turf.

'What are you doing?' Gunnhild hissed.

'Getting ready.' He reached up and bent over, so that he could pull the chain shirt off over his head.

'Don't be stupid,' Gunnhild said as he then removed his shirt too, his pale, strange, and horribly scarred torso eerie in the mist.

'I must face him on equal terms.'

'You *were*. You had your body encased in chain. He had his encased in runes. Now you are at a disadvantage.'

He shook his head. 'This is how it is meant to be.'

She looked horribly disapproving, but clearly she knew when Bjorn had made up his mind, for there was no further argument, and she stepped back. The other two Wolves, watching on with worried interest, both of whom had joined them from Iron Arm's retinue after their journey from Apulia, were suddenly eclipsed by Gunnhild as she turned to them from Bjorn.

'The moment our big friend steps toward that field of combat, move a good distance away.'

'Why?'

'What do you know of the berserkir?'

Baffled looks and shaking heads. 'Put it this way,' she explained, 'once this fight begins, do whatever you have to in order to stay out of the way of either of them, even Bjorn. The next time you approach Bjorn, make sure he's asleep first.'

She turned back to him. 'Are you ready?'

He nodded, and she looked back across the valley into the wall of white. 'I hope Halfdan's having more success.'

Chapter 10

'I think we may have lost our momentum,' Lief noted drily.

Halfdan nodded distractedly, still scouring the ground. Lief's mood had been steadily becoming drier and more acidic the longer he spent away from Anna.

They were lost. That much was clear. The fleeing men of Gunnar's force from the dyke had run west along the dale, and Halfdan had thought to grab the horses, follow, catch them up and either ride them down or harry them to this fort place and deal with them there. Unfortunately, with such thick fog, by the time they were in proper pursuit, the enemy had quite a head start and had vanished into the white. Still, Halfdan had been content they could track the men, but that proved troublesome even for Ketil, the best tracker among them. The ground was of springy damp grass, not of mud, and so the passage of men on foot left very little sign, and the constant damp settling into the grass masked whatever trace there was.

They knew they were on *roughly* the right track from the one sign they had found. Less than half a mile west of the dyke they'd fought at, they came across another one, again rising from the river and climbing to the heights, or so they presumed, from what they could find in the fog. This dyke, though, had not been rebuilt and fortified, and was little more than a man-high grassy embankment. They located a gate, and that gateway was of mud rather than grass, revealing the recent passage of a number of men.

But once again, past that gate and out of sight of the bank in the fog, all traces had vanished. Halfdan had done all he could, then. All seventeen men of the party spread out in a line, down the slope toward the river and upward toward the moors, making sure to each stay within sight of the others, then moving slowly west along the valley side in a long line, looking for signs of enemy passage. So far, the only sign of living things reported in were cattle that grazed at the lower area, close to the river on the flat valley bottom.

It was irksome, he decided as they rode slowly, for though he felt certain they would find the men eventually, this slow approach would give them ample time to recover their wits and courage, and to plan and prepare with the defenders in the fort. Exactly what he'd been trying to avoid.

The other downside of this strange pursuit was the odd isolation. Though he could see Lief and Thurstan to either side, away in the mist, they could only talk by shouting, and therefore did so but rarely, which meant riding in silence in a world of blank white, with only two familiar but distant shapes to rely upon. That left plenty of time for the mind to wander, something that Halfdan had been trying very hard to avoid in all the time since they had landed on this island. This land, these blasted heaths and high hills that were oddly reminiscent of the land of Svears and Geats back home, were also worryingly reminiscent of the hillside that played host to Heimdallr's house in his dream. The idea they were coming close to that fated confrontation was not a comfortable one. All Halfdan had to do was to complete this task for the archbishop in Jorvik, and he would no longer owe any man. He would be free to chase down his vengeance on Hjalmvigi. He would be unbound.

Loki would be unbound.

A small part of Halfdan wanted to argue logic with himself. In the great prophecies of the end of the time of Gods and the unmaking of this world, Loki was freed of his bonds in time to see Ragnarok unfold, and would then meet Heimdallr in battle where both would perish. That Halfdan could not truly say he was unbound until he had completed the task for the archbishop, which would mean meeting, and fighting with, Gunnar/Heimdallr *before* he was unbound, gave him the tiniest sliver of hope that he was attaching greater significance to the dream than it warranted. But he also knew he was arguing semantics and minutiae, and that the weaving of the Norns was treacherous. And he had not the mind of someone like Gunnhild to unpick such things.

He was, once again, deeply mired in the meaning of his personal prophecy, when the call went up. From his left, Thurstan was shouting. Someone had found something. Halfdan sent the message on down the line toward the river, man to man, along with the recall. He waited until every man from the line down the slope had converged on him, then led them up to join Thurstan. From there they moved on up the slope, and eventually all seventeen of them were gathered around Ketil, who had sent out the initial call.

At first, as the Icelander pointed out into the white, Halfdan could see nothing, but then, as the wall of white drifted and billowed, there was something there for a heartbeat. A raised section of the hillside which occasionally, when the white shifted just enough, seemed to be ramparts.

'A good spot, given you have only one eye to spot with.'

'The Allfather has only one eye, and he manages fine,' Ketil replied drily without looking at him.

Halfdan scratched his chin. All hope of a swift strike before the enemy was prepared had long gone, now. He would have to find another way. If this *was* a fort of some sort, then it would be a centre of Gunnar's might, and Halfdan could hardly afford to leave it intact behind him. They needed to clear the enemy out of it first. But his forces were gradually diminishing and with the main goal still ahead of them he really could not afford to lose more men. There had to be another way. He rubbed the serpent mark on his arm. He had to get closer. To know more.

'Lief and Ketil come with me. Ulfr and Thurstan check the injured and secure anything that might make a noise before anyone else moves. Other than that, stay here until we come back.'

And with that, he dismounted and waved the Rus and the Icelander over to him.

'I want to get a good look at what we're up against.'

The three men secured anything that might swing or clatter, removing their chain shirts and leaving them and their shields behind with the horses. Clad finally in just grey cloaks, and moving like silent phantoms, they hurried on into the mist. The terrain was troublesome as they moved, and Halfdan was forced to spend as much of his time looking at the ground, making sure of his footing, as he was looking forward, toward their goal. They were on the slope of the valley side, though still on the part with a reasonable gradient, far below the steep section. Yet moving along that slope was far from easy, especially with patches of heather growing bushy and strong, ready to tangle and trip, areas of fern and bracken wherever water was found lurking in the terrain, dips and bumps, and even scattered rocks from the size of a fist to the size of a small dog waiting to turn or break an ankle. If this was what it was like only this far up the slope, then he was grateful after all that they had not tried to approach across the moors above the dale.

Still, despite the slow going, they were moving on the fort, and it was becoming marginally clearer as they came closer. Of a similar style to the dykes they had seen, the fort was protected by a rampart behind a ditch, though there were two notable differences: the first was the size, for both ditch and mound here were twice the height of a man, making crossing them extremely dangerous in the face of desperate defence. Secondly, the rampart here may be earth, but it seemed to be stone faced at the upper part, presenting an attacker with an additional obstacle. Of course, the place was ancient, and that wall had fallen along most of the circuit, becoming a scree and rubble slope down the side of the rampart. That, in itself, might actually present more trouble than the wall would have.

As they came closer, the other interesting thing became clearer. The gate, which stood on the eastern side, facing them, was protected by twin walls that marched out some hundred paces from the ramparts, creating a funnel leading into the place. Halfdan could only imagine how much trouble an attacking force could get into trapped in that funnel with arrows and sling stones coming at them. Even though the fort was ancient and even those walls had seen better days, as a prospect for an assault, it was not a pleasant notion.

He turned his attention, as they skirted the place, to the fort's occupants. No figures were visible above the rampart, which struck him as odd, and he might have presumed the place deserted were it not for the black plume of smoke rising from a cookfire, unseen somewhere in the centre.

'How many, do you think?' Ketil murmured.

'Our source said twenty or so in the fort. And any survivors from the dyke, of course. I would take a guess at thirty.'

Lief nodded. 'Though it could easily hold a hundred. It's ancient, I think, like the dykes. That means it's unlikely they've built anything more permanent inside. Living in tents, I suspect. Basically a fortified campsite.'

'I saw movement,' Ketil hissed, then made an irritated noise. 'Gone again. I think they have a few men on watch, but they're not standing on the ramparts, just hiding behind them, occasionally looking— There, see? There he is again.'

He pointed, and Halfdan just spotted the head before it vanished this time.

'Down,' he whispered, and the three of them dropped to the ground, still watching. Their grey attire should make them exceedingly hard to spot in the fog from that distance, but there was no point in tempting fate. 'Come on. Keep low.'

They moved on around the northern, lower, side of the fort, keeping some distance from it, and moving low to the ground, pausing any time they saw movement. Not once did the alarm go up, and after a while they reached the far end, climbing the

147

hillside to skirt the fort on its southern side, higher up the hill. The whole place was maybe a hundred paces across, like that funnelled entrance. Quite a place.

As they moved up the slope, the fog began to thin a little, and Halfdan realised they had climbed to sufficient altitude they were coming out above the white that had settled into the dale. Thinner though it was, the world was still far from clear, with a drifting white fleece blurring the land, and they would have to climb a way yet to be able to see properly. Not that there would be much point to that, of course, for all they would be looking down upon was a blanket of white that filled the valley.

They moved around the fort, and here, above it, they had to be careful. The thin mist would make them easier to spot, as was clear from the fact that it also made the fort easier to see from their position. Lief had been correct. Eight tents were pitched around the place, each quite a large affair, with the central area clear and left for a fire. A simple camp. It was hard to ascertain the number of men, for most of them would be in the tents, and only a few were visible on the inner slopes of the rampart.

'Why are they not more alert?' Ketil muttered. 'After what happened at the dyke, I would have every man on watch.'

Halfdan shrugged. 'Perhaps they're content that they're safe in there, and in a way, they are. There are probably twice as many of them as us, and they're in the most secure place in the whole valley. Also, they have no reason to believe we even know about the fort. Anyone coming up the dale will meet the dykes automatically, but only someone who knew about the fort would look for it, especially in the fog. They may just think we are unaware and will blunder right past them. Whatever the case, I think they feel secure.'

'And rightly so,' Lief added. 'You'll lose at least half of us taking that place, even if we succeed.'

Halfdan nodded. There had to be another way. Going over the ditch and ramparts would be brutal and deadly, but the only other option was to be trapped in that stone funnel on the way in.

Trapped.

An idea began to form. What if it were not the *Wolves* that were in danger? He turned to the others, a grin forming. 'What if *we* are not shut *outside*, but *they* are trapped *inside*?'

Frowns. Lief scratched reflectively. 'Well, they *are*, I suppose, after a fashion. But that doesn't help us.'

'Maybe it does. It will be almost as much trouble getting over that rampart and ditch from the inside as for us from outside.'

'Why would they want to?'

Now, Halfdan's grin turned vicious. 'Because it will be safer out here than in there.'

'What?'

'Come with me.'

With the others in tow, Halfdan checked the position of the gate funnel for the fort and used it to work out where the Wolves had stopped before approaching the place. His estimation was close enough for, as they descended the slope some distance from the fort, the shape of their awaiting men gradually became visible in the mist.

'Ulfr,' he said, rubbing his hands in a business-like manner as they re-joined their friends, 'how many cows did you see down in the fields?'

The shipwright's brow folded. 'I have no idea, Halfdan. I didn't stop to count them.'

'But there were more than a few? Say, at least as many as there are of us?'

Ulfr shrugged. 'I would think quite a *few* more, yes. Are you thinking of becoming a farmer?'

'Sort of. For now.' He turned and took in the gathering. 'All right. Here's what I want you to do, Ulfr. Tether the horses. They can wait here, where there's good grass for them. We're going to go down to the bottom of the valley, near the river.'

'That's a long way down, Halfdan, in the fog,' Lief reminded him. 'Getting back to where we were will be hard. We could lose both fort and horses.'

Halfdan shook his head. 'We'll leave a trail. We're going to gather a herd of cows and drive them up the slope. The fort has a funnel entrance between walls. We only have to get the cows into there.'

'And then?'

'And then we give them a scare. If you've ever seen cattle stampeding, you'll be able to imagine what they'll do to thirty men and eight tents in a confined space.'

The few men among them with a history in rural regions winced at the thought.

'How do you know so much about them?' Ketil asked.

'In Gotland I grew up in a village in the middle of nowhere,' Halfdan smiled. 'I spent my earliest years among farmers and hunters and fishermen. I helped Thorfin's lads move cattle from pasture to pasture for years. We can do this. Come on.'

The horses were secured, once more Ulfr at the forefront, and at Halfdan's command half the men hurried over to a band of trees they had passed just before they spotted the fort. A quarter of an hour's work, and they came back each with an arm full of sticks. Lief and Ulfr began tearing five scarves into narrow strips and tying them to the top, and in a short while the party had a collection of markers visible at a good thirty paces even in the fog. Satisfied that they had what they needed, Halfdan planted the first stick-and-rag, and had Ulfr begin leading the group down the slope toward the river. Every time they reached the point where the marker they'd last left was becoming faint, another was planted, and so on, as they swiftly descended the valley side, the terrain beginning to level out as they moved, the landscape easing off from that wild and rugged terrain to flat and lush grass.

Once the first of the cows became visible in the fog, a great brown shape moving through the mist, ambling slowly across the grass, munching in a pasture on the other side of a rough stone wall with a crude timber gate, Halfdan gathered the others.

'I need everyone calm. The first thing to know about cattle is that they can pick up on moods. If you're angry or nervous, they'll start to get angry or nervous around you. Try to be relaxed and calm. No sudden movements, no shouting. For once, I'm quite glad Bjorn isn't with us. All right, let's check the number of cows we have. Cross to the far wall, counting.'

The seventeen of them opened the gate in the wall and then spread out, moving quietly and slowly, with deliberate calm, among the cattle, identifying where the field walls that enclosed the herd were, and tried to estimate numbers. By the time they were gathered at the far wall of the large field, Halfdan had counted six cows on his journey. He looked to the others. 'Estimates?'

'I saw five.'

'Nine.'

'Six.'

'Eleven.'

Halfdan nodded as the numbers returned. Eleven was largest figure given, and surely that man could not have covered the entire field. 'I reckon there are more than eleven. Less than twenty, though. Should be plenty. Right. Here's how this works. The cows will instinctively move away from you when you move toward them. You're not their farmer. They don't know you. You're a potential threat. So, we all move forward from this wall, moving up both flanks of the herd and following on from behind, just urging them on. They will go through the gate naturally. I want two of you to go ahead now, around the edge and out of the field, waiting either side of the gateway. Then, you can just keep the herd moving in the right direction as they leave here, following the line of sticks up the hill. If everyone is sensible, we should be able to get them all back up to where we were within the half hour. Try not to let them stop, as it will be harder to get them moving again.'

He waited as two of the men skirted the herd and moved through the gate into position, then, when he was content they'd had enough time, began to walk toward the nearest cow from the riverward side. Predictably, as soon as he came close, the animal began to move away at a steady, swaying walk. The other Wolves were doing the same, though many looked less than happy with what they were about. He could hear muffled cursing across the field, and from the hushed conversation there, muted by the fog, it sounded as though a few cows were going the wrong way and his men were struggling to correct the matter. Still, in but a short time, he reached the gate, the Wolves closing in as the last few bovines in the herd passed between the walls and out into open moorland.

'All right. Now all you have to do is keep behind them and move up alongside to make sure they don't stray. Remember to keep calm as you do it.'

The others began to move, continuing to herd the animals up the slope. Halfdan moved faster, scurrying along the line toward the head of the herd, counting as he went. By the time he reached Ulfr at the front, he had ascertained they had eleven cows. Not as many as he'd expected, but that was probably down to the mishap getting them moving in the first place. Eleven should be enough.

As they moved, keeping as close as possible to the path they had marked with sticks and rags, Halfdan had to admit that the work was harder than he remembered – or than he'd expected. The cows seemed to continually try and stray to either side, and the Wolves kept having to jog this way and that over difficult terrain to direct them back into the slowly ascending herd. But then, it had been a long time since he'd done this as a child, before even the coming of Yngvar and the death of his father. And even then, that had been in the flat fields of Gotland. This was a vastly different affair, for the slope was steep, and the cows naturally tried to find the easier path all the time, turning from the climb.

Still, in half an hour or so, he could make out the shape of their tethered horses, and knew with some relief that they had reached their former position with the cows still moving well.

'Thank the gods for that,' Ulfr murmured.

'You talk to the horses like they're women,' Ketil grunted. 'Want to swive them, eh?'

Ulfr shrugged. 'They *are* like women, in the way *ships* are like women. You have to look after them, make them think they're special, because if you don't, you'll soon realise how much you rely on them for everything in your life!'

Ignoring the exchange, Halfdan thanked the Allfather, and Loki for his gift of cunning, and then gestured to the two nearest men. Keeping his voice low, knowing they were not that far from the fort, he spoke to them.

'We're nearly there now, but we can't stop. Getting them moving again would be trouble. So, we're going to turn the herd. I reckon I've been at the front long enough to have gained their trust. I'm going to lead the first animal toward the fort, and the rest should follow, but pass the word back to keep control of their movement and make sure they keep following.'

The instruction was relayed, and moments later, as they came close enough to the horses to hear them snorting and stamping, he veered off to the west, leading the cows along the slope instead of up it. To his relief, the cows followed willingly, probably as much for the ease of moving on the level instead of climbing as for their growing trust in his presence. Whatever their reasoning, the herd began to turn all the way along the line, the Wolves guiding, urging, directing.

He could see the fort now, see the open stone arms of that funnelled corridor that led to the gate. The stonework had crumbled and fallen at the outer edge, and the walls were low there, so as they approached, he and Ulfr prepared to climb, making sure the cattle kept to the centre and did not stray up onto the walls themselves.

His heart was pounding now. They were just a hundred paces or so from the fort, as close as they'd come so far. All it would take was one man to look up over the ramparts in the right direction, and they might well spot the herd coming their way.

He expected the alarm to go up at any moment, and the strange, tense silence as they led the cows between the first stones of the passageway began to bite at his nerves. He found himself begging the Allfather to keep the fort's occupants down and oblivious.

Odin was with him.

In another ten heartbeats, he was standing on the side wall above the cows. The lead animals were in the funnel, and the walls to either side here were too high to allow deviation. Content the front was secure, he now turned and hurried back, the others doing the same as soon as the cows beside them were securely in the funnel.

By the time he reached the outer edge, the last few cows were being driven in.

It was then that a call went up in a concerned, and rather baffled tone, somewhere in the fort. Cows had been spotted in the entry passage, though no mention was made of enemy warriors. The fort's occupants were merely confused at the sudden appearance of a lumbering, grunting herd of cows.

Halfdan grinned. When they realised the true danger, it would be too late.

He gestured to the nearest men as he pulled out his sword and sax. The others did the same, and as Halfdan gave them a silent count of three with fingers up, held the weapons apart, some with bearded axes, some smaller throwing axes, some swords, some knives, but all with a weapon in each hand. The shouts in the fort were now becoming clamorous and had turned to an alarmed tone.

With a grin, Halfdan began to smack his sword and sax together with a metallic clang, close to the rear of the last cow. A dozen or so men doing the same, created a din of metallic crashes behind the herd and, to Halfdan's relief, the effect was panic. The herd, until now content and obedient, suddenly leapt and jolted at the cacophony behind them, and started to flee. Their forward momentum carried them – and their fear – into the animals in front, who also started to run, and in moments, the whole herd was racing forward, bellowing in panic.

Halfdan followed, running up onto the entrance corridor's side wall, toward the ramparts. As the long entrance met the banks of the place, there was a climb to make, and, reaching it, he staggered onto the slope. He had no intention of following the cows along the ground level, and getting trapped inside like the fort's occupants. A figure appeared over the bank in front of him and for a moment, Halfdan thought he was in for a fight, but the man's hands were empty, his expression one of desperation, and he took long moments to realise that Halfdan was even there. Fleeing the chaos below, the man slipped on the slope, trying to avoid running directly into Halfdan, and before he could draw his weapon, the jarl had sliced down into the man's arm with his sword and driven his sax into the belly. The man gave a single cry and fell away, rolling down the bank and into the ditch.

Then Halfdan was up onto the bank and taking in the view. The mist was still thick, but he could see enough, just to the rampart at the far end of the fort. His plan had worked as well as he could possibly have hoped. The panicked, stampeding cattle had charged into the open fort and ploughed through tents, knocking aside and trampling anyone who got in the way. The men in the fort had reacted with panic, shouting and drawing weapons, running this way and that, and all the commotion simply made the cattle's instincts to run all the worse, prolonging the disaster. He watched as one of the beasts ran straight into one of the few intact tents. A shouting figure emerged at the tent door, but failed to extricate himself before the whole structure became a tangled net of canvas, the man rolled up and trapped in it as the cow barged it aside. As the tent's remnants flapped to a standstill in the grass, the man, still alive and whole, despite the chaos, managed finally to pull himself free of the tent's folds, but as he staggered back, puffing and panting and with wild eyes, he was ploughed to the ground by another of the animals, and churned beneath their heavy hooves.

The same story was playing out across the fort. Gunnar's men had been caught by surprise, and the stampede was devastating. Here and there, Halfdan spotted a man managing to escape the chaos, some of them limping or nursing broken arms as they managed to get away from the charging, bellowing bovine destruction, scrambling up the banks of their ramparts and fleeing over the top, down into the ditch, where they would then have to climb out and run across the troublesome countryside.

Halfdan let them go. Once again, this was not about complete destruction, but about fear. He had agreed to kill Gunnar for the archbishop, in return for a boon to his own quest, and to remove Gunnar, they would of necessity have to kill the berserkr Arkil and the powerful völva Hrafn, but outside the remit of his mission, Halfdan had nothing against these people. He would rather they lived, and were out of his way, than died. As such, any man who fled the fort here would not only be unlikely to face the attackers again, but the fear he would carry in his heart he would pass on to any he met, making them less likely to stand against the Wolves of Odin.

As Ketil joined him and suggested they chase down the survivors, he voiced this to the Icelander, who nodded sagely, though his one good eye carried a hint of disappointment that reminded Halfdan of Bjorn.

By the time the stampede had run out of impetus, and the cattle had slowed and then stopped, simply milling around, lowing, in the great enclosure, the seventeen men who'd ravaged the entire garrison without once even bloodying a blade were all standing on the ramparts, watching the carnage.

The great ancient fort was now filled with shreds of torn tents, scattered equipment and supplies and bodies, interspersed with quietly lowing cattle. Indeed, the only untouched part of the whole fort was the large fire at the centre, from which the cattle, even in panic, had stayed safely away. Three quick-thinking defenders had hurried to the fire and were huddled dangerously close to it, bathed in its searing heat, but safe from the cattle.

'What now?' Thurstan asked.

Halfdan rolled his shoulders. 'Now, we go down there and deal with the last three. Just disarm them and let them go. If any of them decides to struggle, hamstring them and leave them.'

'And then?' Ketil put in.

'And then we head down to the river, locate a crossing, and see if we can find Bjorn and the others.'

Chapter 11

The past. Magnus's Valley, west of Skara, Geatland.

Bjorn was a free man. Of course, he recognised the fact that any moment now he could instead be a free *corpse*, but even being a corpse was better than being a thrall. The three grandsons of Orm Barelegs stood at the far side of the patch of grass, within the roped area marked out for Holmgång. Each of them was armed with an axe, tools for chopping logs or for chopping enemies, because in a village few men could afford a weapon of war, and some tools had to double up. No one had armour, for such a thing was prohibitively expensive, and so all four combatants stood facing one another with an axe, dressed in simple tunics and trousers.

The thing they did all have was shields. Shields were cheap to make, mostly of wood, and so were painted up with colourful and meaningful designs. Bjorn's was white with a red serpent. He'd not looked at the other two piled up yet. He was to be allowed the traditional three shields, though he doubted he would need the others. Either he would win with his first shield, or he would be dead before he could replace it.

The three villains were hefting their axes ready. Only the one who had accepted the challenge looked remotely confident, and the shorter of the trio looked downright frightened. Bjorn forced himself to commit the trio to memory. He needed to take the confident one first and leave the coward until last, but he also knew that the moment the killing fog fell across his brain, conscious decisions like that would be almost impossible, so he needed to have that sequence in the forefront of his mind going in.

Of course, he had one advantage, which could be enough to counterbalance the three-to-one odds. He was horribly outnumbered, but he had survived many brutal fights now, was frightened of nothing, and had the instincts of a warrior, while the other three were still just village bullies.

He had to make every blow count.

'First blood,' the old greybeard had pronounced, as he set out the rules of the fight. Holmgång could be performed many ways, from a mock fight with blunt weapons to decide who had the right of something, all the way to a duel to the death. The most common was to the blood – the first blow that wounded signalled the winner. Of course, Bjorn had to land three, while they had only to make one between them. But no child of Orm's line was walking away from this fight. That had been Bjorn's purpose in coming here, that and buying his freedom. These three boys were going to Hel's dark hall this day, and that meant that the first blow he landed on each had to be a killing blow.

'Fight,' came the shout from the greybeard, and the gathered crowd of villagers fell silent.

Bjorn rolled his shoulders, checked his grip on his shield and axe, and let himself smile.

The three lads opposite him made no move for six heart-beats, until the older among them, the mouthy prick who'd accepted his challenge, looked back and forth between his brothers and then stepped forward. Once he did, so did the others, though with a more reluctant gait. Some small part of Bjorn, a tiny echo of the boy whose father had gone off to war, felt a touch of shame and regret that he would kill a man's grandsons today, but that echo faded swiftly and was buried beneath the warrior he had become in that pit in Skara.

They deserved it. He made himself remember every beating, every wounding, every shaming, every name, every insult. He replayed it all in his mind's eye as the three approached. He bit his lip, hard, until the blood came, and he tasted its iron tang. He felt the blood on his tongue. Remembered the last day. The thrown rocks.

Saw the three coming at him.

Surrendered himself to the urge.

When he ran, he did so with purpose, fast and hard. There was no fear, nor any plan. Just the need to kill. The other two lads had hung back a little, letting their elder take the lead, and that suited Bjorn just fine. The young man roared, his shield coming up to protect his chest and abdomen. His axe was raised high, ready to drop, as though chopping wood. Inexpert. He had protected his more vital parts with the shield, but in doing so had left Bjorn just the opening he needed.

Bjorn's axe came out to his right-hand side at hip height, pulled back behind him. His own shield went up reflexively, ready to take the blow of the falling axe, though if the two connected, Bjorn would have failed anyway.

He swung his own weapon, keeping it low, a heavy swipe in from the right. His opponent was no trained warrior, and only realised his mistake and the danger when it was too late. As the pair met, he tried to drop his own shield to catch Bjorn's blow, but failed. Bjorn's axe bit into his leg just above the knee, and the swing was hard, carrying not only all the might of Bjorn's now powerful physique, but also of years of hate and anguish. The axe broke the lad's thigh bone clear in two in its passing, and almost severed the leg entirely. What was left holding it together, muscle and sinew, tore as he screamed and fell, blood fountaining from the wound. The leg came off as he hit the grass, axe and shield falling away from his hands, forgotten.

Bjorn was already moving on. The second of the brothers was only a heartbeat behind the first, and the shock of what had happened to his sibling had yet to hit him.

In the pit of Skara, everything was a weapon, from a blade, to a fist, to the teeth if necessary. Bjorn did not have time between the two combatants to bring his axe back around for another hit, but his shield was already up at neck height, ready to take a falling blow. The second brother pulled his axe back ready to swing wide, thinking he had the time, for Bjorn's axe was out of play.

Bjorn hit the young man in the throat with the rim of his shield. Heavy timber edged with rawhide was a weapon in itself, and the blow was good. He both heard and felt the crunch as the shield flattened and crushed the man's throat apple and windpipe.

Spinning, he was beyond his second victim already. The killing rage was on him, and he almost stumbled across the rope marking the contest ground, which would have seen the Holmgång ended with him the loser. He tottered and spun, just staying within the bounds.

The third brother was crying. He had stopped moving, clutching his shield before him and trying to shrink behind it, axe gripped tight, but not ready for a swing. His trousers were soaked through with piss. That dying echo of an innocent boy in Bjorn surfaced again for a moment, the last visit it would ever make, but as Bjorn broke into a jog with a roared oath, the piss-stained weakling in front of him morphed into a sneering, laughing bully, calling him Snowflake as he beat him around the head with a broom handle.

Bjorn hit him, still roaring. He barged into the young fellow, shield to shield. His weight and momentum drove the lad to the ground, his breath knocked from him beneath the shield across his chest. His axe flailed out to the side, still in his grip, but useless. Bjorn snarled, invoking Odin, hooking his own shield behind that of the young man beneath him and using it to push the boards aside, exposing the opponent below him.

Bjorn's head went down. There was no room for an axe blow and the shields were aside, but everything was a weapon when you used it right. His teeth sank into the boy's neck and he clamped his jaws shut and pulled away, standing and spitting out bloody, gristly meat.

First blood.

The boy was screaming as blood jetted in a veritable fountain from his neck. His hand came up to try and staunch the flow, but the sticky crimson simply gushed out between his fingers, unstoppable. Even as Bjorn straightened and lowered his shield, allowing the rage to subside, the boy was going grey, his lifeblood leaving him.

Bjorn turned and looked about him. As the youngest bled out before him, he could see the middle boy already still, eyes glassy and chest unmoving, asphyxiated by the shield blow. The one with the lopped-off leg was still screaming and rolling around. He would probably die. Few men lived through such a wound, and even if he did, he would be a cripple for the rest of his life, and would know he lost the Holmgång. That was enough for Bjorn.

Orm Barelegs was bellowing curses, face almost puce, straining to get to Bjorn to avenge his three grandsons, but the old man was being held back by his friends, probably not for the propriety of the ancient rite, but more because they did not want him joining his lads in death against this monster.

Bjorn spat out more blood, some his, more belonging to his last victim. He watched the younger one die, then dropped the shield to the ground.

'I will not return,' was all he said, as he turned and left the ring, gathering up his gear, his back to the people of Magnus's village, and walking away forever.

He was avenged; and he was free.

Late February 1044. Swaledale.

The fog was thick, a sheet of white that hid the landscape in every direction, though that did nothing to obscure Bjorn's world right now, for at this moment, Bjorn's world was twenty paces across, marked out with skins and ropes. Beyond that inconsequential barrier stood dozens of people. The remaining warriors of Gunnar were silent, pensive, and around them the women, the children, the greybeards, for there was a settlement in this side valley controlled by Arkil for the jarl of Swaledale, and they had all come to see this.

Such a meeting had only happened extremely rarely, even in the ancient days of heroes, and was unheard of in the modern world with its churches and priests.

A meeting of berserkir.

Arkil's reputation was clear, for the crowd stood a good fifteen paces back from the ropes, almost to the point of being lost in the fog, a distance that would allow them to run, should Arkil turn his berserkr upon them when he'd killed his foe.

The giant stood at the far side of the marked-out space. On the ground beside him lay three shields, just as they did beside Bjorn. He doubted Arkil had any more intention of picking one up than he did, but they were there, because those were the rules.

Both combatants were stripped to the waist despite the cold, and both held an axe, waiting for the signal to begin. Gunnhild would give that signal. Even Arkil, despite being an enemy, would grant that right to a völva.

'Prepare yourselves,' she said.

Bjorn nodded. He knew what that meant. Reaching down to his belt, he opened the pouch of the precious compound, licked his thumb and dipped it in. It came out brown and powdery, and he bared his teeth, lips pulled back, and lifted his hand, rubbing his powdered thumb all across his gums and teeth, and then, when they were nicely coated, closed his mouth once more and sucked the bitter magic, letting it suffuse his whole being.

It did not escape his attention that Arkil, twenty paces away, had done almost exactly the same thing. However, while Bjorn continued his personal ritual, dipping the wet thumb once more and drawing Odin's valknut on his forehead with it, the behemoth opposite him picked up one of the shields, which came as a surprise. The reason became clear, then, and Bjorn nodded his understanding. Every man had his own little rituals before a fight, and that he had known since the days of the pit, but Arkil subscribed to an ancient practice.

He was a shield-biter.

Bjorn could feel the compound at work now, and could imagine the same happening to Arkil, as he lifted his shield and sank his teeth into the rawhide edge, gnawing at it furiously. The bitter taste had become sweet in Bjorn's mouth, as always, and he could feel the raw fiery edge of the bloodlust coursing through his veins from his mouth all around his body, his whole being burned, yet with some glorious fire that felt incredible, that felt more alive than it should be possible to feel. The moment was almost upon him. His body was becoming at the same time both over-sensitive and weirdly numb, his blood pounding with that mighty fire that could drive him on, perhaps forever, a dragon's breath in his soul, lifting him…

Then it hit his mind.

He was vaguely aware that Gunnhild had given the signal. It didn't really matter, since he was already moving. Nothing could stop him now, even if he wanted it to. Gunnhild knew the signs, knew the timing. She had let him feel the berserkr take hold before letting him go.

He could see Arkil coming for him. The man truly was a mobile mountain of muscle, covered in his runes of power and his tattooed skull. With the sight of the berserkr, Bjorn could see some of the runes on the man's body glowing as they worked, imbuing their inhabitant with their strength, their will, their stamina. The skull seemed to change, to be that of a bear, then a man, then a bear again.

The two men met in the middle of the roped enclosure.

The fight now would be decided not by careful tactics or skill, but by brutality, endurance, luck, and the whim of gods and Norns.

His axe swung. So did Arkil's. They met with a noise like Brokkr's hammer on anvil, a clang that would ring through the bowels of the earth and wake even sleeping giants. Then they were untangled and swinging again, and Bjorn marvelled in his fogged mind as to how that had happened when he hadn't seemed to do it by design. He felt his axe bite into flesh and muscle, though he couldn't say where, and yet at the same time felt Arkil's axe hit home. His shoulder seemed to burn harder, brighter than it had. Not pain, for pain was something *other* people felt. It was just a sensation that something had changed in his left shoulder. The buried core of waking Bjorn acknowledged that when the berserkr faded, he would have to face what might be a bad wound.

In the meantime, it did not seem to stop him using the arm. With his left, he swiped away another lunge from Arkil, and his right was moving. Somehow the axe was not in his hand any more, but that did not matter, for instinct had balled that hand into a fist, which struck Arkil on the jaw. The blow was hard enough that the mountainous berserkr was knocked back, and the burning joyous fire that burst anew in two of Bjorn's fingers probably meant he'd broken them in the punch. Probably something to do with that skull on the outside of Arkil's face.

Something grasped Bjorn's wounded left shoulder, and suddenly Arkil was right in front of him again, that skull contorting, blood coated, teeth white in red as the thing grinned madly, pinprick pupils in crazed, dancing eyes. The headbutt that came next nearly finished Bjorn. Glorious, wonderful fire filled his head and he was falling backward. It seemed he fell forever, and he wondered if somehow he had fallen off the edge of the world. Perhaps he was even now plummeting past the other worlds, from the branches of Yggdrasil, falling forever.

Then he hit something hard, but Arkil was with him. The world shifted through ninety degrees and suddenly they were both standing again, pummelling.

He felt his fist lash out, felt hard go soft as a rib broke beneath his punch, but felt the fire of joyous war burning afresh in his own gut. He was doubled over now, looking down. Something hit the back of his head and he staggered, then was up. Arkil was a bear now, raging and roaring as it threw its massive arms around him. Bjorn's eyes danced. Beyond the bear, a crowd of *dvergar* watched, silent, waiting, the mist curling around them.

He didn't like dvergar. Except Lief. No. Lief wasn't a dvergr. Not quite, anyway.

Maybe he'd kill some dvergar in a moment.

He was being held in an embrace. Was it love? No, not from a bear. It was crushing him. He could feel the ribs springing, not quite breaking, feel the air being forced from him. Bjorn turned, looking across the space. Freyja was there, in Gunnhild's dress, which was fascinating. When he looked back at the bear that was Arkil, the monster now had his head turned, also toward the goddess. There was only one thing Bjorn could do, constricted as he was in the tight bear hug, not that it mattered, because he had no control over his actions anyway. He returned the headbutt.

His was better.

Arkil's butt had almost put Bjorn out of the fight, such was the power of that skull upon his face, but now that skull was turned away, looking at Freyja, and Bjorn's brow met with the *side* of Arkil's head. The valknut painted on it slammed into the man's temple and things broke. Bjorn didn't *think* the breaking things were his, though he could not be entirely sure. Then the bear was gone from him, retreating into the mist. The *grip* was gone. Bjorn could move. He roared, and took a step forward, and Arkil was there again, in the mist, eyes wild and bulging, teeth bared, his head oddly shaped now, blood and gore coating the left side. The arms flailed at Bjorn, and he realised with odd interest that he'd taken hold of one of those arms with both of his. He gripped it and broke it, though it took great effort, so thick and muscly was the limb.

The other arm hit Bjorn again, and he was spinning. For a moment all he could see was sky, framed with drifting white, and then the worlds passed him once again, as he fell past the branches of Yggdrasil once more. He wasn't sure how he could fall more than once past the world tree and yet keep ending up in the same place, but here he was now, lying in the damp grass. His hand felt oddly cold, which was strange when the rest of him burned with fabulous fire. He looked across, and could see the fallen axe blade beneath his hand. It was his own axe, he realised.

Then, suddenly he was upright once more, the world back as it should be. Arkil was hitting him with his one unbroken arm, and Bjorn could feel the blows landing, pain registering only as hot fire in his flesh that warmed and pushed him on, ever on, into the fight.

He swung the axe.

Even in the berserkr, he registered his own surprise as the axe was pulled from his grip.

He swung two fists, his damaged shoulder burning, though neither blow landed, for Arkil had stepped back. Through the pulsing of his furious blood, Bjorn could see the axe wedged in the huge man's neck. Arkil was trying to look down in confusion at the mortal wound, but his neck would not bend to allow the move, because of the axe lodged in it.

Bjorn found that oddly hilarious, and was laughing now, howling with mirth as he reached out, stepped forward and grabbed his opponent. It was not pretty, and not easy work, but with his left hand on the man's head, he used his right to lever the axe deeper and deeper into Arkil's neck until he felt the resistance give and heard the loud cracks and meaty tearing noises of spine and tendon. Then, suddenly, the head was free. The berserkr's body dropped in a heap, and Bjorn was holding a head in one hand and an axe in the other.

His body burned all over, with the berserkr fire of war, and with the wounds he had taken, but all that came with a massive elation, the joy that only battle could bring. He kissed the severed head on the bald top, almost losing it and dropping it, but he managed to keep hold somehow, which was good, for he did not want to lose his new prize. He had the axe still in his other hand.

Dvergar.

He could see the dvergar again, in the edge of the mist. They looked confused. Stunned.

He didn't like dvergar.

He was running, then, howling like a wolf, roaring like a bear, fire in every vein, another man's head in one hand, axe in the other, chasing the little creatures, looking for something to kill. They fled. Like birds in the sky when the hawk comes, they ran away into the wall of white fog. He chased, he ran, he almost caught one, managed to just touch it with the tip of his axe head with a swing that just about missed.

Suddenly it was not dvergar in front of him. It was the goddess. Freyja.

He almost hit her, but somehow his swing went wild.

Even in the depths of the battle lust, he knew not to kill a goddess, and so he was gone then, past her, hunting more dvergar. He was vaguely aware as he ran, of Freyja following and bellowing at him.

He caught one finally. His axe swung wide and buried itself in the side of one of the creatures. The thing fell, wailing, and the noise was so irritating that Bjorn took his axe and kept hitting the prone creature in the back, again and again, until it fell silent.

Then, something hit Bjorn.

He felt the white fire now in the back of his brain. Something had struck the back of his head, so hard it cut through the fog for a moment. He fell. He rolled over.

Freyja was standing over him, holding a staff.

Bjorn awoke, slowly.

He hurt. Almost all over. Even lying completely still hurt.

He blinked. Even that hurt a little.

His brain swam. How long had he been asleep? What had happened last night? Slowly, the memories of the fight came flooding back, and with them the slightest concern that, with all this pain, perhaps he was dying? The light was fading, so unless he'd slept more than a day, he couldn't have been out very long. Indeed, at the periphery of his vision, he could still see the fog. An hour, then, at most.

And Gunnhild.

She was looking down at him with the sort of expression she'd used when looking at the boot she'd just trodden in dung with.

'Hello,' he tried. His voice sounded hoarse and a little strange. One of her eyebrows lifted quizzically. That was her only reply.

He tried to move.

He yelped.

His right arm was fine, apart from a few scratches and bruises, though one of his legs hurt like a bastard when he moved it. His chest felt tight and painful, and his gut felt as though it had been ground beneath the wheels of a cart. It was his left shoulder, though, that was the problem. He didn't seem to be able to move it.

'Lie still,' Gunnhild snapped.

'What? Why?'

'Because I've had to cover your shoulder in salves and stitch it, and then bind it all, with a strut to help set your broken arm.'

Bjorn frowned, then looked down at his left side.

His forearm had been bent at the elbow and pulled up so that it lay alongside his bicep, his hand on his shoulder. The whole lot was tightly wrapped and smelled of one of Gunnhild's fouler remedies.

'I need to get up,' he grumbled. He was lying in wet grass. And blood, of course. Quite a lot of blood.

'Here.' She reached down and grabbed his other hand, helping him slowly to his feet. He yelped again in the process, for he'd bruised and sprung ribs, and they were agony when he bent. Still, he was on his feet, which was good.

He tried things. He could stand on both legs, though the right hurt with any pressure, and wobbled occasionally. It would be a while before the strength was back. Other than his arm, though, the rest of his injuries would go away eventually.

Unlike Arkil's...

He looked around urgently, causing him to hiss in pain at his injured ribs once more.

'Where is it?'

Gunnhild gave him a look he found hard to describe. Not a good one, though. 'The head? I have it. Stored.'

'Stored?' Why? That was confusing.

'If we are to convince anyone later that Arkil is no more, there is no better proof than his head. And it could hardly be mistaken for anyone else's.'

Bjorn grinned. The reality was suddenly hitting home. He'd *won*. This was the fight of a lifetime, and he'd won it. He had faced a berserkr of greater strength even than himself and he had won. And he had the proof.

'This will be told in mead halls for generations,' he grinned.

'Mostly by you,' Gunnhild said drily. 'And in *your* version, he will be twenty feet tall and have four arms.'

Bjorn could only grin. He would hardly need to embellish *this* tale at *all*. Indeed, embellishing it might even detract from it. This tale would be his greatest, through the purity and simplicity of it being entirely true. He frowned. Although he couldn't remember parts of the fight. And parts of it were blurry. All right, he would have to embellish it a *little*, just so it made sense.

'When you *do* tell it,' Gunnhild said quietly, 'try to leave out the bit where you chase the crowd around the fields and then butcher a farmer.'

She was pointing at the ground nearby. He followed her gesture to see the heap of meat that was all that remained of the poor bastard he'd caught when he thought he was chasing dvergar. It was not a pretty sight, by any means, and once upon a time, Bjorn would have felt just a tiny twinge of sympathy or guilt.

No more.

He shrugged. The man had been in the way. In the wrong place at the wrong time. He was not the first, and he certainly wouldn't be the last.

He turned back to Gunnhild. She was holding out her hand. He frowned.

She jerked her fingers, motioning him to give her something, and it took only a moment to realise what that was. He looked down, which made his neck ache a little. The small pouch was still firmly attached to his belt. He sighed and reached down, undoing the buckle and slowly unthreading the pouch along the belt. As he worked, Gunnhild huffed, looking about, taking in what could be seen in the fog. Not a lot.

Bjorn handed over the pouch, held out on his palm. She took it and he quickly snatched his hand away.

People often took Bjorn for stupid. Maybe he was, a little bit, but not brainless. Not like Agnar Bonehead who had once tried to eat a spear in the belief that would make him impervious to them. And people thought *he* was slow, lumbering. That was because of his size and shape. But his hands could be fast, and so could his wits when he needed them.

That was why, as Gunnhild filed away her precious powder, Bjorn tightened the hand the pouch had been balanced on back into a fist and turned away. He didn't want to lose any of the vital compound he'd managed to palm from the pouch in the process. For speed, he tipped it into his secondary coin pouch at his belt, where he could separate them out later.

He trusted Gunnhild, implicitly. She controlled his access to that which gave him the greatest edge a warrior could have, and he knew why. He didn't care about the pile of meat nearby that he'd caused, but there were times when he couldn't afford to do such a thing. But Gunnhild might not always be there when he needed that edge, and having enough of the compound to become a god-like killer saved for emergencies seemed a good idea.

He turned back to her. 'What now?'

She straightened. 'The people here are cowed. Some ran west, seeking Gunnar, but most went home, to their houses. The impossible happened, here, and they dare not be near you. There is nothing to fear in leaving these people behind us. But what is ahead, I cannot see. Gunnar's völva fogs my mind just as she fogs this valley. I fear we must find Halfdan before he walks into true peril.'

Bjorn nodded.

One thing he would never do was let his fellow Wolves down.

Chapter 12

'What I would give to have my horse,' Ulfr grumbled in the fog, raising murmurs of agreement from all. What had happened to the horses remained a mystery, and ate at the shipwright who had been the keeper of the horses since their moving into the dale. In the aftermath of the fight at the fort, they had made sure all resistance was overcome, and Halfdan had let the men ransack the tents to look for valuables. When it had all been over and done with, he'd gathered the Wolves and returned to where they had left the horses to find the hillside bare. The only thing Halfdan could think of was that one or more of the survivors who'd fled the defences had stumbled across them in his flight and set them free. Still, even if they'd done that, one would expect to find at least one or two horses meandering around the hillside.

They'd wasted half an hour scouring the area and found nothing, becoming increasingly irritable at the fact. It was not so much the transport aspect, for each of them was far more accustomed to walking than riding anyway. It was more that they had lost important goods. Chain shirts had gone, along with spare weapons, spare clothes and cloaks, and a number of personal artefacts. Their elation over their fort victory was rather subdued by the loss, and it was an unhappy party that moved on.

Now, the mood dropped once more.

'In retrospect,' Halfdan said with a sigh, 'we should probably have retraced our steps, gone back to where we separated, and followed the others from there.'

There was a chorus of nods at this. The world was still a blanket of white, but now the light was failing, it was a gloomy evening, and they had no idea where they were. Oh, there were clues. They had found the river, for a start. That much was not difficult. You simply kept walking down the slope until your feet got wet. But from there things had become a little more complicated. They'd walked downstream for half an hour, looking for a way across, by which time Halfdan had fully expected to come across the bridge by the main dyke. They'd found nothing. Not even a sign of the dyke leading from the river, although in this fog and half-light, they could have walked within ten paces of it and seen nothing. With a growing hint of worry, they'd turned around and retraced, past where they'd met the river, they thought, and half an hour in the other direction, looking for a crossing. Still nothing.

Now, they had no idea where they were in relation to the fort, the bridge *or* the dykes. All they knew was that they were somewhere in Swaledale and south of the river.

'We're going to have to think about making camp sometime,' Thurstan put in. 'At least in the morning the fog might have gone and we'll be able to see.'

Halfdan admitted to the logic of it, but Bjorn, the women and the other two warriors were Wolves of Odin, part of his hirð, and while they had duties to their jarl, their jarl also had a duty to them. How could he make camp without finding the others first? Or at least without finding out what had happened to them, if Bjorn had finally met his match.

'No. Not without the others. We cross the river. That map the man drew us showed Gunnar's land on the north side of the river, and that's where Arkil was, so we should presume there's some sort of road between the two. Certainly before the fog came, when I looked across the river up the valley, the northern side was more farmed and had houses.'

'One might wonder why we are on the south bank, then,' Lief mused idly. He caught the look Halfdan shot him and shrugged. 'I know. Following up the enemy, making sure we didn't leave them behind us. Just thinking out loud.'

'Try thinking out *quiet* sometimes.'

Halfdan peered into the mist. He couldn't see the river, but he could see the looming shape of the trees that rose from its banks, and he could just hear the muted rush of water. He'd considered just wading across, but had thus far tried to avoid that. The Swale was maybe twenty or thirty paces across, depending on gravel banks, and it was fast and probably quite deep in the middle. In the height of summer it was probably easily crossable, but this was the arse-end of winter, and the river was still carrying the meltwater and run-off from the hills, so it was as deep and fast as it was likely to get on an ordinary day. Had they still had the horses, crossing would have been considerably easier.

He was stumped. But he had to lead, to make a decision and to look confident about it. He took a deep breath. It was a toss-up, really. Upstream further, away from where the others would be, or back downstream, covering the same bank yet again. The latter, he decided, would look as though he did not know what he was doing, and crossing here would be dangerous, so he would lead them on.

'Right. We move down to the bank, head upstream as long as we still have the light. If it gets truly dark we'll make camp, but as long as we still have light, we'll search for the others. There has to be a way across. If need be, we'll find the narrowest section and wade across, but that's a last resort. When we get across, if we still have light, we'll look for signs of settlement, or a road, hopefully, and follow that back toward the first dykes until we find either the others, or at least signs of them.'

It was decisive, at least. Taking the lead, Halfdan squelched down across the turf toward the trees, the sound of rushing water getting louder with every step. It really was getting harder to see, with the combination of the dying light and the white cloud. When he reached the trees and stopped short of the steep slope down to the water, he examined the flow briefly. It was clear how visibility had declined, for now he could no longer see the far bank, other than as a looming black shape of trees. The water was inky black and flowing at an impressive speed. Once more he put out of mind the idea of wading. Dangerous, but also horrible. They would end up sleeping the night soaked to the bone and frozen, which invited illness.

He turned west and started along the bank.

It was hard to believe this was the same day they had left Catraeth. Last night, they had slept in relative comfort. Today, they had been through Hindrelac, taken down a watch post and signal station, crossed two defensive frontiers and taken an enemy fort, the latter half of the day in thick fog.

He was still marvelling over the day they had had a quarter of an hour later when he almost walked into a great, heavy stone. Frowning, he stopped, taking a step back. The thing was almost chest high, and roughly cylindrical, though weathered and crumbled. Peering at it, he could see words marked out on it. Walking slowly around it, he discovered writing on two sides. The words looked familiar, though he couldn't tell what they said.

'Lief?'

The Rus hurried over and peered close at the stone, on the southern side. He huffed. 'It's quite worn, but the words are Latin. Something about Caesar Galerius something. There's a number, too. Twelve, I think.' He moved around to the other side and smiled. 'This is better. Nice and clear. "*Imperatori Caesari Galerio Valerio Maximiano Pio Felici Virosidio milia passum VIII.*"'

'Thanks,' Halfdan said drily. 'That's much clearer.'

Lief rolled his eyes. 'To the emperor blah blah blah, to some place called Virosidio, eight miles. It's a distance marker. It tells anyone here that Virosidio lies eight miles that way,' he explained, pointing south, over the hills. 'And whatever place has weathered away on the other side lies twelve miles the other way,' he added, turning and pointing north.

A smile spread across Halfdan's face. He walked slowly to the other side of the stone, looking down, tapping the ground with his feet. 'Here,' he said. 'Here the ground is hard. It's a road. Goes up the slope and toward the river. You know what that means? A crossing. There has to be a crossing here.'

With a tangible sense of optimism, the Wolves followed their jarl to the trees that lined the riverbank. The river was still twenty or more paces wide, black and fast, with no sign of a bridge. For a moment, he felt his confidence falter, then looked down carefully and felt it return. The bank here had been cut away in times past so that the road ran down directly into the water. Squinting, he thought he could just about make out a similar dip at the far side, though in these conditions, that might well be wishful thinking.

'It's a ford.'

'It looks bloody deep,' Ulfr said.

'In this light, it would look black and opaque even if it were only ankle deep.' Still, he had to admit the shipwright was correct. It didn't look any different to the other places they'd looked across, apart perhaps from the lack of a gravel area here or there.

Confidence.

Rolling his shoulders and preparing himself, he made his way down the slope to the water and, taking a deep breath and clenching his teeth, stepped into the flow.

Immediately he was in freezing water that reached halfway up his shins. The shock was quite impressive, and along with the biting cold, he was worried by the speed of the flow, for the pressure of the water against his left leg was strong. It felt like someone pushing against him, trying to bowl him over. If the water got too deep, he suspected there would be little chance of holding his position, and every chance of him being swept downstream. He did wonder for a moment whether it was a seasonal ford, only used in the warmer months when the river was low.

Too late to turn back now.

He took another step, and the water level rose, flowing around his knees, exerting immense pressure, its black arms wrapped around him, trying to carry him away.

Trust. Trust in the gods, and in his fate, which said surely he must live to face Gunnar.

He took another step.

The water rose to mid-thigh.

His confidence took another knock. Damn it, but he would find whoever set their horses free and cut them from chin to groin. One glance back at Ulfr suggested that the shipwright was of a similar mind.

His foot slipped on the smooth ford stones beneath him, and even as he tried to right himself, his other foot found a section of the ancient crossing where the stones had come loose and been carried downstream. He dropped to the waist, but managed by some miracle not to fall entirely, and pulled himself back up carefully. He was shivering madly, now.

Another step.

Still mid-thigh.

A crest of hope rose in him.

Another step.

Same depth.

He took four more, and realised with relief that he seemed to have reached the full depth of the ford at mid-thigh. Tentatively, he used his toe in the invisible black depths to locate the edges of the ford. It was quite wide, presumably to allow carts to pass through safely. He wondered how much deeper it was to either side of the underwater causeway, though he had no intention of finding out. Of course, during normal conditions, a man could look across the water to where the far bank dipped, and it would give him the line of the ford even if he couldn't see it beneath the surface.

Halfdan walked on. By the time he was a third of the way across, he could see the dip at the far bank, and that gave him greater confidence to move further. He walked across, carefully. Here and there, he found sections where the stones had gone, and had to search with frozen, numb feet for a better part. Still, it was not long before he was rising from the surface once more, the water level dropping to his knees, then shins, then ankles, and then finally he was stepping onto hard ground.

He turned back and looked at Ulfr, standing on the far bank, little more than a vague shape in the dark and the white.

'It's good. Follow my path, but carefully and slowly. Some of it's slippery, and some of it is missing stones.'

The others began to follow slowly, and Halfdan, content that they were safely on their way, climbed the ford up the north bank of the river between the trees.

The three men took him completely by surprise.

As he emerged from the bank, shivering and shaking, sodden from the waist down, a man leapt at him from his right, swinging a sword. Halfdan only saw him coming in time to get out of the way by throwing himself to the ground in the opposite direction. That left him at the feet of another man emerging from the fog, a third finishing the deadly trio. A sword swung down, and he rolled out of the way, one hand lashing out and grabbing an ankle, pulling as he went.

The attacker fell with a cry of surprise, thumping to the ground where Halfdan had just been.

He had no time to react properly. Another sword was coming down at him, and all he could do was to roll desperately out of the way again. He had no chance to stand, no chance to draw a weapon. Seeing a pair of legs in the billowing mist as he rolled this way and that, he took the opportunity to pause and lash out with a kick, rewarded with a cracking noise from the man's knee as he rolled away and his victim dropped.

The first man he'd felled was back up, now, though. The blows stopped coming for just a moment, and Halfdan was up in a trice, making the most of that moment. He turned, slowly. He could make out the shapes of the trees, but not of his opponents.

He drew sword and sax as he turned, eyes on the billowing white.

When the men came again, it was still a surprise, even though he was expecting it. They'd not made the same mistake of coming one at a time. This time all three men emerged from the fog at once, leaving him nowhere to run, with the exception of the slope back down to the water, which would be extremely dangerous to say the least.

The first blow he dodged, twisting desperately to one side, catching the second with his own sword and turning it just in time. The third hit him in the left shoulder. It was, thankfully, just a glancing blow as he turned, but he felt the edge cut through wool and flesh, drawing a white-hot line of blood.

He flailed, spun, dodged.

He managed to lash out once with his sword, and thought it connected with something momentarily, in the chaos of bodies and swirling fog, he wasn't sure what, and realised in that moment that attacking just left him open to further danger.

A sword hit him in the midriff, but the blow was robbed of the worst by his thick leather belt that caught the blade's edge. Still, he was winded, and knew there would be some bruising. Something hit him in the back, and he felt the pain, but once more, the fact that he was twisting and turning, ducking every blow he could, made it hard for them to land a real strike.

Still, he was losing. He couldn't fight back, he was so busy defending himself, and already they were managing to hurt him. Sooner or later one of them would hit him properly, and then it would be over.

There was nothing for it.

He stepped back onto the slope down to the water, still spinning, ducking and throwing his blade in the way of attacks as he went. He almost lost his footing immediately, slipping on the wet slope, and lurched this way and that. Another blow came, and he ducked. This time he went over properly, landing in a wet heap. As he rolled, he could see shapes halfway across the river, Ulfr in the lead, pushing against the current to get to their jarl. They would never get there in time.

Halfdan struggled round, throwing his sword up and knocking aside one blow, but having to jam his arm in the way of another, risking a broken bone as the sword slammed into his bicep painfully. He slipped again, failing to get properly to his feet, and was forced to throw himself down to the sodden ground to avoid the next flurry of attacks.

He was going to die.

He managed to move, but not enough.

The next blow did not come.

He turned. The three figures had disappeared into the white once more.

As he struggled to his feet, shuddering and fighting to maintain his balance, he heard a blood-curdling shriek not far away. He frowned.

'No,' someone bellowed. 'No, no, no, no, no!'

Then another howl of agony.

There was no third cry, but as Halfdan limped quietly up the slope to the open ground, he heard a strange gurgling, rattling noise that suggested a man meeting a very unpleasant end. Halfdan took a few steps into the fog, shivering. Then a few more.

He found the body of the first man, sword lying some distance from the empty hand. The man's head was a mess, no features visible above the top lip, the face caved in, brain showing amid the mess, suggesting an immense blow of some kind.

Another few steps and he found the second man, though this time that man was not alone. He was dead, even on his feet, for Gunnhild had rammed the wicked point from the top end of her staff into the man's throat. Usually, she used the wooden butt end for hitting people, something to do with the sacredness of the iron spike, he thought, but clearly, she had changed her mind on this occasion.

Gunnhild nodded a greeting as she angled her staff and the man slid from it, a hiss escaping from his ruined throat as he slumped, dead, to the ground. Behind her, Bjorn emerged from the fog like a mobile mountain. He had one arm strapped up and bandaged, folded to his shoulder, was covered in wounds and bruises, and limped as he walked, yet he held the third attacker by the face with his good arm, dangling, dead, a foot from the ground.

The others began to appear from the mist now, and he could hear Ulfr stomping up the slope to join them.

'I cannot leave you alone for an hour without you finding trouble for yourself,' Gunnhild admonished, though without any barb to her tone.

Halfdan felt relief and gratitude flood through him. They were all together once more, and somehow, without any real losses, despite now being deep in Gunnar's lands and fighting his men at every turn. The loss of the horses suddenly felt like a small thing.

He walked over to Bjorn. Never had he felt more like throwing his arms around the big man, though practicality forbade it, even if propriety didn't. He was sopping wet, Bjorn was injured, and held a dead man in his good hand. Instead, he grinned.

'I had feared I would not see you again.' He turned the smile to Gunnhild, to make it clear that he meant all of them, though it was at moments like this that it was hammered home how much Bjorn meant to him. The big lunatic had been the first person Halfdan had ever met who had seemed to understand him and accept him blindly. The first to join him. The first of the Wolves, back in that drinking hall in Uppsala.

'Takes more than a twelve-foot berserkr with his skull on the outside and the power of magic all over his flesh to put *me* down,' Bjorn grinned, as he casually snapped the neck of the dead man in his hand and dropped him to the earth with a squelchy crunch.

'His skull on the outside?' Halfdan frowned.

'Bjorn exaggerates as always,' Gunnhild sighed, turning to the big man. 'I said Arkil would be twice the size when you told the story.'

Bjorn just shrugged. 'He was a big bastard. Hard, too.'

'That,' Gunnhild said, turning back to her jarl, 'is at least true. I actually feared for Bjorn's survival which is not something I find myself saying often.'

As they stood facing one another for a moment, Bjorn reached around with his good hand behind his back. For a moment, Halfdan believed the big man was actually scratching his arse, but then the hand reappeared, and hanging from it was a bag. Bjorn grinned like the lunatic he was, and upended the bag. Out fell an enormous head, landing with a thump in the wet grass. Halfdan stared as Bjorn shoved the bag into Cassandra's hands and reached down, scooping up the head.

The disembodied thing bore as ugly a face as Halfdan had ever seen, made all the more unpleasant by the skull tattoo that covered it, and the runes all across his scalp amid swirling designs.

'Arkil?'

Bjorn's grin widened. 'The berserkr is no more. I am the better man. Not that I was ever in doubt, of course.'

'Of course,' Halfdan laughed, as the others began to arrive from the river. 'Good. We have lost a few men, and, I'm afraid, the horses with our gear, but we are all together, we've overcome the defences of Gunnar's land and beaten his champion. We are almost there. All that remains now is to actually find Gunnar and for me to add his head to the collection, then we can return to Jorvik and free ourselves of the archbishop's service. Then we are away east once more, back to our lands.'

'*Your* lands,' Ketil reminded him. '*My* lands are to the north.'

Halfdan just laughed that off.

'We are close, and nothing can stop us. If Gunnar's warriors cannot, and Arkil cannot, then nothing can.'

He tried to ignore the look on Gunnhild's face, which denied the truth of that.

As everyone joined together once more, and companions parted for the last few hours were reacquainted, plans were set. Despite the fog and the recent attack, which Halfdan had decided was probably three survivors of the fort, they deemed it a low enough risk to camp here. A quick foray into the nearest stands of trees produced sufficient dry wood from the hearts of such places, and so, on the wide grassland north of the river, they built a fire from undergrowth and timbers.

Further foraging by the whole group, while Ketil caught their dinner, brought sufficient chopped branches and ferns to create a dozen shelters sufficient to sleep under, in the absence of the tents which were, of course, on the missing horses.

For two hours, then, as twilight descended into true black, the Wolves of Odin gathered around the blazing pyre that held back the gloom, the fog and the cold, drying wet clothes, warming chilled flesh, cooking coney and a hapless owl that strayed into Ketil's arrow range, and telling tall tales loosely based upon their exploits at the fort and at Arkil's lands. For the first time since leaving the ships at Jorvik, it felt like earlier days, like the whole hirð together in the sight of the Allfather.

Reasoning that if the blazing fire did not draw further danger, then noise was not going to, they even sang old songs in the warmth and light of the blaze. The first to succumb to sleep were Lief and Anna, who retired together to their shelter, drawing raucous and eye-wateringly crude jokes from Bjorn.

Finally, as they all began to yawn and drop off, the Wolves left their seats, much recovered in both spirit and body, and made their way to the makeshift shelters for the night. Halfdan had one to himself, as jarl, while most shared a shelter, barring Bjorn, who took up a whole one himself. He wrapped himself up in the cloak he'd worn all day, now mostly dry, or at least a lot less damp, and lay with the blazing fire ahead of him at the heart of their little camp, its light and warmth a comfort in the dreadful conditions. It was not long before sleep claimed him, the bone-weariness he felt overcoming any obstacle to slumber.

For a moment, he thought he'd awoken, for the world was white and cold and damp and a fire burned nearby, but then he realised that things were not quite the same, and that this was a dream. He was still asleep.

One word echoed across the landscape, spoken in a faint, feminine, scratchy voice, bouncing from hill to hill up and down the dale, despite the fog.

Fimbulvetr.

A shiver. Even in dream.

Why had he not seen that before? They had slogged their way west in the biting cold, downpours and freezing fog, in an attempt to bring bloodshed and death to men who still followed the old gods, who were of northern cold iron even deep in their bones, men who could be said to be the closest thing the Wolves had to kin. The twilight of the gods, Ragnarok, will begin with a winter that lasts three seasons, which will bring the sons of Odin to the edge of reason for survival, pitting themselves against one another.

Fimbulwinter was here, heralding the great war to end everything. Two great wolves would then catch and devour the sun and the moon, bringing darkness and ending any warmth. Jörmungandr, the world serpent, will leave his depths and rampage across the world, while the chains that bind mighty Fenris will break, releasing the great wolf to his work. The giants of Muspelheim will march across the Bifrost, causing Heimdallr to blow his horn. Loki's chains will fall away, freeing him for the end of the world, and the great ship *Naglfar*, full of Jötnar, will sail against the gods, with Loki leading them.

The extended winter, the *Sea Dragon* leaving Nordmandi, the Wolves hunting, the bindings upon Halfdan and the Wolves all loosening when their task was done. It was all too much.

Then the fog fell away, and the dale became clear, as Halfdan gripped his sword and glanced up.

The skies, red as blood, shook and boomed, as though being torn apart. A black crack loomed above him as he stood, sword in hand, watching his enemy emerge from the doorway of the stone hall. On a bleak hillside, a world of men watched as Heimdallr and Loki met.

The guardian of Bifrost was tall, in a glittering shirt of silver. His eyes shone almost gold in the reflected light of the dreadful sky; in his right hand he held a sword that was the death of men, and in his left was a beautiful and terrible horn. It was that which transfixed Halfdan, even deep in the dream, for the very sight of the horn made the Loki serpents on his arm burn, as though he were aflame with the war-fire of the Greeks.

He stepped forward, and so did Heimdallr, and their swords met with a ring that cut through the earth, awaking giants, sending a call to the halls of the slain that the time was nigh.

This time, though, it was not the panic or the shock or the cold sweat that dragged Halfdan from the world of dream.

He opened his eyes suddenly, blinking away the dream which clung in shreds to his mind. For a moment he was still in that dream valley, awaiting the end of the world.

Fimbulvetr.

But then two things insisted themselves upon him. First, the fog had lifted and the morning was lit with a cold, watery sun that illuminated a world hidden from them for over a day now. The second was Lief, who was crouched there, shaking him wildly. The Rus's eyes were wide and riven with panic, which galvanised Halfdan and drew him fully awake, shaking off the last of the dream.

'What is it?'

Lief's face was a mask of horror as he replied.

'Gunnhild has gone.'

Part Three

ᛈᛟᛚᚡᛗᛋ ᛟᚠ ᛟᛞᛁᚾ

Völva

By means of this [Odin] could […] bring on the death, ill-luck, or
bad health of people,
and take the strength or wit from one person and give it to another.
But after such witchcraft followed such weakness and anxiety,
that it was not thought respectable for men to practise it; and
therefore the priestesses were brought up in this art.

Chapter 7: Of Odin's Feats from the *Ynlinga saga*,
trans. Samuel Laing

Chapter 13

The past. Kaupang, Nordvegr.

'Why?' the man begged desperately, dangling from Bjorn's grip, feet kicking wildly in the air.

'Because,' Bjorn answered with an edge of anger, 'it is my birthday. I wanted to drink myself into a stupor, and then you came along and ruined it all when you spilled my beer. So now I'm going to beat you until you squeak when you walk instead. At least I'll have *some* birthday fun, then.'

'But—' the man began, then fell silent as Bjorn's large, meaty fist met with his face, pulverising it and driving all consciousness from him. Bjorn clicked his tongue in frustration. Even this was no fun when the man was gone after one punch. He dropped the limp form and turned to look with irritation once more on the jug of beer that lay on its side next to the rock, its contents having formed a pool in the grass. In truth, it was not enough beer to get him even halfway to a stupor anyway, but it had been all he could afford in Ánslo, and over the past few years he had been forced more than once to come to terms with the fact that his size, shape, colouring and natural bluntness made him a very poor thief. He'd tried to swipe another jug, but the man had seen, and he'd put it back grumpily. These Norsemen were sticklers for law, and there were enough of the king's men in Ánslo that even Bjorn couldn't risk taking them on.

One jug of beer.

That had been all he had, pretty much everything he owned right now, and he'd sat in solitude to wallow in his drink until along came some prat and ruined it.

There was a noise, the clearing of a throat, which suggested that the unconscious blunderer had not been alone, and Bjorn turned in a full circle, trying to locate the source of the sound.

Kaupang was a land of ghosts, of draugar. The town had been gone for generations, now little more than the low ruins of once impressive houses. No one came to Kaupang. It was shunned. The town had simply emptied a century ago, and no one seemed to know why. Stories abounded over mysterious plagues and ghost armies and the like, and it was really just bored curiosity that had drawn Bjorn to it in his directionless meanderings.

He'd not expected to meet even one person here, let alone another, and now that one punch had knocked the villain into unconsciousness, he might never even know why his interrupter was here. But someone else was here, in this shunned land of nothing.

He spotted her a few moments later, beneath a skeletal birch tree growing out of the stony shell of a long-gone home. Just one glance suggested that she had nothing to do with the hapless beer-spiller, which was at the same time frustrating and intriguing. He left his pack and the body of the man, and strode toward the figure beneath the tree. He didn't worry too much about his pack. The chances of anyone else coming across it and stealing it were remote, the unconscious man would be out for hours, and even if it *was* stolen, there was little of real consequence in there anyway. He had his axe tucked into the back of his belt and the pouch of what few coins remained at his waist.

'Who are you?' he asked. Something about her made him shiver.

She regarded him silently. She was short, probably little more than waist height to the enormous albino, but she carried in her being a power that radiated openly, and which gave her a stature far beyond that which nature had granted. Quite simply she was a giant in a tiny form. She leaned upon a staff with a carved haft and a long metal spike decorated with intricate designs. Her hair was the grey of day-old ash, her skin weathered and leathery. She was old, clearly, yet probably sprightly, from the way she held herself. Bjorn found for the very first time in his life that he was in awe of the person before him. He'd faced some of the most dangerous killers in the north lands, and had walked away whistling, yet this small woman made him hesitate as he approached.

'Why the beer?'

He frowned at the question. 'The blaand looked dodgy, and I couldn't afford mead,' he answered, unsure why he was telling such things to this woman.

'I meant, why were you attempting to drink yourself to sleep in a land of draugar on your twentieth birthday.'

Bjorn felt the hairs on the back of his neck rise and bristle. He shivered. He'd been trying to work out most of the day whether he was nineteen or twenty. He only knew his birthday because his parents had always celebrated it on the first day of *Skammdegi*, that season of dark days and winter, and he'd felt the turn in the weather yesterday, and knew it was that time. How in Odin's name did she know how old he was, when even he did not?

He realised he was standing still, silent, staring at her, but before he could answer, she spoke again. 'That small jug of beer wouldn't have got your victim over there drunk, let alone a jötunn like you,' she said with a sly smile.

'I am not good with money,' Bjorn admitted, again wondering why he was doing so.

'And yet you have had much of it over the years, yes?'

He shivered and stared. That much was unpleasantly true. On the death of the grandchildren of Orm Barelegs, and Bjorn's release from the stigma of thralldom, he had wandered without aim or path. For years he had meandered across the world of Svears, Geats, Norse, and even to Daneland briefly. He had grown ever larger, ever stronger, gained more scars and many,

many more kills, none of which had really changed anything. He had tried to settle down, to find any sort of trade he could involve himself in, but it had become unpleasantly plain that his only skills were killing, drinking and telling tall tales. He knew that some men could make a living of such things, but they were usually either obedient men who could serve a lord unquestioningly, or clever men who could navigate the tides of politics. Bjorn was not clever. Not enough for that, anyway. And he had little patience for serving idiots, which every jarl or lord he met seemed to be. Consequently, he had bounced from one place to another for years, never settling, always slightly unhappy with his lot, usually making enemies and having to leave in a hurry. And every time he left, he had money from his endeavours, yet by the time he found somewhere new to try a life, he'd drunk and whored it all away again.

He was lost.

That, of course, was why he was in a town of ghosts and ruins, with a spilled drink and a wealth of frustrations on his birthday.

A birthday this woman seemed to know about.

'Is this Seiðr?' he asked. 'Are you a magic woman? A seer?'

She shrugged. 'I am called many things. In this world of the nailed god, I am mostly called a witch. I am völva. I walk with Freyja. Upon a time, my kind would have the grandest house in a berg beneath that of the jarl. We were respected, trusted, our counsel sought. We were queens of our world. Now that the Christ owns every field and every village, my kind live in places like this, where the nailed god even now fails to hold sway.'

Again, Bjorn shivered. Völva. He'd heard of such women. It had been said in his youth that his own village had once had such a person, though she had died long before his birth.

'What do you want with me?' he asked, a touch of nerves rising, inflecting his voice.

'It was you who came to my home to wallow in self-pity,' she replied, arching an eyebrow, 'not I who sought you out.'

He sagged. 'I want to be alone.'

'That, I think, is a very long way from the truth.' She stepped out from under the tree and closed the distance between them. 'In fact, I think you crave connection, family, brotherhood. I think you have been forced to live alone long enough that you have forgotten how to manage any other way. It is often the way with the sons of Thor.'

'Sons of Thor?'

She smiled. 'Some folk are daughters of Freyja. We walk with the goddess and navigate the warp and weft of the Norns. Others are children of Loki, flighty, clever and swift, given to thievery and the arts, making their way in the world almost as parasites upon it. Some are the sons of Odin, noble lords, or ignoble sometimes, who seek power and lucre. And then there are those who were born to wield axe or hammer or sword. The sons of Thor, warriors in the blood. Such as you, killer of men.'

'Bjorn,' he answered.

'Bjorn is half a name. Time will grant you the rest. And will grant you brotherhood and direction, too.'

He sighed. 'I cannot settle, woman. I cannot find my place.'

She laughed. 'By every god, you fool, you are as hard to talk to as the three-headed beast of Hróarskelda! Your *place* will find *you*. All you need to do is let it. Somewhere out there is a worthy jarl who lacks the powerful warrior he needs. No thread of the Norns' weaving is ever wasted. Every thread forms part of the tapestry. I could walk with the goddess and tell you of the path that lies ahead, but your fate is written all over you, Bjorn-lacks-a-name. You are lost, but that is because you are trying very hard to be something, and you're not even sure what. Until you surrender yourself to the weaving of the Norns and trust in the threads that lead you forth, you will remain at odds with your own fate.'

Bjorn blinked. He was not entirely sure what she meant, of course. He knew he was not the cleverest of men, and the ways of Seiðr were unknown to him, but somehow, what she had said cut through years of waste and confusion and seemed to almost illuminate a path for him. He could not quite see it, but for years he had not even known it was there, and it had taken this tiny woman to reveal its very existence.

He felt a thrill of hope, and something he'd never felt in all the years since he'd been taken captive.

Respect.

Late February 1044. Upper Swaledale.

Bjorn was utterly torn. Around him, the others were bustling in a panic, searching the trees nearby, checking for tracks, asking each other fruitless questions. Even Halfdan, who always seemed to know the answers, or was able to make them up when he didn't, seemed panicked.

Bjorn was not panicked.

He was focused.

He was determined.

But he was torn.

A völva was not to be underestimated. Not to be taken lightly. He had known three in his time. The old woman among the ruins of Kaupang who had found a lost and hopeless wanderer and forged him into a son of Thor, a brief meeting with that powerful woman in Hedeby who had directed Halfdan on his course…

…and Gunnhild. And despite his awe and fear and respect of the first two, there was probably no one in the world Bjorn respected more than Gunnhild. He sparred with her in jest, and he laughed, but he knew true power when he saw it, and there was nothing more important in the face of the plague of nailed god draugar, who spread across this world, than the völvas, who were one of the few remaining direct connections between men and the Aesir and the Vanir in their divine halls.

He was torn.

He wanted to run. He wanted to run and find Gunnhild and save her from whatever trouble she was in. She was as important to him as Halfdan was, if in a different way. He was desperate to bring her back to them.

But he also knew that Gunnhild was powerful. If someone was behind her disappearance, and that seemed the only possibility, then that someone was *even more* powerful than Gunnhild, which was a truly horrifying thought.

'...find the nearest settlement and beat the occupants until they tell us everything they know,' Halfdan was saying as he laid out his plan. Bjorn had only been half listening.

'But this is the darkest of magics,' Anna replied, subconsciously pulling close to Lief, who put his arm reassuringly around her. 'This is not a kidnapping by villagers,' she said. 'Gunnhild slept between Cassandra and I, less than a foot from either of us, and we are both light sleepers. Whoever took her did so without a sound, without a breath of air, left no footprints in wet grass, no trail to follow. Whoever did this, came into our very camp past the eyes of the sentries.'

That much was true, the fact that the women were light sleepers was an exaggeration to say the least. Halfdan had punched the first sentry he'd found. But it was not their fault. Bjorn knew that. They could no more have stopped the villain behind this than they could have stopped Thor or Odin. Because Anna was right. She might call it the Devil's work, or black magic, but he knew the fact that this was Seiðr for sure.

'Hrafn,' he rumbled.

'What?' Halfdan stopped in the midst of his briefing, and turned to Bjorn, as did all the others.

The big man fixed the jarl with a look.

'This is the work of Gunnar's raven,' Bjorn said. 'No ordinary man or woman, in any one of nine worlds, could do this. You know that. This is not the work of men, or of giants, of elves or of gods. This is the work of another völva. Only one more powerful than Gunnhild could have taken her. She is with Hrafn. Why, I cannot say, but I doubt her designs are good.'

There was an odd silence.

'Sometimes you still surprise me, old friend,' Halfdan smiled grimly. 'You are, of course, absolutely right. This is the work of Gunnar's völva. The jarl rules this valley with an iron hand, and he once had the strength of a berserkr at his side, which you have removed. But he also has the power of Seiðr, which keeps this valley safe for him. Gunnhild herself told me that the fog that almost destroyed our mission yesterday was not natural. She said it was the work of Hrafn. Perhaps a whole half day of fog was simply the völva's ploy to put us in a place where she could pluck Gunnhild out from among us. And quite right; as you say, her plan cannot be good.'

'What do we do?' Lief asked quietly.

'We find Hrafn, and we rescue Gunnhild.'

'But what of Gunnar? I remember that map. Hrafn is at the head of the dale, way past Gunnar's seat. We will have to pass him and leave him behind us to find her, and you, Halfdan, are always telling us never to leave a strong enemy behind us.'

'We go for Gunnhild,' Bjorn said, his tone flat, brooking no argument.

'But Gunnar is between us and her,' Lief reminded him.

Bjorn was ready to argue. Even if he did it alone, he was going after Gunnhild. But then Halfdan's gaze met his, and he knew his glorious, wily jarl agreed with him.

Halfdan nodded. 'Bjorn is right. Some things are more important even than our goal. I would let Gunnar live to save Gunnhild. Shit, but I'd let *Hjalmvigi* live to save Gunnhild.'

And there it was. The decision was made.

Camp was struck swiftly, for there was little to take with them since the loss of the horses. As they prepared, Bjorn found his chain byrnie, one of very few still among the Wolves now, and walked over toward Halfdan.

'What?' the jarl queried, looking at the enormous shirt in the man's hands.

'Wear it.'

Halfdan chuckled. 'Bjorn, look at me. At yourself. Ulfr and I could both fit in that together.'

Bjorn shrugged. 'So wear a belt. I have killed my berserkr, and I fear no man even in just a shirt. You will have to face Gunnar, and you know that. Wear the byrnie.'

Halfdan gave him a funny look, but Bjorn held his jarl locked in that gaze. He was not going to let this go. The Norns had a way of settling things, and it was the wyrd of all great heroes to fight the duels that would be told of in mead halls for the rest of days. Bjorn had fought – and beaten – Arkil, and if Gunnhild could not face Hrafn, then between them they would find and somehow beat her, but there were two jarls in this dale, and only one of them could survive an encounter. Bjorn had lost Gunnhild, for now. He damn well wasn't going to lose Halfdan, too.

Halfdan shrugged, and struggled into the chain as they walked.

When they left the meadow, Bjorn was fighting not to smile – despite the disaster they now found themselves in – for the sight of Halfdan was almost too much, drowned as he was in the giant shirt of chain.

The fog had gone, and the morning sun illuminated upper Swaledale, despite its watery paleness. The dale was still quite wide here, fields stretching down to the river from the lower slopes of the north. A road ran along the valley nearby, and farms seemed to be scattered around it. They could make out the location of the dykes they'd crossed earlier, and the small settlement that sat at the junction of this dale and the side valley that had been Arkil's home. Turning to look west, it was clear that the dale narrowed as it rose, and their goal had to lie somewhere up there. They reached the road, a rough dirt and stone track, very soon, and turned west immediately.

Perhaps a quarter of a mile along the way, they passed a poor farm off to the left of the road, and a small group of men stood around a hay wagon, discussing something, falling silent as the Wolves approached them.

Their expressions were filled with fear, something Bjorn had not seen in the locals during their journey, or at least not until Gunnhild had started gutting them in the mist and Bjorn had ripped the head from their champion. He surmised that word of his victory had reached this far, and probably much further, and the confidence of these people who were Gunnar's hirð had been thoroughly shaken.

Halfdan, leading the way, came to a halt ten paces from the men, who shrank back, putting their cart between them and the visitors.

'Where is Hrafn, the völva of this valley?' he demanded.

He was greeted with a nervous silence. The jarl turned, eyes falling on Bjorn. 'Ask him for me?'

Bjorn nodded and walked out past Halfdan, across to the wagon. The men tried to cram behind it, staying out of his reach, but there were too many of them to fit easily, and the big man's good hand closed on a cowering local's shoulder. The man yelped and shouted to his friends for assistance as Bjorn yanked him from cover into the open.

'Where do we find Hrafn?' he asked, and then reached out and casually broke the man's neck. He winced as he did so, for the aches and pains of his duel were still with him, but he ignored them. Pains were like Greek merchants: if you ignored them long enough, they went away and stopped bothering you.

'How do you expect him to answer now?' hissed Lief in exasperation.

'It wasn't him Bjorn was asking,' Ketil explained.

Bjorn's gaze fell on the men behind the cart as the body of his victim collapsed to the ground. The men cowered, eyes wide, yet none spoke. Bjorn took two steps and began to reach around the wagon.

'Head of the valley,' one of the men said, the words tumbling from quivering lips urgently. Bjorn simply held the man's gaze, his fingers twitching.

'Where the dale narrows,' another man said. 'The river runs under some cliffs. You'll see caves. Beyond that, the river turns north and carves its way through the hills. Follow it up into the wilds and you'll find a stone cottage by a spring. That's where you'll find her.'

Bjorn nodded.

'But you're fools to go,' the first man said, as though bravery was returning to him.

'Oh?'

'Hrafn is the most dangerous woman to walk the worlds. Even Gunnar fears her.'

'Then it is time that *she* found something to fear,' Halfdan replied.

'Whatever she has done to you, it is not worth it. Go back.'

Bjorn fixed the men with his mightiest look. 'We are not the mice of the nailed god. We are sons of Odin and sons of Thor and sons of Loki. *You* cower. *We* have fame to seek.'

And with that he turned and started walking west along the road. It was not long before the others were hurrying along in his wake, Halfdan scurrying forward to his side. 'I have never seen such purpose in you, Bjorn, even when you rushed to face Arkil. We are *all* concerned for Gunnhild, my friend.'

'You don't understand.'

Bjorn knew his reputation well. He was the braggart with a thousand tall stories of his life. People assumed he was open, to be read by all. He wasn't. There were some small parts of his past that would never reach the ears of others, and one of those was a time when he had been lost and unsure, and a völva had found him and turned his life around. Even Halfdan, who had in some ways gone through almost the same thing, would never hear that story from him.

'I might,' the jarl replied. 'Tell me.'

'Be content with my presence, Halfdan Loki-born,' Bjorn said quietly, his eyes still on the road ahead. Halfdan apparently understood, for he nodded silently.

'Very well. We will save her.'

'Yes,' was Bjorn's simple reply.

As they walked, Halfdan gave a light chuckle. 'Well if you won't tell me what's really going on, at least take your shirt back.'

Bjorn turned with a frown to see that his jarl had undone the belt and was beginning to peel the great steel weight from his torso. 'You will need it.'

'Even if I do, we don't go to face Gunnar right now, and the weight is the same as a small horse. I'll be exhausted by the time we find Hrafn. And I look like a fucking joke, old friend.'

Bjorn shrugged, and walked on as Halfdan removed the great shirt. He took it as it was handed over, but simply slung it over his good shoulder for now. They walked on for an hour, the valley curving slightly to the right as they travelled, rounding a high moor, and Bjorn began to drift off into a reverie, recalling some of the happier times of his life. After a while, he made a decision, and reached down for the large, heavy bag that swung at his side with every step. Unfastening it from his belt, he lifted it, opened it, and removed Arkil's still fairly fresh head from it.

'What are you doing?' Halfdan asked quietly.

Bjorn shrugged. 'If you had the best brooch in the world, would you keep it hidden or pin it to your front for everyone to see?'

Halfdan frowned. 'Arkil's is the best head?'

'He is the greatest opponent a warrior could face, other than me, of course. His head is a prize beyond most. I do not like it hidden away in a bag. People might not know it was me who killed him.'

'So you want it on show.'

'Yes.'

'But he's bald. You can hardly hang him from your belt by the hair.'

'Exactly. Hold this.' He passed the enormous head to Halfdan, who took it with distaste, and, as they walked, Bjorn drew his sax and spent some time using the narrow blade to work a hole through the head, from ear to ear, across the soft part, and missing the skull. Halfdan grumbled a little at his part in this as the big man produced a length of leather lace and threaded it through the hole. Grinning at his ingenuity, with Halfdan's help, Bjorn tied the lace to his belt so that the berserkr's head was visible to all, bouncing against his leg as he walked. Bits of stuff dangled from the neck and whipped this way and that, and Bjorn could hear Lief making disgusted, gagging sounds behind him as they walked.

Beside him, Halfdan laughed as he wiped unspeakable stuff from his hands. 'You never fail to surprise me, my big friend.'

Bjorn shrugged. 'If you think that, then I've never told you of the time I fucked a Dane girl with five tits.'

'Most men would use their dick,' Halfdan grinned.

Bjorn frowned for a moment, then shook his head and rolled his eyes. 'Don't ruin a good story.' But when he turned to look at the jarl again, Halfdan's grin had gone, and he was not looking at Bjorn, but past him. The big man, brow furrowed, turned and looked in the same direction. All he could see was the valley side. The slope began with lush meadow, gradually rising through scrubby grass and scattered scree, until it reached moorland of heather and fern and open, blasted heath. Up there was a cluster of small buildings, but nothing spectacular or unexpected, just more of the sort of land and housing they had already seen.

'What is it?'

Halfdan shook his head, dismissing the moment, but Bjorn knew more, knew that something was worrying his jarl, and it had something to do with that slope and those buildings. 'Tell me.'

'While you hide your own secrets, big friend?' Still, Halfdan gave a weary laugh, threaded with a touch of uncertainty. 'That is Gunnar's house.'

Bjorn frowned and looked up again. There was really nothing at all special about the place.

'How can you be sure?'

'I just am. I know that house. That moor. I've seen it before, many times, in the weavings of the Norns. Shit, Bjorn, but I'm half expecting the sky to crack open and go red.' Bjorn frowned at his jarl, baffled. Halfdan gave another chuckle. 'Nothing. The jarl of Swaledale's time will come. We'll be back here.'

Bjorn shrugged, putting his questions aside. He was not about to press the matter when he himself was trying not to open up. Instead, the two men walked on in silence at the head of the Wolves, slowly wending their way up the dale, rising all the time, the valley narrowing, the landscape becoming bleaker and wilder. The meandering river drew closer to them as they rounded the hillside and followed the flow north, through an even narrower stretch of valley. Now, the river was but ten paces across, with wide swathes of gravel on both sides. The easy ground between river and slope narrowed until it was little more than a score of paces across, and Bjorn realised the road petered out here. He wondered idly what sort of mind built a road that didn't lead to somewhere. Damn Gunnhild, for such thoughts were her fault, remembering that conversation back at the bridge.

Still, they followed the narrowing river through the narrower valley, now noticeably rising all the time, and the valley once more began to curve to the west. From there, they passed a small side valley, more a glorified gulley, and then the slope to their right began to close and to climb, until suddenly it became jagged cliffs that rose to eight or ten times the height of a man. Content now that they had not accidentally strayed from the path, and were still following the directions given to them by the farmers, they followed along the narrow riverbank under the cliffs. High up, here and there, they could see openings, some perhaps large enough for a man, mostly small, and probably only frequented by birds.

Perhaps half a mile along them, they spotted a cave that was more accessible, a little climb up the slope and large enough for men to enter. Still, marking the landmark from their directions, they strode on, aware now that they were closing on their destination, until finally Halfdan gestured ahead and held up a hand to halt them all.

'What is it?' Bjorn murmured, and followed the jarl as he paced forward and to the left, down toward the river. There, at the edge of the undergrowth, stood a great stone stump, a foot across, and rising from the grass to chest height. On it was a single carving, the image of a raven, quite clear.

'I would like to think this is something to do with Odin,' Halfdan muttered, 'but I think we all know what it means.'

Bjorn nodded.

'We are in Hrafn's land now.'

Chapter 14

'What is he doing?'

Halfdan shook his head at Ketil's question. He had no idea.

The man before them sat outside a small hut, presumably his home, on a tree stump. At first, they thought he was whittling, for he held an arm-length stick between his knees and was furiously intent upon it, but as they got closer, they'd seen that he had no knife to work with. His fingers simply drummed up and down the stick at a steady rhythm, and occasionally stopped, as though he'd lost count of something, and began again. Periodically the behaviour would stop, and he would tug at his ear, bend, pull up a handful of grass, lick it, and cast it into the air.

'A madman,' Bjorn said dismissively.

A nod from Halfdan. It certainly seemed that way. Still, madmen were made mad by something. And something about the man, and the place, had the jarl's senses tingling, the serpents on his arm itching.

They had followed the route they'd been given and turned away from the main valley into a narrower one, not far from the dale's head, trailing a smaller tributary from the north. Following that lesser valley for perhaps a quarter of an hour had brought them to this place by the stream. Initially they had thought they'd reached their goal, but then, quite apart from the madman, they remembered the description of Hrafn's home as a stone cottage, and this place was a poor hut of wood and wattle.

Holding his hand up to halt his hirð, Halfdan stepped out and walked slowly toward the man, hands out to his sides, away from his weapons to indicate peaceful intentions. Close enough for low conversation, he came to a stop. The man never looked up, keeping at his strange work.

'We are looking for Hrafn, the völva,' the jarl said in calm tones. The man did not stop. A strange silence reigned, and Halfdan glanced back to the others, shrugged, then turned and tried once more. 'Friend, is this the way to the völva's home?'

Still nothing. Frustration arose in Halfdan, and he sucked on his teeth, trying to decide how best to change his approach. The man could not take his eyes off the stick, on which he was apparently counting something, other than to taste the grass and cast it away. With such focus, Halfdan might as well not be there. He took a deep breath and reached out, not intending to take the stick, but to stay the man's hands and break the rhythm, to get his attention.

'No!' the man shouted suddenly, hands working furiously on the wood, but eyes now rising to meet the jarl's. Halfdan recoiled. The man's eyes were rheumy pale blue, but around each orb, the flesh was red and sore, as though the man had stopped closing them some time ago, even to blink.

The fingers faltered. The man gave him a horrified look.

'You made me lose count!'

Suddenly the lunatic was on his feet, hands reaching for Halfdan's throat, stick cast aside, forgotten. The jarl pulled away, dancing out of reach as the man fell, starting to sob dry tears, for there was no moisture to those dead eyes.

'What do you count?' he asked carefully, staying close, though just out of reach.

'My hours. All hours. No more hours. All gone.'

Halfdan shivered. The man was counting what was left of his life? That was certainly how it sounded. The figure spun on the ground, still prone, gripping the stick and pulling it close. As he lay there in the damp grass, he began his behaviour once more, and in moments he seemed to have forgotten that Halfdan was there at all, back to his counting and drumming on the stick.

The jarl padded slowly back to his men. 'If this is the work of the völva, I am beginning to see why the people of the dale fear her so much.'

A chorus of nods met this.

'I presume, then, that we continue until we find the source of the water,' Lief suggested, 'since the man we spoke to said there was a spring beside the house.'

Halfdan nodded, and the Wolves moved on, skirting wide around the madman and his house. Soon, he was left behind, blessedly out of sight, a relief to everyone. Madmen often meant the work of elves, and no one wanted to find themselves in the presence of those nasty, dangerous creatures. The valley continued northward, the stream at its centre meandering, sometimes almost looping back on itself, small stands of trees and undergrowth sporadic along its length, tiny trickles joining it from narrow cuttings to either side. For another half hour they followed it, and Halfdan made one observation as he walked. Throughout their journey up the main dale, they had seen settlements, ancient fortifications, various sites of lead-working and systems for its transportation, and numerous pastoral farms. None of that showed any sign in this narrow valley that felt strange and otherworldly. Other than bleak nature, the only thing they had found had been the madman. If nothing else set Hrafn's land apart from the rest of this northern world, it was that it seemed to be untouched by anything except madness.

After climbing for some time, the valley opened out to a wide area of pastureland, a natural bowl among the hills, and the stream here forked, tumbling down from two distinct sources. The Wolves came to a halt at the confluence, frustrated.

'The western stream is the main one,' Lief noted. 'Wider and stronger than the northern one.'

'But that does not make it certain,' Halfdan huffed. 'All we know is that the völva lives by a spring, which presumably is the source of one of them. If we follow the wrong one, we could go miles out of the way, and speed is important.'

Glum nods greeted this, as Halfdan peered off both west and north along the two narrow, winding streams. Logic did suggest following the main one, but something about the other tributary made him twitch and shiver, as though his very being was uncomfortable in its presence, and that led him more toward the northern route. He rubbed the serpents on his arm, hoping for some sort of Loki-sent guidance, but the trickster had nothing to say on the matter.

'*Odin*,' Ketil hissed sharply, and along with the others, Halfdan's head snapped round. The Icelander was pointing, his face a picture of shock.

The jarl's eyes scoured that direction, the valley sides, the trickling stream, the trees and shrubs, and then he too saw it. A figure in a voluminous grey hooded cloak was moving slowly toward them, leaning on a tall staff. The jarl had never seen the Allfather in person. None of them had, though they all knew it to be a possibility, for Odin was known to wander the wilds. Halfdan felt the Seiðr flowing through the very air around them. He looked across at Lief, for the little Rus was a Christian, yet well-versed in the old ways, the wisest and most knowledgeable of them all, but Lief's expression was a mix of shock and disbelief, as might be expected, as they all looked at one another in wonder.

Halfdan turned back.

The figure was not there.

'Where did he go?' He turned again, bristling with nervous energy, to the others, and sagged as he realised that everyone else wore the same expressions of surprise and confusion, shrugging. Somehow everyone had turned away and not seen the figure vanish. Such, Halfdan reflected with a sigh, was the way with gods.

'Look,' Lief said suddenly, and they all turned on instinct back to where the grey wanderer had last been. A figure was there again, though this one was different. A man of middling years in grey trousers and a bright blue shirt, a belt at his waist seeming to hold a sheathed knife, as far as Halfdan could make out from this distance. The figure was walking toward them.

'What is this?' Bjorn grunted.

'I don't know,' Halfdan breathed in reply. 'But we are in the domain of a powerful völva. Nothing here feels right, and I don't know how far we can trust anything or anyone.'

Lief and a number of the others, devotees of the nailed god, drew crosses over themselves with their fingers, a gesture Halfdan had seen Christians use across the world when faced with anything they did not like or understand.

'Be on your guard,' he said, turning and concentrating on the figure. He was already coming relatively close. As he became clearer and clearer, Halfdan picked out more detail. The man was older than he'd thought before, and, though his clean-shaven appearance made him seem younger, his long, wild hair was threaded with large streaks of grey. Still, he walked straight and true, with a steady gait, as he approached.

'*Heill ok sæll*,' Halfdan greeted him, an old phrase, wishing the man health and happiness.

The figure said nothing in reply, but came closer and then to a stop a few paces away.

Halfdan shivered. There was something about the man that was not quite right. He looked the stranger in the eye, and that feeling only heightened. The man's grey eyes were unfocused, even as he looked back and forth among the Wolves, as though he were looking at them but seeing something else, something far away, through the veils between worlds.

'Where is the house of the völva Hrafn?'

The man continued to look back and forth, then finally settled on Halfdan. Still, he was not focused and it made the jarl shiver again to have those eyes looking through him and seeing something else.

'Follow the blood water,' the man said quietly, his voice strange and reedy, almost hollow sounding.

Halfdan frowned. Neither stream seemed to live up to such a description, yet the man turned as he finished speaking, drawing

208

the short knife from his belt and pointing with it, off to the north.

Halfdan nodded. He could not wait to be away from this strange place, and with Gunnhild by his side. Even if it meant facing Gunnar and potential death, at least it would be the death of a man, in battle, where Odin's maidens could find him. Here in this wyrd place, the jarl suspected, Odin held little sway.

'Thank you,' he said to the man, hoping the words would be taken as much of a dismissal as anything.

The man simply stood there, arm still raised, pointing with gleaming blade, and Halfdan's frown returned. He turned to the others, and as he did so, Njal, one of his men stepped toward the stranger, hand up in a gesture of peace. 'Listen, friend,' he began, and in a blur the stranger suddenly spun, knife still in hand, whipping out. The knife cut into Njal's raised hand, almost severing the little finger. Njal cried out in shock and pain as the knife whipped away through the air, blood straying in its path. Halfdan's hand went to his sword hilt in an instant, ready to move, the other Wolves each reaching for weapons, but Bjorn was there first, not even bothering with his axe.

With a huge ursine roar, the albino grabbed the man's knife arm and jerked down, breaking it at the elbow, while his other hand shot out to the man's throat, grabbing it in that huge fist.

'Bjorn, wait,' Halfdan tried, but he knew that even as he spoke it was too late. The man's throat was crushed in an instant and Bjorn simply threw the man away like a rag doll, where he fell to the grass, shuddering and shaking, broken arm flopping about.

The jarl turned to his injured man, but Anna was there already, pulling the finger back into position, and then producing a strip of cloth and binding the fingers together to hold them in place.

'Can you save it?' the man gasped.

'Me? No. But Gunnhild can, so I'm just going to keep you whole and in the right shape until we find her.'

Njal, sweating and wincing with the pain, nodded as she wrapped wadding and bandages around it all. Halfdan looked across at the now-still body of the stranger in the grass, to Bjorn, who was wiping bloody fingers on a scarf, to the stream that meandered off to the right before disappearing into another gill.

'North it is.'

'You trust that man?'

Halfdan rubbed his hands together. 'I'm not entirely convinced the man had any real idea what he was doing or saying. I don't think he was entirely here at all. But the directions he gave were pretty specific, which is something you don't usually get with lies.'

'North, then,' Ketil agreed.

Bjorn was off, then, still wiping his hands. Anna looked up after him. 'Wait until I've finished this.'

'Do it as you walk, woman,' Bjorn replied. 'Gunnhild needs us.'

Halfdan looked back and forth between the two. Bjorn still had in his manner that energy of purpose which he'd had since the moment Gunnhild had gone missing. Whatever the big man's reasons, he was not going to let anything get between him and saving their precious völva. Halfdan made a mental note to keep as tight a rein on Bjorn as he could manage in the coming hours. Bjorn was a force of nature, but he often moved on his desires without sufficient consideration, and that could be enormously dangerous. He would have to keep the big man safe.

'Come on,' he said, and walked off quickly after Bjorn, catching up as he veered off from the stream they had been following, and instead traced the smaller flow to the north. The others hurried after them, Anna still finishing her bindings as they walked. The stream wound past a small stand of trees and then settled into a narrow, steep-banked channel that wound like a serpent up through the land, tumbling across sporadic small waterfalls. The ground was sufficiently open and the stream clear enough that they did not have to traverse every curve, and instead followed the contour of the valley side, above the stream, keeping it in sight at all times.

Halfdan had thought this clever. That by cutting off the loops he was speeding their approach to Gunnhild. As it happened, it was pure luck that found them the way, for they almost missed it in their haste. Thurstan murmured something about needing a piss and that he would catch up. He jogged off down the slope a little and stood at the stream's edge, urinating down into the narrow flow, and then gave a sudden cry.

'Wait!'

'What is it?' Halfdan called back from ahead. 'Lost your dick?'

'No. I've found your stream.'

Pushing aside half a dozen bad jokes that leapt to mind, the jarl waved to the others to follow, and then hurried back to where Thurstan stood by the stream, putting himself away. As they arrived, he raised a pointing finger across the narrow defile that gurgled and shushed.

Halfdan looked and nodded his agreement.

They had left the Swale, following a narrower river into the hills. Then they had, on the latest madman's instructions, left that smaller river to follow this stream. Now, that stream revealed its own tributary, little more than a trickle that flowed from the hillside opposite to tumble down into the one they had been following. The water, as it fell, looked clear and fresh, yet as they looked up at the channel, a foot wide and shallow as it ran down the slope, the stream did have a distinctly ruddy tint.

It had to be the one. Halfdan peered up the slope. He could not see the source of the water, nor any kind of structure, but the horizon formed by the angle of the hillside could well hide anything like it.

Leading the way, the jarl took four steps back, then ran and jumped across the defile, and the stream at its bottom. Landing on the far bank with ease, he hurried over to the trickle that came from the hill. The channel was not wide, nor deep, but the flow was fast and constant, reminding him of the man-made water systems of the Greeks. It certainly could be a flow that arose from a spring, rather than some seasonal runnel. He crouched. The stream's bed and pitiful banks had a reddish tint, with just a hint of ochre, the water itself, too, ran with a red tint, perhaps from the erosion of the red banks where iron was worked. But Swaledale was a lead working area. Did they also have iron here, or was the colour the result of something more sinister?

He shivered and rose once more to look up the slope. That same unpleasant feeling he'd encountered when he looked off north at the confluence now struck him again, peering up the hill, and somehow he knew that this was the right way. He could almost feel the völva's presence there as a shiver-inducing shadow.

'Come on,' he called to the others, though Bjorn had already jumped across after him. The rest followed suit until they were all on the correct side of the stream. 'All right. From here, no talking. Make no noise at all if you can avoid it. We don't know what to expect, and I don't want to give away our approach until we do it by choice.'

'Gunnhild said the völva knew we were coming,' Lief reminded him.

'She said she knew *Gunnhild* was coming,' Halfdan corrected him. 'And we assume that she is the one that has taken her. She may not know *we* are coming. She probably does, admittedly, but even then she cannot know how close we are, or *where* we are.' It sounded good. Privately, Halfdan was half convinced the völva already knew precisely where they were, if she was as powerful as Gunnhild suspected. Still, all they could do was try.

'Stay together, stay quiet, and we will make plans when we know what we're dealing with.'

With that, he started to climb the slope alongside the stream. To their left the land rose high and quick, with a steep bank, the right lower and gentler, and so they stayed to that side. The turf was stringy and thick, and the land was once more spotted with areas of long wild grasses that rose from damper conditions. As they followed the stream and the slope, Halfdan kept low instinctively.

It was as the narrow flow turned north once more, following the contours, that Halfdan first saw it. Ahead there was a crescent-shaped dip in the hillside, just twenty or thirty feet below the grassland above, but it was clearly from here that the stream flowed. As the channel appeared to their view from that depression, so it flowed between ferns and other undergrowth. No trees grew here on this blasted moorland, so there was nothing to obstruct their view, yet that also meant there was nothing to hide them from view. The moment they could see Hrafn's house, she would be able to see them.

Halfdan turned and looked at the other slope, along the base of which the stream had been flowing. From there, he'd be able to see.

'Wait here,' he whispered, and then followed this up with a determined hand held up, palm flat, to stop Bjorn following. The big man looked disgruntled, but nodded and stayed with the others. Making sure his cloak covered him as best he could, Halfdan scrambled on all fours up the steep slope until he reached the point at which it levelled out; there he dropped to the wet grass and lay flat, looking out across the land.

He could see it all. The others waited below the hollow in which the spring lay. In that hollow sat a heavy, grey stone building with a roof of slates. The channel of water that flowed down the slope was, near the house, covered with more stone slabs, in the manner he'd seen used for drains in Miklagarðr. The line of those slabs led from the open stream, up to the rear of the house.

The building had only one floor, but it was of a reasonable size, apparently divided into two distinct parts, each with its own door. The far section had a window, and smoke rose from a hole in the roof, marking it as some sort of living area and, critically, suggesting the owner was at home. The nearer side had only a door, though tucked around behind it, he could also see another small chamber built up against it with its own door and lower roof.

No guards. No walls. No defences.

Yet the home of one of the three most powerful figures in the Dale.

He thought back on what they had seen since passing the marker of Hrafn's lands, and once again noted that they had seen no sign of habitation or life therein, barring two madmen, and the house that belonged to one of them. Immediately, Halfdan came to the conclusion that the völva of Swaledale had no guards or walls or defences simply because she did not need them. That alone was a rather sobering thought.

He lay there for long moments, hoping deep down that they were wrong on some count. That Gunnhild had simply wandered off in the fog and would come wandering back at any time, or that the smoke from that house marked only the hut of a simple sheep farmer.

No. He had not even seen a sheep since they passed into Hrafn's lands.

Oddly, it struck him that he did not remember seeing *any* sort of wildlife at all.

He looked up.

No birds.

Everything about this place made him tremor.

Just how powerful was she?

And dangerous.

He had never considered that before. He'd met only two völvas in his life: Gunnhild and the old woman she'd been training under. Both had been impressive, both strong and sure and with that aura of Seiðr about their very being, but both were wise and had been full of guidance and wit. He'd never really thought what that level of power could mean if wielded by someone with only evil intent. An *anti*-Gunnhild, of a sort. That thought brought an even greater shudder.

Still, he'd seen nothing yet to even confirm that Gunnhild was here.

He looked across at the others down the slope. They had not moved, but they were all looking up at him, and two of them appeared to be trying to hold Bjorn still. He winced at that, and then lifted his gaze to the stone building once more.

He almost jumped, even prostrate as he was, when a figure suddenly emerged from the far door. He felt his flesh prickle at the sight, and knew instantly that this was the woman they sought. She wore a dress of ash grey and black, threaded with silver decoration, and her hair was midnight dark, braided and long, her skin pale. She held a staff with what looked to be a bird skull atop it, feathers tied below the head. She was truly impressive, yet the most impressive, and unnerving, thing of all was how the moment she left the house, she came to a halt and turned, looking directly up at Halfdan.

He felt a chill run through him that had nothing to do with the wet grass.

She knew. She knew he had come, and she even knew exactly where.

A small, cynical, part of his soul told him that perhaps she had been looking out of her window in time to see him scramble up the slope, yet he did not really believe that. She knew. She was truly powerful. The völva's eyes stayed on him for a long moment. He could not see such detail to be sure, but still felt certain that she had not blinked.

Then, suddenly, she turned and walked toward the other door, entering the second building.

The air felt heavy, thick, as it does before a storm, when Brokkr raises his hammer, ready to strike the anvil, sending the sound across the sky. It was the Seiðr. He could feel it, making his hair crackle, his skin itch. This place felt as thick with true power as had that house where he'd first met Gunnhild.

He heard the cry.

From inside the house came a single bark of pain.

Gunnhild.

He had to restrain himself, for he almost leapt to his feet and ran at the sound, but that would be foolish. A horrible thought struck him, and he looked back down the slope to the others, half expecting to see Bjorn charging toward the house, axe in hand. They had not moved. Was it possible they hadn't heard the cry? They were no farther from the house than he. Surely they'd heard? Yet if they had, he'd no doubt that Bjorn would already be running.

He focused back on the house.

Hrafn reappeared from that nearer door, staff still in hand. In the other, she held something. He squinted. It appeared to be a small bowl of some sort. He watched with a sinking feeling as the völva stopped once more, turning to face the spot where he lay. She rammed the staff into the ground by her side and then let go. Without taking her eyes off him, she dipped a thumb into the bowl and withdrew it. She then used whatever was in the bowl to draw lines on her face. Halfdan winced again. Twin lines across her cheeks and one down her chin. Warpaint.

She was preparing to do battle.

What was worse, was that Halfdan had absolutely no doubt what was in that bowl. All he could see from this distance was that the liquid Hrafn was painting herself with was dark, yet he knew it to be blood, and after the cry, he also knew it to be *Gunnhild's* blood.

Hrafn finished her markings, then lifted the bowl as if in salute to the hidden jarl on the hillside, and tipped the rest of the liquid into her mouth. Bowl empty, task complete, she retrieved her staff, turned, and walked to the house and back in through the door, to be lost from sight once more. Halfdan was just about to stand when two women emerged from the house, each in grey, each holding a spear, and took positions to either side of the door.

So, she was not entirely unprotected, after all.

Shield-maidens.

He knew the stories of such warrior women from the tales of old, of course. Shield-maidens had lived and died, gaining fearsome reputations, in the days of the great conquerors and raiding heroes. In these days of nailed god blandness, such women were simply not found. He'd never seen a shield-maiden in the flesh, nor met anyone who had, though his uncle had once claimed his great grandmother had fought alongside Björn Eriksson in Västergötland.

The jarl lay for some time in the damp grass, watching as nothing changed at the house. He knew that Hrafn knew where he was. That meant that the two women by the door presumably knew where he was, too. The moment he stood up, there would be no doubt, yet he could hardly return to the others without standing and becoming plainly visible. He fretted for a moment, wondering whether it would be possible to retreat from the slope and work their way back to the stream then return the way they'd come, hopefully out of sight of the cottage at all times. It would take a while, though, and even then, he was not entirely sure it would work.

A thought struck him.

Hrafn had looked directly at him when not about her work. She had not once looked down the slope. She had known Gunnhild was coming, and she had apparently known Halfdan was coming. Had she not known about the others? Or did she simply consider them irrelevant, not worth her attention?

Either way, she had been focused on Halfdan and on her prisoner, and that gave him one opportunity. If she was focused on him, then perhaps others might slip by her. A slow smile crept across his face, and not only at the bizarre notion of Bjorn being able to 'slip by' anyone. Halfdan could be the bait, drawing their attention, while the others saved Gunnhild. As such, it mattered not if the shield-maidens saw him now.

He rose and began to pick his way carefully down the slope until he was once more out of sight of the house and the watchers, where he reached the stream and jogged back to the others. Pausing there, panting heavily until he caught his breath, he straightened.

'This is the place.'

He described the house as he had seen it, two separate rooms with a small shed at back, and then paused. 'Gunnhild is there. I heard her cry out.'

'Why?' demanded Bjorn, angry eyes narrowed.

'That doesn't matter. What does is that a cry of pain means she is alive.' At this the others nodded. Bjorn looked ready to spring into action at any moment. Halfdan looked from one face to another among his companions. 'Gunnhild is being held in the left room. Hrafn is there, and she is powerful. She lives in the other side. I know not how many people she has, but there are certainly two shield-maidens as they now stand guard at her door. She cannot have seen me, I think, yet she knows I am here. And she knows a fight is coming. I saw her paint her face for war. But I am not so sure she knows about *all* of us. Just me. This gives us our only advantage.'

'It does?'

'It does. I will take the most impressive, biggest, noisiest warriors among us and go to challenge Hrafn and her people.'

'She will kill you,' Lief said in a flat voice.

'I don't intend to fight her,' Halfdan said. 'Not without Gunnhild by my side, anyway. No, I am the distraction. She knows I am here, and she will not believe I am alone. Therefore, I and our loudest warriors will draw her out, away from the house. While we keep her busy, our fastest and sneakiest will steal into her house and free Gunnhild. We can face her in battle later, when we have Gunnhild back. Right now, the important thing is to rescue her.'

Again, the others nodded their agreement in this, though he could see trouble brewing in Bjorn's expression. He looked up into those pink eyes. 'What?'

'I will rescue Gunnhild.'

218

Halfdan took a sharp breath. 'Bjorn, I do not mean to insult you in any way. You are the bravest, most fearsome warrior I have ever laid eyes upon, and I would walk into an inferno for you, but use your wits. You are huge, and not particularly quiet. Some men were born to sneak, Bjorn, but you are not one of them. Your place is with me, drawing their warriors out.'

'No. I will save Gunnhild. With others or alone if I have to.'

Halfdan pursed his lips, running every argument he had through his mind, and there were plenty. He had a score of reasons why Bjorn should not do this, and not one good reason why he should. Yet one look at the big man's face, and Halfdan knew that he could argue until his face went blue, but he would not change Bjorn's mind. He sighed.

'Very well. But let's work this out first.'

Chapter 15

The past. Kaupang, Nordvegr.

'I don't understand. What can I possibly learn doing this? Everyone knows how to chop wood.'

The völva, leaning on her staff and observing him from outside her hut, smiled enigmatically.

'What did I say you needed to learn, Bjorn-lacks-a-name?'

Bjorn sighed. He was getting rather tired of that joke. 'Direction,' he replied.

'Quite.'

'So what direction am I learning chopping logs?'

Her smile twisted slightly. 'What have you done since *Lørdag*?'

He paused, leaving the axe wedged in the stump, rubbing his neck, where the dirt was already starting to build, three mornings from bath day. 'Chopped logs,' he grumbled.

'And?'

'Broke rocks. Pulled up reeds. Dug holes.'

'And you cannot fathom why this is important?'

'Because you're an old woman, and I'm big.'

She shook her head. 'Because to lead the life you wish, you must learn to have a purpose in everything you do. You chop logs, and we have a warm winter. You break rocks and we can build a shed or a pen. You gather reeds and we can thatch roofs. You dig holes, and we can—'

'Have water? Wells? Channels from the river?'

The woman swirled her staff and smacked Bjorn hard on the arm. He marvelled at how fast she could be sometimes, and he fought down the anger at the blow, for it had been meant as a friendly thing, and the grin she wore confirmed that. 'No, Bjorn, you fool. The pits are for the booze. Winter is upon us, and no one should face the ice days without a warm drink in the belly.'

'So, the pits?'

'I will show you, Bjorn, in good time.'

The month that followed held more of the same, though as Bjorn worked the tasks the old völva set him daily, he began to think on them, and on how they could benefit the two of them. Oddly, now that he looked with fresh eyes on such things, he realised that everything the woman had him do, right down to braiding her hair, had a purpose. It was odd, after so long without any purpose to anything he did, but it was also oddly welcome.

She allowed him time to train, too, over the coldest months, to swing his axe at a stake or tree painted with the form of an enemy, to keep his hand in, and she even had odd things to contribute. She may be a woman, but she had lived long and learned a trick or two that Bjorn adopted with relish.

His favourite, though, was the booze. He had mourned beer, for it was many miles to anywhere he could buy such things, and for all his hard work here, he still earned no actual money. But the woman had told him there was more to life – more even to *drink* – than beer. The first day, he had frowned as they lined the small open pit he had dug with cold stone. Then, back in the hut, they had filled a large bowl with apples from the hut's stores, fruit that had been sitting for two months already and was past edible, and he had wondered why they did not simply throw them out. They pounded the apples with a pestle until there was a mulch, added a paste from one of her jars, and then put it through a press the woman kept. The juice that resulted he had sniffed and then turned his nose up at, but it turned out they were far from done. He knew something of fermenting fruit, but the sort of cider formed from rotten apples was not to his taste, yet his frowns only deepened as the bitter-sweet goo was tipped into that cold stone pit behind the hut.

They left it alone for three days, and on the fourth morning, as the first really cold snap filled the world with white and the water butt froze over, she took him to the pit. There, the goo had frozen, a thick white plug forming over the contents. The völva had him crack the ice and lift it from the pit, and he was astounded to find the ice he removed perfectly clear, the brown-green goo remaining beneath it, perhaps shrunk a little in quantity.

The process was repeated for almost a month, and finally, one morning, the old woman gave him a jar and a ladle. Having removed the layer of ice, he scooped the meagre remains of the fruit juice from the bottom into the jar. Back in the hut, the völva strained it to a clear brown liquid, and then tipped some into two small cups, handing one to Bjorn.

He sipped.

His world changed. What the old woman had created by removing all the water each visit was a drink that Bjorn felt burning down every tiny fragment of his gullet, and then sat in his belly, a warm glow, leaving an aftertaste of fiery apple throughout.

The next month they filled three pits with different fruit, and when they celebrated their work a month later, Bjorn experienced the complete loss of an evening's memory for the first time in his life.

The winter passed with good humour and ease. They had sufficient firewood, fiery drinks, stockpiled food, a solid house with a good roof, and Bjorn realised that he was still learning, all the time. The völva told stories that were far beyond credible, yet it mattered not that he did not believe them, for they were entertaining enough to fill the cold evenings. Bjorn was learning. He was gaining a sense of purpose.

One night, he first witnessed a völva walking with the goddess, and was filled with awe as the old woman sang her ancient song and searched for knowledge. When she had finished, and all was silent, she looked at him with narrowed eyes.

'What did you see?'

She shook her head. 'That is not for you, nor for now.' She put away the small pouch of powder she had rubbed upon her lips at the beginning of her rite, and he pointed to it. 'That is your magic powder?'

She nodded.

'Will I ever try it?'

She gave him an even odder look. Finally, folding her arms, she told him of the history of her kind. Of how the one-eyed god had the power, but he could not give it to men, so he gave the sight to women, through which they found their connection with Freyja. But she also told him of how the Allfather had given the same secret to men to use another way, for the same powder that brought women to the goddess brought men to Odin, in the form of the bear shirts – the Berserkir.

He slept unsettled that night.

It was as the world was beginning to warm, the white land slowly receding to reveal the green, when everything changed. One night, the völva sat in her chair and raised a hand, gesturing to Bjorn, who was busy eating the last of the broth with fresh-baked bread.

'What is there left to learn, Bjorn-lacks-a-name?'

The big albino paused, then dipped the bread and chewed thoughtfully. Finally, he shrugged. 'I do not know.'

'Why?'

His brow folded as he pondered this. How could he know that, too? 'Because if I knew what there was to learn, I would already know it, and so would not need to learn it…' He paused, frowned, and scratched his pate. 'That's stupid. That makes my head hurt.'

The old woman cackled. 'Self-realisation is an important part of the path for every man or woman, Bjorn. You have much still to learn, of course. All people should never stop learning. I am as old as the mountains, yet every day I question something. You are never done learning, and that is an important thing to learn.'

Her smile at that made his head hurt a little more. He rolled his eyes. 'So what will be next? Archery? The carving of runes?'

'That, Bjorn, will be your choice. What I am trying to tell you is that you have learned what you needed to learn when you arrived. When I found you out there, you were broken. A cracked jar that could not hold water. Now you are mended. You can hold whatever you wish. And you know how to do it. How to get what you need.'

Bjorn had a horrible feeling he was being dismissed. 'But I still do not know what to do.'

'That will come. You will be tested, Bjorn, and you will gain the name you lack. You will know it when it comes. And when you pass that test in the sight of the Allfather, you will be ready.'

'But ready for what?' Was she really going to throw him out?

'Ready for where the path leads. The Norns have woven it ready, and the coming days will guide you to that path. You may not even realise you are on it for a while. But remember this, Bjorn: while the Norns may be tricky, the threads they weave cannot be avoided. Yours is a great thread, Bjorn, that joins a glorious pattern. I will miss you.'

'I am going nowhere.'

She did not reply to that, which unnerved him, and he spent the rest of that evening working into the conversation ways of pointing out that even if she was done with him, *he* was not done with *her*.

But the Norns' weavings can be neither evaded nor undone.

The next morning was chilly, still, confirming that while winter may be passing, it had a few iced barbs to throw yet.

Bjorn dropped the last grayling into the bucket, tipped out a little of the water to compensate, and then lifted it and began the mile-long walk back through the scattered ruins of Kaupang to the völva's abode. He found himself whistling as he walked, which took him by surprise. He was not a natural whistler, and that realisation brought with it another: that he was actually happy. He'd never been happy, to his recollection. Although in truth, that happiness was still overshadowed with a worry that the old woman was ready to evict him.

He knew something was wrong before he saw it. The sound of whooping voices and painful cries echoed out across the green-white world. Male whooping. Female pain.

The bucket hit the ground and rolled, fish flopping free to die in the open as Bjorn broke into a run. He reached to his belt, but there was nothing there, for he had left his axe in the hut. He'd only been catching grayling, after all. He rounded the corner of a ruined building at full speed, a feral growl accompanying his pounding feet. Since the days of the pit at Skara, Bjorn had never been afraid. Oh, perhaps there had been some gnawing worry in those days of wandering, and some real actual panic last night at the thought of leaving, but if it came to a *fight*, fear was unknown. Bjorn had faced everything the world could throw at him and had torn his way through it all. No man was strong enough to stand against him, and larger numbers merely meant a fight would take longer.

But even Bjorn, somewhere in his subconscious, registered that there were just too many here to beat.

A priest in his nailed god robes stood on the bench of a wagon, snarling his hatred, surrounded by well-armed king's men from Ánslo. More men bristling with weapons and gleaming with iron filled the area around the hut, and a small group were clustered around something Bjorn could not see, but had no doubt about the identity of. He did not stop running. There could be all the men and axes in the world, but they would not get in his way. A column of smoke arose from that place, which boded ill, and the men of Ánslo cried out in surprise as the albino giant barged them aside, carving a path through the gathering by dint of his sheer size.

They began to claw at him, to try and stop him, but with little luck. Bjorn burst through the ranks of whooping soldiers to see Christian morals at work. The old völva lay on the stone table in the garden. The table had been used for meals on warm days, for gardening, for all sorts of tasks, and now… for torture. The slab that formed the table top was around a palm-width thick, and the soldiers had lit a fire beneath it, likely several hours ago from the look of it. The völva had been stripped naked and tied to the top, and had lain there, skin pressed against stone, as the table had gradually warmed with the heat until the point at which it had become blistering agony.

Looking back on the scene at later times, Bjorn realised that the woman had been doomed long before he returned. She was just clinging to the last vestiges of life, perhaps long enough to see him one more time.

Bjorn tried to run to her, but there were just too many hands grabbing him, pulling him back and down, keeping him away from her as she slowly baked to death.

'Let her go,' he bellowed in fury, struggling to free himself of many gripping fists.

'She is free to go,' the priest said in airy tones, 'in one more hour. One hour for each apostle she denies. If she survives the ordeal, the Lord has given us his will that she be free. If she perishes, then we know she is not saveable, and the Lord cares not for her.'

Bjorn opened his mouth to argue, still pulling against those hands, but things began to smash into his head, and by the sixth blow, black peace was claiming his thoughts.

—

He awoke at twilight.

The fire was still burning, now just embers. The men had gone. Given the state of Bjorn's body, they had probably left him for dead. Ignoring the immense pain it brought, Bjorn struggled to his feet and staggered to the table. What was left of the völva was horrible to behold. He accidentally rested his palms on the table as he examined her, and they began to sizzle almost immediately, forcing him to pull away.

He watched her. All night, he watched her.

He had failed her.

In some ways, he realised that she had known it was coming. That was what last night had all been about. She had known, and therefore she must have been ready, unafraid. But if she had told him last night what was coming, he could have saved her. They could have gone from this place.

All night, he watched her.

In the morning, he managed to peel most of her from the slab. It took three days to bury her, for he would not bequeath her anything other than the great mound of a völva, and it took much work. In the chamber he placed her staff and all the goods he could find in the house that she might want. It was as he was searching the house that he found his own pack, already filled with goods. She had prepared him for a journey even as she prepared her own.

He said farewell to her that morning and walked away. Perhaps he was on a path. Perhaps not. But one thing he knew: he would make those men pay for what they did.

Late February 1044. Hrafn Sætr, Swaledale.

Bjorn lay on the wet grass, the others stretching off to his left, all prone, all watching, just like him. The others, led by Halfdan, were visible from this lofty viewpoint above the house, marching up the tiny stream bed toward Hrafn's home, seventeen of them in open ground, approaching as though they feared nothing. Bjorn knew differently. Despite his desperation to go after Gunnhild, even he feared this Hrafn, so what might lesser men feel?

The Wolves stopped at the lip of the depression that held house and spring, ready, armed. They had looked better, Bjorn considered, for they were tired and had lost most of their armour, yet the mettle of the men was of far more import than the metal they wore. The albino was content that there were no better people on this whole island to do what they were doing than the Wolves of Odin at this very moment. Halfdan stopped and walked out ahead.

'Face me, Hrafn, völva of Swaledale, chosen of Gunnar.'

Even Bjorn, never the sharpest of men, caught that. 'Chosen of Gunnar' clearly set her one peg below the local jarl. A provocation, quite simply.

There was a long silence. Bjorn could not see the two shield-maidens by the door from here, behind the house as he was, but they did not emerge into clear sight, presumably remaining where they were. Finally, Halfdan tried again. 'You have taken our friend. Return her and we will go in peace. Fail, and we shall leave this place a stinking pit of carcasses and ruin.'

Bjorn blinked as Thurstan, standing beside Halfdan, suddenly dropped to the ground. He'd seen no missile loosed, no weapon in flight. One moment Thurstan was standing proud, the next moment he was lying in the grass, unmoving. Seiðr? Just how powerful *was* this woman? He frowned. Thurstan was a Christian, but he was also one of the Wolves, and had proved himself more than once. Thurstan added himself to the list to be avenged.

'Come on,' Bjorn said, and rose, with the difficulty of using only one hand, to descend the slope.

'We haven't seen the völva yet,' Lief hissed.

'But Thurstan is down, so it is her who is dealing with them. Now is our time.'

The others began to move behind him. Though they should have a good approach from behind the house, unseen, it would only take one mistake for the völva or her people to discover their plan. Now that the enemy were concentrating on Halfdan, it was a matter of timing. They had only as long as the jarl could keep Hrafn busy. Bjorn had been late to save a völva once in his life, he would not make the same mistake again.

He slid and skittered down the slope, the ferns and mossy grass damp and treacherous, but momentum did much of the work. The aches and pains of his recent struggles bloomed with the activity, but Bjorn had long since learned to ignore pain when there was something more important to concentrate on. Behind him came Lief and Anna, Cassandra, and one of the Apulians, each sliding down the slope, leaping here and there to keep their feet, each with a weapon in hand.

When he reached the flat behind the house, Bjorn stopped, waiting for the others to join him. In the momentary stillness, he listened. He could hear distant shouting and clanging. With luck, the others had drawn Hrafn and her people from the house. Taking a deep breath, aware that he was far from the subtlest of people, Bjorn jogged over to the rear wall of the building, his run still a lopsided lope. His leg had largely recovered now, but it still strained when he ran. There were no windows here, and he edged along to the small shed built up against the rear of the main building. There was a doorway, without a door, and he peered inside, ready for trouble. The room was but five feet across and in pitch darkness, but sound alone told him what it was. The burble and stammer of water bubbling up from beneath the ground and forming a pool said this was the spring, the source of the stream. Satisfied that there was little of interest here, Bjorn moved along the house toward the corner.

'Let me,' Lief tried, but Bjorn thrust out his good arm to hold the Rus back. Yes, Lief might be sneakier, but no one was getting between Bjorn and the task at hand. Without waiting, he reached the corner and peered around it to the side of the building. No sign of life. He was so close he could almost feel the presence of Gunnhild in the room on the other side of this wall. In moments, he had moved along that wall to the next corner. Bracing, he peered around it.

The front of the house was deserted. Indeed, he could see no movement. The sounds of a brawl echoed back up the slope from further down the stream, but it seemed as though Halfdan's plan had worked. He had drawn the völva and her people from the house.

Wasting no further time, Bjorn dashed along the wall and dipped into the first doorway, only pausing there to let his eyes adjust. That tiny delay was almost the end of him. Instinct alone made him duck as the weapon swung out across the doorway at head height. He spun, almost falling as his leg gave, coming up in front of the assailant who had been to one side of the door, only to realise that he might actually be in trouble.

His opponent let out a low growl, snout wrinkling to show huge fangs as it pulled back its massive, clawed paw. Bjorn blinked. He'd no idea they had bears in Angle land. Oh, in the *real* North, yes, and perhaps even in Rus lands, but these pampered places in the south and west had seemed to be devoid of such wild creatures. Not so, apparently.

Before the bear could lunge again, Bjorn acted. The one thing a man should not do when faced with an enraged bear was allow it to go for the head. He threw himself at the creature, one good arm going around it in a semi-bear hug, the other arm in sharp pain at the collision as it was knocked against the shoulder to which it was bound. Wrapped in a lovers' embrace with the creature, he made sure to tuck his head in and down so that it was beneath the beast's jaw. A big iron collar around its neck was attached by a chain to the wall, though it would do him little good, for even chained, the creature could reach almost anywhere in the room. Already, he could feel it trying hard to get its mouth around his face, the bear's natural attack, preventing the enemy from biting in return.

Behind him, Lief shuffled into the room and cried out in alarm. 'In God's name!'

Bjorn could picture the others backing away, or edging past, but he had his own problem. On a good day, Bjorn would give little for the bear's chance of success, but he was down to one arm, which made the prospect of victory considerably less likely.

He was in trouble. He could ignore the injuries only so much, and a bear was a fearsome opponent. The moment the animal realised that all it needed to do was to enfold Bjorn in a hug and crush him, that was precisely what it would do. He was too close to draw a weapon and use it, and if he tried to back off, he would open up his head as a target. Right now, the creature couldn't bite his face, lodged as he was beneath its chin.

This situation was not going to last for long.

No one was coming to his aid. Of course, that was largely his fault. Over the years of sailing with the Wolves, he had made it clear that no one was to interfere when he was fighting. In retrospect, he should probably have made some caveat or exception about bears. And it wasn't as if he needed this heroic kill as he had with Arkil. He had already killed one bear in his time, after all.

His eyes rolled wildly while he made sure not to move his head and imperil himself. His gaze fell upon stone. The walls were of stone blocks, not cemented together as the southerners did, but piled and wedged with ingenuity using only pressure and gravity to create the wall. As such, a few of the stone blocks jutted out a little.

He stopped hugging the creature with his good arm, and that hand snaked out, up the wall, to the most protruding of the stones, around half the size of his forearm. His fingers wrapped around the stone, and he tugged. Nothing happened. The stone was wedged hard, and he did not have sufficient position to work it out. The bear was changing its tactics, now, too, trying to pull back out of his embrace, and if it succeeded, it could easily gain the upper hand. Another tug and he felt the stone loosen a little. The wall gave a worrying groan, and Bjorn saw a large cloud of grey dust billow out into the room, suggesting the disturbing possibility that removing the stone might collapse the wall. Still, it was not as though he had a great deal of choice right now.

He pulled again.

The stone came free, the walls shuddering and scattering dust, with a creak. With a roar, Bjorn brought the block down on the back of the bear's head. It was not easy at this angle, and the blow was not hard. Indeed, it seemed simply to anger the bear, who roared and shoved him away.

Bjorn had one heartbeat to act before the animal was on him and his head was gripped between powerful jaws. He swung the rock with all his might, slamming it into the side of the bear's head. The animal let out a strange, unearthly scream and lurched back. Bjorn, stunned, stood in the doorway, watching the bear as it retreated, howling, to the rear wall, where it stood, shaking its head, in a great deal of pain.

The big man staggered, exhausted and hurting, as his opponent lurked back in the shadows, neither of them possessing of a great urge to recommence their dance.

'Shit, Bjorn,' Lief breathed, suddenly next to him, looking at the monster, hand on the hilt of the sax at his belt, 'I've never seen anything like it.'

'Bears.' It was all the albino could say, his voice a little shaky. The pain was flaring now, and in the strange lee of battle, it flooded his mind before he could push it away.

'I'd always assumed your story about the bear and your scars was a tall tale,' Lief breathed. 'It wasn't, though, was it?'

'It's how I got my name. This one is a little smaller, though,' he added, the need to enlarge his own achievements getting the better of him.

'I think you need to put the rock back before the house falls down.'

Bjorn glanced over at the wall. There was a definite sag to the stonework. He shrugged. 'It'll last 'til we leave.'

'Finish the bear,' the Apulian hissed.

Bjorn shook his head, eyeing the injured beast. 'It's not his fault he was chained up by a völva. I would let it loose, but I don't think going near it now is a good idea.'

For the first time, Bjorn turned and took the room in. The bear had somewhat interrupted his reconnaissance when they'd arrived. The room was perhaps twenty feet across. The bear occupied a niche not far from the door. The rest of the room was open, with tables around the edges. On those surfaces he could see bottles, jars, bags, racks, rune-carved stones – all the accoutrements of a völva – but also knives, cleavers, hooks: the tools of either a butcher or a torturer.

And Gunnhild.

Even as Bjorn had struggled with the bear, Lief watching in shock, Cassandra and Anna had hurried over to the völva. She had been hanging upside down at the far side of the room, ankles roped together, dangling from a roof beam. Similarly, her wrists were bound where they dangled almost to the floor. She was barely conscious, making groaning noises, yet incapable of true speech. Bjorn's overwhelming joy at finding her alive was tempered by his realisation a moment later that both her wrists were bound tight with wrappings soaked through with blood. Her skin was paler than usual, not much healthier than Bjorn's own. She had been bled. More than once, too. Almost dry. In fact, while Bjorn might not be an expert in such matters, he was willing to bet she was just one or two more bleedings away from death.

Anna and Cassandra had untied the rope and were trying to lower Gunnhild slowly to the ground, while the other two hurried to help her up. Bjorn stomped past them all, grasping Gunnhild in his one working arm, then throwing her over his shoulder with a grunt of discomfort.

'Work as we run,' he barked at the others. He had to duck considerably to leave the room. He could still see no sign of the others, nor of Hrafn and her people. He glanced momentarily at the woman over his shoulder. Though she could do little more than grunt, there was something odd, something missing, out of place. He paused, looking this way and that, knowing that Hrafn and her people could be back at any moment.

'Bjorn, *come on*,' Lief hissed, pointing at the slope.

Still he paused. It was not right. He cast his mind back to Gunnhild as he had last seen her, and somehow all he could see was that old woman at Kaupang, raising her cup of fruit liquor. What made them völvas?

He turned, suddenly, finger jabbing at Lief. 'Her staff. Find her staff.'

'In there? With the bear?'

'The bear's hurt. It won't attack you… yet.'

He stood, tense, shivering body over his shoulder, as Lief vanished back inside, looking rather worried. There was a wait that lasted an eternity in which Bjorn half expected Hrafn to return at any moment, and then finally the Rus emerged, gripping Gunnhild's staff.

That was it.

Done.

Task complete, Bjorn turned to the slope and began to stagger up it with difficulty. As he did so, Cassandra and Anna followed him close, hands working, busy untying the bonds at Gunnhild's wrists and ankles, and by the time they were halfway up the slope, the völva was free, the rope falling away in their wake. After what felt like hours, they reached the crest of the hill and paused to look back briefly. There was still no other sign of life at the house, and Bjorn nodded to himself and turned with the others, heading away down the other side of the hill, following a long, circuitous route that would bring them back to their meeting place.

They were to rejoin the others at the house of the madman at the entrance to the valley, the nearest landmark. Bjorn ran, pulse racing, the others alongside him.

There was trouble lying ahead yet, but at least when they met it, they would have Gunnhild.

Chapter 16

Halfdan watched as the two shield-maidens in front of the house became four, and four became six, each pair emerging from the doorway armed for battle. He swallowed. There was something that sat badly in him at the thought of killing women, especially brave and powerful women, shield-maidens of old. And, of course, there was the nervousness. Just as he feared what Hrafn was capable of, these warrior women of hers were also an unknown quantity, and potentially powerful themselves.

Then there was the question of the odds. Since Bjorn had gone with four of the Wolves to rescue Gunnhild – he could just see the big man on the crest of the hill above the house – Halfdan had been left with the other eighteen, but three of those men were walking wounded, still nursing injuries from the dyke fights, and another had a hand out of commission after the lunatic with the knife. That put their effective fighting strength down to fifteen. Normally he would not blink at that number taking on six spear-bearing warriors and their leader, but when that leader was a völva and those six were shield-maidens, it became less certain.

Hrafn, after all, was clearly content that she was perfectly safe.

All the Wolves needed to do was draw them out and away from the house. This was not intended to be a proper fight, but a decoy.

The six shield-maidens watched them impassively from the front of the building now. Silent. Eerie. Still no sign of Hrafn herself. Two other tiny figures joined Bjorn on the ridge above the house, watching, waiting. Halfdan could quite imagine Bjorn twitching with the need to leap into action. If they didn't achieve anything down here soon, Bjorn might just take matters into his own hands.

He took a deep breath and bellowed up to the house. 'Face me, Hrafn, völva of Swaledale, chosen of Gunnar.'

There was a long silence; still no activity. Halfdan thought he saw faint movement in the darkness of one of the windows of the house, but he could not be sure. He waited, but he knew Bjorn would move soon. He took another breath, tense.

'You have taken our friend. Return her and we will go in peace. Fail, and we shall leave this place a stinking pit of carcasses and ruin.'

This time, the silence felt loaded with danger. Was that the völva's anger settling across the land? Halfdan shivered. He certainly had no intention of facing this Hrafn for real without Gunnhild by his side.

'I...' Thurstan began, just to his right, and then frowned.

'What is it?' Halfdan murmured sidelong through tight lips.

'I...' the man said once again, and then suddenly dropped like a rock, hitting the turf with a damp thud. As he landed, gravity took him and rolled him onto his back. His chest was blossoming with soaking red from a wound that Halfdan could not even see. He blinked, as the Apulian died with a single sigh right next to him. He'd never even seen the attack. If there had *been* one, he reminded himself, given that this was the work of a völva.

Then she appeared. Hrafn, the Raven, all grey and black and silver, impressive and frightening in equal amounts, emerging from the door with staff in one hand and sax in the other.

'Fools,' she said, loud enough to be heard, but only just. 'Fools or madmen. Which are you, jarl of nowhere?'

Halfdan shivered. His eyes rose past her. There were no longer figures atop the slope. Bjorn had begun to move. Damn the man, could he not wait? Halfdan fretted. He needed to get the enemy moving, away from the house. Away from Gunnhild.

'Arkil Bear-shoulders is dead,' he called up. 'The valley's defences have fallen, and the berserkr is no more. Even Gunnar now hides in his hut, for his wyrd approaches. You do not have to be part of their fate. Give us Gunnhild and I will consider letting you live.'

'Bring me the blond jarl,' she said to her maidens. 'The others are unimportant.'

The shield-maidens began to move now, lithe and fast. Halfdan, along with the others at his side and back, watched them carefully, sizing them up. They jogged easily, unperturbed by their armament, unfazed by the battle awaiting them. They were truly warriors.

Instinct made him look back, past them, and he cursed himself for his gullibility. He had naturally focused on the maidens – they *all* had – and when he looked back, Hrafn was gone. Where? Back into her house? If so, she could be a lot of trouble for Bjorn.

The maidens were running now. Halfdan turned to the others. 'Stand fast. They are only six. We are eighteen.' *Four of those injured, all of them scared, one dead, so now seventeen...* the jarl added silently to himself.

The shield-maidens were fast, reaching the top of the slope before the house swiftly, and Halfdan braced, felt the others doing the same.

The first to crest the rise halted at the slope for two breaths mid-run, using her momentum to add weight as she brought her spear overarm in a powerful, practised throw.

Off to Halfdan's left, he caught the result in his peripheral vision, Ernaldus taking the spear in the belly, hurled back from their ragged line to fall in the wet grass with a cry of horror and pain. The man had travelled with them from Apulia and become a Wolf of Odin in the lands of William the Bastard. Now he was no more, just another corpse in their wake on the hillsides of northern Angle land.

Halfdan swallowed as the others crested the hill. Battle had not yet been joined and he had already lost two men. How long did he dare hold this line? But if he did not, what of Bjorn and the others?

'Fuck this,' someone shouted off to his left, a great deal of feeling in his voice.

'*Valkyrjur*,' Ketil hissed. 'Halfdan, we *cannot* fight Odin's maidens.'

'These are *Hrafn*'s maidens, *not* the Allfather's,' he called back, though he was having similar doubts in the silence of his own heart. More so, as the women came into closer view, and he could see that each bore a rune of power on their forehead. These were more than just warriors.

More spears came. Ulfr cursed as he just managed to deflect one with his axe, though it carved a line across his shoulder in passing. Two spears missed their targets by a hair's breadth, one taking a piece out of a man's leg. Along the slope, the last of the six spears took Sveinn in the thigh, knocking him back, out of the line. If he died, Sveinn would be happy to have fallen in combat, but would curse to the end of days that his last regarded words had been 'fuck this'.

Three men gone already.

Halfdan fought with himself, but the decision was made for him a moment later. Two of the more recent Apulian recruits turned and bolted. In truth, he could hardly blame them. It was easy to call it their weakness, as children of the White Christ, while the older Wolves were true children of ash and elm. But their flight broke the dam. As the shield-maidens came on, now drawing swords for the close, others were running, too. Before it became a rout, Halfdan turned and bellowed 'retreat'.

At least even those who were sporting injuries from the dykes could still run, and while the shield-maidens might be fresher and more energetic, few things give a man an extra turn of speed than running for his life. The Wolves not only stayed ahead of the six shield-maidens, but were gaining distance as they ran back down the valley. Not so Sveinn, of course, whose leg was done for, and who merely crawled away from impending death. Báulfr, who had taken a glancing wound in his thigh, was managing to keep up, with a little help.

Halfdan felt guilt, and even shame, hitting him from all sides as they ran. His decoy had likely failed, since Hrafn had apparently not followed them. He had lost three men already without a fight. They were running from battle like cowards. And Bjorn and the others could be walking straight into disaster now. More guilt came at the gurgling scream behind them, as one of the women finished the wounded Sveinn, whose leg injury had prevented him from running.

He fought to gain control. He was jarl here, master of the Wolves. Yes, they were running, but was that not their plan anyway? To draw the enemy away from the house? Apart from Hrafn herself, it seemed that they had achieved just that. And no man could be blamed for the fear of fighting something unkillable. Even Ketil, who had looked down the fire-tube of Byzantine flame weapons, was not likely to draw steel against the shield-maidens of Odin.

Halfdan needed a plan, though. They could not run forever, and if they reached the house where they were to meet Bjorn and the others, what then? Battle would just come again. He looked around at the others. Fifteen men remained with him, five of them wounded. That left an active shield wall of eleven, and he was not sure how far he could rely on the Christian Apulians now. This would have to be led by the core of the Wolves. The fight was theirs to command. How Halfdan wished Bjorn was with them again.

In addition to the Varangians and Apulians with them, Halfdan had Ulfr, Ketil and Farlof, some of the oldest crewmen among the Wolves. The four of them together should be able to stand strong in almost any fight. As they ran, Halfdan jogged this way and that, gathering each of his three friends.

'When we near the house, let the others take shelter. I will face the shield-maidens. All I need is the three of you to stand at my back. To look unafraid and strong. We need to give the others enough heart to fight. Even not counting the wounded, we are eleven good men, while they are six, but the others need the push to become involved. Wait until I kill the second of them, then shout the others and join the fight. Then we'll be almost three to one.'

The others nodded their understanding though each clearly harboured his doubts, something Halfdan could entirely understand. To give his men heart and get them to join, and win, the fight, he would have to kill two himself, and that would not be easy. He found himself reasoning it through as he ran. The shield-maidens were good warriors, but not all had hit with their spears, so they were not *perfect*. And they were lithe and strong, but the Wolves were all born warriors – the workers Ulfr had recruited were with the ships back in Jorvik – and they too were powerful and quick. What the enemy had over them was fear. Their almost legendary nature, the runes of power they bore and their connection with Hrafn. These were the things that set them apart, and which had made the men flee.

He broke into a cold smile as he ran. He would beat them at their own game. He reached down to one of the leather pouches at his belt, the one that held kohl. Once, as a boy, he had questioned his father why all the men edged their eyelids with the black powder. His father had taken him to the pool below their garden. He had bent Halfdan over and told him to look at himself in the water. Halfdan had done so, and seen only his face. His father had then straightened him and applied the black all around his eyes. Taking him back to the water's edge, he said 'give me your war face, then look again.' Halfdan had done just that, and had almost recoiled at the warlike monster staring back at him from the surface.

Black-rimmed eyes could be impressive, but there was more that could be done with it. After all, had not Hrafn painted her bloody warpaint just now just as a show for him? It was not easy applying such things while running, but Halfdan trusted to Luck. Dipping his finger into the pouch, he began to draw as carefully as he could, given the pounding feet and uneven ground, imagining with some difficulty what the design looked like from the outside.

Finishing, he breathed heavily and wiped his finger on the sword-cleaning rag tucked into his belt. He turned to Ulfr, running beside him.

'Well?'

'Loki?' the shipwright replied. Halfdan nodded. 'Pretty good,' Ulfr commented. 'A little touch up will help.' Again, Halfdan nodded. The man was an artist in many ways; the decorations he had applied to his vessels were true works of art.

Halfdan turned to see how close the shield-maidens were, and slowed a moment. The six women had dropped back. They were still running, but not so much chasing now as following. Maintaining their wind and strength, he presumed, knowing they would need an edge when the fight came. Good. That bought the Wolves a few precious moments.

Finally, he saw the house come into sight. A new idea struck him, and he gestured to the others again. 'Ulfr and Farlof at my shoulders. Ketil? You get into that tree. You know what to do.'

The Icelander nodded and veered off to one side as they neared the house. The others hurried over to the building and prepared, pulling weapons, regaining their breath and gathering close, backs to the walls so that no one could surprise them.

Halfdan stopped short of the hut, with Ulfr and Farlof. The moment they were still, the shipwright went to work, using wet thumb and blackened finger to correct Halfdan's shaky face paint, and to neaten it. It was the work of but moments, and by the time the six women were closing, Halfdan had turned to face them, sword in one hand, sax in the other, Ulfr and Farlof also armed, and at his shoulders in support.

The jarl felt his pulse quicken as he noticed a new shape. A little up the slope, behind the shield-maidens, Hrafn stood, leaning on her staff. Relief and worry fought for precedence.

That she was here made it very likely that Bjorn and the others had a clear run to rescue Gunnhild. That she was here also put every other Wolf in the valley in danger.

His direct challenge seemed to be understood, and the six women came to a halt twenty paces away, shoulder to shoulder, each armed with a long, northern sword, left hand empty.

'Hear me, shield-maidens of Hrafn,' he called. 'I see your markings. I know the tales. You are daughters of Freyja and of Odin Spear-shaker. Well I am Halfdan of Gotland, child of Loki Hveðrungr, trickster and father of monsters. I am stronger, faster, cleverer than the best of you, and I stand ready to prove as much.'

He knew they would be looking at the swirled serpents and webs drawn across his face, sizing him up. Though their expression betrayed no fear, he felt a shift, as though their unshakeable confidence had slipped a little. Good. In this upper dale, Hrafn's hirð would have been unopposed until now, feeling secure in their power. Now they knew that Loki had come, and Loki was *always* an unknown quantity, even among gods.

One of the six turned back to the völva. Whatever her expression asked, Hrafn answered it with a nod. Halfdan watched the maiden as she turned back, for as spokeswoman, surely she was also their leader. And any leader faced with a duelling jarl could only answer their call directly.

She was the tallest of the six, if only just, perhaps half a head taller than Halfdan. She was pale, with reddish hair braided, the braids wrapped around her head and tied behind. Her forehead bore the Uruz rune, granting her strength in battle. He almost gave the call for Ketil already, but held his tongue for now. It would be best to make his own mark first. He settled into the duelling stance, arms by his sides, held slightly out, a weapon in each, feet planted slightly apart. His eyes he let defocus a little. There was nothing further to be gained by studying her in detail. Now he needed to be aware of every nuance of her moves and looks. Focusing, he might miss something. Allowing a general view of her, on the other hand, meant he could see everything, would miss nothing.

She, on the other hand, was still carefully sizing him up. Even as she took two steps toward him, her gaze went repeatedly from his eyes to his sword hand, to his sax hand, and then back. He forced himself not to smile, to stay carefully expressionless. She had tells; she was giving things away. He would not reciprocate. She was focusing on his weapons and his eyes, trying to identify what he would do first.

He paid attention now to his peripheral vision, while remaining carefully defocused, and there, he saw it: a small grey shape in the grass in front of him. A rock. If Loki was with him, it would be loose. If not, it would be half buried, lodged in the earth, and Halfdan would likely die a few moments later, looking a fool. With the trickster god, you could never be sure. Yet Loki had given him what he needed to come this far in life.

Trusting to the cunning and luck of the Trickster, Halfdan took two careful steps toward the advancing shield-maiden. They were only four or five paces apart now, almost close enough to strike. She was still paying attention to his eyes and his weapons, while his gaze had not moved, yet he had come to a halt at the grey shape of the stone.

He stood there, waiting.

The shield-maiden's eyebrow flicked up briefly, uncertain about this Loki-born man who had stopped, calm as a mill pond, and was waiting. He lifted his sax hand very slightly, which drew her gaze. All he did was hold it there. He was weighing it slightly in his hand. It was not specifically designed as a throwing blade, but its balance was good enough that he'd used it as such more than once. He had to be lucky, of course, but then that was what being a child of the Trickster was.

She came at him very suddenly, with impressive speed. Her sword came out as she leapt forward, her other arm ready to try and knock aside any thrown knife, eyes still on his sax arm.

He kicked up the stone at his right toe, and tried not to laugh out loud. Loki was with him, around him, within him.

The stone was loose and of medium size and weight, and his kick was true. As the woman flew at him, the stone whipped out and struck her hard in the kneecap. As her next step came down, the leg that took the weight failed, the knee weakened by the blow.

She almost fell. It took her precious moments to regain her balance and stay upright. She looked up at Halfdan in shock as she recovered.

The sax struck her in the neck, sharp point thudding deep into flesh and gristle. As she gasped, stunned by the unexpectedness of his attack, her empty hand came up to the knife, her sword falling from her grip. Halfdan took two steps forward as she tottered. She managed to pull the sax from her neck, which simply sent torrents of blood flowing free. He reached out and plucked the knife from her grip as her eyes began to glaze, and she toppled backward.

There was a strange pause. The shield-maidens looked at one another in confusion and shock. Two of them recovered quicker than the others, and leapt forward, both going for Halfdan. The jarl's gulp of relief was audible as Ketil's arrow whipped out from the tree and took one of the two in the chest. She fell by the wayside with a cry, as the other met Halfdan. The balance had shifted. Atop the hill, when the women had attacked, surprise and fear had been with them, shattering the resolve of the Wolves. Now it was working entirely the other way.

The warrior woman met the jarl in battle a moment later, but he was no longer in awe. Loki was with him, while Odin and Freyja both seemed to be ignoring his opponent. She swung. He ducked. His counter-blow was caught by her parry, and they struggled on, blow after blow, each either dodged or turned, clangs and bangs and curses their orchestra. But she was getting slower, while Halfdan could only feel his own strength and speed rising, his energy surging as the god threw power into his blows.

It was only a matter of time, the result inevitable. A few moments later, her swing went a little too wide, and she opened up her side with insufficient time to react to the next strike. Halfdan's sword sank into her ribs below the armpit. He felt the jarring grate as it slid across bone into the crucial organs inside. She staggered, and he lifted his foot and kicked her away, pulling his blade free.

'*Odiiiiin*,' bellowed Ulfr, suddenly next to Halfdan and leaping at a startled shield-maiden with his heavy axe. It threatened to raise a smile on Halfdan's face how many of his hirð took up the battle cry of the Allfather's name, including the Christians among them. In moments, even those men who had been quick to flee down the hill were busy piling into the shield-maidens.

Halfdan managed to land a few blows in the melee that followed, though he did not seek glory, letting the others fight this for him. He'd had glory enough with the two women he'd personally killed, and he could feel that post-fight exhaustion closing on him, pumping lead into his limbs as the exhilaration of battle wore off.

By the time it was all over, and the six shield-maidens were dead, Halfdan had begun to breathe calmly once more. A thought struck him, and he looked up.

Hrafn had gone. Shit, but that woman could move silently and suddenly.

He smiled at the others as they cleaned weapons and spoke quietly to one another. Wimarc the Apulian lay unmoving among the fallen, another Wolf gone to the Allfather's hall in this one fight. Four now. But then, Halfdan would be willing to lose as many again if it meant getting Gunnhild back. And the Wolves standing around him, fourteen of them, did not look dismayed at the losses. There is a certain elation, even after such bloodshed, at being one of the survivors, and this was expanded upon by the simple fact that they had been victorious. Despite their losses, the Wolves had faced the chosen warriors of a völva, shield-maidens out of legend, bearing runes of power, and they had won. This was the stuff of tall tales in mead halls, and each man here would proudly tell of his part, leaving out the bit where they had run away in the first place, of course.

In the absence of Gunnhild and of Anna and Cassandra, they gathered in the lee of the hut and tended the wounded as best they could. They stayed on the far side of the hut to the lunatic and his counting-stick, of course. No one wanted to be involved with him again. Ketil had rejoined them from his tree, receiving congratulatory slaps on the back for his well-placed and well-timed arrow.

There were a number of fresh wounds, but nothing that would kill a man, as long as wound-rot did not set in. An hour passed, three of the uninjured men set at a distance on watch, and wounds had been cleaned with stream water and bound as skilfully as possible. The bodies of the six warrior women were lined up by the stream, and Ulfr went about each, putting weapons back in hands so that if Freyja or Odin came to gather the fallen, they could be taken. They may be the enemy, but such women deserved a great afterlife. And, just in case, one of the Christians said a few prayers over them, too.

There was no further sign of the völva.

Halfdan was starting to worry about their friends when they finally returned. He had rarely felt such relief as when the call went up from one of the sentries, and the jarl hurried over to see Bjorn slipping and leaping down the slope from their circuitous route, cursing with every step, the body of Gunnhild over his good shoulder, the others at his back.

Cheers went up from all present, as the great albino leapt the stream without pause, and landed on their side, hurrying over with his precious burden.

'Is she...?' Halfdan began, almost breathless, noting the deathly pallor and limpness of the woman over the big man's shoulder.

'She will live,' Anna pronounced, her tone carrying that self-importance that only one brought up in Byzantium could achieve. 'She has been bled close to death, but not *too* close. Time and sustenance will bring her back to strength.'

'How *much* time?' Halfdan asked quietly. He was horribly aware they were still in very unfriendly territory and not far from extreme danger.

'I do not know. In some people, heavy blood loss can take a month or two to fully recover, though they could be reasonably active in half that time. Some will be only days in recovery. This is Gunnhild. I doubt she will be kept down for long.'

Halfdan nodded. He had no idea how Anna knew such things, beyond the possibility that she had learned as much from Gunnhild in the first place. A few days they could perhaps manage. Any longer than that, and all the achievements they had gained in Swaledale would be lost. Hrafn and Gunnar would rally their people, and the Wolves would face an army.

Lief planted Gunnhild's staff in the ground and laid out a blanket, upon which Bjorn lay the unconscious völva. Halfdan could see now the bindings on her arms where the multiple blood-lettings had happened, and his mind furnished him with that image of Hrafn standing before her hut, applying Gunnhild's blood as warpaint and then drinking the rest. A surge of anger washed through him. This völva of Swaledale had to pay for her actions. He would not leave the dale until the local völva's glassy eyes stared up at the sky, unseeing.

He turned, looking back. Hrafn would be there, at her cottage. She no longer had her shield-maidens. Now, it was just her. Maybe they could do it?

He turned to the others. 'We need to kill the völva. Revenge for what she has done. She has no warriors now.'

'She has a bear,' Lief replied, which made Halfdan blink.

'Yes,' the Rus confirmed, 'an actual bear. Bjorn knocked the bloody thing out. Never seen anything like it. But now she's back up there, she will have the bear to guard her.'

'I'm sure we can put a bear down, too. I want that woman dead. Who's with me?'

'No one,' said a quiet voice, almost a whisper, hollow and reedy.

Halfdan's head snapped round to find Gunnhild awake on her blanket, unmoving, but eyes open now. 'What?'

'You will leave the völva of Swaledale alone, Halfdan Loki-born. Hrafn is *mine* to kill.'

Halfdan blinked. 'You cannot even *stand*, Gunnhild.'

Hurrying over from where they had started to re-apply dressings, Anna and Cassandra were nodding. 'He's right, Gunnhild. You are too weak to face *anyone* right now, let alone *her*.'

'It will take days of rest and food to get you stronger.'

'Tripe,' Gunnhild snapped. 'One day. A meal for the evening. Find calves or sheep. Get me their livers. Do not cook them – feed me them raw – and dandelion leaves if you can find them, too. I am not as weak as you might think, and these foods will give me sufficient strength.'

Halfdan was already shaking his head automatically. The völva looked close to death. In her current state, he could hardly imagine her fighting off a cold, let alone a more powerful Seiðr than her. It was ridiculous. 'Gunnhild...'

She fixed him with a look. 'When you fail to heed my advice, Jarl Halfdan, how does it go for you?'

He faltered. 'But you are weak. Hrafn is so strong.'

'I have my sisters, now. No arrogant little dove in raven colours can face me and win.' Her eyes slid past him, and Halfdan followed her gaze. She was looking at the man who'd had his finger almost severed by the lunatic. 'Watch him,' Gunnhild said quietly. 'Watch him carefully.'

Halfdan nodded, casting one more glance at the wounded man, but when he returned his gaze to Gunnhild, her eyes were closed once more. He turned to Ketil, who was testing his bow string. 'Take a couple of others. Find good meat for tonight. Make sure you don't pierce the liver.'

Chapter 17

The past. Ánslo, Nordvegr.

'I know you,' the soldier said, rising from the bench at the far end of the *skytningr*, the drinking club in Ánslo's secondary market. His right hand still clutched his cup, though the fingers of the left danced close to his sword hilt. He straightened, looking down the length of the hall at the big figure in the doorway. Bjorn took half a dozen steps inside, axe in hand, water pouring from him to the reed-strewn floor, the rain slanting in behind him. The few other locals in here at this time of day took the opportunity to slip wide around him and back out of the door into the downpour, leaving the hall empty, bar the two men.

'Yes, you do,' Bjorn replied.

'I thought you were dead in that haunted town.'

'Maybe I've come back to haunt you. Not for long, though.'

'Oh?'

Bjorn may not be the subtlest of men, but he was strong, and he was surprisingly fast. The man realised what he was doing at the last moment, and tried to dive out of the way as the albino's axe suddenly whirred through the air. He failed to move fast enough, though a combination of factors meant that at least he did not die instantly, something that suited Bjorn perfectly. His axe was not designed for throwing, and he was not particularly good at such a move anyway, but he'd tried, just to prevent the man turning and running for the rear door before Bjorn could get to him. As it was, the axe spun badly, hitting the man butt-end first, and on the shoulder, as he tried to leap away. It was, on the other hand, a hard enough blow to break the shoulder, and the man screamed as he hit the ground between two benches.

By the time the man had recovered his wits enough to start rising, Bjorn was suddenly above him. The big man reached down. The soldier tried to draw his sword with his good remaining arm, but was hampered by the benches to either side. Then, Bjorn had the man's head held in one giant paw, fingers wrapped around the back, and he slammed his face into a bench with a sound of breaking bones and teeth. The man was unconscious from the first blow, but that did not stop Bjorn repeating the process a score more times until there was no longer enough head left to hold, and the man could not be identified even by his nearest and dearest.

Bjorn walked over to the counter, noting the skytningr's owner cowering behind the rear door.

'Sorry for the mess,' he said, washing his hands in the communal bowl there, then retrieving a few of the coins he had saved from the völva's house, and dropping them to the counter.

He turned and left the room.

It took him some time to track down the rest of the soldiers who had killed the old woman. There were many soldiers in Ánslo, and this was a matter of revenge. Bjorn did not particularly want to start a war with the king. Just the men responsible, and the priest who led them. Over the following month, he located and killed every soldier he could find who had been part of that unit sent to Kaupang. He was neither careful nor discriminating. They all died, messily and fast. He picked up a few fresh scars, but nothing to worry about. Bjorn was a true warrior these days, forged in the crucible of combat, afeared of nothing, and the death of the völva had given him a new purpose, something he had lacked since the day he'd bought his freedom over the bodies of Orm Barelegs's grandsons.

Bjorn would never be sure he had killed them *all*, of course. He'd learned plenty of names from the first man he'd found, and killed his way down that list, but there may have been men who escaped being added to the list in the first place. He'd done what he could. With one grand exception. The name at the very top of the list, he'd saved until last.

Finally, he found the priest, visiting a church in the village of Skedsmo, not far to the north-east of the city. The man who had led the trial of the völva would die badly. Bjorn waited until the man was alone, his congregation dispersed, and then crept into the wooden church and thumped the man on the head, heaving him over a shoulder and carrying him away, kit bag on the other arm.

The rain had stopped, and in the silence of the spring countryside, sound could carry well, so Bjorn made sure to lug the priest some miles from the village, into the thick woodland dotted with lakes nearby. By the time he was deep among the trees, the clouds had gathered once more, and rain threatened again, so when he spotted the entrance to a cave formed by a heavy rock fallen across a dip long ago, he dropped the unconscious priest to the ground, and dragged him inside. There, in the dim grey light afforded by the small entrance, he laid the priest face down. In a perfect world he'd slowly bake the man on a stone, just as the priest had done to the völva, although that smacked of nailed god things. Still, had it not been damp and dismal, he might have been tempted. But he had something else in mind. Something old – *very* old.

The tale of Harald Fairhair and his warring sons had been a favourite of Bjorn's father, and he had listened intently as a boy, waiting each time for the violent young prince Long-legs to receive his punishment for burning sixty men to death in a hall. A 'blood eagle' had been performed upon the young man, something that had not been done now for centuries. Well, tonight, Bjorn was going to reinstate the practice.

He worked hard that afternoon. The priest woke with a scream as Bjorn broke his legs first, then both arms. This, of course, was not part of the ritual, but he did not want the man to escape, and this seemed the simplest way of keeping him where he was. For half an hour then, as he worked, the priest continued to scream, an endless noise that cut deep into Bjorn's ears, giving him something of a headache. Still, he laboured on, using the screams as motivation. With his sax, a fine weapon purloined from one of his soldier victims, he drew an eagle in the man's fleshy back. Then he pulled the skin wings aside to reveal the man's inners, and began to work, snapping the ribs away from the spine. He did it slowly, with a long pause between each, so the man could savour every moment of agony. This was revenge, and this was justice. Just as Long-legs had suffered this for burning men alive, so the priest suffered for burning a woman. This was old justice.

He was rather disappointed when the man died after the third rib, but he shrugged and went on anyway. The whole thing was quite experimental. His father had told the tale many times, but had never detailed how quickly it should be done. By the time he'd laid out the lungs in the open and finished, the priest had been dead for some time.

Revenge was complete.

Bjorn was not entirely sure why he was still rather unsatisfied.

He made to leave, but the rain had begun in earnest while he worked, and darkness was beginning to fall, and so he unpacked his kit and began to settle in for the night in this dry space. He wrapped himself in his blankets and was asleep in moments.

He woke in the dark, though he couldn't say why. What he did know was that despite not having eaten much that day, thanks to his work, he needed a shit, and quite badly. It was still pouring outside, and so, despite the fact that he'd have to sleep in the smell the rest of the night, he edged over to the far side of the cave, tripping over the shattered priest and cursing as he went, and then dropped his trousers and answered nature's call. When he had cleaned up with moss and leaves, he padded over to the cave entrance to give his hands a little wash in the rain.

There, he almost died in an instant.

The huge brown bear, whose den he had suborned for his own purposes, returned at a rush, hurrying to get in from the rain, and dived in through the doorway, only to find a big human meeting him at the entrance. The bear had clearly had a bad day himself, for without any preamble, as Bjorn squawked with surprise, eyes wide, the beast slashed out.

Bjorn felt the four great claws rake across his face, feeling his ear tear, astounded that his eyes both seemed to have survived the blow. The four wounds burned instantly with a pain unlike any he had ever felt in a fight, even in the pit at Skara. But the blow had been a reaction by the bear upon seeing Bjorn, and the creature reeled, backing away slightly, weighing up its opponent in that moment. Bjorn knew little about bears, but he recognised the danger and the opportunity. When the beast came again, he would probably die, so he had to take advantage of that moment. He dived back into the cave, rolling across the uneven ground, fingers closing on the haft of the axe he had left untended to one side.

The bear roared. It came barrelling in, making straight for Bjorn, now intent on finishing the interloper who had invaded its cave. Even prepared and armed, Bjorn might have died then, had there been room in the cave for the bear to stand full height. But there was not, and the great beast had to remain on all fours, which made it difficult to use its forepaws in the fight. As such, its great jaws came snapping at Bjorn. He reacted. There were no planned moves, no finesse of combat. He saw the great head coming for him, and he swung the axe as hard as he could.

The bear died in that first blow, for the great iron blade slammed into its head and buried itself deep in the thing's skull and brain. Bjorn still backed away, panting, not trusting that the creature wouldn't come again. He backed to the cave wall and sat there, shaking.

His face burned as his hands had done that day he'd placed them on the fiery stone slab.

An hour passed, and then another. Sleep came then.

He woke to find dawn light shining in through the cave mouth, the rain gone. The golden rays passed across the massive bulk of the dead creature whose home this was. They passed across the mangled corpse of the priest whose tomb this was.

They fell upon Bjorn, who realised something, with a touch of surprise.

He was no longer Bjorn-lacks-a-name.

Late February 1044. Near Hrafn Sætr, Swaledale.

Bjorn sat close to Gunnhild. Halfdan had forbidden the others from disturbing her, with the exception of the other women, of course, for he had said she needed as much rest as possible to recover her strength. He had taken one look at Bjorn, though, and had let him in without a word. Halfdan knew there was something to Bjorn's relationship with the völva that was important. He didn't understand it, for that tale was Bjorn's own private one, but he knew it was there, and he respected it.

This time, Bjorn had not been too late to save her.

This time there would be no costly revenge for her demise. The old völva had led Bjorn Bear-torn on a path of revenge that had almost cost him his life, for all that it gave him both his name and his purpose. Oh, there would *be* revenge this time, of course. Hrafn would pay dearly for what she had done to Gunnhild, but it would not be *Bjorn's* revenge to take. Gunnhild, in her early moments of waking lucidity, had made it perfectly clear that she would deal with this herself, and Bjorn respected her right in this.

Of course, if it looked like she might fail, Bjorn was still well prepared to step in and tear the black-garbed woman limb from limb. But this was not to be Bjorn avenging a dead völva. This was to be a living völva avenging her own wrongs.

'Anna tells me I have you to thank for my staff.'

Bjorn bowed his head.

'I doubt many others would have thought to save it,' she said, smiling. 'Halfdan would have, for he remembers me without the staff, and what it means.'

'It means you are völva,' Bjorn said simply. He remembered reverently collecting the old woman's staff at Kaupang, and laying it beside her in the grave he'd made. She and the staff had been tied together. With her staff, she had been a völva, a figure of great power and wisdom. Without it, she had been an old woman with some good stories.

Gunnhild nodded. 'It is what I am. It is me.'

Bjorn smiled. 'You will kill her.'

'I will.'

'Do it well. She should not die fast or easy.'

That made Gunnhild chuckle lightly, then roll her eyes. 'It is not my way to tear the arm off people and beat them with it, Bjorn Bear-torn.' He simply held her gaze. Finally, she nodded. 'She will die hard.' She pulled herself into a seated position. She still grunted with exertion, and was still a little weak, though much of her colour had returned over the evening and the next day, and she had been up and about half a dozen times, if slowly and shakily.

'Why did she do this?'

Gunnhild frowned, then looked down to her bandaged wrists. 'This?' He nodded. She sighed. 'Do you not know of the tales of the great wyrm Fafnir and his demise at the hand of Sigurd?'

Bjorn shook his head. Dragons had not been a favoured subject of his father.

'When Sigurd slew the beast, Regin drank its blood, and he and Sigurd cooked its heart, and they gained powers beyond the ken of normal men, such that they could understand the birds, and their wit, will and body were sharper. As Regin drank of Fafnir for power, so Hrafn drinks of her victims, should they be of sufficient power themselves to deem it worthwhile. She seeks to gain my power through my blood. I am grateful, Bjorn, that

255

you came before she got as far as my heart. That wound might have taken more healing.'

He laughed at her levity, but still there was an air of seriousness above it all. Hrafn was extremely dangerous already, and even though he might not be the sharpest wit among the Wolves, even Bjorn had noticed that Gunnhild had not denied such a practice might work. If it did, then Hrafn would now have a part of Gunnhild's power alongside her own. He wondered idly if drinking the blood of his enemies might do the same for him, then realised he was drifting while she was still talking.

'...don't suppose you found it?' she asked.

He winced. 'Sorry. I'd stopped listening.'

'Of course.' She rolled her eyes again. 'And no, Bjorn, drinking blood will do nothing for you but give you a bellyache. I said that Hrafn took from me my pouch. You know the one,' she added, meaningfully. 'You found my staff. Did you find my pouch?'

Bjorn silently cursed himself. He'd never thought about that. He'd not looked at the room really, beyond the bear and Gunnhild, and it had been *Lief* who'd found the staff. None of the others had mentioned the pouch, though, and he was sure they would have done if they'd seen it. He shook his head. It was not as if he could go back and look now, either.

The völva sighed. 'I will still kill her, but it would have been easier if I'd had my entire armoury to hand. Without my pouch it will be more difficult, but I will still do it.'

Bjorn felt a small smile creep across his face, and Gunnhild's eyes narrowed as she saw it.

'What have you done, Bjorn Bear-torn?'

He reached down to his belt and unfastened one of the pouches there, a small, simple drawstring bag, and held it out to her. She frowned, then reached out and took hold. Withdrawing it, she pulled open the strings and peered inside. Her brow creased again.

'How?' she asked, looking up at him.

He managed a rather sheepish smile. 'When I gave you the powder back after Arkil, I kept some. Just in case,' he added, holding up his hands in defence at the accusatory look she shot him. She softened immediately, and he tried a warm smile this time.

'Freyja does sometimes use others to change things. I could never have guessed she would use *you*, Bjorn.'

He grinned. He wasn't sure whether that was supposed to be a compliment or a jibe but, it being Gunnhild, he decided he would take it as a compliment anyway. She dropped the small pouch to the ground beside her and relaxed a little. 'This will make the coming fight a little easier. Thank you.'

Before Bjorn could say more, they were interrupted by Anna and Cassandra, who came in with a bowl of some mushy green stuff, sat next to a glistening lamb's liver. Bjorn pondered on what power the völva was trying to gain. As she ate, and the three women talked, he found himself musing on whether lambs were magical. If she was consuming its liver to heal her missing blood, just as Regin had gained power from Fafnir, was a lamb's liver a mystical, powerful thing? If so, that perhaps made lambs magical.

As he drifted off into his internal meanderings, the other two women took the bowl, let Gunnhild wash her hands in the ewer they had also brought, and then left. Gunnhild closed her eyes.

Bjorn's thoughts were stringing along now. Blood somehow remade itself over time. This he knew, for over his lifetime he had lost a body's worth of blood a number of times, yet had always recovered. He wondered if there was some way of taking another person's blood and adding it to your own to speed up the process. Some wounds leaked blood, while others pumped it. The pumping ones led to a quick death. Was it possible that blood could somehow be pumped into the other ones? That if a man half-bled to death, he could take half the blood of another and add it to his own and immediately get back to the fight?

257

It was an intriguing idea, and he leaned forward, dragging himself back to the present, ready to ask Gunnhild her thoughts on the subject, but stopped himself as he realised she had fallen asleep. He smiled and leaned back against the cave wall.

Funny, he thought to himself, how things tended to repeat. Once, long years ago, he was involved with a Seiðr woman, had spent a night in a cave, and had fought a bear. And here he was once again, with Gunnhild, recovering from his struggle with Hrafn's bear, sitting in a cave.

They had come back to the main dale, past that marker that defined Hrafn's lands, figuring it was safer spending time here as Gunnhild recovered. The cave was one of those in the cliffs above the river, which they had passed yesterday while searching for Hrafn's home. The cave was more or less two rooms, formed almost like a figure '8', the outer one larger and housing the Wolves in cramped conditions, while the inner one was given over to Gunnhild for her recovery. Over the recent hours, with an improvement in the weather, the others were tending to stray outside a little, for breathing room, and to keep an eye on the valley and make sure no one came for them.

Everything was so peaceful that Bjorn was drifting off to sleep, sitting in the corner of Gunnhild's cave room. Only the two of them. The outer room was busier, but most were outside. It took moments for him to realise that what he was hearing in his near-slumber, buried beneath the muffled sounds of the Wolves, was footsteps.

He idly opened one eye.

It was not Anna, nor Cassandra, coming in, bearing their next gift. Nor was it Halfdan, checking on his wise woman.

It was a figure Bjorn didn't immediately recognise in the gloom.

His other eye shot open the moment the light from the cave entrance caught the sax blade in the man's hand, and flashed bright.

With a roar, Bjorn was up in a heartbeat, barrelling across the room.

The man turned in shock, clearly not having known that Bjorn was there in the shadows.

He brought round his sax to defend himself, but it was too late. The big man hit him hard, knocking his weapon hand away with his one good arm. The two men hit the wall at the far side of the cave, and the interloper's breath left him explosively with the collision. The sax fell from his hand, and Bjorn's gaze fell to the other arm, wondering if he was armed with more than one weapon. His eyes picked out in the gloom the two fingers bound tight together, and he realised with a start that it was Njal, the man who'd had his hand cut by the knife-wielding lunatic when they were crossing Hrafn's lands. Bjorn had killed the lunatic who'd done that. But Njal was one of the Wolves.

Bjorn stared in shock at the man pinned between him and the cave wall. The man had been with them since the beach near Taranto, five years and half a world ago. What could have made him do this?

But Bjorn was a man of simple logic. Whatever was at work here, and however much this man had been one of them, he had been about to put a knife into Gunnhild, and that was enough to condemn him. Bjorn reached up and grabbed the man's face, fingers and thumb wrapping around his head to each temple, then proceeded to smash it backward repeatedly against the cave wall, each time with a reverberating thump. The second time there was a loud crack, and by the fifth, unmentionable stuff was pouring out, and the man was shaking his death shakes.

Bjorn knew the attacker was dead, but he kept going for a while just in case, before dropping what was left to the floor. He stood for a long moment, looking down at his victim, then turned, slowly. A smattering of horrified faces were gathered in the entranceway between the two cave rooms, and when Halfdan pulled them aside as he pushed his way through, his own face was a picture of shock. As the big man turned the other way, the only person in the room registering no shock was Gunnhild.

'What the fuck is this?' Halfdan began, looking back and forth between Bjorn and the heap of bloody mess on the floor, via the brain stuck to the rock, and the trails of blood running down it. He then looked across to Gunnhild.

'I told you to watch him,' she said quietly.

Recovering himself quickly, Halfdan turned and ushered the gathered spectators away, back into the outer cave. Lief nodded to the jarl and took charge, herding them away and leaving Halfdan, Bjorn and Gunnhild alone in the inner room.

'He came for her,' Bjorn said, 'with a sax.'

Halfdan's eyes were wide. 'It is a blessing of Odin that you were here, my big friend.'

'It is a blessing of *Bjorn*,' corrected the völva, sagging back with a sigh.

'But he was one of us,' Halfdan said, scratching his head. 'He joined us when we landed from Miklagarðr, with Maniakes. He fought Fulk and the gold-hungry Normans with us. He fought with us in the Bastard Duke's lands. Shit, he even fought with me across dykes and forts in this very dale a couple of days ago.'

Gunnhild nodded. 'Do not blame him,' she said. 'He has paid the price for his actions, and more besides.' She turned to Bjorn. 'Give him his chance at *Valhöll*.'

'Really?'

The albino would just as soon kick the carcass into the river and leave him to rot.

'Really,' Gunnhild agreed. 'This was not his mind. Not his decision. He has been a Wolf of Odin among the best of us. Let the Allfather take him if he sees fit.'

Bjorn shrugged, looking unhappy about it, but he did crouch and slip the unused sax back into the man's hand, and close the fingers around the hilt. When he rose, Halfdan was looking at Gunnhild with concern.

'This is Hrafn's doing,' she explained. 'I told you she was powerful. More powerful than I. Remember that I was just a fledgling but a few short years ago when you found me in

Hedeby. I was not trained, not fully völva. This woman is as powerful as the mother in Hedeby was, and probably more so. I fear she is no true woman, in fact. Perhaps she is troll, with her dark Seiðr. I cannot tell you how she made him do this, but logic alone says that she did. Why else would a man wounded in her lands turn on me directly?'

'Perhaps it was some sort of poison on the knife he took to the hand,' mused Halfdan, 'but that would not explain him targeting you specifically.'

'If *I* cannot understand her ways,' Gunnhild said with a raised eyebrow, 'how do *you* expect to do so, my jarl?'

Halfdan nodded at that, but Bjorn was thinking. 'Others have been wounded here,' he said. 'By spears and more. By the shield-maidens. Do we need to watch *them*, too?'

Halfdan blinked. 'Ulfr was wounded by one.'

Gunnhild chewed her lip for a moment. 'I have noticed nothing in Ulfr that worries me, but until Hrafn is no more and her influence scattered to the wind, I would strongly advise that every one of us watches the others carefully.' She looked back and forth between Bjorn and Halfdan, and slowly pulled herself to her feet.

'What are you doing?' Halfdan snapped, reaching out to her.

She brushed him off. 'The time has come. We can delay no longer. I have to face Hrafn.'

Bjorn shook his head. 'You're weak.'

'And you're irritating, but if we have to wait until you're not, I'll be an old woman.'

Bjorn couldn't help but chuckle. 'Like this, you will lose.'

'No, Bjorn. Not with Anna and Cassandra. You and Halfdan keep the others safe. Come with us, in case Hrafn has other warriors, but her death has to be mine.'

'It's getting late in the afternoon,' Halfdan said, concern in his tone. 'We have only a few hours. Perhaps we had better wait until morning, and consider this then?'

Gunnhild fixed them both with a look. 'How many Wolves would you like to see turn on us in the coming hours? This needs to end now.'

Bjorn nodded. When a völva had her mind made up, no one was going to change it.

All he had to do was keep a bear out of the way while she did her work.

Chapter 18

Halfdan was as prepared as he could be.

Hrafn's house still belched smoke from the roof, and dull golden light showed in the right window as they waited for a sign that the challenge had been heard. The Wolves of Odin stood arrayed on the hillside now, awaiting the coming fight... or at least, *most* of them did.

Gunnhild, Anna and Cassandra stood at the fore, the völva in lead position, with her companions at either shoulder. A little further back and to one side stood her jarl, with Lief at one shoulder and Farlof to the other, mirroring their stance, twelve more warriors lined up behind. Eighteen. Three were missing. Would Hrafn notice?

Of course, Gunnhild had argued. She had told him flatly that this was *her* fight, not his. She would brook no interference. Halfdan had agreed, with qualifications. He was not going to let her die today, and so, quite apart from the fifteen of them backing her on the hill, ready to charge Hrafn and take her down should it be required, he had set three extra plans in motion long before they arrived in this place.

The most immediate was Bjorn, who had taken the long and wide approach with Ulfr, coming up around the hill and then down behind the cottage, just as he'd done when they rescued Gunnhild. This time, though, his focus was on removing any defences Hrafn may have: other warriors, other shield-maidens. They would be Bjorn's to deal with, as well as the bear, should it be let loose.

Ulfr had gone with him. Warned of what had happened when Bjorn hit the bear with the rock from the wall, the clever engineer had told Halfdan that buildings of such construction could quite easily collapse in on themselves if the wrong stones were removed. He would study the walls, identifying those stones. Should Hrafn retreat to her house, Ulfr and Bjorn should be able to collapse the building on her head.

But the most direct and simple backup plan Halfdan had in place was Ketil, who stood wreathed in bushes and under-growth just thirty paces away from the open space in front of the house, bow out and ready. The moment Gunnhild was in danger, he had his orders to loose and put Hrafn down.

In short, Halfdan had done all he could.

'Face me, Hrafn of Swaledale,' Gunnhild shouted once more. 'Or do you need your mists to hide in, so that you do not have to face your enemies openly?'

There was another long silence. Halfdan saw the heads of Bjorn and Ulfr poking around the side of the building, going about their own business, unknown to Hrafn. Of Ketil, he could see nothing, which was as it was meant to be. For a time, they all waited, tense, and then finally, just as Gunnhild was cupping hands to mouth to yell once more, there was movement.

Halfdan had never seen a bear in the flesh, though he'd heard plenty of stories. Still, he was quite surprised at the size of the thing. It emerged from the left doorway of the building, ambling on all fours. A moment later, Hrafn appeared from the other side, with three shield-maidens in her wake. The völva barked some unintelligible command, throwing out a pointed finger at Gunnhild and the Wolves on the hillside before them.

The bear suddenly roared and reared, then dropped to all fours once more and began to run.

Halfdan felt his pulse race at the sight, and then even more so as Bjorn emerged from the side of the house, axe in his good hand, running with all his lopsided might. Hrafn's head snapped round to the albino, but she did not move. Instead she watched, impassive for a moment as Bjorn hurtled after the bear. No matter what commands it had been given, the animal sensed the danger at its rear and slowed, turning, to face Bjorn.

Halfdan glanced back across at Hrafn and felt his skin prickle at the realisation that one of the völva's companions had lifted a bow, with arrow nocked, and was tracking Bjorn as he closed on the bear. The woman with the bow tensed, stretched the string tight, counted, edging the tip of the arrow a little further in front, to account for Bjorn's speed, took a deep breath, and…

…disappeared backward into the grass with a cry, bow snapping tight, arrow thudding into the turf a few paces from where she stood. Ketil's own arrow had been true. He had ignored his instructions, which were to remain hidden until he was needed to put down Hrafn, but the man was ever impulsive and hard to control, and Halfdan could hardly blame him. There was little doubt in the jarl's mind that had Ketil not loosed that arrow, Bjorn would have been dead long before he got to the bear.

As it happened, the big white warrior reached his target entirely unaware of the danger he'd briefly been in, and his axe swung, striking the bear hard in the shoulder, causing a massive roar. The creature was so large and powerful that it never even staggered or fell under the blow, but bellowed and lashed out with the other paw, sending Bjorn flying. Before it could get to him, though, the albino was already back on his feet, axe coming around for a second swing.

Halfdan watched, impressed, as Bjorn slowly took the bear down. The big man was slower than usual, suffering from his injuries, yet they did not stop him as they would most men. Even when his bindings came loose and his broken arm hung free, he did not stop. When Bjorn fought, all that existed was victory or death. The big man was hit three times himself, sent flying back each time, but each blow of his own was true, and both he and the bear were bleeding and losing strength with every movement. It was as much a matter of who would succumb first as of fighting skill. When the beast finally collapsed first, shaking, and lay still on the grass, Halfdan smiled to himself. This was another story for Bjorn's arsenal of personal greats. When this was finished, they would spend months hearing ever more embellished tales of both Arkil and the bear.

Still, for now, that was over. Bjorn was done now, for a time, exhausted and injured, and he dropped to the grass beside the dead bear, leaning against its bulk, regaining his breath. Hrafn would be seething, the jarl decided. She had left the house with three women and a bear, and she had lost two of them already.

The völva of Swaledale began to walk toward Gunnhild. She briefly turned and glanced toward the undergrowth where Ketil lurked, perhaps trying to identify his location, but her attention soon returned to Gunnhild.

'You are foolish, child of Hedeby,' the völva said as she approached.

'Perhaps. But I am set upon my course.'

'I was stronger than you even when we first met, but now I am *twice* as strong, and you are *half* as much. You would have done better walking away and saving your hide.'

Gunnhild shrugged in answer.

'It is not your place to save these people,' Hrafn told her.

'You think I am here for someone else? No, Raven, I am here because of what you are and because of what you put me through. You are an affront to the goddess. You walk with one foot on Odin's path, as though the Aesir and Vanir were one. I am here to end you, Hrafn of Swaledale.'

'Then let it be done.' Hrafn eyed the arrayed figures of the Wolves. 'You and I, alone.'

'Agreed,' called Gunnhild.

'You said you could win because you have Anna and Cassandra,' Halfdan hissed from behind her.

'They will yet play their part,' Gunnhild replied quietly. 'Let Hrafn break her own rule, first.'

Halfdan felt his pulse beginning to pound once again. He did not like this.

Across the open space, Hrafn produced a pouch and dipped her hand inside, removing it and using the russet powder within to draw runes and markings on her face. Halfdan recognised the valknut, symbol of Odin and favoured by the berserkr, something he could not imagine Gunnhild favouring. Indeed, in answer, Gunnhild produced a pouch from her own belt and marked herself. Halfdan could not see the designs, as she stood facing away from him, but he was sure there would be no symbol of the Allfather there. Gunnhild was Freyja's daughter. She respected Odin, of course, but she would never trust him, nor devote herself to him the way Hrafn clearly did.

He thought back over the stories Gunnhild had told him over the past few years. The völvas had been given their power by Odin, but had gone their own way, unbeholden to him. Indeed, Odin had cause to consult völvas in time, even to learn of the fate of the gods. The gift he had given them at the dawn of days would be repaid with knowledge at their end. But in between, the völvas were Freyja's creatures, not his.

The two women stepped forward, approaching one another warily, each with staff in hand, each with two women in support, though these four slowed, hanging back, letting the two völvas face one another alone, as per the conditions.

Halfdan was as tense as he had ever felt. He truly had no idea what to expect from this meeting. The two women stopped, finally, six paces apart, and stood straight and still. Something began to pass, unspoken, between them, and Halfdan could feel the Seiðr beginning to build, and to fill the very air around them, a strangely energising thing, giving the air a thick, greasy feel, as though in a warm fog, or waiting for a great storm.

Nothing seemed to happen for the longest time. Halfdan's attention wandered, from the pair to their women, to Bjorn and his dead bear, to the trees where Ketil remained hidden, to the house, where Ulfr would be preparing to collapse walls, and finally back to Gunnhild and Hrafn.

The tension was reaching an unbearable point when suddenly something happened. What caused it, he could not say, but both women cast their staffs down to the ground before them with cries, as though the ash hafts had become painfully hot to hold. Both weapons hit the turf with a thud, though the two women never took their eyes off one another.

'Fuck me,' Farlof barked, pointing.

Halfdan followed his gesture, his gaze dropping from the women's faces to the grass beneath them. He could not see the staffs, but what he *could* see was a single snake, rising up, rearing from the grass. He acknowledged that perhaps he could not see the staffs because of the long grass, but the notion that one had been turned into a serpent was hard to ignore. The thing rose, neck flattening, cobra-like, and suddenly its head seemed to explode, what looked like blood and bile flying to shower Gunnhild's legs. To her credit, the völva did not even twitch at this, never taking her eyes from Hrafn. Halfdan was impressed. If that had happened to him, he'd have been running for the stream by now to wash whatever it was off.

The snake dropped to the grass and disappeared amid the tufts.

Everything fell silent once more. Halfdan found he was holding his breath.

Hrafn took a pace forward. So did Gunnhild. The two women stopped once more, just over an arm's-length apart, eyes locked together. Halfdan could see nothing happening, but he could feel something in the very air, and not just the strain or the ever-present Seiðr. It was so silent and tense that he almost jumped when Hrafn suddenly issued a furious hiss. Gunnhild yelped as though scorched, and wobbled for a moment, before righting herself.

Both women began to speak, then, though what they said was unintelligible. As though speaking in some ancient, forgotten tongue, the two women began to chant, each murmuring different phrases, their voices dropping so that they were little more than whispers. They took another step, together, now so close they could almost embrace.

The chanting became louder now, more intense, almost snarling, as though every ancient phrase in that long-gone language were a curse levelled at the opponent. Halfdan marvelled. Both of the völvas were starting to sweat with effort, although the strain was showing far more visibly on Gunnhild than on Hrafn. There was a rigidity to the format of the struggle that reminded Halfdan of Holmgång. *Let Hrafn break her rule first*, Gunnhild had said, but even then, that was only a trigger to allow her two companions into the duel, not the rest of the Wolves.

Halfdan watched, the tension in him mounting moment by moment. The two women seemed to be locked in an edgy and dangerous struggle, yet without a single blow being struck as far as he could see. They had even stopped chanting, now. Yet *something* was happening, for Hrafn issued periodic grunts, and her feet shuffled, repeatedly planting in new positions, as if bracing for a charge, while Gunnhild was silent, immobile, but the strain was showing increasingly in the sweat and grimace of her face, as well as an increasing tremor in the rest of her body.

When the pair took another step forward in perfect time, as if triggered by some unheard command, Halfdan actually jumped a little, so tense was he. He felt his pulse speed once more as the two women both reached out and grasped one another's heads, fingers gripping to each side on temples, cheeks, ears. There they remained, still locked in that strange, eerie battle, just their lips moving in silent combat.

Gunnhild cried out, then, and Halfdan took a step forward automatically, before restraining himself and holding back. He wanted nothing more than to intervene, even if it cost him his life. He looked about. Bjorn was on his feet again now, moving slowly toward the combat. Ulfr had appeared around the house, apparently content that this would not now end within those walls.

Still, Anna and Cassandra stood a few paces back, as did Hrafn's women.

The struggle was reaching a crescendo. Both völvas were now grunting and cursing, chanting and hissing, though through it all, Hrafn seemed composed, while Gunnhild was increasingly struggling. She was weak. Hrafn was strong. The woman had been quite right about that. Foolish. Foolish to have gone into this fight knowing that it was so uneven. Now, Halfdan was going to lose Gunnhild. He might lose a number of other Wolves, too, when that happened, and he inevitably had to end Hrafn.

The two women were moving, then, still locked in that strange embrace, gripping each other's head. They turned, slowly, though Halfdan could not tell whether it was by mutual design or whether one or the other of them was turning the pair. He almost ran to her aid again, but his common sense warned him not to this time. Not only would the rules of this contest be broken, and Gunnhild furious with him, but as they turned, he could see that from where Hrafn had her hands, one wrong move and her thumbs would be in Gunnhild's eye sockets, blinding her. He was effectively constrained by that. If he made a move, the völva would cripple his friend.

He realised, as he fumed impotently, that the two had now switched places in their circling, and he could see directly into Gunnhild's face and eyes, across Hrafn's shoulder. What he saw tore his heart asunder. Gunnhild was struggling. She looked like a dying woman, fighting to hold on to her last heartbeat. He could no longer see Hrafn's face, but he could easily imagine her smiling a cruel smile.

Then he saw the move, and he understood.

The two women who had come forward in support of Hrafn were leaping into action. Even as the two völvas had turned a half circle, the women on the far side had drawn blades from their belts, each holding a sax of short design, gripped by the tip. Throwing blades, properly weighted. Gunnhild was unaware, locked in her struggle, her back to the fresh danger. Halfdan was too far away to do anything.

His eyes widened as the two women lifted their blades and pulled back their arms. Two other figures were moving now, Anna and Cassandra, who had been but a pace behind the two Seiðr women, creeping forward already in anticipation of treachery. Halfdan felt frozen to the spot, watching the tableau like some voyeur, unable to affect what was happening.

Hrafn had planned a sneak attack that would kill Gunnhild, very likely unnecessarily, given that she could probably have killed Halfdan's friend with little effort in good time. This was her backup plan, just as Bjorn, Ulfr and Ketil had been his.

One of the two women threw her blade with a truly expert arm. The other never had the chance. As the second woman's arm came back, ready to throw, Ketil's arrow thrummed through the cold air and smashed through the raised limb, lodging itself between the two bones. The woman cried out and fell away, knife uncast, and Halfdan found himself sending silent thanks to his Icelandic friend, true as ever, who had made the decision to intervene of his own accord. The other woman succeeded, though. Her knife flew true, and would likely have ended Gunnhild in a moment, had Cassandra not been there. The Byzantine woman was just in time, throwing herself between Gunnhild and the gleaming death flying her way. She hit the grass with a cry, blade lodged in her front, around which she curled.

The rules had been breached. The contest was over, if not the battle. But Hrafn had cheated, and now Gunnhild could do what she wished. The rules had been cast aside. For a moment, Halfdan wondered whether to intervene. He was fairly sure that he was now permitted by whatever esoteric code they worked, yet somehow he felt that Gunnhild would tear him a new arsehole if he tried, no matter how the rules stood. He dithered, in a panic.

Bjorn was there now, having picked up pace on his approach the moment the fight had changed. Since he was coming from the house direction anyway, the big man was behind them, and therefore quick. He hit the two women of Hrafn's hirð like an angry bull, powering into one and sending her sprawling into the grass with a cry, as his one good arm smashed into the other woman, breaking her face in a single blow. Bjorn started to rampage, like the beast he was. Halfdan almost smiled, in spite of himself. His big friend was one of very few men who knew the berserkr, who had worn the bear shirt, but he was the *only* one that Halfdan knew of who could reach that state without the aid of the mysterious powder they all consumed.

He took his eyes off that fight. There was no point in watching further. Whatever Hrafn's two companions did now, they were dead women, even if they still yet breathed. Bjorn would pulverise both, and no force on earth was going to stop him now.

But there was still a fight going on.

Cassandra was down, on the ground, the knife wound clearly brutal, yet she was not dead from the way she rolled this way and that. Anna, on the other hand, was clinging to Hrafn from behind, one hand round each of the völva's arms, pulling them away, trying to prise free Gunnhild from her grip. Despite everything, Halfdan was impressed. Had they not been commissioned to clear Gunnar from power, and had Hrafn not already wronged his friend, he might well have left her to her own devices. In a world where the feeble treachery of the nailed god was the norm, it was oddly satisfying to see such power of an old sort, even if it was wielded by an enemy. But she had bled Gunnhild, and if he wanted Gunnar gone, Hrafn had to go first. Again, though, he felt that impotence, for now he could move to help her, yet he knew that this was not his place, and he should not. Nor should Ketil, yet his response had been appropriate to Hrafn's betrayal, and Gunnhild would forgive him. And despite Bjorn's direct intervention, Halfdan knew that Gunnhild would forgive the big bastard almost anything if it came down to it. But not her jarl. Halfdan was the leader of the Wolves, and his place was to make laws and live by them, not to break them like a thief in the night.

Gunnhild was still losing. She was close to breaking, he could hear that from her gasps, let alone see it in her expression, her sweat, her shaking body, as the pair slowly turned again. Everything that had happened was not going to make a difference if it was left to the two völvas. Hrafn was just too powerful.

He watched Cassandra rise from the grass.

He felt his pulse race. This was like the sagas of old. Like magic and gods. He saw the small, black-haired Byzantine woman rise from where she had fallen. As she turned toward him, he could see the blade still lodged in her chest, somewhere between heart and collarbone, almost certainly a killing blow. That she was moving at all was incredible.

Cassandra touched the blade, winced, did not remove it, and Halfdan understood. The blade was holding her together now. It had struck well, a death blow, but for now its steely bulk was stopping the damage from showing. The moment she removed the blade, the blood would flow, the organ collapse, and she would die. But for a few more heartbeats, with that blade in place, she was alive. He felt the work of gods then, as Cassandra walked slowly around the revolving völvas, and then grasped one of Hrafn's wrists.

Freed of the need to divide her efforts, Anna now let go of that wrist, and used both hands to grab the other. Slowly, and with great effort, as though tearing the hide from a bear, the two Byzantines pulled Hrafn's hands from Gunnhild's head. Even as they did so, the Swaledale völva bellowed a cry of fury, and tried hard to gouge out her opponent's eyes with her thumbs. She was too late. The two women had her wrists and were pulling her hands away from Gunnhild's face.

The völvas had turned once more, enough for Halfdan to see his friend's face, and what he saw there almost made him feel sorry for Hrafn. No one, no matter what they had done, should have to face Gunnhild when she was truly angry.

Cassandra and Anna had pulled the völva off their friend, and Gunnhild was stepping back, taking a single, long breath. The two Byzantine women lifted and twisted their captive's arms, almost bending them painfully behind her, causing Hrafn to curse in heaving breaths. Bjorn was there now, too, having left little of Hrafn's women but smears in the grass and a field of bone shards. The big man roared as he stepped toward the völva who had caused all of this, who was held tight.

'No,' Gunnhild said, her breath coming in short gasps.

Bjorn stopped, just short of bringing down one meaty hand on the völva's head. He paused, taking a step back.

'Let her go,' Gunnhild said.

Halfdan was torn. Hrafn was still strong. She had barely broken a sweat yet, and the only reason she had not won already was her foolish treachery that had allowed Gunnhild's friends to intervene. He had no doubt that, given a moment to recover her breath and wits, Hrafn would come back just as strong. What was Gunnhild thinking? She was allowing her enemy to regroup.

But he could see her face. And what he saw in Gunnhild's eyes left him in no doubt that he was superfluous to all of this. That, no matter how it looked, the balance had tipped Gunnhild's way.

Despite the Wolves having gained the upper hand, there was something in Gunnhild's tone that had Bjorn, Anna and Cassandra all backing away, letting go of the vicious völva. The three of them stepped back, Cassandra staggering. Her work done, death was claiming her now, but she fought it to the last to watch her friend survive.

Hrafn was free. She was, in fact, unharmed, and not even all that tired. She rolled her shoulders like a fighter readying for a bout. She was regaining her confidence by the moment. Halfdan looked into Gunnhild's eyes again. Hrafn was wrong. She was *over*-confident. She thought she could win now. Thought, as Halfdan had done briefly, that Gunnhild had made a terrible mistake in freeing her.

No. Everything Gunnhild did was by design.

And she had no fear.

Suddenly, Halfdan felt a little pity for the völva of Swaledale.

Hrafn was growling, as her dead bear once had, rising to her full height. She was impressive. Halfdan wavered.

Gunnhild smiled, and her smile was the cold realm of Hel. Her smile was a death with no promise of feasting halls. Her smile was the unforgiving sea storm, the falling blade of the executioner, the boom of a tomb door closing.

Halfdan hoped dearly never to see that smile again.

She did something. He couldn't really tell what. He was in a state of confusion, agitation and almost fear, the Seiðr in the air so thick he could almost swim through it. She made a series of small motions with her hands, which Halfdan had absolutely no idea about. Whatever they were, they meant something to Hrafn, for the völva let forth a blood-curdling cry, the like of which Halfdan had never heard.

'No,' she cried at Gunnhild, fight forgotten, arms coming up in a gesture of supplication. 'No. You *can't*.'

But Gunnhild did.

Halfdan watched, silent and stunned, not even daring to breathe, as his völva friend took one step forward, arm coming out. Gunnhild extended her index finger. Hrafn was shaking now, as though sobbing uncontrollably. The völva of Hedeby said one word, so quiet that Halfdan stood no chance of hearing it, and her fingertip touched Hrafn's eyeball.

The völva of Swaledale toppled, falling to the turf, dead in an instant.

Halfdan stared. Still he did not breathe.

Hrafn hit the ground, rolling onto her back, and the look on her face, he was fairly sure, would haunt him at night for the rest of his life. Whatever it was Gunnhild had done, it had been as terrible a thing as could be done in this world.

Hrafn lay still.

Gunnhild took a long, slow breath, then walked straight past one body without looking at it, to the next, beside which she knelt. Cassandra's breathing had stopped. She was gone. Lief was there, a moment later, a man who not only prayed as Cassandra had done, to the nailed god, but even shared her specific church, for the Rus and the Byzantines were of a mind in this.

'She will want the last rites,' the little Rus said. 'It should be a priest, really, but I think God will understand if I take his place this once.'

Gunnhild looked up at Lief. Usually, her reaction to such Christian assertions was one of dry sarcasm. Halfdan could see no such thing in her right now. The völva fixed the Rus with a look. 'You may do as you wish, Lief the Teeth, and I am sure she will be glad for the offer. But whether she looks to the new god or the old, I will tell you now that there is a place in Sessrúmnir set for her, for she is welcome and anticipated greatly in Freyja's hall, and the world's unmaking will see her rise once more.'

Halfdan felt the hairs rise on the back of his neck. He had never heard such a thing about a Christian. He had never heard any such thing from Gunnhild.

He shivered.

Gunnhild crossed the grass once more to the site of her victory. She reached down into the grass, and Halfdan almost cried out in shock when she pulled up a snake, shrugged and snapped it at the neck, throwing it away. She then collected two staffs, hers and Hrafn's, and crossed once more to her friend. Crouching, she put Hrafn's staff, the symbol, tool and heart of a völva's power, in Cassandra's hand, closing her fingers over the ash haft.

'At Ragnarok, I will have a völva friend,' Gunnhild said, rising once more with a sad smile.

Even Lief, Christian as he was, had his head bowed reverently as he rose.

'That is it,' Gunnhild said, turning to Halfdan. 'It is done. Now you must face Gunnar, and then we can go home.' She turned to Bjorn, pointing down at Hrafn. 'Take her head.'

Part Four

ᚹᛟᛚᚠᛖᛋ ᛟᚠ ᛟᛞᛁᚾ

Heimdallr

There shall come that winter which is called the Awful Winter…

The Wolf shall swallow the sun; and this shall seem to men a great harm. Then the other wolf shall seize the moon, and he also shall work great ruin; the stars shall vanish from the heavens.

When these tidings come to pass, then shall Heimdallr rise up and blow mightily in the Gjallar-Horn, and awaken all the gods…

Loki shall have battle with Heimdallr, and each be the slayer of the other.

Extracts on Ragnarok from *Gylfaginning* in *The Prose Edda*,
Snorri Sturluson
trans. Arthur Gilchrist Brodeur

Chapter 19

The recent past. Somewhere in the land of forests and lakes.

'Watch yourselves,' the leader said, unseen from Bjorn's hiding place. 'Look for the signs – valknuts and serpents and the like – and note them all, but watch yourselves and don't walk into anything dangerous.'

Bjorn nodded silently on the other side of the wall. 'Like me,' he grinned, secretly.

'Sir, haven't we crossed the border now?'

Again, Bjorn nodded. By his estimation, they were in the lands of the Svears and Geats, probably not a long walk from his birthplace, in fact. He reckoned he'd crossed back from Nordvegr yesterday afternoon, but up here in the lands of forests and lakes there were no official markers or guards to say you were in one or the other. He hunkered down to listen once more, fingers running along the haft of the great axe in his hands. Soon...

'Who cares?' the leader snorted dismissively. 'You think Onund Jakob cares about a few idolaters in the woodland on the edge of his kingdom? Besides, Magnus of Nordvegr is powerful enough now that the Svear king wouldn't dare anger him. And Onund wants his land clear of pagans every bit as much as Magnus, anyway. Just find them and report back. And watch out for the Bear-torn.'

Now, Bjorn grinned wider. A man could count his worth in many ways, in silver or in sons, or in land and hearth, but Odin ever favoured a man who could count his worth in fame. And that was what Bjorn was gaining now.

It had begun when he'd hunted the nailed god soldiers who'd murdered the völva, and he'd carried his vengeance as far as the priest in charge. He'd thought himself done then, especially since it had taken several months in the middle of nowhere to recover, applying salves he vaguely knew from his time in Kaupang while his ravaged face healed, leaving four great scars. He'd fretted and mused over what he was going to do next, as he recuperated. He felt certain that he should know the answer to that. He had his name now, and the old woman had seemed adamant that once Bjorn reached that point, he would be on a path woven by the Norns and would simply have to walk it. But yet again, Bjorn had had no idea what to do next.

Until the day he returned to civilisation.

Taking his pack and his pouch of silver, largely purloined from his victims, he had headed back toward Ánslo to resupply, for he was sick of living on stream fish and animals he could catch and skin in the woods. There, he had discovered that his antics with the priest and the soldiers had become rather infamous. The unnamed pagan brute who had torn through the authorities in the town and performed 'unholy rites' on the priest was being sought by the king's men, and with a solid price on his head.

That had made him smile. It had made him happy. Some men might panic and try to run, to hide, at such tidings. Not Bjorn, for this was a challenge. A new goal. It wasn't that he'd ever set out to put himself against the children of the nailed god. He'd always assumed them to be harmless and misguided, and a little bit wet. And even after his father's death and that time of captivity among Christians, he'd laid the blame squarely with Orm Barelegs and his people, not their religion. Even with the völva at Kaupang, he'd not set out to kill Christians on principle. It had been justice for the old woman, revenge on a specific group.

But no matter that Bjorn had never set himself against Christians, the day he returned from the forests, he discovered that *they* had set themselves against *him*. The new king of Nordvegr, no less, had agreed the bounty on his head. Soldiers all across the land were hunting what was being described as a 'great white giant of a man'.

Thus had begun his new path. He had moved from place to place, making sure to be visible at the right time and the right place to draw out soldiers. Then, when they began to hunt him, he'd play a game, turning the hunt upon them, picking them off, for men like that were at home in towns with churches and palaces, but far from their element in the woods.

Oh, he'd had a few close scrapes, for certain. At one point he'd found himself being chased by twenty horsemen, and had only got away by stealing a fishing boat and rowing like mad until he was out to sea. He'd got lost, then, out on the whale road, for he was no great sailor, and instead of landing along the coast somewhere south of Ánslo, he'd spent three days at sea and then discovered the coast of Daneland quite by accident. He had spent half a year in Daneland, then, fighting for one lord or another, keeping his beliefs to himself, for the Danes were the most Christian of all Northmen. His true feelings had been revealed one day at Hedeby, when he'd been drunk and called some Christian a 'cross-humper' in a mead hall, and he'd been forced to flee again, crossing northward once more aboard a merchant knarr, and landing in Nordvegr.

There he'd discovered, to his delight, that in half a year's absence, the campaign to hunt the 'great white giant' had changed. It had taken on something of a mythical edge, and Christian parents were frightening their children into line with the threat that the 'Bear-torn' would come for them.

But myths and legends tended to fade in the world unless they were periodically given new life, and so Bjorn popped up the next winter near the Svear border. A village there had been suffering bad harvests for three years, and though they muttered at their cross in the square, he had spotted Mjǫllnir pendants around many necks, suggesting that they paid only lip service to the nailed god while keeping their private faith in the Allfather. Bjorn had sacrificed nine of the twelve soldiers who found him that winter, hanging their bodies from the great ash tree to the north of the village in a gesture to draw a good harvest next year.

They were not removed until the authorities came, hunting him.

His legend grew once more.

So did the bounty.

And the number of men after him.

And that was what had brought him back over the border this winter and into the land of his youth. That was what had led him here, hiding in a ruin by a crossroads and listening to the men hunting him. There had been ten riders in that group but, as he listened, he heard the distinct sound of hooves departing, and counted three pairs of riders dispatched along each different way at the crossroads. That left four behind, including the commander.

Bjorn grinned. Time to bring the legend of the Bear-torn into Svear lands.

With a roar he rose, axe in hand, and raced around the corner of the wall, toward the startled Norse soldiers.

Late February 1044. Swaledale.

Bjorn felt good, and one look around at the Wolves of Odin as they made their way back down into the main dale only made him feel better.

Halfdan walked tall, a true jarl in the model of the old heroes, leading his hirð toward another victory to recount in the mead halls. Bjorn had begun this journey with the fear they were no better than thralls to the archbishop, doing the work of the nailed god. But, somehow, they had instead found themselves pitted against enemies truly worthy of the sagas. Bjorn had proved himself in the greatest fight a man could have, and had even been able to best a bear into the bargain – twice! His stories would be told for years to come. Since the day they had taken ship in the *Sea Wolf*, they had not stayed in one place long enough for their fame to become known, but that time was approaching, and the Bear-torn's legend would be greater than any hero since Sigurd.

A lot of that was because of his place as Halfdan's champion, and he knew that. Without him, Bjorn would probably still be bumbling about the Northlands, playing hunt-the-hunter with the soldiers of Christian kings. Here, he got to best berserkir, and bears.

The jarl walked alongside Farlof, Lief, Ulfr and Ketil – all good men, particularly the Icelander, who was strong and brave enough to almost wear the bear shirt himself sometimes. He supposed it ought to matter that two of those men prayed to the nailed god, but the strange fact was that... it didn't. Bjorn would never bow to the Christ, would never be a thrall to him, but neither was he a persecutor like the Christians. Let them hunt non-Christians over their beliefs. Bjorn had only ever fought men who deserved it. Lief did not deserve it, despite being one of them. Nor did Farlof, or any of the other Wolves walking with them.

Gunnhild, who *really* held no love for the White Christ, was still comfortable walking alongside Anna, who wore a cross around her neck.

Even Bjorn, who had never truly got on with Cassandra's beliefs, had to acknowledge her bravery and sacrifice when she saved Gunnhild. He did not speak against transporting her back to Jorvik for burial in a Christ-tomb. Besides, who was *he* to complain about burdens? Cassandra was now tightly wrapped and tied to the horse they had stolen from a field back in the upper dale.

The others walked in a group, chatting quietly as they travelled. They sounded optimistic. There were plenty of wounds among them, Bjorn's own arm starting to itch irritably beneath all the bindings, for one, and Gunnhild was still pale and weak, but the völva had been content to declare that no one still walking with them was in danger of death. Really, for what they had been through and had achieved, their losses had been little short of miraculous.

He wished he could change arm. The two-wheeled hand-cart he was pulling was heavy, and it was becoming increasingly tiresome being limited to pulling it with one limb. He'd argued that the horse should have pulled the cart, and the Christians among them could have carried Cassandra's body. But Halfdan had fixed him with a firm look.

'You want it, you carry it, my friend.'

And so he had. A bear weighed quite a lot, though, even on two wheels and downhill. He'd tried to persuade several others to take a turn, but no one had taken him up on the offer, even when he'd counted silver into the deal.

'Why would you want a dead bear?' Lief had asked.

Bjorn had frowned at the stupid question. 'A pelt. Fur. The teeth for necklaces. The skull for a prize. Bone to shape into needles and combs. The meat, if nothing else. You might question me now, but when you're eating roasted bear tonight around the fire, you'll all be praising old Bjorn Bear-torn and his prize.'

He smiled nastily to himself. He might just keep all the meat for himself, and watch them drool at the sight of his dinner, since they wouldn't help him carry it. That thought brought with it renewed strength and determination to bear the burden, despite his ongoing aches.

The other burdened walkers among them were Anna and Ulfr. Cassandra had been wrapped up with the völva's staff after the fight, but everything else of value or interest from Hrafn's house had been gathered up and stuffed into bags. Gunnhild had prepared to take them with her, for they were hers by right of conquest, and she would now have the makings of a great völva's house, but she was simply too weak to carry them, and so Anna and Ulfr had shouldered the bags for her. Lief had politely tried to carry them for her, but she'd been adamant. This was her job, not his.

One thing they had found in Hrafn's home, which had been a great discovery, had been a sizeable stock of the bitter brown compound that the völva needed for her journeys with the goddess. Bjorn had been subtle enough to slip a handful into his own pouch once more, before it was taken for Gunnhild's bags. He smiled at that. He wasn't entirely sure that Gunnhild had not seen him do it, but she'd not commented. Perhaps, since he had given her some when she had needed it to defeat Hrafn, Gunnhild was willing to accept him carrying the powder now. So long as they all remembered to stay safely out of the way when *he* needed to use it…

He grinned again at the thought of the battles he had fought these past few days, and the fights that might yet be to come, when his arm was better.

A rhythmic clonking drew his gaze over his shoulder and the sight that greeted him there only broadened his grin. Two heads bounced against the wooden side of the cart, beneath the swinging paw of the great bear: Hrafn's, tied to the rail by her hair, and Arkil's, tied by the lace that ran through the middle of the skull. Two of the great powers that had made Swaledale unassailable were now trophies. Soon they would find Gunnar and his head, and then their mission here would be complete.

And how powerful could this Gunnar be? By all accounts, the people of the land had been largely cowed by the strength and brutality of Arkil Bear-shoulders and the spite and magic of Hrafn, the two of them lending their jarl all the power he needed to rule. Without them, Gunnar was just a man. He might be a jarl, but he had no Seiðr at his command, nor the strength of the berserkr.

A small part of his consciousness reminded him that Halfdan, too, was 'just a man', but that he was also his jarl and the wiliest and wisest of men, and Bjorn would rather carry a dragon boat over his head than face Halfdan in a duel. Still, how dangerous could Gunnar be?

The big difficulty for Bjorn was going to be staying out of it. Arkil had been his to deal with, and while Hrafn had been Gunnhild's, Bjorn had been involved, for he'd had the bear to kill. When they met Gunnar, though, the fight had to be Halfdan's, and Halfdan's alone, jarl to jarl. Bjorn would have to step back and watch. That was not going to be easy.

At least the jarl was well armed now, he supposed.

Among the other goods they had found in the völva's house had been some of the equipment of her hirð. Where the shield-maidens had lived, they could not figure, for there was not enough room in the house, but some of their gear had been stored there, and one of the chain shirts had fitted Halfdan, if a little snugly at the shoulders. They had also found spears, cloaks, two good helmets, and four shields, all of which had been distributed among the Wolves. Now, Halfdan was attired like a warrior once more, with chain shirt, a good iron helm with eye covering, and a shield bearing the design of a raven. Lief had promised to paint over it with wolves the moment they had the opportunity, but it would do for now.

Halfdan was as ready for battle as he could be.

Or, at least, he looked it.

Bjorn suspected that his jarl's mind was unsettled. On the way up the valley, they had passed a house on the hillside that Halfdan had said was Gunnar's, and he had sounded both certain of that and, surprisingly, a little nervous.

But Bjorn shrugged it off. If ever there was a man he trusted to get the job done, it was Halfdan Loki-born.

'That's them!'

The call took them all by surprise, and the Wolves stopped sharply, looking ahead. A figure had appeared, slightly up the slope at the valley side, from a stand of trees that overlooked a rough, stone-walled sheepfold. Even as the man came out into the open, pointing at them, two more stepped out behind him.

'Get them,' Ketil said, suddenly.

'What?' Halfdan replied.

'They'll warn Gunnar you're coming,' the Icelander said, turning to his jarl. 'How much time do you want to give him to prepare?'

Halfdan frowned for a moment, but Bjorn was only half listening, and was already moving. The moment they'd stopped, he'd let go of the cart handles, the whole thing tipping forward, the great carcass sliding forth until it thudded to the ground. By the time Ketil had said 'get them,' Bjorn was already running.

As he passed the front of the group, feet pounding, axe coming out in his good hand, he heard Halfdan shouting at him to wait, but it was too late. He had already given himself up to the Lord of Battle and he could no more stop his charge now than he could grow a second head.

He could hear the others moving to support him, then, pounding feet behind him in the distance, and he growled in irritation. No. He was not going to get to fight Gunnar, but here were three men who needed to be put down, and he could savour that.

As he ran, he kept his eyes locked on the men ahead. They were armed, though not armoured. They stood still for a few moments until a mixture of fear and common sense put them to flight.

Bjorn was aware he was beginning to tire from the run, but he'd already covered half the distance to the men. Then, pounding footsteps were beside him. He turned his head to see Ketil the Icelander pulling alongside him, the man's massive stride allowing him to catch up where most stood no chance.

'Back off,' Bjorn growled.

'No.'

'This fight is *mine*,' he snapped.

'They have horses,' Ketil replied, pointing ahead. 'We can't let them mount.'

Bjorn grumbled aloud. The bastard was right. Bjorn had no doubt that he could bring down the three men himself, but he probably wouldn't be fast enough, and all it would take was one of them to mount up and he'd be free to race away and warn Gunnar.

The two Northmen bore down on the trio as they began to hurriedly untie their horses' tethers. Two were nearer than the other. 'Take the far one,' Bjorn said to the Icelander as they ran.

'But he's the *small* one.'

'I can't catch him in time.'

Grunting his agreement, Ketil suddenly started to run faster. There were two things about Ketil that impressed Bjorn. One was his archery, given that Bjorn would be lucky to hit the side of a house with an arrow, and the other was his height and speed. The Icelander was the only man Bjorn had ever met, before Arkil at least, who he had to look up at, and when he ran, it was like watching a racehorse.

He left the Icelander to it. Instead, he made for the nearest man, who had untied his reins and already had a foot in his stirrup. The man was on the far side of the horse, though, which made any attack difficult. Still, all Bjorn had to do was keep him here for a moment. As he ran, he pulled his great axe back across his body, then dropped low and swung with a massive backhand.

The horse's leg smashed and ripped into two pieces just below the hock joint. The animal screamed as it fell, one lower leg entirely severed. The man who'd been trying to mount it was thrown clear, landing on the turf with a thud.

Bjorn left the man and beast behind, making for the second figure, who had just finished untying his reins. The man turned in shock at the horse's scream, only to see the great albino bearing down on him, bloody axe in hand, crimson mizzle filling the air around him. The rider looked to the shield strapped at the horse's flank, clearly trying to decide whether he had time to free it, but then abandoned hope of that. Instead, he drew his longsword. The delay as he'd contemplated the shield was his undoing, for he had barely managed to get his weapon free of its scabbard before Bjorn was on him. He thrust the blade in the way of the albino's powerful swing, but the axe simply struck the sword near the crossbar and sent it flying from the warrior's hand, away into the grass.

As Bjorn pulled the axe back for a second blow, the man desperately tried to draw the sax at his belt, but it never even left the mouth of its sheath before the axe bit deep into his chest, smashing ribs and pulping organs. The rider was halfway to dead before he'd even fallen to his knees, and hurried the rest of the way as he fell further, to rest on his front, shaking, blood forming a lake in the grass around him.

Bjorn turned to see the man who'd been thrown from his horse rising to his feet, sword in hand. He looked a little dazed, but was recovering fast, shaking the fuzziness from his head and rolling his shoulders, readying for a fight.

From somewhere along the line of trees, Bjorn heard a cry of pain, and it didn't sound like the Icelander, suggesting that Ketil had dealt with the third rider.

Bjorn marched on the remaining man, axe running with blood and gore, face locked in a deadly rictus. The man looked a little nervous now, as his daze lifted, but he did not run. He readied his sword. Bjorn ran at him, but at the last moment, the man jumped two steps to his right. Bjorn's swing narrowly missed him, for the man had moved to Bjorn's left side, where his injured and strapped-up arm was. Bjorn turned with a curse to face the man again, but the man danced right once more, staying on Bjorn's injured side.

'Fucking stand still,' Bjorn snapped as he turned again and again, trying to face the man, axe swinging sporadically, always narrowly missing him. Twice, the rider stabbed or slashed out with his sword, and it was only with a great deal of luck that Bjorn avoided taking a fresh wound. The bastard was clever, and quite fast, and it was riling Bjorn, until he realised something. The man was taking advantage of Bjorn's bandaged arm, but was paying no attention to his feet.

The big man grinned as he turned yet again, but this time he turned the *other* way, sweeping his leg out as he did so. The man, so used now to ducking right again and again, did so before he realised things had changed, colliding with Bjorn's outstretched leg and almost falling. He tried to stop himself, staggering this way and that, attempting to keep his footing, foolishly, for that gave Bjorn the opportunity he'd been waiting for.

His axe swung again, catching the man just below the shoulder and shattering his arm, removing any remaining balance he had and sending him falling to the grass. As the man landed on his back, he somehow managed to maintain hold of his sword, and Bjorn moved to deal with that instantly, before he could use it. The big man's boot stamped down on the rider's wrist, and stayed there, pressing down with the giant's weight and holding it in place. As the man cried out, bones crunching in his wrist, Bjorn lifted his axe.

'Good night,' he grinned, and let it fall on the man's neck.

The cries ended suddenly.

Bjorn looked around. Both his men were dead now, and Ketil was strolling back toward him, leading a horse, a third figure lying immobile in the grass a short distance away. The only cries now were those of the crippled horse, and Bjorn walked over toward the animal. Some *men* deserved to suffer, but no *horse* did. He brought his axe down hard, butt-first, on the top of the horse's head and was rewarded with a loud crack. In moments the horse had stopped thrashing and bellowing and lay still.

'Nice fight,' he announced, as Ketil grabbed the reins of the other surviving horse and led him over.

'Why will you never accept help?' the Icelander sighed. 'Not *all* our enemies are yours alone, Bjorn.'

The big man shrugged. 'The fight coming is the jarl's. Mine were the stuff of legend, but they're done, and fame only lasts if you keep it alive.'

Ketil snorted. 'It's been just hours since you killed a bear and what, two days since you killed the berserkr? I don't think you're in danger of people forgetting you just yet, you big fool.'

Bjorn grinned. 'Good.'

'We've acquired two new horses,' Ketil announced as the Wolves caught up, two of the others pulling Bjorn's bear cart for him.

'I tried to tell you to stop,' Halfdan snapped.

Bjorn frowned, confused. 'What?'

The jarl shook his head, raising his eyes skyward for a moment. 'I want the killing to stop now. Remember, we're not here to depopulate the dale, just to kill Gunnar. Shit, Bjorn, but we didn't even officially need to kill Arkil and Hrafn. We just did it to lessen Gunnar's power. Now, it is all about the jarl of Swaledale, and him alone. I need to add his head to the others and take them to the archbishop in Jorvik, then we can get our ship and sail after Hjalmvigi and Harðráði.'

'You want to leave live enemies behind you?'

'When Gunnar dies, they will not *be* my enemy,' Halfdan said. '*Think*, Bjorn. We've lost good men here, and we were short of true Odin-bound warriors to start with. This valley is full of them.'

'But they're *Gunnar's* warriors,' Bjorn reminded him, scratching his head in confusion.

'For now. But when Gunnar is gone, and the archbishop sends his men to settle the dale and start mining lead, what place will there be here for true Northmen?'

Bjorn's frown deepened. 'So?'

'So we *need* these men, Bjorn. Now, they fight for Gunnar. I want them fighting for *me*. Soon, we will meet Harðráði again, to take back our ship, and we will need a crew for it, for then we'll have two. And soon we'll move against the bastard priest back home, and I guarantee you he will be prepared for us. And even then, what of the future? We need a true hirð of Northmen.'

Halfdan smiled suddenly. 'I know, Bjorn. Mercy is not your natural state. But I want the killing to stop, unless we are attacked. No more butchering men who could have a future with us. From now, the only man carrying a death mark in this valley is Gunnar, and he is *mine* to deal with.'

Bjorn huffed irritably. 'All right. As long as there's no danger of my deeds being forgotten.'

Halfdan laughed, and pointed past him. Bjorn turned, to see the handcart bearing two swinging heads and the carcass of a bear.

'There's little chance of that,' the jarl said.

Chapter 20

'There,' Halfdan said, pointing off east along the valley side, into the fading light.

'Are you sure?' Lief asked.

'Certain.'

The small knot of stone houses stood far up the slope and perhaps a mile down the valley, overlooking Swaledale from their lofty eyrie, three sizeable buildings with associate sheep-folds and sheds. No ostentatious hall for Jarl Gunnar. His was a simple house of stone with a thatched roof, those buildings of his retinue gathered around, a side of the enemy jarl that Halfdan respected. A small settlement of timber buildings sat below in the valley floor, alongside a stream that ran down from the slopes to join the river nearby.

Lief looked up. 'It's almost dark. Too late to start climbing hills into enemy lands, I'd say.'

Halfdan nodded. He couldn't take his eyes off that all too familiar sight on the hill. Behind him, he heard the others dropping their bundles and preparing to make camp for the night. Part of him wanted to go on, to get it done with, but he knew the sense of waiting. These hills, with their bracken and heather and scattered stones, were not lands to wander at night.

The jarl stood for some time at the periphery as the Wolves set up camp, gathering firewood and preparing for the evening, their chatter light and excited. The mission had so far been a success, and it was almost over. Or, rather, for everyone but Halfdan it was almost over. Lief wandered across.

'Ketil is preparing a cook-fire for the night. I told him to wait. We are close enough to that settlement that anyone looking up the dale will see our fire. We could be inviting a night attack.'

Halfdan shook his head. 'They won't come tonight. They already know we're here, I think. They will protect their jarl, but I do not think they will move to the offensive. Let Ketil have his fire. I think we will all be grateful for it tonight. Have four men on watch at any time, though, just in case, up and down dale, uphill and down to the river.'

'Yes, Halfdan. Are you coming?'

'I'll be along in a moment.'

In the end, he stood for another half hour or so staring at the houses on the hill, where he could see no sign of movement, until the sun set fully and evening rolled over them, hiding the hillside from view. A few fires burned in the wooden-house village below, but there was no movement or noise visible there, either. Still, he could sense they were being watched.

When he finally moved into the camp, Lief and Ketil had done a good job. They had used an old wall and a stand of trees just off the road, making temporary shelters from them. The fire was already going well, the wood having had over a day to dry out now. The sky was cold but clear, the ground dry, barring a little settling of evening dew.

Bjorn was in high spirits, turning his exploits of the last few days into raucous self-congratulatory songs as he repeatedly carved lumps of meat from his dead bear and roasted them over the fire, only handing them out when someone congratulated him on his victories and sang along with his mad, lewd verses. It made Halfdan smile, even as he accepted a hunk of dripping meat without having to pay his due – he was jarl, after all. The more he wandered this world, the more apparent it was becoming that the children of the nailed god considered the future to be their domain. Everywhere were churches and crosses, everywhere the old ways were being rolled back to remoter lands. But there were still beacons of tradition to be found, and one such was Bjorn Bear-torn. In their travels, Halfdan had met great warriors and heroes, dukes and emperors, but none of them stood as even a shadow against Bjorn. The albino might as well have walked straight out of the song of a skald, from an ancient lay, of the time when Odin walked openly among the hills of the North.

He shivered, remembering that figure he'd seen up near Hrafn's house. Perhaps in the more remote areas, away from the houses of the Christ, Odin *still* walked in the open.

It was anathema to Halfdan. He could understand how these Christians worshipped their god. There was much mysticism and power to him, and if he did half the things they claimed he did, then his hall should be every bit as packed as those of Odin and Freyja. What he *couldn't* understand was how the Christians could deny the existence of the ancient powers that had come before him. Halfdan *knew* Odin to be real. Knew Thor for a power, Freyja for her wisdom. He needed no belief, for he knew the gods still walked, because he had been marked by Loki himself, and could *feel* the god's influence on him. He could feel the Seiðr in the very air when Gunnhild worked her designs. And who could deny Odin, Lord of Frenzy, when they watched Bjorn at his work? No, there could be no denying that the old gods still held power in this world, no matter what the Christians said. He frowned. Perhaps the Christians actually *did* believe in them, regardless of what they said. Why else would they work so hard to stamp out their names, after all?

His gaze slid up to that hillside once again, the heights little more than a dark shape against other dark shapes. And he could feel the Norns weaving, feel every thread as they bound together to draw him into his fate.

Bjorn's voice cut into his thoughts as the man shouted to overcome the general noise of the camp. 'Did I ever tell you of the time I met the Queen of Danes? She liked it rough, you know?'

'Piss off, you outrageous liar,' shouted Lief with a good-natured grin.

He returned to his contemplation of the hill and what it held for him. He could feel the good humour ebbing, and the tension of what he must face, and what it might mean, taking its place, a sour taste in the mouth.

'He's a man,' a voice said.

Halfdan turned to see Ulfr behind him, offering him a cup of ale. He took it, gratefully. 'What do you mean?'

'You're troubled, Halfdan. I can see it. We all can. But whatever you fear tomorrow, remember that. In your head he might be a monster or a giant, to his people he can be a jarl or a king, but standing on the grass with a sword in his hand, all he is is a man.'

'A powerful man. A dangerous one.'

'Has he stolen ships and gold from heroes and princes? Has he fought wars and saved empresses? Has he put dukes on thrones, built a crew of legend from nothing, faced Greek fire, and hunted a criminal jarl halfway across the world?'

Halfdan laughed sheepishly. 'When you put it like that...'

'All he has done is find powerful people to support him and make the law in this dale. Of the two of you, I'd rather face *him* any day.' The shipwright smiled encouragingly, downed his drink, and clapped a hand on his jarl's shoulder. 'Come to the fire. Drink and celebrate. Do not stand alone and mope. Alone in the dark is where fear does its work.' With another smile and a squeeze of the shoulder, Ulfr turned and walked back to the fire.

Halfdan follow, and passed the evening with easy smiles and quiet good humour, singing along to Bjorn's ditties, listening to his increasingly unlikely stories, eating and drinking. It was a façade, of course, to keep his people content and confident. Beneath the shell he created, though, and despite Ulfr's valiant efforts, the jarl was still riven with doubt. It was almost a relief to turn to his shelter and to cocoon himself in his blankets against a chill the fire couldn't quite dissipate. Sleep came slow, but at least it came.

–

He gripped his sword and glanced up again.

The skies, red as blood, shook and boomed, as though being torn apart. A black crack loomed above him as he stood, sword in hand, watching his enemy emerge from the doorway of the stone hall. On a bleak hillside, a world of men watched as Heimdallr and Loki met.

The guardian of Bifrost was tall, in a glittering shirt of silver. His eyes shone almost gold in the reflected light of the dreadful sky; in his right hand he held a sword that was the death of men, and in his left was a beautiful and terrible horn. It was that which transfixed Halfdan, even deep in the dream, for the very sight of the horn made the Loki serpents on his arm burn, as though he were aflame with the war-fire of the Greeks.

He stepped forward, and so did Heimdallr, and their swords met with a ring that cut through the earth, awakening giants, sending a call to the halls of the slain that the time was nigh.

Loki unbound...

–

Halfdan started awake suddenly, and almost lashed out at the figure before he realised it was the völva. She crouched over him as though ministering to wounds.

'Gunnhild?'

'You were talking in your sleep. I knew why.'

Halfdan looked about sharply, worried, but Gunnhild shook her head. 'Everyone else is asleep, apart from those on watch, and they are outside the camp. We are practically alone.'

He sighed with relief and sagged back. The last thing he wanted was for the Wolves to know he was suffering with night terrors – if that's what they were. Perhaps they were more accurately memories of something that hadn't happened yet.

Whatever Ulfr might say, he was fairly sure that Gunnar was more than 'just a man'.

'What do you know of the Twilight of Gods and Men, Gunnhild?'

The völva pursed her lips, rocking back on her heels in that crouch. 'Ragnarok? I know the prophecies, as do all the wise. The Mother in Hedeby recounted the tale over every meal for a year, to be sure I knew it by heart. Most people know *some of it*, I expect. You yourself are aware, I think, of most. And there are parts that even I am not permitted to explain.'

'Tell me.'

Gunnhild frowned. 'You need rest. Sleep. Tomorrow is as important a day as you have ever faced. Perhaps even more so. Not only your future, but that of all your hirð ride on the events of the morning.'

Halfdan snorted. 'Thank you, Gunnhild. A little extra pressure was just what I needed, but I'm not sleeping any time soon. Tell me.'

She huffed and then sat properly on the grass and folded her legs, her back to the fire, a comforting silhouette against the golden dance.

'When the time approaches, Odin's maidens will assemble the Æsir and those who feast in Valhöll. Freyja will gather the fallen from her own hall, and all shall await, eager, champing at the bit. Odin's son, Baldr, shall be the first of the slain, taken with a mistletoe arrow by the trickery of Loki.'

She paused here, looking up sharply at Halfdan. 'What you have to remember is that whatever you feel, Halfdan, you are *not* Loki, any more than I am Freyja. Loki may at times guide your hand for good or for ill, but it is not your will or actions that affect such weaving. It is his.'

'Tell me,' he said again, shivering.

'The Æsir shall punish Loki for the death, binding him to a rock beneath Yggdrasil with the entrails of his son, while Sigyn, his wife, sits by his side and catches the serpent venom that drips from above. Thus is Loki's bondage forged.'

Loki bound. Halfdan nodded.

'With Loki constrained, the corpse fields of Nástrǫnd will open, and great Fenrir shall pull at his chains. The jötunn in Ironwood releases her children, Skǫll and Hati, who consume the sun and the moon and plunge the world into darkness. There will follow a terrible time of storms and blood, and fire and death, ravaging all nine worlds. Fjalarr shall crow to wake the giants, and the dvergar and the jötnar will gather in their dark halls, a mirror to the gods.'

Was it Halfdan's imagination, or could he see shapes coalescing in the dancing flames of the fire behind her, coming and going in the blink of an eye, wolves and dwarves and giants and cockerels? He shivered again as he almost saw Loki break his chains in the flames. One of Gunnhild's eyebrows rose. He had heard the old tales, of course, but never with such detail or such clarity, usually embellished in the form of song. 'Go on,' he urged her.

The völva's eyes narrowed. 'Are you sure? Some knowledge is best kept from the ken of men.' When Halfdan simply nodded, she folded her arms around her knees and continued.

'Gullinkambi will crow then, to ready the gods, just as the unnameable cock crows for the hirð of Hel. The gates of Hel will burst open at the howl of her hound, and Fenrir shall break free of his chains and come into the worlds once more. So shall the war begin in Miðgarðr, as brother slays brother and kin slay kin.'

She fixed him with a look, and he found himself bracing automatically. 'Then,' she said, 'shall Heimdallr blow the Gjallarhorn and call the gods to war. At the horn's sounding, Loki will escape his bonds and find the great nail-ship of *Naglfar* and its crew of jötnar and Hel's fury, and sail against the Æsir, above the world serpent and beneath the eagle. With them shall join mighty Fenrir and great Surt, and the war of Gods and Giants will rage.'

Again, she fixed him with her piercing glance. 'Would you know more?'

Halfdan nodded, transfixed.

'Odin shall fall to Fenrir's mighty jaws, and Freyja to Surt's blade. The sons of Odin will avenge their father, Vithar on the great wolf, and Thor against the world serpent, yet the serpent's dying breath will kill its own slayer and Thor shall be no more.'

Another pause as the völva locked him with a silent gaze. Then she picked up in little more than a whisper. 'And Loki and Heimdallr shall meet, blade to blade, and both shall perish.' She sighed, and leaned back a little. 'Few of the gods will survive, and *none* of the great powers, and with the death of the Æsir and the Vanir and the giants and dwarves, so shall the war end. The stars will die and the earth will sink beneath the waves. And when, after nine days, the last of the gods meet, they will make the world anew, beginning with the golden hall of Gimlé. And so ends the saga of Ragnarok.'

She fell silent. Halfdan found that he was trembling, and hoped it was the cold and that she could not see it. Finally, she spoke once more. 'This is the story of the end of the worlds of men and gods. It is not *your* story, Halfdan Loki-born.'

'It feels a little like it.'

'Are you völva?'

The jarl frowned. 'No.'

'Then why think you to navigate the threads of the Norns? How can you know more than a hundred generations of wisdom, tied to the goddess?'

He winced. 'It's just...'

'Nonsense is what it is. There is prophecy in your dream, for certain, and common sense tells you that, for you must face Gunnar in life, even as you do in your sleep. Have you ever seen the end of the duel in your dreams?'

'No.'

'Then how can you even hope to know what you face? Halfdan, leave the working of Seiðr to the Seiðr workers. Odin gave the gift to women and kept it from men for a reason. I shall strike with you a deal for all our time together. You will not attempt to work my works, and I will not challenge you for the leadership of your hirð. I remain völva and you remain jarl, yes?'

Halfdan could not help but smile.

'Sometimes I need to hear your wisdom to calm my spirit, Gunnhild. Can you feel the goddess now? With Hrafn gone, can you walk with her, see the weaving?'

The völva shook her head. 'It will clear, but Hrafn's spirit here, her dark work, has poisoned the very Seiðr of this place. I would not walk with the goddess here if I could.' She gave him *that* look again. 'But I need neither Seiðr nor Freyja to know that you are not Loki, and your actions cannot start the Twilight.' She breathed in and out, slowly, a few times. 'In Miklagarðr, I spoke with the empress Zoe of many things. She is a true daughter of the nailed god, but bright enough to see that there is more to the world than her religion. When we talked of gods and of faith, she spoke of something called a simile. It is where one thing resembles another, and can be used to explain it. This, I think, is what your dream is. What your fate here is, too: a simile. This is not the end of the world and the birth of a new. This merely heralds the end of *this* path and the start of a new, for we know that your saga draws to a close. For years, the Wolves have grown and changed in their quest. What began as vengeance upon Yngvar must end with vengeance upon Hjalmvigi, but that is not the end of Halfdan Loki-born. Just of that path in his life.'

She reached out and cupped his cheek in her hand, a curiously affectionate gesture he could never have anticipated. 'As Loki is freed,' she said, 'so are you. As Loki faces his enemy, so do you. But as the world of gods is remade, so will yours be. This is the moment of change, Halfdan. It is not an end. It is a beginning.'

With that, she gave him an odd smile, then reached for her staff and rose, turning and walking away. The jarl lay in his blankets for a while, sleep still elusive, his gaze playing across the sleeping forms of the Wolves of Odin.

When he slept, finally, it was peacefully, for the first time in months.

–

Halfdan awoke feeling energised and refreshed, his spirit calm, his confidence full. The dark purple of night was slowly giving way to light, but that light was not uncontested. Across the valley, clouds boiled and rose to thunderheads, piled like wispy rocks in the sky, reaching for the fading stars.

Fading stars…

Thunderclouds…

Thor was here to watch what was to come, he realised.

Yesterday he had seen Odin wandering across Hrafn's domain, and now Thor was here, too. Would Freyja come to Gunnhild and watch with her, he wondered. Was Loki still bound after all, unable to watch?

He rose, and the Wolves each greeted him as they roused from sleep. Within a short time, they had collapsed the shelters and gathered up their things. Bjorn had heaped what was left of the bear onto his cart, upon which those two heads were starting to look a little waxy and grey. The light was just beginning to change as they stepped onto the road once more.

Ahead, the dozen or so wooden shacks that formed a village still sat by the stream, lights long since extinguished. Even as the Wolves moved toward it, figures began to emerge, blocking their path. Halfdan made sure to walk a little ahead of the others. Yesterday there had been three deaths that may well prove to have been needless. He would avoid as much today, if possible. Even as he strode forward, Bjorn was moving up beside him, cart abandoned. He turned to the big man.

'No, Bjorn. This is time for the work of diplomacy, not war. Your talents may yet be required before the day is done, but for now I seek to build a new world, not to destroy the old.'

Frowning in incomprehension, Bjorn shrugged unhappily, and dropped back to collect his hand cart once more. For a moment, as they walked, Halfdan wondered whether he'd done the right thing there. The figures at the village were massing, and they outnumbered Halfdan's hirð already. Moreover, they were variously armed with spears, swords and axes, some in good helmets, some in chain byrnies. They were men attired for war. That could not be an accident.

Confidence.

He needed these men for what was to come, and when Gunnar's head swung beside those of Hrafn and Arkil, *they* would need *him*. He made sure to step even further forward, to leave them in no doubt that he was not afraid. He could not look back, but he could almost *feel* his closest friends gathering at his back: Bjorn and Ketil, Gunnhild and Lief, Ulfr and Farlof.

The Wolves of Odin.

But today no wolf would consume the sun.

'There is a price to pay,' a man shouted from the gathered locals.

'We have silver.'

'A price in *blood*,' the man clarified. 'Your hirð has invaded our lands, killed our people, and so far you have been lucky. But your luck, and that of your master in Jorvik, ends here. The price will now be paid. Gunnar rules these lands, and no child of the White Christ will drive him out.'

Halfdan waved to the others to stop, while he himself continued another five steps.

'You misunderstand me,' he said. 'The cunning of *Loki* is what brought us through your lines, not the Christ. The cunning of Loki, the strength of Thor, the wisdom of Freyja and the might of the Allfather, Lord of Frenzy.'

There was a weird silence. This apparently had not occurred to the locals. They had assumed Halfdan and his people to be Christians. Good. Now he had them disconcerted, it was time to hit them with a few truths.

'I am Halfdan Loki-born, son of Gottland. This is my hirð, the Wolves of Odin, and we are not here as servants of Jorvik, nor as conquerors or settlers. We do not want your houses, we do not care about your livestock or your lead mines. We are hunters, not invaders.'

He turned to give a shout to the others, but to his delight, Gunnhild was way ahead of him. She and Bjorn had untied the two heads from the cart and were walking forward with them, each holding their victim high.

'See the fate of Arkil the Berserkr,' he announced, gesturing to the heads, 'of Hrafn the völva. So shall be the fate of Jarl Gunnar in time, but no one else in this valley needs to share his fate.'

The silence was now expectant, wavering somewhere between shock at the sight of the heads and interest in what this enigmatic stranger was saying. Halfdan pulled himself a little straighter. 'You have defended your lands well, like good Northmen, like the men of rock and ice, of ash and elm. But there is so much more. You protect the lands of Gunnar of Swaledale, but no more than that. Gunnar seeks only this cold, bleak niche in the world, free of the children of the nailed god. Cattle and grass, rain and stone. Where is the whale road? Where is the adventure of the old world?'

He paused. Sometimes, he knew, skalds would pause in their story, for the silence heightened the tension of their tale and brought their audience ever closer. He was rewarded by a few of the locals stepping forward. Their weapons, he noted, were lowering. Not going away, but taking a less avid, belligerent stance. He *had* them.

'The Wolves of Odin are more than you see here, *much* more. We have fought with kings and emperors, *against* kings and emperors. We have raided the gold of Miklagarðr. We have fought dragons and giants and draugar at the very end of the world. We have made the earth quake in our travels, and we are in your lands for so brief a time, taking one more head. Then we move on, our dragon ship crewed and ready in Jorvik, for kings and priests in the land of the Svears tremble, knowing we come for them. Our deeds are already worthy of saga, our silver and gold already the riches of kings.'

Another pause to let that sink in.

'When Gunnar dies, the Christians of Jorvik will come, as they must, inevitably. Those good children of ash and elm who live here will be made thrall farmers for the archbishop, will kiss the cross to keep their land. There is no future here for children of the old ways.'

Another pause. He felt he was getting good at this.

'But that matters not. For any true child of ash and elm, of rock and ice, will always take adventure and fame and riches before damp farmland. Come with me, sail the whale road. Be a wolf in a world of sheep. I offer you an oar on the *Sea Dragon* and a journey such as you have never dreamed.'

Now he fell silent, and stayed silent. He could not resist turning, briefly, to look over his shoulder. Gunnhild gave him a firm nod. Bjorn looked faintly irritable, as though Halfdan had hidden his favourite toy, which, to some extent, was exactly what he was doing. The others waited, expressions hard, pensive.

'Only one jarl will leave this valley,' Halfdan said, then. 'It is your decision which one you will follow. Whether you will leave to explore the world and seek riches, or to avoid becoming a servant to the priests.'

Another long silence, and then half a dozen of the locals went into a huddle. There was a quiet, furious debate, and then they returned to their stance. Their weapons remained bared, but they also remained lowered.

'You come as a man of the North, not as a thrall of the Saxon dogs?'

Halfdan nodded. 'I do.'

'Then you will challenge the jarl the way it should be done. In Holmgång. Three shields, one victor.'

Halfdan nodded again. 'I shall. Though it will be a match to the death, not to blood or blow. Gunnar or I must leave this valley, not both.'

A chorus of assent arose from the locals. One of them gestured to another. 'Eiðr, go find the *hersarnir* and tell them a man comes to challenge Gunnar for his command.'

The second man nodded and turned, sheathing his sword and jogging away between the houses. 'We wait here?' Halfdan demanded.

The speaker among the men shook his head. 'Word goes ahead of us. You come to the jarl's seat, and there we mark out the green for Holmgång.'

Halfdan nodded, and the villagers all spun, then, many sheathing their weapons, and began to walk ahead. Halfdan turned and beckoned to the others, who came along behind him, following the locals. Reaching the edge of the houses, a grumbling drew his attention. Bjorn dropped the handles of his cart, the half-corpse of the bear once again sliding forward until it smacked into the ground. 'Not wheeling this thing up there,' he explained, pointing up the hillside. 'But it'd fucking better still be here when I get back, or I'll leave nothing in this valley but meat and bones.'

Halfdan smiled. 'I doubt they will take your mouldy heads or bear carcass, Bjorn.'

'Better not,' the big man growled, looking around and rubbing his hands.

'Come on.' Once again, Halfdan led the way, walking off through the village in the direction of the locals, who were already climbing the slope on a narrow, switchback path.

'You realise they're putting you at a disadvantage,' Leif murmured as he came alongside.

'Oh?'

'You'll have climbed a steep hill. Gunnar will have opened a door at most. Make sure they give you time to rest and recover before it begins.'

'You will be our law-speaker, Lief. You always have been, anyway. You will take our side in setting the challenge.'

Lief nodded, looking a little relieved. 'There is one thing to remember, though, Halfdan. Until you have stood face to face with Gunnar and issued the challenge, Holmgång has not been declared, and no law is in place. Be wary when we reach the top, for if Gunnar prides his survival more than his honour, we might find ourselves attacked before you can open your mouth to speak the challenge.'

Halfdan nodded. 'Make sure Bjorn and Ketil and the others realise this. But tell Bjorn not to go wading in without being told to. He is not to start anything, just to defend, should *they* turn on *us*.'

Lief turned and jogged back to the others, ready to issue his jarl's orders. Halfdan continued to stride ahead of the Wolves, following some distance behind the locals. The track was still steep, despite winding back and forth up the hillside, and Halfdan forced himself to slow to a very steady pace, preserving his breath and his energy. Lief was right. No one knew what to expect up there, and the sort of man who relied upon the support of people like Arkil and Hrafn was perhaps not to be trusted. Halfdan needed to be as ready and as prepared as he could be.

He jumped a little as a crack of thunder loud enough to wake the world serpent rang out over the hills to the south. He had an odd flashback to the dream, then, and his newfound confidence faltered for a moment. His eyes strayed to those thunderclouds. They were coming no closer, drifting lazily up the valley. The dawn was now in full swing, though the sun, which gleamed red-gold, showed only in a narrow line beneath those ominous clouds.

As he climbed, that blood sun began to paint the sky, rising through indigo to pink, and then to a strange, otherworldly red.

Just like the dream.

This is not the end of Halfdan Loki-born. Just of that path in his life.

Halfdan took a deep breath and steeled himself. There was no time now – no room – for doubt. Atop this rise was the house of Gunnar, Jarl of Swaledale, and if Halfdan ever wanted to look down the length of his sword at Hjalmvigi, Gunnar had to die.

One more breath and he bent to the last part of the climb, even as the blood sky swelled above and the thunder boomed.

Chapter 21

The recent past. Uppsala.

Bjorn knelt before the stone, head craned, and pulled out his axe-cleaning rag. The name was there, clear enough when he rubbed. *Sigviðr*. It had to be him.

It had only been when Bjorn cautiously made his way between the first buildings of the place, and asked a local what town this was, that he had realised the stone would be here at all, but once he knew, he'd had to find it. 'Uppsala,' the local man had replied, equally cautiously, edging around the huge, white, scarred man with the gleaming axe in his belt.

Uppsala.

The last known home of his grandfather.

He had no recollection of the old man, for he'd left the village before Bjorn was born, but he did remember some word arriving that the old warrior had been reported killed, for his father had raged and shouted for a time, and had then taken a friend and made the journey from their village to this town of kings to learn more. His father had come back with a bitter look to explain that there was no sign of the old man. He'd left Uppsala more than a year earlier on some fool quest and died abroad, and his father had dallied in the town only long enough to raise a rune stone in the old man's memory.

In a way, he was lucky to have found it at all.

The rune stones in Uppsala were being uprooted and moved, smashed and reused. There were still those in the town who trusted the Allfather and shunned the young Christ-god, continued to hold the ancient rites at the royal mounds and temple, hid what stones they could from the rabid Christians, rescuing ones that had been taken, but each month more signs of the old world were disappearing. The tide in Uppsala was turning against the Æsir and the Vanir.

It had taken three days, a small fortune in silver, and five punch-ups to locate the stone.

He found it in the church, of all places. While defiant men tried to halt the spread of the nailed god's faith, their opponents had raised a new wooden church overlooking the old temple, and had even taken the stone of Sigviðr from its place of honour, tipping it flat and placing it atop other broken rune-stones to form the altar on which their god's work was to be done.

So here was Bjorn, crouched in the church, right at the altar, looking up at the underside, where his grandfather's name was the only clear part. He rubbed at it again with the rag, squinting. There was more there, something about his grandfather going to the land of the Angles. That, at least, was something Bjorn had not known. His father had not spoken much of the old man's travels.

Angleland. An exotic place over the sea to the west. Even in Bjorn's now-wide travels he'd never got that far.

'Can I help you, my son?' asked a calm voice.

Bjorn frowned. Turned. Rose.

A priest stood a short distance away, a benign look on his old, beak-nosed face. His clothes were neat and basic, his hair shorn and heavily receding.

'I doubt it.' Bjorn hesitated. He was sorely tempted to pull his axe free and cut the man in half, as the Christians here had done with someone's rune stone to make the legs for the altar. Really, Bjorn felt he would be entirely justified in pounding the priest to snot for dishonouring his grandfather's memory.

But looking at the old man, who was smiling with an open, trusting face, he realised he didn't feel like it. He'd never intended to crusade against the nailed god, just to stand against his followers when they did something wrong. It was justice, and occasionally vengeance, that he sought, not murder.

He saw the priest quail for a moment at the sight of Bjorn's startling colouring and the four great scars across his face. To the man's credit, he recovered remarkably quickly, and the smile never really faltered. No, this priest could live. Looking at the man's hands, he'd clearly never done a proper day's work in his life. In retrospect he'd clearly not moved and broken the stones himself, and it was quite likely he was never really involved. It was not justice to kill someone for a crime you *suspected* they'd been involved in.

'I was just leaving,' Bjorn said.

The priest gestured to the altar. 'The bread and the wine are blessed, ready for the service and the eucharist this morning. If you cannot stay for the service, perhaps I can give you communion now? You could partake of the flesh and blood—'

Bjorn's nose wrinkled. 'Urgh. No thanks. The only flesh and blood I eat comes in stew bowls or on iron spits.'

The priest frowned, uncomprehending. Bjorn nodded to the man and started to walk past him.

'Will you turn your back on God, my son?' the priest said, and now there was an unexpected edge to his voice that had not been there before.

Bjorn paused, then, breathing shallow, controlled. He was holding on to his temper, though the priest was starting to test that. The man would shut up if he knew what was good for him.

'Not everyone bows to your cross, old man.'

He turned back, and was astonished at the change that came across the priest then. Where he had seemed serene, beatific, even welcoming, a moment ago, suddenly his face was filled with righteous fury, his eyes hard, blazing, his finger rising to point at the visitor.

'Heathen! You, a heathen, dare to foul this place with your filth?'

Bjorn shrugged.

'Filth? It's been hours since I shat, and I wiped and washed, too.'

The priest faltered again, confused at the abrupt change of direction, but quickly recovered. 'Out. Out of my church before I send for the authorities.'

Bjorn's eyes narrowed. 'I don't often kill priests, but it's not unknown. Careful, old man.'

'Out, spiteful son of the pit. Out, filthy demon-loving vagrant. Out, foul one. Out!'

Bjorn's punch was hard enough to send the priest floundering, staggering back toward the altar. He fell to the ground on his backside, still furious, still pointing. He rubbed his jaw, tasted the blood pouring down his lip from his nose. Bjorn felt quite pleased with himself. Despite provocations, he'd pulled the blow so that he didn't break too many bones.

'I know who you are, demon,' the priest hissed. 'The Bear-torn. Who else could you be? May the angels rip you limb from limb for your sins.'

Bjorn rolled his eyes and turned away once more, walking from the fallen man back toward the church door, and the more fragrant air beyond it.

'I pray you burn for your heresy, in this world, and in the next.'

Bjorn ignored the ranting priest on the church floor and strode to the door. His fingers closed on the handle. Gripped. Turned. Pushed.

The air outside was as cold as Hel's breath, flakes of fresh fallen snow whirling up and around in eddies. The sky was iron grey, filled with clouds that promised a fresh blizzard. Bjorn stopped. His eyes fell on the four men in russet uniforms standing across from the church, swords and spears in hand.

'Your time has come, Bear-torn,' one of them said.

The main house, clearly that of the jarl, stood more forward than the other two, and was larger and of better quality. A solid building with a good roof, its position granted it phenomenal and unobscured views up and down the dale, as well as up the small side valley of the tributary stream. Before it, a wide-open area sloped only very slightly, creating more or less a terraced area above the hillside. A perfect place for Holmgång, where a cordon could be strung out around the fighting area.

The people of the village they had followed up from the valley bottom were already falling into place around the edge, in a manner very reminiscent to Bjorn of the crowd around the fighting pit of Skara. The jarl's door stood wide open, darkness within, as the strange red light of the storm-morning bathed the stonework to either side.

Bjorn knew that Halfdan considered this his fight, and so it was. It would be jarl to jarl, and the moment the challenge to Holmgång was given, Bjorn would be no more involved than any other bystander. But Lief had pointed out that *until* the challenge was given, anything went, and had warned the Wolves to be on their guard, to keep their eyes open and be aware of everything here, in case the whole thing turned into some trap before rules could be laid down.

Bjorn found himself hoping, wishing, praying that someone here might start something before the challenge was issued, but no one here looked likely to try. Even those warriors they'd followed up from the valley bottom had sheathed their swords and were simply standing and watching, waiting for events to begin, pensive, worried. There was the murmur of conversation within the house. Someone was animated in there, *several* someones. It sounded, to Bjorn, like the moments of raised voice when a discussion is about to break out into open argument.

Whatever was being hotly debated, someone had clearly had enough, for there was a snapped curse in there, and everything fell silent.

Bjorn could feel possibilities growing. They could only be arguing over the new arrivals, and if there was division, that almost certainly meant that *someone* was spoiling for a fight.

He almost grinned as two figures suddenly emerged from the door of the house, for both were armed for war, shields on display and blades bared, and both immediately turned and pointed at Halfdan and his Wolves, snarling something to each other.

They stopped.

The whole world stopped.

The two men stared at Bjorn and the others, possibly sizing them up. Bjorn's glee began to crumble. The two men had seemed belligerent and ready for a fight the moment they appeared, but now, with sight of the Wolves, they had faltered. The fight was going out of them. Perhaps Gunnar, inside, had ordered them to stand down, and now they were of a mind to obey.

'I would speak with your jarl,' Halfdan shouted at them.

The two men stood, silent, both watching. The one on the left was slightly taller than his friend, but the one on the right was broader at the shoulder. Bjorn was acutely aware that Ketil was now standing beside him, and was almost vibrating with the need to fight.

'They're mine,' Bjorn breathed quietly.

'They're no one's when Halfdan shouts his challenge. Until then, one of them's mine.'

'Bollocks.'

'Bollocks, legs and everything else. One is mine. I'll take the tall one.'

Bjorn frowned. There were times that he felt people took advantage of his slow wits, and this was almost certainly one of them. If Ketil wanted the tall one, then Bjorn wanted him too.

'Tall one is mine.'

'I am the taller of us. It makes sense.'

Bjorn growled. 'I'm almost as tall as you, you streak of piss.'

'Fair enough. *You* take the tall one. I'll take the short.'

Bjorn's frown intensified as he peered at the two men. What was the Icelander up to? He fought the urge to retort with 'No, *I'll* take the short one,' but there was always the possibility that Ketil had done that just to talk him into the very choice. A double-bluff. The big man fumed.

'Good,' he said.

'It's moot anyway. Listen.'

Halfdan was repeating his call. 'Jarl Gunnar, I am here to challenge you for command of your hirð and the right to rule this valley.'

More furious conversation issued from the house, though again it was muted and inaudible.

The two warriors out front were muttering together now, occasionally looking across at Bjorn and Ketil.

They were hersarnir, Gunnar's commanders, the men who led war parties, men who – if Gunnar had boats and access to water – would have skippered his ships. They were the best men Gunnar had, and that was clear by their nature. A man who lived to take the role of *hersir* did so because he was the best warrior and the best leader a jarl had in his hirð. The day they were no longer the best, they would probably end it as a corpse, as their killer took on the role. It was in their nature to be the best.

Bjorn felt himself begin to smile and forced it back down. Too much eagerness might draw Halfdan's anger. Bjorn had killed Arkil, Gunnar's champion berserkr, and while he had no claim over Hrafn, he had killed her wild brown bear, which was perhaps even better. Now, in front of this house, stood the two men who were the best warriors in all of Swaledale… apart from Gunnar himself, of course. This was an opportunity, and Bjorn was not about to let it slip through his fingers. Halfdan would shout at him, no doubt. 'These men could have been allies,' he would say. 'They could have been Wolves of Odin.' Bjorn was prepared. He could manage a counter argument. These men were bound to Gunnar in a way ordinary warriors were not, for Gunnar had granted them their position, and without him, they *were* just ordinary warriors. He smiled to himself at that one. That was the sort of logic that Lief and Gunnhild usually used on him to talk him in circles. He was quite proud of it.

But for all those two men were proud warriors and looked distinctly ready for a fight, neither was yet making a move. That, of course, would have been what all the argument indoors would have been about. They did not like it, and wanted to fight. And that meant that, if the other side of the argument had been their jarl, which it almost certainly was, Gunnar was considering a straight duel with Halfdan for control of Swaledale.

The men looked at him again, and he saw their eyes narrow as they talked together in low voices.

These two would never submit to Halfdan. Even if everyone else here embraced a place as a Wolf, these two wouldn't – *couldn't* – because of what they were.

Bjorn hid the smile once again.

Provocation. Like that priest in Uppsala a few years ago. Bjorn had been ready to walk away that day, but the balding little bastard had just needled him too far.

Bjorn waited until the pair were watching him closely, then he turned. It was a leisurely thing, slowly moving as though to speak to Anna, who stood behind him. The moment he was facing the surprised Anna and with his back to the hersarnir, though, Bjorn proceeded to hitch up his shirt, jam a hand down the back of his trousers, and have a good rummage in his arse crack.

Once he felt certain it had been long enough that both the hersarnir had to have seen him delving, he pulled his hand free once more, shirt dropping over the top of his trousers, turning back to face them. There were a few things he'd learned in Greek lands, most of them insipid and dull, but the one he'd liked, he now employed. As he turned back to the hersarnir, he raised the finger he'd jammed in his arse, which was now none-too-clean, and lifted his arm, bent at the elbow, the back of his hand to the pair. Folding three fingers below the thumb, he extended the middle one high and proud, smeared with shit.

He stayed like that, grinning.

The pair were clearly getting the idea that this was an insult, even if they did not know the Greek habit, and just in case they did *not* get that he was imitating their penis, worryingly slender and covered in another man's excrement, he turned his hand a little and let the finger droop comically. His grin widened.

The burly one of the pair snarled something and took a step forward. His friend, also looking less than happy, held him back.

'I call you a third time,' Halfdan shouted, 'Gunnar of Swaledale. If you are a man, come and meet my challenge.'

That, too, was a provocation. Bjorn felt time moving too fast. If Gunnar appeared to answer the challenge, any hope of a nice little fight disappeared, for Bjorn would never dishonour Halfdan by breaking Holmgång etiquette. He looked about. Almost everyone was watching either Halfdan or the house's door, expectantly. Only the two great warriors were watching Bjorn and Ketil. They were ready to fight, but still holding back.

'You smell like a shitter,' the Icelander commented and recoiled with a gasp from Bjorn's stained finger as he turned to him.

'You want the little one, you need to piss him off.'

Ketil frowned, then realised what Bjorn meant, nodding. 'If only I could sink an arrow into his groin. *That* would piss him off.'

Bjorn grinned, and turned back to the hersarnir. He had only moments. He needed more provocation. Grinning, he pointed to the tall one, then mimed dropping his own trousers and taking the man roughly from behind, slapping his buttocks.

The man glared balefully at him. Bjorn almost laughed. He'd known plenty of men who'd liked a cock from time to time, some of them men who were lonely after weeks of voyage, some Byzantine warriors who seemed more naturally inclined that way. It didn't bother Bjorn a bit, but he knew just how much it bothered some people, notably Christians, or snotty men who considered themselves important warriors.

He was rather enjoying his lewd mime, and starting to turn it into a song in his head, when his labours bore fruit. Suddenly the two hersarnir were running across the open ground toward them, the tall one bore an expression of utter fury, while his shorter friend, though clearly also angry, was trying desperately to stop the man running.

Bjorn stopped his mime in an instant, falling still and effecting what he hoped was a look of total innocence. Bjorn had not been even remotely innocent since the day he'd been taken as a war slave. Still, he must have got it reasonably right, for even though both Halfdan and Gunnhild, having seen the warriors run, turned to look directly at Bjorn, neither said anything, and their suspicious gazes swiftly moved on.

The two warriors struggled as they ran, one trying to stop the other, and Bjorn looked across at Halfdan with a question that the jarl answered with a resigned nod. Bjorn and Ketil moved to stand between Halfdan and the hersarnir. This clear move to prepare for a fight stripped the last reserves of care from the two men, and now both were running, weapons out, teeth bared.

Bjorn smiled grimly. He'd managed to engineer one last fight for himself. True, he had to share it with Ketil, but he could live with that, especially since he still wasn't at his best. As the two warriors closed on them across the open ground, the world slowly slid into chaos around the hillside. The gathered locals murmured and shouted, unsure what to do, some taking a step forward, hands going to weapon hilts, others trying to hold back their friends. They were at odds. Did they hurry in to support the two captains, or did they stay back, awaiting orders, for the two men had not called for a general attack?

A moment later, a voice began bellowing from the house for the hersarnir to stop, but there was no chance of that now. The pair were warriors of the old ways, and just as happened with Bjorn, their blood was up, and nothing short of a thump on the head was going to stop them.

The two picked up pace, just a few footsteps from Bjorn and Ketil, weapons coming back for a swing.

A horn call suddenly blared from inside the house, a deep, resonating 'Booooooo' that blasted across the hillside like a tidal wave, drawing the attention of almost all present. Four men did not heed it, for they were about to collide, though out of the corner of his eye, Bjorn saw Halfdan go pale, as though something momentous had happened.

Then the fight began.

The pair came at Bjorn and Ketil, one on each, and the big albino paid attention to his own fight, confident that the Icelander could handle the other man. The hersir swung his sword, bringing his shield around to face his opponent. The shield, red and white, bore a triquetra design, an interlaced, three-pointed knot, and at each point was painted a rune of power – Uruz for strength, Hagalaz for stamina, Sowulo for victory.

As the man's sword came around, a solidly aimed swing, given Bjorn's current one-arm disability and lack of shield, the albino threw out his axe in that direction. The two blades met with a metallic clang, both slipping away together, shredding the air.

Even as Bjorn moved slightly to prevent a follow-up in the same manner, he was planning his next attack, for he was as yet in no danger of the battle mist descending upon him. The shield would be unbreakable, with those runes placed as they were. He knew damn well that he could hammer at it all day with his axe, but he would get nowhere. That shield had been designed by someone with the Seiðr knowledge, probably Hrafn. The man knew it, too, for he was keeping the shield between him and Bjorn, like a wall of power.

If he could not destroy the shield, he had to get it away from the warrior so they could fight properly.

Another swing came, and this time, Bjorn did not put his axe in the way. Instead, he took a huge step to his right and forward a little, putting him at the man's flank, near the shield that came around to face him, as expected. And as Bjorn took the massive step, his axe, pulled back at hip level, swung round. The blow, unchecked, would either hit the lower edge of the shield and knock it askew, or possibly slip under it and bite into the man's pelvis.

The problem with men who had good shields, and knew it, was that they often relied on them too much. Even as the hersir's sword swiped through the air where Bjorn had been a moment earlier, missing him by less than a hand-width, the man instinctively dropped his shield by just half a foot, enough to catch the low swinging axe.

That, though, was just what Bjorn had anticipated. In dropping his shield, the man exposed his arm for half a foot above the upper rim of the shield. Bjorn's swing may have looked low, for it started that way, but as the axe swung it was rising, coming up unstoppably. The man realised his error too late. He tried to lift the shield again, but the great axe slipped over the rim and smashed into his upper arm.

The man's chain byrnie had good, elbow-length sleeves, which prevented the powerful blow completely severing it, but the sound of the bone shattering within was audible even over the din of combat. As the two men leapt back, Bjorn to reassess and plan his next attack, the hersir in shock, leaping out of the way of any follow-up strike, the powerful shield with its magic protection fell from that shattered, agonising arm to the grass below.

The two men stood for a moment, facing one another, two strong warriors, each now with one arm and no shield. The

320

man was panting with the pain, gritting his teeth, but like a true warrior he had not backed away or submitted.

Off to his right, Bjorn could hear cursing in an Icelandic accent atop the sounds of grunting with effort, the ring of iron on iron and the clonk of wood being struck. Beyond that, he could hear Halfdan and Gunnhild both talking loudly, but could not quite make out what it was they were saying over the din, and then, again, he could also hear that great 'Booooo' of the horn in the house. The crowd had not moved.

None of it was Bjorn's concern right now. Right now, he had a hersir to kill.

His opponent watched him carefully as he, with some difficulty and a lot of hissing, tucked the hand of his broken arm in his belt to stop it swinging wildly as he moved. Then, impressively, the hersir made the next move. His arm came up, sword over his shoulder, and then began to swing forward in a chopping motion as he took a step forward to bring him within range of his target.

The sword came down, and Bjorn had been ready to dodge to the side, but the man's chop curved as he swung, the sword cutting across at an angle, so that as Bjorn tried to step out of the way he was, in fact, just stepping into the blow. Clever, almost a copy of the blow with which Bjorn had broken the arm. He had no choice but to throw his axe up in the way, letting his grip slip toward the head and presenting the haft to the descending blade. The man's weapon struck the ash handle hard. The parry was not strong enough to entirely deflect the sword, and the blow struck Bjorn on the shoulder to which his damaged arm was strapped, though the axe haft had robbed it of most of its power. Still, Bjorn grunted at the pain the blow sent through his broken arm. It would clearly be some time before he could rely on that arm.

Both sword and axe were now down by Bjorn's left hip, and both men pulled their weapons back for another strike, but Bjorn had no intention of letting another blow land. Even as they pulled back, his right foot came up in a hard kick. His aim was true, and his enormous leather boot swung up between the legs the man had planted apart for stability. Long ago, in the pit at Skara, Bjorn had learned a hard lesson: there was no such thing as a *heroic* fight; there was just a fight.

This fight was over in the moment his boot connected. His foot smashed into the man's privates, the chain shirt doing nothing to stop it, only cloth undergarments within. Bjorn fancied he even heard the crunch as his opponent's manhood was irreparably crushed.

The sword fell from the man's grip as his eyes bulged, cheeks going red in a suddenly white face, his howl of horror and agony cutting out across the landscape and the gathered folk. The hersir dropped to his knees, fresh agony rippling through him as the motion sent shockwaves up his broken arm and through his ruined groin. His remaining good hand came down to the hem of his chain shirt, and disappeared beneath. The look of horror on the man's face only worsened at whatever he found.

Bjorn toyed with the idea of leaving the man like that, but decided against it in the end, not for reasons of ethics and sympathy – a coup de grâce – but because if the man lived, he would inevitably become a revenge-seeking enemy, forever lurking in Bjorn's shadow.

As the man rocked back and forth gently, clutching his privates and making strange mewling noises, Bjorn took a step to the side and pulled back his axe. His first swing did not entirely remove the head, but it got as far as being wedged in the spine as the man gasped and shook. The victor pulled the weapon free amid a spray of blood, and took a second swing. This time the head rolled free, face still white, eyes bulging, mouth an O of shock. What was left of the man toppled gently to the side to lay there, unmoving, in the grass, dead arm still cupping his privates.

Bjorn turned, wondering if he might get away with finishing Ketil's fight for him too, but only in time to see the Icelander's opponent kneeling on the ground, Ketil's axe buried in the angle where his neck met his shoulder. The tall man put one boot on the hersir's other shoulder, pulled the axe free and then swung again, this time taking off much of the man's face. The shaking body dropped to the ground, unrecognisable, and shuddered there for a while as Ketil tutted at a nick in the axe blade. He turned to Bjorn.

'No, you can't have him.'

The two men straightened, both retrieving their cleaning rags from their belts. They looked around for a moment, to make sure no one else was moving to the attack. No point in cleaning the weapons if they were about to be used again. The crowd were standing silent, immobile, around the edge of the gently sloping terrace, mostly ashen-faced. The Wolves were still, gathered in a band, close to the scene of destruction, Halfdan out front, hands on hips, silent, waiting for the chaos to end.

Nodding to one another, Bjorn and Ketil cleaned their axes, then slipped the weapons back into their accustomed places.

Bjorn sighed with satisfaction. He'd thought there would be no more fights. Now there wouldn't be. It was not that he could find nothing else to do from time to time to entertain himself, but drinking and whoring were unlikely up in this barren, wild place. Killing was about the only viable pleasure here.

But the killing that was left now wasn't to be his.

The horn calls had stopped at some point during the fight, and there was fresh movement. Beneath a sky the colour of blood, with mountains of white-grey cloud on the horizon and the rhythmic boom of thunder bouncing across the valley, Gunnar of Swaledale emerged.

Even Bjorn found that he was holding his breath.

Chapter 22

Halfdan had had half a mind to put a stop to it. The moment Gunnar's hersarnir appeared from the house, it was clear that they wanted nothing more than to give a call to the various gathered warriors, then lead a charge to put an end to the newcomers. The fact that they did not do so made clear that Gunnar had sufficient power over them to hold them back, but from their very attitude, it was obvious that hold was weakening by the moment.

And he'd stolen a surreptitious glance at Bjorn and Ketil, and knew in an instant that they too were spoiling for that fight. Halfdan could see past this day, insofar as he could see anything past the portentous events of his dream, and could see how perhaps it was better to keep the more indiscriminate killing to an absolute minimum, and let this all ride on his challenge. Unfortunately, he knew damn well that Bjorn did not have that kind of foresight, and Ketil was a slave to instinct. That the pair had not already screamed obscenities and run at the hersarnir with axes held high was quite impressive.

He turned back to the house and cleared his throat. Time to start this. 'I would speak with your jarl,' he bellowed.

His attention switched back and forth between Bjorn and Ketil, eyes locked on those two warriors, and the doorway that as yet gave up no enemy jarl. Silence ruled for a moment, until he broke it.

'Jarl Gunnar, I am here to challenge you for command of your hirð and the right to rule this valley.'

There was another tense pause, and then Bjorn started acting up. Halfdan could see what the man was doing, though Bjorn probably thought he was being clever and getting away with it. He and Ketil – mostly he – were goading the two warriors into a fight.

As jarl, Halfdan could stop it. Probably *ought* to, in fact. But there were four things that prevented it. Firstly, he had too much on his mind, and needed to concentrate on the coming fight, not on Bjorn's lunacy. Secondly, he might actually *not* be able to stop the two fools starting the fight, and that would make him look like a powerless jarl to the enemy. Thirdly, the two hersarnir actually did look belligerent, and may well not accept the results if Halfdan did win, so it might just be better with them out of the way. And lastly, quite simply, he owed both Bjorn and Ketil so much that it was a small matter to let them loose on the enemy now, to make them happy.

Thus he did nothing as Bjorn taunted the men. He jerked his attention back to the house.

Time for another try.

'I call you a third time, Gunnar of Swaledale. If you are a man, come and meet my challenge.'

Frantic activity broke out across the space in front of the house, as Bjorn's taunts finally goaded the hersarnir into running, bellowing, into the fray, everyone else uncertain whether or not to join in. In fact, Halfdan was actually starting to enjoy the spectacle, and had to force himself to pay attention to his own business, particularly when Gunnar started shouting from inside the house, ordering his men to stand down.

Then came the horn.

A deep tone echoed out from the house and all around the dale, echoing from slope to slope, filling the world, or at least filling *Halfdan's* world.

Then shall Heimdallr blow the Gjallarhorn and call the gods to war. At the horn's sounding, Loki will escape his bonds and find the great ship of Naglfar, and the war of Gods and Giants will rage.

Halfdan shivered. He risked one glance up at the blood red sky, half expecting to see a black crack open across it, then at the house, and he was almost back in the dream. Small details were different, perhaps, but it was all so familiar.

Off to one side, Bjorn and Ketil were busy with the hersarnir, but Halfdan paid that little attention. He had no real fear for either of his men, and it was clear that this was an isolated incident, and that neither the Wolves nor the waiting locals were inclined to escalate matters. Even when the booing of the horn stopped, to the background of the fight, the held breath of the locals, and the crashes of thunder, the jarl of the Wolves stood, trembling slightly, eyes never leaving that door.

Gunnar appeared.

Halfdan found himself sizing up the man the moment he stepped from the house and stood in the strange morning sunlight. He was of slightly above average height, muscular and well-built, without the enormity of Bjorn or the barrel chest of Ulfr. He was not a young man, for the dark hair that hung long, shaved at one side and braided at the other, was shot through with streaks of grey. His beard was short and clipped, unlike most of the men Halfdan had met in the dale. He wore a blue shirt and grey trousers, over which hung a chain byrnie of exquisite manufacture. Even from a distance, Halfdan could see just how astounding the armour was, for the links were so small and tight that the whole thing shimmered more like the scales of a fish than a normal chain shirt. The armour reached halfway down his thighs and the sleeves to his wrists, girt about with a belt of leather and gold, from which hung sword and sax.

Apart from the quality of his armour, there was actually nothing astounding about Gunnar of Swaledale. He was, physically, quite average. He was no giant like Arkil or wielder of Seiðr like Hrafn. Yet there was about him a presence that filled the whole hillside the moment he appeared, as though he too were a sun, his light falling upon the people of the dale as he appeared.

Quite simply, Halfdan could understand in an instant why people served this man. Why they would die for him. Why a crazed killer like Arkil would bow to him. Why the powerful Hrafn would bind herself to him. In an odd way Halfdan was as jealous as he was impressed. He was fairly sure that if he lived to reach a hundred he would never have half the presence of the man he now faced.

Gunnar's gaze drifted across the hillside and then fell on Halfdan. It was probably a trick of geography and light, for the jarl stood bathed in the sun's rays as it shone beneath those thunder clouds, but his eyes seemed to gleam and burn, which made Halfdan's flesh crawl, for it was so reminiscent of the dream.

He felt the Loki serpents on his arm burning.

As they stood, appraising one another in front of two hirðs, silent against the backdrop of thunder, the fighting over to one side finished as Bjorn and Ketil both dispatched their opponents, looked around, and then began to clean their axes as they watched.

Silence.

'Who are you?' Gunnar called across forty paces of death-ground.

'I am Halfdan Loki-born, a son of Gottland, Jarl of the Wolves of Odin.'

'Gottland? You are a long way from home, Halfdan Loki-born. These are lands of the Norse, not Svears, Geats and Gottlanders. What brings you to my home?'

Halfdan shivered slightly. His home. That notion had not settled in him before. He'd considered these people invaders in the lands of the Angles, but if they had been here for generations, which clearly they had, then in truth, this was as much their home as that of the Angles, which made the *Wolves* the invaders.

'I am here for you, Jarl of Swaledale. I need your head to fulfil my end of a bargain.'

Gunnar simply nodded, no surprise. 'You strike a deal with the priest in Jorvik and thus invade my lands, and put my people to the sword.'

'You do not sound as offended as you might.'

Gunnar shrugged. 'In other worlds, in other times, it could be me standing there and challenging. Though I cannot think of any bargain I would strike that would see me do the bidding of the nailed god's lap dog.' He sighed. 'Still, there is little point to argument or persuasion. You are here, your friends carry the heads of my closest, and the bodies of my hersarnir lie mouldering before us. I do not think a man who has come so far will be turned back.'

Halfdan nodded. 'You speak true.'

'Then hear me now, Halfdan Loki-born of Gottland, I am Gunnar Thorkilson, Jarl of Swaledale, and I have never lost a fight. I will accept any challenge you care to make, but know this: I will kill you. On this hillside, you will die. Knowing this, state your wish.'

Halfdan felt his skin prickle. Everyone on the hillside, friend and foe alike, had been looking at Gunnar, and now every pair of eyes turned to him. Gunnar was not boasting idly. What he said was plain truth the way he saw it. He was stating fact, absolutely certain of his skill and the outcome of a fight.

Loki and Heimdallr shall meet, blade to blade, and both shall perish.

So be it. The Norns wove the world, and men could do naught but follow their thread.

He took a breath.

'There has been no insult between us, and there is no cause for Holmgång, yet there must be a duel, and only one of us can win this day. I would avoid *Einvigi*, or warfare of our people. I need only your head and would spare your hirð. Need I insult you to offer Holmgång?'

Gunnar's expression did not waver as he replied in calm tones. 'You have invaded my valley, killed my people and stolen their goods. I would say the insult is already given, enough even for feud. Let this end in Holmgång, as you say. Let my people see you pay for what you have done, Jarl Halfdan. You need not challenge me, for I challenge you.'

Halfdan nodded, trying to control the urge to shiver. It was done.

Lief stepped forward now. 'I am Lief Ivorsson, sometime skald of Kiev, once companion of Prince Jarislief. I claim the right to act as law-speaker here, for I know the Holmgångulog.'

Gunnar glanced at Lief only once, before nodding. Halfdan too nodded.

Lief stepped a few paces forward, then, looking across the ground. Compared with much of the dale's upper reaches, this patch of land before the jarl's house was flat, with short grass, no bracken or heather, and cleared of rocks. It was as good a patch of land for a duel as could ever be found. He pulled from his belt a bundle of sticks. Halfdan had not seen him gather them, but there had been plenty of opportunity. The Rus jammed one hard into the ground, pulled out his axe and used the haft to hammer it solidly into the grass.

'Let this mark the Holm,' he announced, and then took position next to the stick, still holding the others and his axe. He then took four large paces, and repeated the process, then turned and did so again, and then a fourth time, creating a square some twelve feet across. He nodded to Ulfr, who walked over carrying a bundle. As Lief wound a narrow cord around one stick and then ran it out to create a cordon around the sticks, Ulfr moved to the centre of the square and laid out a large cloak to form a square within it, some nine feet across, pegging the corners down.

The task done, Ulfr returned to the others, and Lief stepped outside the square and came to a halt, folding his arms.

'The Holm is ready. Let both men choose a shield bearer.'

Halfdan's gaze played across the Wolves. Bjorn and Ketil would not do. Both had already killed Gunnar's men on this hillside and might therefore be unacceptable to the locals. Lief could not be called upon, as the law-speaker, and Ulfr seemed to have automatically taken a role as his aide. Of Halfdan's oldest companions, then, that left Gunnhild. He didn't know whether there was any rule against a völva being involved. There very well might be, given the unpleasant idea of Seiðr being used, but he didn't know, and so he turned and gave her a nod. Gunnhild bowed her head in response, and then went among the Wolves, collecting shields from two of them. She then walked across to Halfdan and added to them his own shield, making a pile close by. The jarl also removed his helmet and placed it on the ground outside the Holm. If this was to be a meeting of equals, he would be equipped the same as Gunnar.

The man standing on the far side of the roped-off area gave a humourless chuckle.

'Something is funny?'

'Not really. I find that every name that comes to mind as a shield bearer is either lying in the grass over there, or their head dangles from your men's hands. Yes, I think you have given enough insult for Holmgång.' He turned to the locals, and gestured to the man who had spoken for them in the village. 'It seems I am in need of a new hersir, Eygrímr. Will you be my shield bearer?'

The man gave a single nod, and gathered three shields from the men around him, carrying them over to Gunnar with some difficulty and then dropping them by the roped area. As he did so, Ulfr and Lief took two swords from their people and unsheathed them, jamming them into the ground within the Holm, between the pegged cloak and the rope, at opposite corners.

Without the need for a command, Halfdan and Gunnar both stepped to the rope, beside the pile of shields. Lief came to the third side, between them, with Ulfr at his shoulder, while Gunnhild and Eygrímr each stood behind their master.

Silence fell, split only by a massive crack of thunder, south across the valley. The light was changing now, though not for the better. The sun had risen sufficiently above the hills to now be buried behind the thick, boiling white clouds, and so while the gold-red of the sky had faded, the world had darkened considerably. Halfdan wondered at that.

The jötunn in Ironwood releases her children, Sköll and Hati, who consume the sun and the moon, and plunge the world into darkness.

He suppressed the latest in a long series of shivers.

'I am the law-speaker,' Lief called, then, his voice clear and strong. 'The nature of Holmgång is known to all, but each land has its rules. The warriors here are of Gottland and of Angle land, and so I shall set the rules here for all to know.'

Nods greeted this all around. Everyone knew Holmgång, and many would have witnessed one at some point in their life, but when a duel was as rigid and strict as this, it was important that everyone worked to the same rules.

'Once the two warriors enter the Holm, there will be no interference from others, and no violence outside the Holm, for such things can distract the warriors. Any man or woman who deliberately distracts either of them shall be scourged for their crime. The only outside contact either warrior will have will be by my voice, should I need to halt or pause the fight, or by their shield bearers when they change shields.' He then turned to his own jarl. 'Halfdan Loki-born, you bear a short blade. Do you wish to exchange it for a longer sword, to match that of your opponent?'

Halfdan shook his head. Perhaps his short blade would prove to be a disadvantage in this, but he would fight to the end with the weapon he had won in the east.

'Very well. Once both men are in the ring, I shall give the call to begin. From that moment, should either warrior leave the roped area, he forfeits the duel. Holmgång is commonly to the wound or to incapacitation. On this occasion, there can only be total victory. On this day, here, Holmgång can only be declared complete upon the death of one warrior.'

He fell silent again, and this time the silence felt like lead. After a sufficient pause, he began once more. 'The warriors will alternate blows, beginning with Halfdan as the challenged party. A pause will be granted upon the need to discard a ruined shield, and for it to be replaced by the shield bearer. Once the shields are gone, the second sword, found in the corner of the Holm, can be taken up and used to parry. There will be no running or tripping or physical contact other than with the warrior's weapon. If either man needs to pause for a valid reason, he will hold his shield aloft as a signal. Are the rules understood?'

Both Halfdan and Gunnar nodded, and called the affirmative.

'Then warriors, take your first shield and enter the Holm.'

Gunnar and Halfdan both collected a shield from the pile. That of Gunnar was of a simple design, quartered with black and red, while Halfdan's was the raven one they had found at Hrafn's house. Both men stepped over the rope and walked forward until they were standing on the cloak area. There was silence again, then, split once more by the crash of distant thunder.

'Begin,' Lief called, and Halfdan hoped he was the only one who noticed the slight quaver of nerves in the Rus's voice. A great deal rode on this fight.

Halfdan and Gunnar walked forward until they were but two paces apart.

'Would that this did not have to happen,' Halfdan said. 'There are too few of us left of the old ways.'

Gunnar said nothing in reply, but rolled his shoulders and lifted his shield, sword held down by his side. Halfdan looked his opponent up and down. A heavy Northern sword could break a shield like this in three blows at most, one if the wielder was lucky or careful. His smaller Alani blade, while glorious and sharp, was going to do little to damage the shield. Never had he needed Loki cunning more. He took a deep breath. He was never going to break the shield, and that was obvious. Thus, he had to strike past it. Gunnar would know that just as well, looking at Halfdan's blade, and would be ready for such a move.

The secret was going to be tricking Gunnar into expecting one thing, but delivering another. That would take time. He could only hope that his own shields would last long enough. He was young, and he knew it. A veteran warrior like Gunnar might expect him to be predictable or less experienced. Not *too much*, of course, for he was a jarl, and had been successful so far up and down dale. Apart from the shield, there was the question of Gunnar's chain shirt. He was exposed only from the neck up and from mid-thigh down. The chain shirt's arms were long-sleeved, to the wrist. There were few places he could hit to wound, and a sword blow against the chain was less likely to cripple with broken bones than was Gunnar's long sword. Still, there was no more time to waste. He took a breath.

Head or legs. They were the only real targets, and so he would have to be inventive.

He lunged. His first blow was a slash from right to left, dropping down to knee height mid-swing. Gunnar simply dropped his shield to meet the blow, the hide edging turning aside Halfdan's sword, a small tear in the hide all he had to show for the attack. Halfdan pulled his blade back in, eyes narrowing, and readied his shield, sword now down at his side.

Gunnar was plagued with no such doubts. There was no delay. As soon as they had separated, the jarl took a step forward, bringing his sword down overhead with all his might. Halfdan threw his shield up to catch the blow, which it did, but felt the shock echo all the way up his arm to his shoulder. As they stepped away once more, Halfdan looked at his shield. The blow had dented the boss, taken half the facing from the shield, cracked one of the boards and torn a whole section of edging away. It would last another attack, but probably only one more. That was a worry. This could be over quite fast.

He knew that Gunnar would be expecting a variation, now. But as they stood facing each other, Halfdan instead repeated his previous strike, though he began it with a feint, as though he were going for the head this time. Gunnar dropped his shield,

333

taking the blow once more, this time scraping a line across the design and tearing more edging. Again the blow came nowhere near the target.

To his credit, there was no glee or grimace on the man's face. Gunnar was being careful, and not overly-confident. He must know he was getting the better of this every time, yet he did not gloat.

Good. Because Gunnar was going to die. And now, Halfdan thought he knew how. He had to test his theory a couple more times first, though, for he'd only get one shot at this.

He braced, as the jarl of Swaledale swung his sword wide, coming in at Halfdan's left. He threw the shield out to block the blow, and was careful to angle it so that the circular board took the strike edge-on. The sword slammed into the shield and hacked away a chunk of hide and board, though the majority of the shield remained intact. Halfdan shook himself, the ache from the blow palpable.

The two men separated again. Halfdan chewed his lip. His next move, if he wanted to test his theory, would be a stupid one. Would Gunnar believe for even a moment that Halfdan was naïve enough to make such a move. He would have to trust to luck.

As Gunnar readied himself, Halfdan braced, then leapt forward, sword lancing out in front of him, straight to Gunnar's chest. If he'd been making a serious attempt, then it was a very foolish one. Even if he got past the shield, the chance of hurting Gunnar badly through that chain shirt was very small indeed.

Yet it seemed luck was as with him as ever it had been. Gunnar clearly thought he was feinting and meant to raise or drop the blade mid-thrust. He lifted the shield to cover his face, and Halfdan's blade thrummed just under the rim, slamming into metal links. The jarl of Swaledale let out a grunt of pain at the blow, which was a long way from causing serious injury, but would bruise, and had winded him.

Halfdan had to control his face to prevent the grin breaking out. Not only had he scored the first actual hit, which showed

334

that Gunnar was not as untouchable as he'd seemed, but in doing so, Halfdan had more or less proved his hypothesis. He would try another two or three blows to be sure, but he was happy this was the case. When Halfdan struck, Gunnar responded by moving his shield to block, as one would expect, but natural instinct was making him move his sword in parallel. When his shield came up, the jarl's other arm brought his sword high; when his shield dropped, his sword-arm went low.

Gunnar took a few moments to recover this time, but once his breathing was slowed again, and he was ready, he narrowed his eyes, reassessing the younger jarl. His next blow was a repeat of his first, overhead in a chop. Gunnar had little need for subtlety, for he could rely with confidence on simply smashing Halfdan's shields until he had none.

Sure enough, this hit was sufficient. As Halfdan staggered back from the blow, he shook the shield in his hand, which was little more now than a dented metal boss with some broken wood around it. He raised it in the air, causing Lief to bellow for a pause, then shuffled back to the rope, throwing the broken shield away as Gunnhild held out a replacement.

'I see what you are doing,' she said. 'Good luck.'

Halfdan nodded, hoping that Gunnar was less perceptive. Once Lief called for them to resume, Halfdan stepped forth as though he were going into a crouch, but at the last moment threw the sword forward just as he had last time. Gunnar was prepared. The shield remained central, angling to knock aside Halfdan's blade. The blow failed to connect this time, but he continued to prove his theory, which was the main thing. Once again, Gunnar's sword arm was in concord with his shield, staying central, at his side.

Once more should prove it sufficiently.

He braced himself, as Gunnar circled his sword, exercising his wrist. The big sword scythed out, then, coming for Halfdan's side. He managed to get the shield in the way, but the sheer power of the blow split the hide edging, and cleaved the boards apart until it hit the boss, almost taking Halfdan's hand off in the process. He felt the numbing of his arm and the ache all the way up. That one had been bad. It had destroyed his second shield, for the chances of another blow simply going through it and into the arm were quite high. Lifting it, with some difficulty, he stepped back as Lief paused the match once more, and threw the ruined board away as Gunnhild held the last shield out for him.

'Be quick,' she said, somewhat unnecessarily. He was running out of shields fast, and had done little more than dent his opponent's. Stepping back in, he took a steadying breath as Lief resumed the fight. A swing once more, this time at Gunnar's head.

The jarl's shield came up, sword echoing the move. The board blocked Halfdan's hit, the shield taking a nasty gouge, yet still holding up well. But that was it. Halfdan was in little doubt. He knew what to do, but would get only one chance, and would have to make it count.

He barely had time to step back and ready himself before Gunnar's next strike, his third overhead chop. Halfdan's shield exploded under the impact, and only the metal boss saved his arm. He cast it aside, pieces of board all around. The shield had clearly already been weakened prior to the fight without any of them knowing, but there was nothing he could do about that. Three shields was the rule, regardless of quality.

He felt his pulse pound. Next time, he would have two swords, but no shield. His chances of stopping Gunnar's blow would drop drastically. He needed to finish this now. It seemed unlikely there would be a later.

The jarl of Swaledale readied himself to take Halfdan's next strike. Still, the man did not gloat, despite being a hair's breadth from victory. Halfdan braced himself. He needed Gunnar to know what move he was going to make, to react as he had already done.

He leapt, stabbing straight out.

Gunnar's shield moved only slightly to protect his torso, his sword arm level, blade held out at chest height. Halfdan's aim changed at the last moment, only very slightly. It was an insanely small target, but no smaller than that great arrow shot of Ketil's a few years ago that had ruined a fire-throwing tube.

Loki's own luck was with him.

The blade slammed into the cuff of Gunnar's extended sword arm, almost becoming trapped within the chain sleeve. He pulled it free, content in the knowledge that it was going to do as much damage coming out as it had going in. He was rewarded, as the blade slipped free, with a great wash of blood from the torn flesh of the jarl's inner wrist. Even as Gunnar pulled his arm back, yelping in surprise, another gush flowed from the sleeve.

The head and legs were the only *sensible* targets, but they were not quite the *only* targets.

Halfdan kept a check on his elation. It was not over yet. That was a mortal wound, as long as it remained open and unbound, but it would take a short while. Even with the immense damage he'd done, Gunnar would have time for at least one more blow, and the way the jarl gritted his teeth and stepped forward, blood pouring from his sleeve, he intended to take it.

Halfdan scurried over to the corner of the Holm and pulled the other sword from the ground, hefting it in his hand as he returned to the centre.

Gunnar was paling by the heartbeat, his life ebbing away at an astonishing rate, but a look of fierce determination had fallen across him. He had told Halfdan flatly that he would die here, today, and it appeared he meant to keep that promise.

Marshalling every tiny drop of strength he still had, Gunnar swung his sword. Halfdan moved the larger of his blades to block. The two swords met with a clang, but the Norse jarl had the edge. His blow was robbed of some of its power, but, smashing Halfdan's sword aside, it continued on its way. The large, heavy sword, knocked upward by the parry, smashed into the side of Halfdan's head with a pain he'd never experienced. His vision blurred, and he heard two distinct cracks. He staggered to the side, shaking, stunned. He tried to focus his eyes. Everything was blurred, but he saw Gunnar fall. Saw the jarl of Swaledale collapse to the ground. Saw him lying there, utterly still.

Halfdan felt shaky. He tried to turn his head to Lief, but when he did, there was another crack and his vision became even swimmier. The pain burst through him like a fireball, then, and he staggered. Even through the agony, he realised that he had to outlast Gunnar.

'The victor is Halfdan Loki-born,' Lief announced. 'So say I, so say the gods.'

'Much good it will do him,' shouted Gunnhild, with real alarm in her voice.

It was the last voice Halfdan heard as he fell to the ground.

Funny thing about a heartbeat, he thought to himself as the blackness engulfed him. *You don't really notice it until it stops.*

Chapter 23

The recent past. Uppsala.

Bjorn swung hard with the knobbly walking stick that he'd picked up from beside a house doorway, smacking it into the russet-tunic'd man's head. It struck his temple, and the man spun, eyes rolling, and fell to the ground in a heap, sinking into the settling snow.

The big man watched for just a moment. He contemplated finishing him off, for it was never a good idea to leave live enemies behind you, but too much killing in a town tended to bring down the authorities, and he could do without having to flee Uppsala in a hurry.

The four men who'd been waiting for him outside the church had thought they could bring him down between them. He'd disabused them of that notion quite quickly. His axe had felled the first right in front of the nailed god's wooden house, and he'd put down the second quickly afterwards. He'd taken a nasty slash in the process, and a couple of thumps that would leave a bruise, but nothing that would cause lasting harm, unlike the two men who now lay around the church, mouldering into their tedious Christian afterlife.

The other two had watched in shock as their friends fell, and had looked at one another, then taken to their heels and fled the big man as fast as their legs could carry them. Bjorn had chased the men through the streets of Uppsala, then, cursing and threatening them, snow whipping through the air to chill the bones. The pair had stayed together, presumably feeling safer that way, until they reached the last corner. There, they had split up, and Bjorn had followed the fastest one until he cornered him here in this dead end, where he'd now put the man down with the stick.

With a sigh, Bjorn turned and ran back after the last man. Rounding the corner, he could just see the man off ahead, along the street, running like a coward, piss-stained trousers and bulging eyes as he looked back over his shoulder. For a moment, Bjorn believed he would never catch him, but then, while looking back, the man tripped in a pothole hidden by the snow and went crashing to the ground with a cry.

Thanking Thor for his timely interference, for Bjorn knew that he was favoured of the Thunderer, he put on an extra turn of speed as the man struggled to rise again, slipping in the snow. As the big albino bore down on the man, a small crowd watched from the doorways and windows, wisely staying out of the snow, even more wisely staying away from the fight.

The man was just up again as Bjorn reached him, and quite astoundingly, as he rose, he spun, fist coming out. Bjorn blinked in surprise as the man's fist slammed into his jaw, his mouth open as he cursed. He felt two teeth break under the blow, quite painfully, the most pain he'd felt in some time.

He roared as the man recoiled, staring in shock at his own fist, in which a tooth was now embedded. Bjorn spat blood at the man, and returned the favour, his massive fist planting square in the man's face. He both felt and heard the nose break, and blood sprayed out to join his own. A mizzle in the air, red droplets settling into white snow all around them.

'I'm going to kill you slow for that,' Bjorn snarled, through the blood.

'Fuck off,' was the man's eloquent reply.

Bjorn had to hand it to the man. He was brave. Not for long, though. As Bjorn roared, the man turned and tried to leg it again. This time, though, he had no advantage of distance, and as he reached the door of a tavern, Bjorn was on him.

He punched again, this time hitting the man in the chin. The combatant fell back against the door, which swung open. The man staggered backward into the building, between tables of locals bathed in golden light, nursing mugs of drink, many swearing at the sudden interruption and the snow that swirled and whipped inside like the breath of Hrimgrimnir.

The man lurched backward toward the bar, by some miracle managing not to fall, just staggering, looking this way and that, swearing in mild panic.

Bjorn took a step to follow, but at that moment, something hit him in the back, and arms were suddenly around his neck, the sleeves a familiar russet. He cursed. The man he'd left unconscious clearly hadn't been, after all. Damn it, but he knew not to leave enemies alive. Ah well, it just meant the fun would last for a little longer.

Roaring, he staggered into the tavern, one man clinging on around his neck, the other lurching away from him. All eyes in the hall turned to him as he dealt with his immediate predicament. He turned, fist bunched, and elbowed the man on his back in the ribs. The limpet let out a whoosh of breath as he let go and fell away.

'Fucking cross-humpers,' Bjorn snarled, then concentrated on the one before him again. A few steps forward and he reached down and swept up a stool from beside an empty table, swinging his makeshift club back and forth as he bore down on the man. He heard the footsteps of the one he'd just shaken off, then, as he came on once more, and Bjorn simply stepped aside and watched the russet man barrel past.

There was an odd silence. Bjorn stood and watched as the two men stood side by side, fists bunched, ready to fight on, knowing they were trapped.

The first he knew of the fresh danger was a squawk of surprise behind him.

Bjorn turned, frowning, and recognised the third man in a russet shirt, one of the pair he'd left at the church, falling to the filthy, wet tavern floor. Behind the man, a young fellow still had his leg stuck out, having tripped the man, and quite possibly saved Bjorn's life, given the sword that even now fell from the downed man's grip. He watched the man only long enough to see the young drinker stand and deliver the fallen Christian a kick to the temple that sent him into the black, then turned again.

The two men he'd been facing had taken advantage of his distraction. One had tried to duck past him to escape, the other snaking fast between tables to pass him by. Bjorn swung with the stool and broke it over the man slipping past him. The man cried out as Bjorn lifted the broken stool with a roar, but he was still up and running. One fleeing man met the other near the door.

Bjorn narrowed his eyes as he caught the gaze of some of the patrons at their tables. A number of them wore crosses around their necks. He made a quick mental calculation, and decided that perhaps it would be better not to kill the three men in here and trigger another fight with the majority of the mead hall's population.

He brandished the broken stool at the men and roared, but made no move to chase them as they bent and grabbed the arms of their unconscious friend, dragging him away. Moments later they were gone, out into the snow. A skinny fellow with a lazy eye swore crudely and rose, crossing to the door and slamming it shut to keep out the snow and the freezing wind.

'Why d'you bring your arguments in here, you great hairy heap?' the owner of the tavern snapped angrily behind him, causing Bjorn to turn. 'Look what you've done to my furniture,' the man said. 'And there's blood all over the floor. I hope you've a purse full of hacksilver.'

Bjorn was about to explain that he was a little short of coin at the moment, as usual, when the young man who'd saved him before strode up beside him and held out a sword to the innkeeper.

'It's no jarl's blade,' the young man said, 'but it's solid and well balanced. Worth more than a stool and a quick scrub of the floor. Maybe even worth an evening of ale?'

The man's eyes narrowed as he took in the blade being offered. Clearly it would be a very advantageous trade, yet while a Svear might be a warrior or a craftsman, fisher or farmer, first and foremost he will always be a trader.

'Four ales,' the man said, still eyeing them up carefully.

The young man smiled. 'Done. For four ales each.'

As the owner blustered, claiming he'd never said 'each', the young fellow placed the sword on the counter and returned to his table. The other chair sat empty, and so, after a pause and with a furrowed brow, Bjorn stomped after him and sank into the recently vacated seat. A moment later the owner was there with two mugs of sharp ale and no further argument. He might have been outmanoeuvred in a barter, but he had still got the better deal, and he knew it. The sword would more than pay for an evening for these two.

'Your help was timely,' the big man said finally.

'A fight's a fight, but murder's different,' the stranger said simply, taking a pull of his ale.

Bjorn nodded and followed suit. 'Christians,' he snorted quietly, though not quietly enough, for several heads turned and regarded them warily for a moment before returning to their own conversations. 'They cannot let a man worship his own way. Everything has to be crosses and eating their god's flesh and drinking his blood. I don't care what foul things they do in their temples, but I'm not eating the flesh of their nailed god. They say he's a thousand years old. How rotten will that flesh be now?'

The young man chuckled. 'Our sort are not popular these days, my big friend.'

Bjorn's eyes narrowed. 'Except where you come from, I think. I know a Gotland accent when I hear one. I'm Bjorn, who they call "Bear-torn".'

The man smiled.

'Halfdan. Who they call Halfdan.'

Late February 1044. Gunnar's Sætr, Swaledale.

Halfdan lay still.

Bjorn felt something then that he had not felt in a very long time, reaching right back through the years and across the worlds he had travelled, past his days of hunting and being hunted, past the bear and the blood-eagled priest, past the völva in Kaupang, past the fighting pit of Skara, past his time of slavery, right back to the day a small boy had asked why his father had to go off and fight.

He felt panic.

He *owed* Halfdan Loki-born. In fact, he owed the jarl so much that had he eight lifetimes, he would never be able to repay him sufficiently. Bjorn had been a powerful man by that day in Uppsala, and had been on a path of sorts, but it had only been as he sailed east with the Wolves, aboard the *Sea Wolf*, seeking the blood of Jarl Yngvar, that Bjorn had realised that Halfdan and his hirð *were* that path before him of which the völva had spoken. Halfdan was their leader, and Bjorn had found direction, cause, fellowship and friends, all through him. If Halfdan was dead, what would happen? Bjorn could not contemplate going back to that world, wandering aimlessly, hunting and hunted. With Halfdan, he was *more* than the Bear-torn. He was a Wolf of Odin.

He bent to lift the broken form of his jarl from the blood-soaked cloak.

Around them, everything was chaos and noise. The Wolves were arguing and shouting in worry, Lief trying to bellow for calm and quiet across the top of them, largely ignored, Ketil crossing to the body of Gunnar of Swaledale and repeatedly kicking the shit out of it in fury. The locals were watching silently, not knowing what to do, whether to avenge their fallen jarl, or to mourn both combatants, who had fought so bravely and cleverly to a mutual demise.

Bjorn ignored it all.

He didn't care about anything right now except the young man before him, who had once tripped a man in a tavern and brought order to Bjorn's life. Halfdan's head was a mess, and his neck was going black. Bjorn didn't know much about such wounds, but he had seen men get up and walk away from head and neck injuries. Yet Halfdan was motionless, eyes closed, and his chest did not move, no breath coming. He was dead.

Bjorn reached down to slip his arms beneath his jarl and lift him, but a voice at his ear stopped him.

'Don't you touch him, you big clumsy oaf.'

Bjorn blinked and turned as Gunnhild hauled on his arm, pulling him out of the way. He let her, for no man should stand in the way of a völva at work. He stayed beside the jarl, though, as Gunnhild crouched. The others were there, now. Ulfr and Lief and Anna and Farlof, all huddling around Halfdan and Gunnhild. Even Ketil had stopped taking out his anger on the other warrior and was here with gore-stained boots. They created almost a cocoon around the fallen jarl and the völva.

Bjorn watched in horrified, panicked fascination as Gunnhild leaned over and drew the Dagaz rune on Halfdan's head with her charcoal stick. She raised a small phial of green-brown powder and tipped a small amount into his mouth. She then lifted a small amount of that precious compound from her pouch, dusted it to her lips, then bent over the jarl and whispered something in a language Bjorn had never heard, before, to his astonishment, leaning further and kissing Halfdan full on the lips, lingering for a moment. She then rose once more, the imprint of her own lips on his in that compound that Bjorn knew all too well.

She counted slowly, silently, to seven, Bjorn thought, and then, in a move that shocked him even more, she suddenly clasped her hands together, tight, with interlaced fingers, and brought them down hard in a thump onto Halfdan's chest.

There was an astonished silence, all the Wolves watching in shock. Even the locals had fallen quiet, the only sound the distant rumble of thunder.

Halfdan's eyes shot open, wide, a gasp emerging from those dusted lips, and suddenly his chest was rising and falling.

Bjorn stared.

He had never seen the like. Had never even believed such a thing could happen. The Christians said that their god had died and risen, that he had raised another man from death, but Bjorn had not believed such things. He had presumed it to be a falsehood.

Yet what had Gunnhild just done if not that?

Bjorn could count on one hand the number of times he could remember crying in his life, yet a tear welled up in the corner of his eye at what he was seeing.

Halfdan was gasping still, eyes rolling wild, but slowly his breathing seemed to return to normal. His left eye seemed impossibly pink, almost red. He made to turn, but Gunnhild reached out and held his head tight.

'Slowly, gently, carefully. There may be broken bones. With luck it is not your spine, Halfdan, for there is no recovery from that. I do not think your wounds are fatal. It was the shock that did this to you. The shock and the pain, which sent you away from us. It is not often possible to bring a man back, but you are touched by Loki, my jarl, and the Norns are not done with you yet.'

She let go of him, and Halfdan very slowly turned his head. He hissed with pain, but managed to turn to the side and then back. Even as Gunnhild warned him against it, the jarl then put his hands to the bloody cloak beneath him and started to push himself up.

Despite the völva's protests, Halfdan managed to reach a seated position with a few grunts and curses, and slowly turned his head. He wobbled, for that almost sent him back into oblivion, but he managed to stay with them, much to Bjorn's relief.

'Stay still,' Gunnhild snapped. 'Your neck is not broken, and you are alive, but until I clean all this off your head, I cannot assess what you yet need.'

Halfdan fixed her with a look. 'I will rest in a moment. First, Gunnar's people need to see me strong. Need to see me alive and standing. We won this day, but when we leave this dale, I want these warriors with us, as Wolves of Odin, ready to crew our ship.'

Gunnhild was still arguing as Halfdan reached out to Bjorn, who grasped his hands. With a series of hissed curses, Halfdan pulled himself to his feet. Bjorn wanted to speak, wanted to say something to Halfdan, but he just did not know what to say, and so he watched in reverent silence as his jarl let go, wobbled for a moment, then planted his feet apart.

'My sword,' Halfdan whispered.

Bjorn looked around and spotted the fine, short, unusual sword lying in the grass next to the cloak, blade still red with Gunnar's blood. He swept it up and passed it to the jarl, who nodded gently, then winced, regretting it.

The Wolves parted to allow him through, and Halfdan walked, a lot more steadily than Bjorn expected, to stand facing the gathered crowd of the Swaledale men.

'Gunnar and I met in Holmgång,' he said. 'All was done according to law and tradition. Gunnar lies dead, and I stand the victor. As such, I claim that which was decided before: rule of the dale, and command of all Gunnar's hirð.'

This was greeted by silence. No cheers or affirmatives, yet no argument or curses, which was hopeful.

'I do not intend to rule Swaledale,' he said. 'That is not my fate. But you must know that the archbishop and his Jorvik men will come, and soon. It is they who will rule this land now, and I care not. I will hand it to them gladly, for the archbishop will owe me, and our deal will be concluded.' He paused to let this sink in. A future under the rule of a Christian priest was unlikely to appeal to anyone here.

'And I will press no man to my service,' he announced. 'You each have a choice as free karls in his land. You can stay here and wait to serve the church men from Jorvik. Or you can stay and prepare to fight a last stand for your world. Or you can leave these lands and seek somewhere new to settle, perhaps, if there is anywhere else on this island the nailed god has not yet touched. Or you can come with me.'

Another pause. Even Bjorn could feel the air almost crackling with expectation and anticipation.

'I do not offer you land, homes, farms and a roof and fire as Gunnar did. But I do offer you that which is in your blood: the whale road, battle, glory and silver, the stuff to fill mead hall stories and the mouths of skalds from now until Ragnarok. We go east to kill a priest, to challenge a prince and to steal back the best ship that ever sailed the whale road. We leave this afternoon. If you would come with me, gather that which you cannot leave and join us.'

With that, he turned and made his way back between his people, who closed up behind him. Back among his hirð, Halfdan staggered for a moment, and almost fell. But he did not. He stayed upright, turned, pointed to Gunnar's house, and began to walk in that direction. The Wolves of Odin followed him, close on, Bjorn making sure to be at his shoulder, while Gunnhild was at the other. Halfdan may have made an impression on these people and appeared invincible on his return from the grave, but Bjorn could see how he was shaking now, how his legs constantly threatened to buckle beneath him. Halfdan had managed to put on a good show, but he was weaker than a kitten in truth.

As they passed inside the house, which stood empty, its owner lying on the ground twenty paces from its door, Halfdan let himself stagger, out of view of the locals. He managed to avoid falling only because Bjorn and Gunnhild grabbed him, then helped him over to a seat. He sank into it with a grateful sigh.

'You need to be a lot steadier and take a lot more care,' Gunnhild snapped. 'Much more of this, and you'll repeat everything that happened. I won't be able to undo it a second time. Heed that warning.'

Halfdan nodded gently, and hissed at the pain again. 'It had to be done, Gunnhild, and could only be done then, and by me,' he said. 'Now, we have given them the choice. With luck, some will join us, and we will return to our friends with more men than we had when we left. What is coming back home will need a sizeable force, I think.' He sighed. 'But now that it's done, yes, I will rest. My neck feels like someone is standing on it, and I have a headache the likes of which I have never felt. Will it go away or is this life now?'

Gunnhild shook her head. 'It will pass, and I have a few things that might help. But you have damage you cannot see. I will examine you as best I can, and I will try to make you comfortable. Go over to the bed and lie down. You will stay there until we have fed you at noon, and then we will think about how best to get you back down the valley. You cannot walk it, clearly, and I fear that riding a horse will be the end of you. It may be a journey in the wagon for you.'

'They have to see me whole and unharmed.'

'They already have. They also saw you win an impossible duel, and they saw you die and rise again. They are not likely to consider you weak for riding in a cart for a few days.'

He looked ready to argue, but Gunnhild turned to Bjorn.

'You can do something useful for once,' she said. 'I am going to examine Halfdan and then leave him to rest. You will stay with him, and make sure he does just that. If he sits up, you have my permission to punch him on the arm and push him back down. If he needs anything, you get it. He lies there, still, for the next four hours. Understand?'

Bjorn nodded.

He stood, watching, as Gunnhild hustled everyone else from the room and shut the door. She then crossed to Halfdan once more and crouched beside him.

'Water and a cloth,' she said.

Bjorn stood for a moment until he realised she was talking to him, and then looked around. Gunnar had a water butt outside, near the door, he remembered. He found a large wooden bowl and a cloth in the room, then dipped outside and collected the water before returning and placing it beside the bed and Gunnhild, then closing the door once more. As he did so, he caught a momentary sight of Ketil taking Gunnar's head to add to the other two as proof of their success for the archbishop.

Back in the gloom of the house, for a moment, he panicked that Halfdan had died again, but then saw the chest slowly rising and falling. The jarl was asleep. He continued to sleep, even as Gunnhild began to wipe the blood and gore from his face and neck. Bjorn watched as she worked, tutting every now and then at what she found.

'Is he all right?'

Without looking around, the völva nodded. 'The bone around his left eye broke when the sword hit it. I think there might be a small break in the cheek, too. I might have expected him to be blind in that eye now, but there was no indication of that while he was awake, so I think the break must be small, and the damage limited. If he can still see, I believe these breaks will heal in due course. There was some damage to his neck, and it clearly pains him, but nothing that will not repair. He is, in fact, incredibly lucky. He could very easily have been wounded irreparably. Had he not been struck by so much pain and shock it stopped his heart, he may never even have fallen. Truly he is Loki-born. Let him rest now,' she added, rising from the side and lifting the bowl of pink water and the stained cloth.

She rooted around for a moment in her pouches and produced a small bottle of what looked like grains, a pot of paste and a waterskin, all of which she put on the table. 'While he sleeps, I cannot help his headache. If he wakes, get him to take a pinch of the henbane and wash it down with water. I will apply the salve the next time I come.'

She stepped across to the door, fastening pouches once more, and levelled her gaze at Bjorn.

'If he cries out, or anything unexpected happens, come for me. Otherwise I shall return when we have good hot food for him. For now, I must go to walk with Freyja for the first time in this land, whether Hrafn's influence lingers or not. Do not fall asleep or mess this up, Bjorn Bear-torn, or I will strip the hide from you with my sax.'

He nodded as she left the house, closing the door behind her. Hardly had she left before the jarl whispered. 'Is she gone?'

Bjorn, frowning, turned to Halfdan, to see him lying still, one eye open and rolling toward the door.

'You were asleep?'

'I was pretending. I was getting sick of the lectures. And yes, I can still see out of the eye, and my head hurts, and my neck hurts, and I feel shaky and achy, and cold. But at least I will heal. How does it look?'

Bjorn shrugged. 'You're still prettier than me.'

The jarl laughed quietly. 'This is not a difficult thing to achieve, my friend.'

Bjorn grinned. 'You died. You actually *died*. And you live. Maybe you are the nailed god?'

'Ha. I think not. And it is Gunnhild's Seiðr that is the glory here, not me.' Halfdan fell into a serious look, then. 'I asked you, before we found Gunnhild, what was on your mind, and you wouldn't tell me. You asked me what was bothering me, when I looked up at this house and I said I knew it. Bjorn, I've told this only to Gunnhild, for I didn't want to alarm anyone, but for months, I have been dreaming of this place and this day, even when we were in the Bastard's castle in Nordmandi, and it was a Norn-woven dream. In the dream, I saw Gunnar, though at first I did not know it was him for we had not even come to Angle land then, but I saw him as Heimdallr, while I was Loki. I saw us meeting here, beneath a red sky.'

Bjorn frowned. He may be no skald or great reader, but he was not stupid, and he knew the tale as well as any Northman who had heard the stories of gods and heroes since childhood. 'Ragnarok,' he said, quietly.

'Of a sort. For Heimdallr and Loki slay one another, and I could not believe such a thing was to happen. But given that is exactly what happened, I have no doubt that Gunnhild has gone to speak with the goddess, now that she is able, to find out whatever she can.'

Bjorn nodded.

'You feel like telling me what was on *your* mind?' the jarl said with a small, sly smile.

Bjorn pursed his lips. That he had been lost, confused, just a directionless child, even as a grown man, until a völva had pointed him in the right direction? That it had not been until a snowy fight in Uppsala, and a chance encounter in a tavern there, that Bjorn had truly felt he was home and that he knew what to do? No. Even now, some things were his to own, forever. He gave Halfdan a smile.

'Just don't ever die again.'

Chapter 24

Halfdan walked across the compound toward the large meeting hall, the Wolves of Odin at his back, Bjorn protective as ever, Gunnhild there as his advisor, Ulfr, Ketil and Farlof big and dangerous looking, Lief with his Anna bringing up the rear, along with Eygrímr, new to the hirð, but already becoming an essential part.

Five days had passed.

In actual fact, he had fallen asleep only a few moments after Gunnhild left the house, and had needed to be roused at noon to eat. Defiant as always, he had tried to ride a horse that afternoon as a test, but five paces on the beast was enough to convince him that Gunnhild knew what she was talking about, and so he glumly accepted a place in one of the wagons they were taking from the village.

In the end, twenty-seven warriors had chosen to join them, nine of them bringing along their wives and children. Halfdan was not entirely sure how that was going to work, especially on board the *Sea Dragon*, but he'd made the offer without stipulating the conditions, and would not go back on his word. They would find a way.

The journey had been slow. Five days: two down Swaledale, then one south to Burgh town, and two more along the old road to Jorvik. It had, however, been an easy and uneventful trip. There now being forty-eight armed and dangerous men in the column, few chancers would take the risk of causing trouble with them.

In addition to taking the wagons from the village, as well as supplies for the journey, Halfdan had been overjoyed to discover that their missing horses, lost after the fight at the fort, had turned up, for they had been taken by three enterprising men of Gunnar's, and had been kept nearby. That meant that now they were back with their owners, as well as all the kit and armament they had thought lost. Ulfr, too, was relieved, for the horses had become to some extent his responsibility over their time in the dale.

The twenty-seven new men had taken the old oath, in the sight of Odin, and been accepted into the Wolves as brothers, with any past conflict ignored, and Eygrímr, who had been their spokesman and the shield bearer for Gunnar, had become their leader, under Halfdan, as Farlof was for his fellow Varangians. The bolstering of the Wolves with men of good Norse stock who shunned the Christ and watched for Odin's ravens was a boon for Halfdan.

They had arrived at Jorvik late in the evening, and the archbishop had been busy with his church business. A nervous, suspicious-looking priest had informed them that they could use the same guest accommodation they had occupied when they had first arrived, and that the archbishop would meet with them in the morning.

Despite everyone's discomfort at spending the night in the lands of the Jorvik Christians, Halfdan had to admit that an actual bed made it all worthwhile. The new Wolves who had come from Swaledale had hardly slept, though. Gunnar and his people had been all but at war with Ælfric Puttock, Archbishop of York, for as long as he had been in the position, and indeed for generations before. To be accepting his hospitality sat badly with them all. It was Bjorn who smoothed things over with them, for he liked it no better than they, but he knew the importance of the visit.

This morning, the Swaledalers had been a little more positive, especially when servants in the place had turned up at their quarters with huge platters of bacon, eggs, bread and sausages. The food had gone a long way to buying goodwill, and Halfdan's worries over them had faded somewhat by the time he left them and took his closest people to the meeting.

The great hall was decked out with the same banners and colours as the last time he had been here. Ælfric sat in a large, ornate, wooden chair across from them, while stools and benches had been laid out around the same table for the others. The archbishop's guards stood around the periphery, well-armed and alert. This was to be a meeting of allies, but only a fool was not prepared for trouble when pagans came.

Halfdan was shaking as they arrived, from the effort. He was still not right, and his head had hurt for five days solid. Gunnhild said he would heal, but it might take weeks, perhaps even months before he was back to his old self. Still, he would not let the locals see his weakness, and he forced himself straight and steady as they entered the room, essaying a short bow to the archbishop before he crossed the room and took the stool in front of the man.

As the others took their seats, Halfdan looked across the table. Three bottles of wine stood there ready, along with a collection of ornate glasses, though it was the other objects that interested him. A letter on vellum, rolled up, but with a seal visible at the corner, beside a leather scroll case. A map that, if he was not mistaken, covered not only Angle land, but everywhere east across the sea as far as the land of the Finns, and even Rus territory. Two great iron keys, and a document in small writing with a large blank space below.

'Good morning, Jarl Halfdan,' the archbishop smiled.

Halfdan watched the smile for a moment, to make sure it was not masking anything sinister. The world would end before he would ever truly trust this man, yet his smile did indeed seem genuine, and there was good reason, for Halfdan had held up his end of the bargain.

'Good morning. The work is done. The evidence is available, out in the yard with the carts.'

The smile slid slightly then. 'Yes,' Ælfric said with a slight tang of distaste, 'my assistant directed me to your three mouldering heads before I had even broken my fast this morning. Not the most pleasant thing to wake up to, but I appreciate the sentiment and your steadfastness in proving your success. I acknowledge that you have carried out everything I asked of you, and done so with aplomb, and not without personal loss, I fear.'

Halfdan frowned. Did he mean Thurstan, who'd been here last time but had been lost to Hrafn, or was he referring to the bruising and scars on the side of Halfdan's head. He shook it off. It mattered not.

'We had a hard fight, but the Allfather watched over us, and all went well in the end. So, to our bargain...'

The archbishop nodded. 'I was going to offer you wine and a little conversation in preamble, but I had forgotten how direct you Northmen can be. Very well, yes. Just as you are a man of your word, so am I, and more besides. In breaking the power of the pagan in Swaledale, you have opened up for me a lucrative mining region. The king will be immensely grateful, and Jorvik will prosper, even as the region grows and settles. As such, I believe that excommunicating a man, who so clearly deserved it anyway, from what you tell me, is poor payment for such a victory.'

Halfdan frowned, and then regretted it. His eye hurt so much when he did that. Was the archbishop about to find a subtle way to double-cross them?

'Go on,' he said, suspiciously.

'My assistant reported many things to me last night upon your arrival, including what he considered to be rather worrying wounds visible among you.' He pointed to Halfdan's face, to Gunnhild's wrists, to Bjorn's bound arm. 'It would be very unchristian of me to send you out into the world in that state.'

Again, Halfdan's eyes narrowed, but he said nothing.

'You need not worry,' the archbishop said with a sly smile, 'I have nothing to offer but magnanimity. You have done me a great service, and I pay my debts.'

He reached out and took the sealed document and the scroll case and held them out to Halfdan. The jarl rolled his eyes. As if he would be able to read it. Without even unrolling it, he passed it along to Lief, who unfurled it and scanned the contents.

'The all-important letter,' Ælfric explained. 'This document is legal and sealed confirmation that one Hjalmvigi of Uppsala, priest of the King of Swedes, is hereby excommunicated, removed from God's grace and cast out of His Church. Three copies have been made and sealed with my seal. The first departed Jorvik an hour ago by escorted courier, heading for the office of a friend of mine, the Bishop of Roskilde in the Dane Mark. The second is on its way to Lundenburh, where it will join the convoy of my fellow archbishop on the way to Rome, where it will be lodged with the Pope. There is no undoing this. The document has sealed your enemy's fate. He is no longer a bishop. No longer a priest at all. No longer a Christian, even. The deed is now done. The third copy is the one in your hands, for you to keep, as confirmation, perhaps, or even to present to your enemy when you meet him finally.'

Halfdan glanced down the table at Lief, who was rolling the letter back up. He slid it into the case and placed it before him, nodding at Halfdan, confirmation that it was exactly what the archbishop said.

'Thank you,' Halfdan said simply.

'I have also decided,' Ælfric said, 'that I must extend to you my offer of hospitality for a number of weeks.'

Halfdan moved to refuse, but the archbishop held up his hand. 'Hear me out, Halfdan. For my part, having guests for a few weeks is a small price given what you have done for me. And you need have no fear in this place. I have laid down the law in Jorvik that you are my personal guests. No man will even insult you, let alone cause trouble.'

He leaned back. 'Firstly, it would be precipitous of you to go charging off to seek your revenge without leaving sufficient time for my work to be realised. Staying here until the summer comes will allow time for this Hjalmvigi to receive his fate, and for the Pope and Rome to confirm and lodge the records. Otherwise, what value is there to my letters if you race off to face him before they themselves arrive? Logic, my friend. Logic.'

He gestured to the window.

'You will also note the weather. It is somewhat changeable. I doubt you have ever attempted to cross the sea between Jorvik and the lands of the Danes and the Norse, but any man will tell you only a fool attempts such a voyage in winter. The seas will be safe to sail by summer, without having to cling to the coast and pray the whole way.' Ulfr looked over to Halfdan and curtly nodded the truth of that.

The archbishop leaned forward and steepled his fingers.

'And thirdly, whether you will admit it or not, you have some rather alarming injuries among your men. Only an idiot runs off to sea, to hunt, without allowing time to heal properly. I have priests who are adept at the healing arts, who are at your service for as long as you need them, or, if you will not have them, then I will make any supplies your own witch-woman needs to do the same. Common sense says you have nothing to lose from delaying your departure, and everything to gain.'

He fell silent. Halfdan, already knowing what he was going to see, turned to the others. Gunnhild nodded her agreement. She knew there was work to do to have her friends hale and hearty, and it would be far easier to do it here than at sea. Ulfr was still nodding. He clearly agreed with the archbishop's assessment of sea travel. Lief nodded, too. He agreed with the need to let the letters go on ahead. The only one who looked unhappy was Eygrímr, who was not going to be comfortable being a guest of his former enemy. Still, on balance, even Halfdan had to agree to the sense of it all. He would certainly like his headaches to have gone before he tried sailing.

'I accept your offer, Archbishop. Thank you.'

Ælfric Puttock smiled. 'Good.' He slid the two keys across. 'Anticipating that your men would be considerably more comfortable in the town than within the church boundary, I have taken the liberty of securing two sizeable halls near the river for you. However, given that Brother Swiðhun tells me your numbers seem to have swelled since your return, I have already started looking to secure a third hall. They are yours to do with as you wish, your homes until you decide to leave us.'

Halfdan inclined his head in thanks.

'And this?' he asked, gesturing to the other document.

'This is an agreement I hurriedly ran up this morning, when I was told of your increased numbers. I have seen the *Sea Dragon* for myself, remember, and I know well that you will not fit all your men aboard. Keep this document with you. The day you decide it is time to leave, you will be able to secure any one of several vessels in Jorvik to transport your people across the sea alongside the *Sea Dragon*, with any charge levied to the Church.'

Halfdan gave him a sly smile. 'Because the last thing you want is sons of Odin sticking around when I've gone, yes? Get rid of all the inconvenient heretics at once?'

'The thought had never crossed my mind,' the archbishop replied, with a smile that made a lie of his words. 'That leaves only this,' he said, pointing to the map. 'We have little contact with the lands of Svears and Geats, and not a great deal more with the Norse, but we do have regular contact with Dane Mark. If I remember rightly, you have spent a number of years in the south, and I wondered whether you were up to date with news of your homeland?'

Halfdan merely shrugged. He'd only heard snippets in Nord-mandi.

'I believe,' Ælfric said, 'that currently Magnus, King of Norway, also sits upon the Danish throne, while Onund Jakob, son of Olof Skötkonung, rules your homeland. My friend, the Bishop of Roskilde, believes that conflict approaches. There is certainly no love lost between Onund and Magnus, and there are plenty of claimants to the Norse throne with at least as much right to it as Magnus. I have been perusing the map this morning, and I fear that any war between these kings will inevitably cover the narrow channel and the mess of islands that lie between the three countries. Only a fool would make for the Svear lands from here, knowing that. Your best bet might be the Dane Mark to begin with. There you will be able to judge how best to proceed. Should you see value in this, I will provide you with letters of introduction to the Bishop of Roskilde, which could prove to be a solid staging post for your expedition.'

Halfdan peered at the map, nodded, and sat back. He was still suspicious. The archbishop was being extremely helpful and accommodating. Did he want something? Was he hiding something?

The jarl simply could not tell, but one thing was certain, Halfdan had never been closer to Hjalmvigi since that day in Georgia. The man's day to pay his debts was approaching swiftly, and even a few months in Jorvik would pass quickly, with that in mind. By the summer, the Wolves of Odin would be stronger than ever, fully healed, well-equipped, and with direction and purpose.

As silence fell, the archbishop reached out and poured two glasses of wine, handing one to Halfdan. He lifted his own. 'To a mutually prosperous deal.'

'To vengeance,' Halfdan added, and waited just a moment to make sure Ælfric drank first, before taking a swig.

Vengeance.

Time for Hjalmvigi of Uppsala to die.

Epilogue

Sweyn Estridsson, exiled King of Denmark, stepped toward the dock. The king's guards moved to intercept, but Onund Jacob, King of Svears, Geats and Gotlanders, waved them aside and Sweyn came on. The exiled hero of the Hedeby raids moved to stand beside his fellow king. Of the lands of the Northmen, Sweyn and Onund represented two of three great rulers, the man who had ousted Sweyn, Magnus of Nordvegr, the other. But just as Magnus had pushed Sweyn from Daneland, so he had also taken in Nordvegr a throne that was not his, and the man who *should* sit upon that throne was coming now, his ship darting across the harbour, looking for somewhere to rest, oars splashing, sail booming as it filled with wind.

The ship was small for its design, and old-fashioned, but it was fast, and it was a thing of beauty. It cut through the water like an arrow and pulled alongside the dock with ease, and before it had even fully come to rest, its master moved to the prow and leapt over the two-foot gap to the land, striding toward the two kings. The man was impressive, from his tanned handsome face, past his ash blond beard and hair, to the silky garments that sat beneath a glittering coat of chain, gifts of the lord of Kiev. The daughter of Jarisleif, heiress of Kiev and wife of the new arrival, stood in the ship, watching her new husband with the doe eyes of the young and obsessed.

'Your ship sits low in the water,' Sweyn commented as the new arrival joined them.

'But it is a ship to be reckoned with, I think,' Onund added.

Harald Harðráði laughed, then. 'The *Sea Wolf* sits low because she carries half the gold of Byzantium, my friends. She is a ship to be reckoned with because she was built by a true craftsman, but sadly, she is not mine. I was forced to borrow her, and if I know its owner, I will have to return her soon, before he comes looking for me. With a little luck he will bring his witch-woman with him, though.'

The man's grin widened. The new wife in the ship seemed to miss the leeriness of Harðráði's look. Sweyn and Onund shared a glance, both rolling their eyes. The new arrival was everything his legend suggested, for good or for ill.

'So,' Harðráði said, taking a few steps forward and wrapping an arm round each of their shoulders, 'what are we going to do to get my throne back?'

Historical Note

From the very outset, the Wolves of Odin series was planned to be six books. From an initial premise that explored the less well-known regions of Viking exploration, to the east and south, I knew I would naturally have to take them to Constantinople, whose very name is inextricably intertwined with Vikings. And by the end of the first book, let alone the second, I would have a number of unresolved quests for our heroes to complete. They would have to retrieve the *Sea Wolf,* Hjalmvigi would have to pay, and somewhere, Gunnhild was going to have to see Hardrada again. That meant that they were going to have to eventually do full circle and go home. As such, even as I started writing book two, the rough plans were in place for all the others. Yngvar, then Constantinople, then Varangian involvement in Sicily or southern Italy. At that point, I was going to start bringing them north, while still exploring the Viking world in the mid-eleventh century in its waning days. That meant the unmissable opportunity to introduce them to a certain bastard Duke of Normandy who we think of as medieval, yet who was just a few generations removed from being a Halfdan himself. And for the last book, of course, there were going to be things to resolve.

This book's story came about born of two things, then. One was the need to lay the groundwork for the last book that would complete the cycle. At this point, the Wolves have been far removed from the troubles they'd experienced in Georgia and Constantinople. They have grown strong, become wealthy, expanded. But they still could not easily move to Scandinavia and involve themselves in the affairs of kings and their high priests without having a little more of an edge. I actually began weaving this in during Normandy in book four, but it very much comes to the fore in this novel, as you'll now be aware.

The other influence is Swaledale. The valley of the Swale in the northern Yorkshire Dales is my local area, and a place I have visited all my life in which I have great interest. It is also a curious dale in its history. It has ever been a lead mining centre, bringing Roman, medieval and early modern works there. It is a place of strange fortifications. No one can say for certain when the various dykes around Reeth and Fremington were constructed and used. The best estimate to date is that they belong to the early medieval, post-Roman era, from the fifth century on, and that they mark the limits of a semi-legendary kingdom in the area. The fort I use in this book, Maiden Castle near Reeth, is likely Iron Age, present during the Roman invasion. But the fort is unusual in having a stone walled entrance, and the dykes show some signs of use in the early medieval, pre-conquest era. This, of course, is just the time I have my Vikings coming this way.

Better still, Swaledale is the meeting place of two cultures. At the lower end of the dale, the names are Saxon, and churches abounded, showing the strong influence of the Anglo-Saxon powers expanding from York. In the upper dale, though, the names are all Old Norse, for the Norwegian Vikings who had settled northern Scotland, the Hebrides and then Ireland and the Isle of Man then began to expand into Lancashire and Cumbria, spreading up into the Pennines. It is therefore from the west, atop the hills, that the Vikings entered Swaledale, and their influence waned as they closed on the arable Saxon lands of the lower dale.

Names in Swaledale have had me entranced for a long time, but now, writing this series, they began to whisper to me, building a plot from their very etymology. Gunnerside – Gunnar's Sætr (a sætr being an area of pasture land). Arkengarthdale, from Arkil's Garth. And perhaps the most fun of all,

Ravenseat, from Hrafn's sætr. These three places alone gave me my three main villains in the tale, while the notion that someone pagan had fortified upper Swaledale in the early medieval days, reusing ancient fortifications, more or less gave me my plot. Because, yes, the plot to this book is not overly complex, as some of mine are. It is really a straightforward war story. Nonetheless, I felt it of great value to explain to the reader why this book is what it is, and whence it came. Almost every location in this book is real, and most of the characters are based on names from history or the region. The plot even loosely ties in with the vague hints we have of what was happening at this time. Before I move on to the detail, though, I would like to talk about Bjorn.

Since the second book, I have expanded this series to allow each of the core characters their moment in the light. Gunnhild had her imperial friend in Byzantium, Ketil had his war and inner struggle and Ulfr was allowed to build another boat. I was about to write a war story. What better milieu in which to see the world through Bjorn's eyes. He has become something of a caricature as the series has gone on, and I am aware of this. He is the source of most of the lewdness, the rib-ticklers and the outrageous violence. In fairness, I wanted him to be no different in this book, but in *Loki Unbound*, I also wanted the reader to understand Bjorn. And that meant knowing how he became this caricature. None of the other characters, other than Halfdan at the series's opening, has had their background revealed in detail, but Bjorn has built up such a fascinating series of questions that I wanted to answer them. Why was he attacked by a bear? Why was he smashing Christians to bits when he first met Halfdan? Why is he so full of tall tales? Why does he have such a strange and complex relation with Gunnhild? Well, I guess this story answers all of that. And it explains why he does what he does throughout the tale. Thus, before I go through the Wolves' latest adventure blow by blow, I will do the same for Bjorn's past.

The tale of a boy who lost his family in local wars and was taken as a slave is simple. That he escaped, grew strong, returned and avenged himself is straightforward. I doubt this needs any extra elucidation. It is what happens afterwards where Bjorn's story gets interesting, I think. The town here mentioned as Ánslo is, you may have guessed, Oslo, at this stage a young but expanding place. The king of Norway had converted his kingdom to Christianity rather harshly, almost by the sword, and there was no grace granted to pagans the way there was for a time in Sweden or Iceland. Norway was Christian. I had Bjorn wandering, uncertain what to do with his life. I wanted him to meet a völva and learn a path. I set this in the ruins of Kaupang because their very history is fascinating, and I could just imagine a magic woman, in a world where she would be hunted relentlessly, living in such a place. There is to this day no record or confirmed reason as to why Kaupang was abandoned. Like an ex-parrot, it just ceased to be.

In this era, in many places, magic was still vaguely acceptable, if frowned upon. But in some lands, open paganism already earned the sort of witch-hunts Britain wouldn't see for another half a millennium. At this time, the Norwegian king would still be busy stamping out heresy, and thus the torture of the witch. Medieval Viking justice in such cases is sometimes recorded as the 'trial by...' variety, again as it would be later with witches in Britain, and so the völva is baked to death, setting Bjorn on his anti-Christian path and on a hunt for those responsible. The place where he catches the priest is Skedsmo, a few miles north-east of Oslo, and home to a wooden church built in 1022, later replaced by a stone one. He then moves up into what is now the Høgsmåsan nature reserve for the incident with the cave and the bear.

From there we have Bjorn's legend growing in Norway and Denmark before he comes back to Sweden, hunted by Christian authorities, explaining, perhaps, why Bjorn had been to Hedeby before and why he was already well-travelled before taking up with Halfdan. The story from there, as he stumbles along his path and into that of Halfdan, brings us back to where we first encountered him in book one. Bjorn's history is complete.

On, then, to the main tale. We open with a flashback of Gunnar's attempt to frighten the Christians into leaving him alone in his dale. This is based on vague historical detail. The monastery involved, one Ghellinges, was long thought to be that of Gilling West, north of Richmond, close to the lower reaches of Swaledale, though now considerable doubt is cast on this. Still, Gilling was an important village in the Dark Ages, as the seat of the Earl of Mercia, and one of the best Dark Age swords ever found was found there. That monastery is said to have been sacked by Vikings, and so, I had my prologue.

York (Jorvik) is a well-explored place, and I won't linger there, other than to point out how hard it is to envisage post-Viking but pre-medieval York. A strange shambling town amid ruins was the best I could do. From there, my characters follow the old Roman road to Aldborough, where they meet the Reeve of Ripun (now Ripon). From here they follow Dere Street (now the A1) as far as Catraeth (modern Catterick). A once Roman town, Catterick was by this time a small village outside the Roman circuit, though it already had a church. In time it would have two Motte and Bailey castles, both of which can still be traced, one opposite the church and one out of bounds on military land. But with Christian control over the area, I had a pre-Norman ringwork fortress there on the site of a later castle. That is my conceit and I stick to it.

Moving into the dale, our friends first visit Hindrelac, a settlement mentioned in the Domesday Book that must be located somewhere beneath later Richmond. Moving on from there, they attack a small fort that holds a beacon. This is now found beneath Whitcliffe Scar, near Willance's Leap (a place with its own superb story). This place was the site of Roman lead mining, with adits in the cliff. A square fortification of earth and stone embankments has yet to be explained, but might be a slave pen, a walled guard station, or even a small military fortlet. It is this that Halfdan and friends take control of.

They then move further up the dale and encounter dykes near Marrick, Grinton and Fremington. These dykes cross the valley at various places and effectively seal off upper Swaledale, or would have done when they were in use. Their remains can still be seen, some of them quite impressive. A trip around that area of Swaledale is highly recommended, by the way. The characters then move on to Maiden Castle (mentioned earlier). My descriptions of the terrain are based upon my own treks over those hills, and the description of the half-day fog based on personal experience.

Bjorn fights Arkil around High Fremington, at one of the northern dykes. The form of the Holmgång is well recorded in sources, and beautifully portrayed in the movie *The 13th Warrior* (watch it if you haven't), but I found myself rather nonplussed when faced with the idea of two berserkir (men who were as chaotic and unpredictable as could be) involved in a rigid, structured duel. Well, you've read the result as I see it – order swiftly descending into chaos. At about the same time, Halfdan and friends are lost. They only cross the river because they find a ford indicated by a Roman milestone. The ford is the one recorded at Scabba Wath, a little downstream from the bridge of the same name, which certainly dates back to before Halfdan's time. It may be Roman, but is actually more likely of Viking origin from the name (specifically, Vikings who had a touch of Irish!) But a known Roman road runs from Wensleydale to Stainmore, crossing Swaledale in this area. Its course has been traced by Lidar to a crossing a mile or so to the west. I conflated the two for simplicity.

We then move into Raven's lands. This is the very top of Swaledale, near Keld. I spent an afternoon scouting out the area when I wanted to place a home for my völva. I could find plenty of blasted heathland, and some narrow rivulets, but I wanted something that stood out. The answer came to me when I was in Wales, of all places. We visited the holy well at Ffynnon Gybi and just the sight of the place had my skin itching. There was a curious feeling of magic and antiquity about the place, and I immediately envisaged Hrafn living there. Well, this is historical fiction, and so I translated the building at Ffynnon Gybi to my location at Ravenseat: Raven's cottage was born. Some might argue that Viking houses were of timber. I would point such folk to the many stone rectangles in the Pennines that are the remnants of Viking farmsteads. Walls of stone were common, and perhaps even the precursor of the now-famous Yorkshire dry stone walls.

Exsanguination and blood drinking were not the norm among Vikings, just as among Saxons, but that is not to say it never happened. Indeed, as I note, the saga of the dragon Fafnir includes just such a thing. My Hrafn needed to be bad. Really bad. And powerful. The bear was actually an afterthought, yet it is worth noting with a sly smile that brown bears are thought to have become extinct in Britain in the mid-eleventh century. Did Bjorn kill the last one?

I was then faced with probably the biggest headache of the book. I had planned this book with three duels in mind as the focus for the story. Bjorn against Arkil, two berserkir, Halfdan against Gunnar, two jarls... and Gunnhild against Hrafn, two völvas. The problem is that the other two can be relatively easily envisaged and portrayed, but the latter had to be a magical battle. You remember Disney's *The Sword in the Stone*? Well, this also had to be Merlin and the witch, but probably with less actual shape-changing and things that go 'Poff!' History is actually replete with such magical struggles, two of the best being Saint Patrick against the Druids, and the Buddhist Milarepa against Naro Bönchung (and that's without even approaching Biblical possibles). But one thing I have tried to do in Wolves of Odin is to keep the whole thing grounded and real. Yes, it involves gods, berserkir, and even witches dreaming the future, but everything I have written thus far has been explicable if you felt like it. Nothing is overtly magical. As such, I needed to stick to that. I hope you appreciate the result. Gunnhild's duel is probably the hardest one-on-one fight I have written in twenty years of scribbling, yet when I finished and read it through, I was beaming from ear to ear.

I do not think much needs to be said of Halfdan's duel. All is fairly straightforward, and the details of Holmgång are lifted directly from sources. I knew from the start that Halfdan had to win, but to complete the story of Loki and Heimdallr, he would also have to die. For the record, though to those present, it was Gunnhild's Seiðr that brings Halfdan back from the dead, a modern reader should be able to recognise a crude version of CPR. The green-brown powder she administered would be made from the plant ephedra, which naturally contains a form of epinephrine (or adrenaline), which combined with CPR can certainly restart a heart which has only recently stopped beating. Though CPR has only been properly recognised and practised in the current form since the mid-twentieth century, its roots go back much further, and Persian physicians were aware of the procedure in the fifteenth century. References to the breath of life go back so much further, to the Bible and beyond, and so it does not seem such a far reach that a wise woman and herbalist, magician and healer like Gunnhild would also be aware of the possibilities.

So, Bjorn, Gunnhild and Halfdan have all had their duels, their heads are in Jorvik, Swaledale can move on and be Christianised. Halfdan has died and risen as his dream foretold, and the Wolves are now stronger than ever, ready to bring the saga to a close. See you in book six.

Simon Turney
September 2023

Glossary

Aesir – one of the two groups of Viking gods, including Thor, Odin, Loki and Tyr

Berserkr (pl. berserkir) – lit. 'bear shirts'. The berserkers of Viking fame who were overtaken by battle madness in the name of Odin

Draugr (pl. draugar) – the zombie-like restless dead, occupying graves and guarding their treasure jealously

Dromon – a Byzantine warship powered by sails or by banks of oars akin to the Roman trireme or Ottoman galley

Excubitores – an elite Byzantine regiment with an origin as imperial bodyguards, by this time part of the garrison of Constantinople

Freyja – the most powerful goddess of the Vanir, whose realm includes magic, fertility, war and the gathering of the slain to her land of Fólkvangr

Gotlander – one of the three peoples of modern Sweden, the Goths occupied the island of Gotland

Holmgang – an official, ritual form of duel between two opponents

Jarl – a noble of power (the derivation of the English 'earl') who receives fealty from all free men of a region

Karl – a free man. Neither a noble, nor a slave

Katepan – regional governor of the Byzantine empire

Loki – a trickster god, a shape-shifter, who is destined to fight alongside the giants against the other gods at the end of days

Miklagarðr – Viking name for Constantinople, the capital of the Byzantine Empire, now Istanbul

Mjǫllnir – Thor's hammer

Norns – the female entities who control the fates of both men and gods

Odin – most powerful of the Aesir, the chief god and father of Thor, who gave an eye in return for wisdom and who has twin ravens and twin wolves, and an eight-legged horse

Ragnarok – the end of the universe, including a great battle between gods, giants, monsters and the slain who have been gathered by Odin and Freyja

Rakke – A Viking version of a mast parrel, the sliding wooden collar by which a yard or spar is held to a mast in such a way that it may be hoisted or lowered

Rus – the descendants of the Vikings who settled Kiev and Novgorod and areas of Belarus and Ukraine, from whom the name Russian derives (Rusland)

Sax – a short sword or long knife of Germanic origin, known to the Saxons as the seax

Seiðr – a form of magic that flows around men and gods, which can be used and understood by few, the source of divination

Svear – one of the three peoples of modern Sweden, the Svears occupied the northern regions of Sweden, around Uppsala

'Tafl – a Viking board game akin to chess or go, where one player has to bring his jarl piece to the edge of the board

Theotokos [Pammakaristos] – lit. 'Mother of God'. Greek terms of Mary, mother of Jesus

Thor – son of Odin, the god of thunder, one of the most powerful of the Aesir

Thrall – a slave with no will beyond that of his master, often a captive of war

Valknut – a symbol of interlocked triangles believed to bind an object or person to Odin

Varangian – the Byzantine imperial bodyguard, formed of Northmen

Varangoi – Greek term for the Varangian Guard

Völva (pl. völvur) – a wise woman or witch or seeress with the power of prophecy and the ability to understand and manipulate Seiðr